Praise for *The Vegan*

"At once bracingly contemporary and deeply strange . . . *The Vegan* channels the queasy paranoia of an era when the fear of human extinction via machine learning can make even masters of the universe feel like trapped animals."

—Judy Berman, *Time*

"[*The Vegan*] sets a series of dead-serious moral traps for its protagonist . . . but is also very funny, and Lipstein's writing voice is sleek and constrained." —Emma Alpern, *New York*

"[*The Vegan*] reads like if Martin Amis wrote *Money* about a more distinguished salesman . . . Lipstein asks us to investigate what's harmed and what's lost in our relentless progression, and what sacrifices might be necessary to stop the forward march."

—Mary Childs, NPR

"One of my favorite books . . . Poignant, but it's also really funny and lightly written . . . [It] grapples with ethical questions in a really sensitive way." —Lulu Smyth, *Financial Times*

"[A] wildly engaging look into a business and tech powerhouse on the brink of major success." —Shelbi Polk, *Shondaland*

"One of the year's finest novels." —*Largehearted Boy*

"Exquisite . . . Perfectly pitched between farce and poignancy."
—Michael Delgado, *i*

"Andrew Lipstein's *The Vegan* is a meaty comedy with a bleeding heart, highly recommended for all animals who read."
—Joshua Cohen, Pulitzer Prize–winning author of *The Netanyahus*

"You will want to tear through this ingenious tale in one sitting, but I urge you to resist and wallow in the strange, hilarious, whip-smart world Andrew Lipstein has built. Exacting, upending, and constantly surprising, I loved this novel."

—Cynthia D'Aprix Sweeney, author of *Good Company*

"*The Vegan* is the weirdest novel I've read in ages. In a good way. A genre unto itself. Skillfully written and strangely addictive."

—Lionel Shriver, author of
Should We Stay or Should We Go

"Andrew Lipstein's hilarious, acid-tart, spot-on, and deeply unnerving novel *The Vegan* follows its privileged narrator as his inability to tolerate his own guilt and complicity deranges him. We can't turn away as he follows his impulse, both righteous and ridiculous, to burn it all down. Lipstein has written a precise, weird, and wildly propulsive take on modern American ethical and moral bankruptcy."

—Dana Spiotta, author of *Wayward*

"In his engrossing new novel, Andrew Lipstein has produced a feverish, fantastically surprising parable about guilt, money, and (curveball) the lives of animals. It reads like the unholy offspring of Saul Bellow's *Seize the Day* and Julio Cortázar's cosmic short fiction, or *Crime and Punishment* for the Brooklyn brownstone set. I tore through it."

—Andrew Martin, author of *Cool for America*

"I ignored house and home to read this propulsive story of impulse, guilt, and resolve. A dazzling and resonant allegory for our moral moment."

—Julia May Jonas, author of *Vladimir*

Andrew Lipstein
The Vegan

Andrew Lipstein is the author of *Last Resort* (2022),
The Vegan (2023), and *Something Rotten* (2025). He lives
in Brooklyn, New York, with his wife and three sons.

ALSO BY ANDREW LIPSTEIN

Something Rotten

Last Resort

The Vegan

The Vegan

Andrew Lipstein

PICADOR • FARRAR, STRAUS AND GIROUX • NEW YORK

Picador
120 Broadway, New York 10271

Title-page art:
Japanese grass lizard © Purix Verlag Volker Christen / Bridgeman Images.

The Library of Congress has cataloged the Farrar, Straus and
Giroux hardcover edition as follows:
Names: Lipstein, Andrew, 1988– author.
Title: The vegan / Andrew Lipstein.
Description: First edition. | New York : Farrar, Straus and Giroux, 2023.
Identifiers: LCCN 2023001281 | ISBN 9780374606589 (hardcover)
Subjects: LCGFT: Novels.
Classification: LCC PS3612.I677 V44 2023 | DDC 813/.6—
    dc23/eng/20230203
LC record available at https://lccn.loc.gov/2023001281

Paperback ISBN: 978-1-250-33572-2

Designed by Gretchen Achilles

Our books may be purchased in bulk for promotional, educational,
or business use. Please contact your local bookseller or the Macmillan
Corporate and Premium Sales Department at 1-800-221-7945, extension 5442,
or by email at MacmillanSpecialMarkets@macmillan.com.

Picador® is a U.S. registered trademark and is used by
Macmillan Publishing Group, LLC, under license from Pan Books Limited.

For book club information, please email marketing@picadorusa.com.

picadorusa.com • Follow us on social media at @picador or @picadorusa

1 3 5 7 9 10 8 6 4 2

To Joshua Mikutis

After all, the sky flashes, the great sea yearns,
we ourselves flash and yearn

The Vegan

C hirp. Gong. Ding-ding. Ocean waves, ding-ding.

The alerts were coming more frequently now, sounding from the overhead speaker system every few seconds. Something was happening, a lot of activity even for market close. It was perfect timing, a blessing; this barrage of sound was just the kind of quirk Foster might appreciate. I was always looking for ways to underscore our nerdy kind of brilliance, our rejection of the old maxims. In fact I'd had a banner made: *Toto, I've a feeling we're not in Greenwich anymore.* Milosz, my partner, told me to take it down. I knew he was right because he said anything at all. Milosz gave what could be called *an opinion* about twice a year. He spoke only facts, facts that could be backed up with more facts, a chain of unimpeachable logic that I assumed culminated in either the meaning of life or the number zero. They say the best person to start a quantitative hedge fund is someone who can both manage the hell out of other people and master any sort of math thrown their way. Milosz and I were that person, divided in two.

I hurried across the trading floor to the speaker, fiddling with some knobs as Peter, our receptionist, watched patiently. *Do you want me to turn it off?* he asked. I laughed, I couldn't help it, my performance adrenaline was already spiking. *Louder*, I said, and he tapped at his computer.

Chirp, ding-ding. Cash register sound. It was a bit loud, that was okay. But a cash register alert was too on the nose—what did that one stand for, anyway? I told him to change it ASAP.

I turned around and saw Asja, Yuri, and Jake, three of our associate-level researchers, hunched over a table; their posture, their furtive glances, made them look like teens copying homework. I was about to send them back to their desks when I noticed the scrawl on the blackboard. It was a seemingly simple algorithm they'd been discussing for weeks, often for hours at a time, always with a piece of chalk in hand, although they never made a mark lest they disturb such an elegant formulation. *Why don't you three go to the board and have a lively discussion about the, uh*—I drew my finger in a circle until Yuri said, *The Baum-Welch algorithm.* He didn't mind that I could never remember the name, he was glad to teach me something new. *Right*, I said, and smiled. I looked at my watch, 4:01, and then at the door, where I saw Foster standing, his suit jacket over his arm, his hand flattening his hair. I renewed my smile and strode over, pointing to Peter and delivering our tired joke about gearing up the light show. He was game, Peter, his laugh sounded nothing like vocational obligation.

I opened the door and gave him my hand.

Ian? I asked, as if I didn't know what he looked like.

The great Herschel Caine. He didn't wait for an invitation to walk in; actually, I had to move out of his way.

Let's head to my office, I said, stepping past him. I preferred we not loiter, I hardly knew who he was. Well, I knew almost everything about him, I'd scoured the internet—just not what exactly he was doing here. He wanted to invest, that was what he said in his email, but he had a way of phrasing things— *I'll be in the area Monday, might I stop by?*—that suggested conspiracy. And was it just a coincidence that he was also invested in Webber? That part didn't make sense. We had nothing in common with them, the whole point of our firm was to be the antithesis of Webber; in fact Milosz and I often made business decisions by asking ourselves what our old employer *wouldn't* do. Of course I'd never say anything of the sort in a pitch, let alone mention Webber Group, unprovoked, by name. This wasn't just because no investor wanted a David in a sea of Goliaths—they all wanted a Goliath with an excess return slightly higher than that of the other Goliaths—it was because vindication and the associated passions simply weren't the stuff of moneymen. They preferred to hear something more along the lines of *We've discovered a quantitative scheme that, we believe, once perfected, can generate untold wealth.* This line I knew by heart; it was my opener no matter the audience, a nice balance between supper club restraint and carnal greed—Wall Street's stereotypes for WASPs and Jews united at last.

I turned around to find him staring at the floor, as if to make a point of not seeing anything he shouldn't. This only fed my paranoia, that he was so attuned to our need for secrecy. Actually I hoped he'd glimpse enough to see we weren't another Dockers-and-beige-carpet hedge fund, some isolated *campus* with priority parking spots. We had designed our office for creativity, for thinking; we surrounded ourselves with plants: not ferns or cacti but fiddle-leaf figs, variegated strings of pearls, wandering Jews, *Monstera obliqua*. We had no dress code, official or implicit; employees were encouraged to come as they were. Yuri was our case in point: he didn't even wear shoes, and I frequently found strands of his long, dry hair around the espresso machine or on the coffee table with the art books. It was with this mindset that we chose to rent three thousand square feet in SoHo, on Wooster off Broome, even though we could have spent the same amount for thirty thousand up Metro-North. It was why we mandated (and paid for) once-a-week therapy for each of our fourteen employees, myself included (Milosz was a harder sell). You had to be careful, though, not to fall on the wrong side of the obnoxious-tech-startup divide, so we forwent the furniture so modern you dared not sit on it, the murals, the liquor (I doubt our researchers even drank), and decided on Vintage seltzer over LaCroix.

Still or sparkling? I asked. He leaned in, he hadn't heard. I told Peter to turn the alerts down and, with my hand on Ian's back, shepherded him into my office.

Some people here think it sounds like a song, I said, walking behind my desk. *Some say it's like listening to a cartoon. But I think if you really pay attention, it starts to sound like language.* He nodded and gave a perfunctory smile—rather, a smile meant to convey that it was perfunctory. Fine, so it wasn't such a profound thought. I would have thought someone with a master's degree in English from Harvard (earned at age forty-two, no less) would appreciate the grace note, but apparently he had more straightforward tastes. *It sounds funny, gimmicky even, and yet, every time you hear, say, a studio audience clapping, that's our algorithm telling us there's a public stock that's more than sixty-two point five percent likely to rise at least two percentage points by market close.*

He gave a more genuine smile now. *If only 62.5 were 100.*

Of course, I said. *And that's why we hear a sound at all. Because we need someone with ears—albeit someone quite smart with ears—to hear that studio audience clapping and walk over to a computer and do something I certainly don't understand, something they could have spent a dissertation on, something that, applied differently, might have made a real difference in the world, but instead it's being used here, in this office, to generate guaranteed profits for people who are already too rich.* I sat down, held my palm out, inviting him to do the same. *Well, that was some kind of introduction. Let's start over.*

Ian Foster, he said. *Nice to meet you. But perhaps I shouldn't waste more of your time. By the sound of it you're basically printing money, and money is all I come with.* He didn't sit. Was he for real? I took him in, matched him against all those preening men I'd met at Webber, at business school—no, surprisingly the best fits were from college; yes, he was a bit immature, insecure, he wasn't at home in the world. He couldn't act natural so he withheld himself, became someone else, covered his unease with affectation—like that hand, his right, which swam in front of him constantly.

Well, we're not printing money just yet. We still need to raise enough to buy the printer. But once we've got it, once we can cover the ink and maintenance fees, et cetera, I promise I'll let you walk out of here. In fact I'll stop returning your calls.

Ah, taking a page from the RenTech playbook. Renaissance Technologies was one of the first hedge funds to use quantitative modeling, and still is an industry paragon. Decades ago, their Medallion Fund became so lucrative they kicked out their own investors, and now only employees and executives reap their unprecedented returns. *You know I met Jim Simons*, he said. Who hadn't? I acted impressed. *But let me be a bit more up front. I'm here to invest, yes, but I'm also here as a favor to a friend, Colin Eubanks. You know him, I assume?* I nodded, as if it were some name that fell on my ears now and again—my dentist, my wife's ex-fiancé—and not the Colin Eubanks whose support the firm needed to survive, $220 million, money he'd guaranteed was ours, guaranteed not in a promissory note, which I would have preferred, but with a firm hand on my shoulder and intense eye contact one night at the Harvard Club, a venue I didn't know was taken seriously—let alone by British financiers who hadn't attended Harvard—at least not $220 million seriously. But he was serious. I believed that, I'd already rewritten the clinching line of my boilerplate pitch: *To date we've filled out most of a fund of $400 million*, a line that had helped generate almost the additional $180 million, though this was all uncommitted, and assumed people wouldn't drop out. They would, I knew how this went, I'd gone through the fundraising cycle end to end four times at Webber. But of course pitching Webber to investors was an entirely different proposition: *In this market? You want tried and true.* Webber had beat the market seventeen years out of the past twenty, and usually by a good margin. We, Atra Arca Capital Management, had beat the market zero years out of zero; we were exactly the kind of risky proposition I'd spent my past life warning investors against: a firm that relied on numbers and numbers only, a quant hedge fund that was truly a quant hedge fund, and not what firms like Webber claimed to be—a quant hedge fund wrapped in rationale. We didn't want rationale, we wanted to build a black box so opaque, so dense with algorithm and data—50 petabytes of it, computed at 105 teraflops, eventually (we already had the servers, $1.5 million worth, so said the insurance we took out on them and the information they would hold)—that none of it could be explained, not with words or numbers or even overly abstract schemata (the currency of overeducated researchers). Yes, it was sexy, and investors loved to love it, but when it came to putting down a check they wanted to see historical returns, hopefully decades of them. In other words, I was plenty aware of the stigma, and it was my mandate to prove we were not just a room full of PhDs, data servers, and chalk. Hence the name Atra Arca, which means *black box* in Latin, a detail I thought might serve me well in meetings just like this, with people of the Ian Foster sort, the *learned* sort, the sort who, if they didn't know Latin, at least revered it.

Colin, I said. *He's a good man. And I'm intrigued: What's this favor?*

Oh, he said, as if he hadn't guessed I'd ask. *Colin has superb taste, great instincts. But sometimes he needs help pulling the trigger.*

Right, I said, and smiled. *So you want a bit of due diligence. We'd start with an NDA, of course.* A bluff of my own. The only nondisclosure agreement we had was for employees; it was needlessly punitive and meant for people who'd know our strategy inside and out—not something that would ever be on offer, even to Colin.

He waited a beat. *No NDA*, he said. *I'm not here for due diligence. I'm not a numbers guy, I trust I know even less than you about*—the hand wave again—*all of this. And I'm not some fink, not that I've never been called that in so many words. It's just that . . .* Now he began talking at great speed, words that were mostly for himself, I could tell by the way he lit up, the self-sneer he couldn't hide, he obviously enjoyed having a captive audience. He spoke about regulation, finance in the eighties, *Den of Thieves* and *Barbarians at the Gate*, books I grew up on that now seemed so outdated I doubt anyone in the office had even heard of them—and he clearly had a keen mind, his sentences were clever, unexpected, I found myself laughing, a real laugh, which I didn't get every day, at least not at work. *And every other character in these books is either tall, thin, and silent, or short, fat, and egregiously loud. No, I don't think things are so cut and dried, and, likewise, I don't know why exactly Colin trusts me. Probably because we think alike, so with me he gets an objective version of himself. So let's say that's why I'm here, to be Colin when Colin's somewhere else. And we'll proceed with that.* He gave a quick nod, an abrupt end to his little soliloquy, and suddenly it felt like our meeting was all but over. Did he only need to be listened to, humored, flattered? That I could do. He smoothed his hair again, looked for his coat and found it already on his arm. I was going to say something, wind the meeting down with some formality, but that didn't seem to be his way; from now on my only purpose with him was deference. He made to leave but stopped at the door. *I have to ask: Why Atra Arca?*

Ah, it means black box. As in—

No, he said. *I know that. But I'd think it would be* Niger Arca. *Atra is more . . . gloomy, dismal even.*

Really? I'd used Google Translate. I'd confirmed it with a friend. A Hail Mary: *Do you know why they call economics the dismal science?*

Something about population growth, limited resources—no?

Exactly. To profit in any market you have to take from others. But that predator-prey mindset presumes intent, which we've taken out of the equation. Only our algorithm knows why it does what it does, and so the dismal science is kept in a box.

He laughed. He shook his head. *Herschel,* he said, *that's evil.*

———

I bought a six-pack at a grocery store outside the office and drank one in the Uber back to the house. I needed some sort of reset before the big dinner; that meeting had left me disoriented, in a mild stupor, as if I'd just woken up. When Ian left I'd felt good, that I'd done well, but by the time I myself left, about thirty minutes later, I wasn't sure precisely what I'd done well *at*. I almost called Colin but thought better of it; when we'd spoken last week he'd made clear, in so many words, that he'd commit when he was ready. It didn't help that there was a swarm of protestors just outside the office: next door was some tech company that had recently signed a deal with China that would, somehow, enable them to expand the tracking and surveillance of their Uighur population. They booed me as I entered the black SUV, even though I'd obviously come out of a different building, further proof that their protest was just an outgrowth of a more generic frustration; I was wearing slacks, that was the problem. They weren't radicals, they just wanted to feel alive; their animus wouldn't change the world outside, it only expressed a void within. I could forgive the young ones, they didn't know how the world worked, but on those my age, almost two decades out of college, I let my spite exhaust itself, I needed it out of the way. After all, it was the twelfth of May.

May 12. Franny and I had used the date as shorthand more times than we'd ever admit to the evening's guests. It was, by this point, a code name for our mission, one we'd been planning for months, a feat that would guarantee that our life here in Brooklyn, in Cobble Hill, would be all it needed to be:

we would make new friends, best friends, in our late thirties. And we would do this by showing our neighbors, Philip and Clara (née Miller) Guggenheim (yes, that one; his great-great-etc. had founded the museum), that we were not only just as interesting as they were, but fun, good people, married with kids on the way, next year if everything went to plan, which they were shooting for, too—an intimate detail revealed on just our second rendezvous a few weeks ago, as both couples lounged in the narrow, shared courtyard that separated our (nearly identical; I'd found their floorplan on StreetEasy) brick townhouses. The similarities were uncanny: Jewish husband, gentile wife, none of us actually religious; we'd bought our homes within two months of each other; Franny a furniture designer, Clara an interior designer; husbands runners, wives in book clubs; both couples shopped at Trader Joe's despite being rich. Even our differences were complementary. Outside the office there was nothing I liked talking about less than finance, and Philip was a film director (and actor, but only in his own movies), my secret (I don't even think Franny knew this) dream profession. And their dynamic perfectly counterbalanced ours. Whereas Franny was our chief executive officer, it was clear from the first time we met that Clara was beta to Philip's alpha. It wasn't so much that there was an imbalance between them, just that their personalities produced a natural equilibrium: Philip was the consonants, establishing order, setting terms, and Clara the vowels, sliding through the indeterminate middle, applying her apparent vagaries to a neatly prescribed life. For the past few weeks, when we saw that they were outside, we would come up with an excuse to join them—claiming that the gardeners didn't water the lilies enough but we were happy to do it, or noting that it was the only hour of the day when our thin patch got direct sun. We clicked, there was no denying it, but their social life seemed more than full (practically a dinner party a week, it appeared) and we wanted to be much more than casual acquaintances. We wanted, we needed, to impress them.

May 12 was also, not by coincidence, the night we were having over Franny's freshman roommate, Bertie "Birdie" Barnes, a prominent British playwright, in town under the pretense of the opening of a friend's show, but really because she was finalizing her (second) divorce and needed something to do—hence the contacting of old, lost connections. Birdie and Franny had been inseparable at Brown for exactly one semester; since then their relationship had consisted of a phone call every few years (albeit one that lasted half the day). I'd never met her but had the impression we wouldn't share much common ground; Franny used the term *outsized* whenever she described her. But this was a perfect opportunity, kismet, Birdie was the whole package, a posh accent and a dazzling career in the arts, the idea came to Franny and me at the exact same moment: yes, May 12 would also be the night we'd finally invite Philip and Clara into our home. With Birdie's charm coloring the evening, they would witness firsthand our lives, our taste, Franny's artistry; while they ate they would sit on her trademark chair, the one featured in *Architectural Digest* not six months ago (did Clara subscribe?). The invitation was delivered offhandedly, as if Franny had just come up with the idea. *Yes*, Clara had said right away, *that would be lovely*. Franny gave me the news that night as though she were recounting a special at Paisanos; from then on we agreed, tacitly, to play it cool.

When I got home I found Franny in the kitchen wearing

her teal linen dress, her hair shorter than I'd ever seen it. In fact she was trying and failing to tie it back while frowning at her laptop, which sat dangerously close to the lit stove. On the screen was an email written in her assistant's signature blue font. Franny had worked from home to prepare for the evening, and it now seemed, as I'd expected but did not suggest, that she hadn't been able to balance the two. I noticed steam rising from the trash bin: the still-hot memory of a false start. I stopped myself from asking how it was going, I knew the answer and anyway she was obviously in—as she herself called it—her *do not fucking disturb* mode. If she slid into that gear more often than she liked to admit, still she only did so when necessary, when there was too much to do in too little time. This penchant was so ingrained in her that I'd always assumed it was inherited from her family—until our wedding last year, when I met them, or rather, the few who chose to attend. That our ceremony was to be held in a temple was enough for most to decline the invitation. They were devout Lutherans, all living in or around her hometown, Fergus Falls, Minnesota. She still spoke of them as the spurned do, with vulnerability but also with the conviction that comes from forging a life of one's own. Even her accent, an indistinct composite of Northeast modulations, had been fully scrubbed of its quasi-Scandinavian roots. But unlike most every transplant I'd met from that part of the country—all of whom seemed to view their lives through the eulogizing lens of their families—Franny had something indelibly *New York* about her. It was as if she captured the spirit of the city, embodying all those threadbare sayings. She unironically believed in the concept of *making it*, which both moved and inspired me, probably because to her it wasn't a concept. She had nothing to fall back on, she couldn't imagine any other life for herself than this one; for her, failure did not mean settling for something more realistic—there was no such thing.

I went up to the shower, taking another beer with me. Even in the bathroom I could smell the meal, a menu we'd finalized the night before: escarole with pancetta and hen of the woods, sweet potato and sage ravioli in parmesan broth (the idea shamelessly cribbed from Frankies, an Italian restaurant up the street), and bone-in pork chop saltimbocca (ditto); this last item had been subbed in at the eleventh hour for a needlessly complex and ultimately desperate beef Wellington.

After I got out, just as I was rubbing the mist from the mirror, I heard an unusual sound, a sort of siren. My first thought was that it was the new security system, which I'd nearly forgotten about despite the fact that it was almost as expensive as our home insurance. I opened the door and identified the source: Birdie. This was her God-given voice, one I'd previously heard only through a phone receiver across the room. It was clarion, there was no other word for it, I pictured those metallic statues on the covers of Ayn Rand novels. But after I got changed, finished my beer, and went downstairs, I found in our family room a woman who might have been the very inverse of those gilded musclemen. She was round and short, her hair ginger but darkened with age, with stubborn curls she forced into a high ponytail. On her person there seemed to be every color, every pattern, every fabric; against all that chaos her face looked like one big pinkish pearl. She turned to me, flashing her emerald eyes—they were so brilliant I inhaled, nearly a gasp.

Hersch-el. Darling. You've absolutely outdone yourself.

I glanced at Franny, whose face had fossilized into a genial smile. I'd seen that look before; she'd been taken conversational hostage. I tried to speak—to say what, I didn't know, I didn't have the slightest clue what she meant—but before I could, she said, walking over to me, *Now listen. You take this.* She disrobed her shawl, jacket, gloves, and sweater, and handed me the pile.

Thanks, I said, and she laughed heartily, a staccato triplet, pulling me in for a hug and then letting go only to appraise me, her hands on my shoulders, as if I were a nephew she hadn't seen in ages. With the weight of her clothes in my hands I nearly forgot it was spring until I made it downstairs to the foyer, where I hoped to take a moment to regain my composure. But I never got the chance; through the glass of our front door I saw Philip and Clara. The dismay I felt at having them witness me in such a disoriented state was washed away by my pleasure in seeing that they too were treating this night as something special: he wore a turtleneck, she a beige blouse and red lipstick, each held a bottle of wine. I opened the door and extended my hand, an awkward enough maneuver, and on top of it I let Birdie's shawl fall to the floor. I bent down to get it but Clara got there first.

Laundry day? she asked, placing it on top of the heap.

This came off a single woman, I said, *and she's still not naked.* They laughed but nervously; as they walked up the stairs I cringed, hearing my words again.

My God, Philip said, *you didn't tell us your friend was Birdie Barnes.* He gave her his hand. *We saw* A Feast of Seconds *in London, it was this time last year. Loved it, of course.*

Well, that's something coming from Philip Guggenheim, Birdie said. He looked down, a show of humility; he'd done the same when I mentioned *The Phoenicians*, his limited-release but highly acclaimed motion picture of three years ago. *Franny told me all about you two. You know, I once dreamed of getting into the Guggenheim, and now I have, in a way.* She glanced at me and yipped. I tried not to look at Philip's face but couldn't help it, his feigned modesty dripping off to show tainted pride beneath. *I was born to be a painter, that's what my mum always said. I believed her up until I was twenty-four and had given it a go. Yes, some talent—but I digress. Anyway, I have a Carrington in my office,* she said, blinking at him. No, he didn't know what that meant, none of us did. Birdie acted surprised and then told the entire saga, a tale of great love between surrealist artists—Max Ernst and Leonora Carrington—torn asunder by the Nazis, never to meet again. Carrington apparently spent time in an insane asylum, receiving electroshock treatment, and then escaped to Mexico, while Ernst began a marriage of convenience (in Birdie's telling, at least) with Peggy Guggenheim.

I didn't know that story, Philip said. In those minutes he'd retrieved his grace.

Well, Birdie said, eyeing the bottle of wine in Clara's hand. *If I've got any chance of staying up we must pop that open. It's almost midnight in London and, let's be frank, my life is crumbling to dust.* She made a clownish frown none of us knew what to do with; to move the moment forward Franny ushered us into the dining room and handed me a corkscrew.

As we took our seats—me at the head between Philip and Clara, with Franny and Birdie across from each other—Franny apologized for the state of the house. *We're changing everything,* she said. *That is, if we ever get our building permits back.* The city's approval process had been her albatross, it was now the only thing that lay between her and her dreams: a home crafted by her own hand. We had both been thrilled to buy, but as we moved through the closing process we came to realize it was for opposite reasons: I wanted an investment, she wanted something that we'd never sell—that would, eventually, be passed down through generations. It was with this in mind that she'd worked with a contractor to reconceive the space, ditching all the modish effects in favor of something more, as she put it, *permanent*.

I just want a simple, honest home, she said, her eyes softening, or blurring, whatever it was they did when she was seeing something that didn't yet exist. But as she came back to herself, squinting at the other side of the room, her face hardened, a look that had only increased in severity since we moved in. *This house is basically a WeWork. Everything's* smart. *The fridge is* smart. *As if we need an app to tell us when the milk's expired. It's like we're trapped in some nouveau riche purgatory, waiting for the gods at the Department of Buildings to look our way.*

Franny wishes our home was carved from a single block of wood, I said.

Birdie looked at me and said something in French I didn't understand, at which only Philip laughed, and not exactly kindly. Franny responded in kind—years ago she'd apprenticed with a cabinetmaker in Paris—and gave me a sympathetic look.

I split the bottle into five glasses and then, as Clara watched, took a sip. I told her I loved it, and then something about the full-bodied flavor, though her smile indicated that wasn't quite right.

No, I said, *I know nothing about wine.*

There's nothing to know, she said, the sort of thing said by people who knew just how much there was. *Just don't tell that to my parents, they spend most of their waking hours in the cellar.*

So it wasn't just Philip's family that was rich. I wondered why they didn't get a nicer place, given theirs was the same price as ours. (Again, StreetEasy. And actually it was a bit higher, $3.1 million; even though ours was a two-and-a-half bath to their two, their balcony had an unobstructed view of Manhattan and their living room was, apparently, a sanctuary of light.)

But let's talk about anything else, she went on. *The market, for starters. We haven't the slightest clue where to put our money.*

I glanced at Philip, who simply looked down; no, he didn't want my investment advice. *I'm hardly the one to ask,* I said. Her look demanded more—didn't people like me fill their funds with just her type? But even without Philip's tacit *No thanks* I would have quashed my instinct to make a pitch; I'd heard too many stories of mixing work and play in just this way. *The S&P would be the most boring place for it, and that's exactly why I'd invest in—*

This wine, Birdie said, her voice rising to break the conversational barrier, *was fabulous.* Was? She'd finished hers; I hadn't even had a second sip. Philip was game, he raised his glass and practically downed it. I took a gulp and so did Franny, but Clara just looked at her husband. Before it became too obvious, Philip put his hand on hers. *Well,* she said, *we have something of an announcement to make.*

Franny cooed, I said *How wonderful* or something just as anodyne, anything to hide my unease; the previous weekend Franny and I had talked for hours about when we'd have children, agreeing, finally, to postpone for six more months. It wasn't ideal—we were both eager to start a family—but in a year and a half the firm would be in a state where I could take some time off, a full two months I'd promised her, we'd bring the baby to Italy, Spain, Morocco. The usual questions were asked, I listened to their answers with a smile, choosing to divert my anxiety, leave enough space to *uncover the upside*, as Magda, my therapist, would say; thinking of her Hungarian lilt comforted me. Their kid would be a year or so older than ours; that didn't mean they couldn't be best friends. Ours might always lag somewhat—a little weaker, a little less smart—risking the development of submissive tendencies, sure, but the upside was much greater: our child would always be challenged, competing in the next weight class.

Well, let's enjoy your freedom while you still have it, Birdie said, lifting her empty glass. *I'm sure the other bottle is just as good, but I think I'll take something stronger.*

And we'll need some food to sop it up, Franny said, excusing herself to the kitchen.

Birdie wiggled the glass and raised her eyebrows at me, like I was waiting on her, like the whole world was. But why did it feel, what—earned? Was it just her accent, her witty little aperçus? Or was it because she never second-guessed herself, never let on a hint of doubt? Whatever it was it arose from her wealth, surely, a lifetime of it, such imperiousness could only be inherited—like the freedom to single-mindedly pursue a career in the arts. Even though Birdie had only garnered success in the past few years, Franny said she'd never had a job, a real job anyway; since college she'd mostly written when she felt moved to and otherwise attended to an apparently packed social calendar. Perhaps I envied her, resented her, even. I never felt empowered to do anything but make money, that being the one glaring lack all through my own childhood. We weren't poor, per se, and yet vacations were riddled with anxiety around eating out, getting our security deposit back. I'll never forget my parents gathering at the dining room table every Sunday night, sorting out their finances in hushed, tight tones.

I'll make you something, Birdie, I said, and followed Franny into the kitchen. I caught up with her at the stove. She glanced at the doorway and said, sotto voce, *She's not normally this, you know, overpowering.* I shook my head and she squeezed my arm, imploring me to remain positive. *She can be good company*, she said. *Great company.* I smiled and looked at the liquor cart. *If I've got any chance of staying up*, Birdie had said. Yes, the booze was enabling her. I searched the fridge for our strongest mixer and took out the black currant syrup. I added it to a tumbler of seltzer and poured on the smallest splash of our cheapest vodka. Finally, I cut an orange twist, squeezing it and then dropping it in, and brought out the drink.

When I sat down Clara asked me what the S&P was, which made me feel better about my uninformed comment about the wine. I talked about mutual funds and indices, reciting the standard recommendations while I watched Birdie. She'd yet to take a sip, she waited until Franny had made it out with the first course. Then she lifted her glass.

To all of you, for having such coherent, respectable lives, she said. *My mum would have been much happier with a daughter like you. All she ever wanted was for me to breed.* She took a drink. *Marvelous, Herschel.*

We started to eat. I was thankful for the quiet, the chance to reset. But it wasn't fifteen seconds before I realized there was too much of it. I looked up to see that Clara had stopped eating, that Philip hadn't even started. He turned to me. *I don't eat meat*, he said, plainly enough that I realized it was something I already knew, he'd told me a week ago, outside in the courtyard.

I'm so sorry, Franny said, glancing between him and me.

It's my fault, I said. *You told me that, but I failed—*

Surely not the biggest surprise, Birdie said. *I didn't eat meat for weeks after I saw* The Phoenicians. *Well, that's a lie. But really, the man had Kristen Stewart served in a stew. Wasn't too ethically ambiguous, now was it?* No, it wasn't. And now it seemed as though, on top of forgetting he was a vegetarian, I hadn't seen the film, which I had.

I separated the art from the artist, I said, lamely. *And also I forgot that simple fact. We'll just give you the next course.* I looked at Franny, my mind was blank.

Ravioli, she said. *Vegetarian.* She got up and went to the kitchen.

The entrée is pork, I said, *unfortunately. But we're happy to pick you up anything you like, we're right by a great Italian restaurant.*

I thought you were neighbors, Birdie said.

Right, I said, swatting away a fly. *We are, I've just had a mental lapse. I'm sure they have those in London, too.* Franny passed a glare as she entered the room.

It's all fine, really, Philip said. *Ravioli sounds lovely.*

Franny set a plate before him. *Sweet potato and sage ravioli,* she said, *in a parmesan broth.*

We all watched as he took a bite. *Wonderful,* he said. *A meal in itself.*

So you're not full-on vegetarian, Birdie said. He looked up. He didn't know about rennet, clearly, or didn't care, that was made obvious by the fact he had ears and had heard the word *parmesan,* like the rest of us.

No, Birdie. I'm not. He kept his eyes on the food, he took another bite. He swallowed, placed his fork down, clasped his hands, and finally looked up at her. *And I trust that even as the writer of* A Feast of Seconds, *you don't think every dinner party should end with someone vanishing into thin air.* It was the perfect retort, a joke strong enough to put everything to bed, but that wasn't his intention, the line came muttered through barely split lips. I saw on Clara's face not just worry but understanding, she'd seen such a reaction before. Was that all it took—his artistic integrity barely ruffled by a stranger? But I was surprised to find that Clara's empathy had made its way into me, too; he was struggling, that was clear, hurt but not wanting to be.

Well, I said, *I hope you wouldn't peg me as a full-on capitalist just be—*

If you must know, that wasn't the original ending, Birdie said, lifting her glass, which was now half-empty. *I had something there that was much better, but a very arrogant, obtuse producer told me he wouldn't do it, it was too close to something Joanna Hogg had done first. I've never even seen her films, actually, but I heard from a friend it was far . . .* She showed no sign of stopping, she was only picking up speed. At this point she didn't need an audience nor did she have one; she was slowly transforming our collective distaste into tedious, flavorless boredom. As I watched her ugly British mouth widen and bend and skew, dancing around her crooked white teeth, something began nagging at me, pulling at me like a child demanding my attention. *Something Joanna Hogg had done first.* That was the line. Unlike Birdie I'd seen Hogg's work. That was what was bothering me, the thought I had to reclaim, it was a scene from a film of hers I'd seen many years ago. It was unforgettable— yes, I saw it now in such high fidelity I could even make out the edges of the screen. A character pretends to faint in order to leave an unpleasant dinner party. The scene had invigorated

me then, and even now in recollection, it wasn't only hilarious, it was just lifelike enough, it could happen, it stretched
but stayed inside the boundaries of possibility. But then I was
shaken out of my reverie, literally; the screen disappeared, and
right where its center had been was a glass, shaking. Birdie had
finished her drink and wanted another. *One just like it*, she said,
now in full focus. I tried dipping one last time back into my
thoughts, but before I could, she said, *If you make me make it
myself you'll have no liquor left.*

I stood up. I saw that Philip had finished his plate, they
all had. I took her glass and walked into the kitchen, where
I leaned against the island. In the microwave door I saw my
reflection, as dark as obsidian. Outside I heard the first pat-
ter of rain; hadn't the forecast said tonight would be clear? I
returned to the Hogg scene, the colors of the room suddenly
matched that palette, soft and drained but crisp. I laughed to
myself, a real laugh; it had to be stifled so they wouldn't hear.
It was then that the idea came to me, at once, wholesale, like
the ones I have for Atra Arca, a painting too big to see but in
pieces.

I turned the music louder. I took off my shoes. I picked
up the glass and left the kitchen through the hallway, walking
slowly up the stairs—they didn't creak, thankfully, something
our broker had pointed out more than a few times—to the
bathroom off the master bed. I closed the door and urinated.
I washed my hands and opened the medicine cabinet, where
I found a bottle of NyQuil and two of ZzzQuil. I didn't know
the difference though the ZzzQuil had two cartoon cherries
on it. I put one of the bottles in my pocket but it jutted out so
I held it in my palm as I walked downstairs. In the kitchen I
poured the ZzzQuil into her glass, filling it halfway, and added

a few ice cubes. I smelled it. I thought a bit. On the counter I saw two lemons, I quartered them both and juiced every segment. I swirled the cocktail with my finger over and over again. I was just about to go back into the dining room when I saw the bottle of cheap vodka, and put a small splash on top, as before.

As I walked the glass stayed in the center of my visual field, as if my internal camera was stabilized. I delivered it and returned to my seat, where I found the next course, the ravioli. I looked up at Franny, her face was blank, her expression gone, as if she were alone, as if we weren't making eye contact. I winked at her and she reanimated. *We've decided you'd be the one to disappear*, she said.

A fly landed on my hand, I lifted it and it flew away. *What?* *Like in Birdie's play. We were joking about who would be the one to vanish into thin air. I said that with that Cayman insurance you have, it would serve us all if it was you who went poof.*

Key man, not Cayman. But even so, you'd have to already be invested in the firm and . . . I trailed off, Birdie had picked up her glass. *Never mind.* Franny followed my eyes to her friend. Birdie took a sip, she let too much in, she coughed, wiped her mouth, tilted her head to the side in mock relief. She swallowed and her eyes lit.

That is— Herschel, it's— My God, it tastes like divorce. I lifted my wine glass, newly filled. She matched, they all did, in silence we drank, Birdie nearly half her glass. *When Franny said Cayman insurance, I thought of my father's pied-à-terre in St. Barts, which is just like the Cayman Islands except it's French— and, well, for people with taste. Not that* . . . I took the time to eat the ravioli, which were delicious, the parmesan broth much more than a gimmick. I savored it, I rarely savor food, but now

I let each mouthful practically dissolve on my tongue. I took a big swig of wine and watched Birdie yap. I blurred her image, her abstracted form was so much more harmless: a symbol, if anything. It was amusing, seeing her head bob up and down, her wrists swivel. I enjoyed the rest of the dish in a sort of solitary state. In some way we were each of us alone.

By the time I finished Birdie seemed to have lost just as much interest in what she was saying as we had. I waited, took advantage of a rare pause and jumped in to change the subject. I spoke about our lone meeting with the previous owners of the house, just after we discovered that they had an outstanding building permit; this was the reason, Franny thought, we were still struggling to get ours through. Franny jumped in, she couldn't help it, she still lost sleep over the incident and had already cultivated a not-quite-accurate impression of the wife, who was German, a professor, and deliriously pretentious. *Vee had no idea! This is for vat? Zee toy-uh-let? No, it did not clugg vonce, vie vould vee need to change zee toy-uh-let?* I egged her on, playing her part in the disagreement: *Frau Schneider, a permit is a permit, and we'll never be able to build our triplex treehouse made of Japanese maple if you don't—* Back and forth we went, until Franny stammered that neither she nor her *hoos-band* had ever taken a shit in their lives. We got genuine laughter from Clara and especially Philip, who I'd worried had turned a bit dour. No, we only needed the right setting, needed that windbag to quiet down for a bit. And now she was more than quiet, she'd all but left the room. Yes, the drink had taken hold, and before I could suggest it myself she said, *Franny dear. I'm terribly sorry but with this jet lag, you know, at my age you just— Well, you are my age but you're much younger, too. Anyway, I don't think I can stay for the pork. Philip can have mine.* She gave him a lazy, nearly flirtatious smile and stood up.

Franny frowned, I matched. I went to get her things and by the time I was back her Uber was just two minutes away. She'd input the wrong address, a block away, she gave Franny and me kisses and then, just like that, drifted out of the house.

From that moment on the night shifted, there was an air of newfound freedom, as if our parents had just left for the weekend. As we finished our meal, the misfortune of Birdie's presence became, in retrospect, comic, in fact all of her little comments seemed funny now; we laughed like we were getting away with something. After dinner we went to the family room and had rugelach with milk and then cognac. The slap-happiness faded, but in its place came real conversation, shared intimacies, Philip talked about the film he was working on, they told us how long it had taken them to get pregnant, even showed us pictures from their ultrasound. Franny pretended to refuse to play the piano, and when she finally did it was lovely, we weren't drunk but had had enough to be able to listen in silence, get carried away. There was no longer a feeling of performance or manners. Clara even admitted to having *low-key stalked* Franny, she was an admirer of her work—to which Franny, never one to miss a window of opportunity, replied that she would love to talk about some sort of collaboration. At this point Philip suggested that we call it a night, that we do it again soon, and we all shared a look that meant *And please let's keep it us four.* As I closed the door Franny and I stood beaming at each other. The night had been, ultimately, a success; we wouldn't have done it differently if we could have. We hugged, we kissed, it was more than a happy kiss;

I became hard and didn't hide it. She told me to meet her in bed and went to the bathroom. I turned off the lights, shut down the stereo system, and finished my drink. In the kitchen I found the ZzzQuil, I brought it up with me to the bedroom, where Franny was, nude, the lights on, her legs spread, her face flush from drink.

The night's saving elixir, I said, sloshing the bottle. Her eyes widened, she laughed, her cheeks wide and plump, it was exactly how she looked in a picture I took when we'd first met. I drank a small sip and then a swig; I needed something to combat the alcohol, which always ruined my sleep. *My God, it tastes like divorce*, I said, my British accent terrible. But she was done with the jokes, she pulled out a condom from the bedside table. I stared at it. My toes gripped the rug. I felt an unusual stroke of gaiety, whimsy even; life was surprising again.

Maybe we start trying, I said. She didn't react, wouldn't allow herself to until she knew for certain I wasn't kidding. I wasn't, I told that to myself and then to her: *It's all we've ever wanted. Why should we wait?* I took off my pants and shirt, my underwear, I stood before her naked, surprised to find that even after such a night, even on the precipice of something so life-changing, I still felt a twinge of shame. I went to the door, closing it slowly, and then turned off the light.

———

I'd never seen Milosz don a tie before, not to mention a suit, if you could call it that. A family heirloom, certainly; I could imagine him shaking hands with Stalin. When had he put the outfit on? He hadn't been wearing it this morning. He was nervous, I could tell because he was making intense eye contact, but at least he shared it equally among everyone in the room, at least it would keep them awake. Seven potential investors, six men and one woman—the wife of a Chinese bottled water magnate—their stares as blank as their Atra Arca–branded notebooks, which had been virtually untouched since Peter arranged them on the conference room table. But how could they be expected to take notes? They'd been plopped into a graduate-level math lecture. Ostensibly he was talking about the market and risk reduction, but really he was expounding on the tenets of machine learning and data—what the term even meant, how there was no such thing as *data* but actually *information* and *noise*, one being the lifeblood of his sort of mathematics and the other a blight, a crop-killing fungus, dangerous not just for its poison but for its invisibility. He didn't put it this way though, didn't care to make things entertaining; instead he opted for variables, Greek letters, formal logic. I myself majored in math and could hardly grasp the symbols he was slashing on the chalkboard. But if Milosz thought he was making sense, the illusion was maintained by everyone present. At Webber I learned that investors can be of any temperament, inclination, or political bent, but they all share one belief: that money is equivalent with intelligence. No matter if their wealth had been created by their father's mother's father—just one-eighth of their genetic pool—and no matter if they had no idea what, actually, we were doing with their investment, they all thought they had an intrinsic understanding of finance, that they could sniff a dollar and pinpoint its provenance, its undertones. So this was flattering to them—this pale, sweaty, poorly dressed Slav who might have been a world chess champion in his past life; this chalkboard full of theorems; this air of erudition. It was why I let him give it a go—yes, he'd asked to do this, explain his work, he loved nothing more than to explain—and also so that my presentation, in contrast, would seem practically erotic.

When he moved on to computational linguistics I knew we were almost home. He discussed hidden Markov models—systems we can use to predict the next word in a given text, systems that, in theory, could be used to predict tomorrow's stock prices given today's and all of those preceding—and then made a brief detour into Brownian motion, a subject he thought was overrated; he tried to convey as much, but his emotive range was too limited and anyway the room was half asleep. I thanked Milosz and we all clapped. He couldn't help but blush; he was beaming with pride. When Peter came in with espressos he even allowed himself a congratulatory cup, for him not an everyday treat.

My very appearance at the board reinvigorated the room, I'd timed the coffee exactly to enhance this effect. I needed one myself, by this point I regretted the ZzzQuil, regretted not sticking to my system. I never took a sleep aid two nights in a row, and I made a rule of cycling through them: melatonin (though it always woke me up early), antihistamines, Ambien, CBD oil (hardly did anything), valerian root (ditto), half a Xanax (the gold standard), and NyQuil (the next best thing). This way I wouldn't have the same drug more than once a fortnight, and could stave off tolerance and withdrawal. But I'd had NyQuil just three nights ago, and last night's dose had not only lost some of its magic, it put me on edge, too.

Predicting prices isn't just difficult, I said, scanning the room. *It's impossible. Some firms will tell you that with enough research, with enough understanding of fundamentals, they can predict some winners—or, at the very least, hedge you some risk when they're wrong. In my past life I sold such a firm to investors such as your-selves, the kind that was sure to beat the market—and not much else. We hung our hats on covering our management fees and a little more, and then our day was done. I believed I'd spend my life at that firm. That's the truth.*

But then one day at lunch I met a brilliant man in the cafeteria. I understood maybe a tenth of what he was saying but couldn't stop thinking about the small bit I retained. And so the next day we met again. And then the next. And then Milosz and I started to talk at night, too, and texted each other ideas when we couldn't sleep. My wife got worried. Small bit of laughter. *So I showed her his photo; problem solved.* A bit more. *Now we listen to his lectures together when we need to get some sleep.* Bingo.

For such a rational man, Milosz absolutely abhors *rationality, at least when it comes to picking stocks. It's true. Nothing makes him more suspicious than investment strategies based on concrete reason-ing. People buy and sell stock for the same reasons they pick their spouse, their profession, the names of their children: circumstance, superstition, fallacies, and whimsy. How can the value of any of the world's largest, most-traded companies change by ten percent, twenty percent in the course of a month without an earnings report or anything else of note? Yes, Milosz abhors people who can tell you why they're buying this stock or shorting that. But we're sure as hell thankful for them. Because every time some* bowtwy *puts his life savings into—*Milosz flagged my attention, right on cue, a better actor than I ever would have guessed. *Sorry. We have a term here:* bowtwy, b-o-w-t-w-y, *short for "bored office workers and the too-wealthy youth." It's a stand-in for all those retail trad-ers scouring Reddit for tips, checking Robinhood thirty times a day. This is our modern-day patsy. Fifty years ago you'd find them in a roadside diner, tell them some sob story about your foreclosed house,* *your sick sister. Now you can write an algorithm—well, not anyone can, hardly anyone actually, but at least one person in this room can—and you can pour into this algorithm ten million gallons of data, and figure out what these patsies, these bowtwys are going to do minutes before they know it themselves.*

By now you're probably wondering: How exactly does it work? Or, more to the point: Why are we asking for money when apparently we can print our own? The answer is data. Milosz has built a machine that's ready to fly, but it needs fuel, it needs data—a lot of it. It needs the most potent, most— Sick of the metaphors? Me too. What we do is track a select set of public companies, matching their price movements in real time against historical data. Our algorithm is trained to find similar patterns and alert us when it can say, "This has happened before." But nothing is ever so simple. Math may be elegant; reality isn't. We can't just match a given stock against one from the past, we need to find hundreds, sometimes thousands, which our algorithm will Frankenstein together to give us something eerily similar to our target. And this, of course, only becomes possible with an immense trove of data to draw from. On your way out, take a look into the room to your right. There you'll find the server space required for such a trove, 50 petabytes in total—enough to store every movie ever made, assuming each was shot in ultra-high definition. Our mission now is to fill those servers with market data—but, as with movies, not all data is good. In fact, Milosz prefers I stop using the word altogether. Information is what we're after, and to this end half of our technical team is dedicated to cleaning and sorting the data we acquire. At other firms, this work usually goes to the most junior researchers, but here it's our secret weapon. We categorize information in a way no other firm can—legally, I mean; it's patented. Milosz's proprietary system all but frees information from the bounds of rigid, right-angled models, allowing our algorithm to make inconceivable connections between drastically disparate sets of information. If it sounds like magic, well, welcome to Atra Arca.

I motioned to Peter, who began passing around copies of our prospectus, a thirty-page document with projections, risk profiles—everything they'd expect and much more, like a one-pager on time and the market, how to warp it, rethink cadence, understand that minutes pass differently through-out the day, that the wrinkles set by man's collective caprices could be ironed out. *If black holes can twist and bend time*, it started, *if God can, why can't a supercomputer?*

I had these made because I have to, because you've received some-thing similar at other presentations you've attended, or will. But I don't want you to think of us as another hedge fund, with an ex-pected return and the like. I run Atra Arca like a technology startup, one that has the vision and talent to build something that doesn't yet exist but soon will, once we have the right resources behind us. And when we do— Here was the moment. I inhaled, let my-self hear my own words—*when we've constructed the world's largest repository of good, clean financial information, replete with every modern market movement known to man, every fundamental, every performance indicator and more*—I felt the tears, they never failed, a fact that didn't just make me happy, and confident, it was proof that what I was saying was true, that I was not some salesman but an inventor, someone who might actually change the world—*well, we will then, quite simply, see into the future.* I let it come, a single tear that made it halfway down my cheek before I wiped it away. *Perhaps we'll force the financial world into a reckoning. Perhaps there won't be a single fool left who thinks he knows which stocks to choose. But no matter, by then we will all have become impossibly, unimaginably wealthy.* I clasped my hands and smiled at Milosz, who was furtively looking at the phone tucked in his lap. *Thank you all for coming.*

Applause, finally, or at least as much as seven remarkably privileged adults could muster. I had hit all my notes. I had made them believe in me, in us. I had even inspired some of them, that I could tell. And yet, and yet and yet and yet, after they stood up, and put on their coats, and pretended to leaf through the prospectus, after they shook Milosz's and my hands, I knew this batch would yield nothing. If they made eye contact it was fleeting, they departed with polite nods— *polite* anything was the death knell. The only one who even spoke to me was the French-Israeli man, and that was to ask for the bathroom. No, this crowd did not consider themselves tech investors, if they thought the firm's approach was intriguing they still just wanted a standard hedge fund, this was their money after all, something that, even if treated conservatively, could generate enough wealth to enable their kids and their kids' kids to continue living without a whiff of work. Why would they do anything but hedge risk?

I smiled as they walked out, I tried not to care. No, these weren't our top prospects; that was why we'd met them seven at a time. Even if I'd bagged them all, they wouldn't bring me half of what I was going to get with Colin. And once he committed, the second the ink was dry, I'd shore up the rest of the $180 million, they'd fall like dominoes, I'd only need to set a deadline, put some fire under them.

The last one filed out and it was just Milosz and me. By the way he was erasing the chalkboard, large strokes over territory that hadn't even been written on, I could tell he'd seen what I had. I knew what he'd say, or at least insinuate—that we should reconsider the pitch, especially my half of it—and to avoid that interaction I told him he'd done a great job and went straight to my office.

I sat at my desk and checked my phone, which showed a message from a potential investor and six missed calls from Franny. Before I risked clouding my head further I dialed Colin. He picked up immediately, an auspicious sign. *Monsieur Caine*, he said, even more promising.

Monsieur Eubanks, right. I'm calling because the mail's just arrived, and it seems your signed contract was lost along the way.

He forced a laugh. *You know I wouldn't trust your country's post offices with something like that.*

Well, I wouldn't trust anyone with anything these days, but still business must be done.

You're odd, Herschel. It's why I thought you'd like Ian. I trust he stopped by?

Indeed.

Sharp as hell, isn't he?

So sharp, I said, mindfully unballing my fist.

So he's doing a bit of due diligence on my side, I hope you don't mind. He's got some money of his own, you know. I believe he could put up a million or so. This was half of our minimum, but I'd take it; I'd take anything from someone who was doing *a bit of due diligence* for Colin, or even his laundry.

Well, perfect.

We'll all do great things together, I don't doubt it. But Herschel, I hate to be rude. If this is just a courtesy call I'm running a bit short on time.

Oh, I said. *Well, I've just gotten out of a terrific meeting, delighted* to say we now have some Saudi interest, some interest from Beijing, and right here in New York if you'd believe it, and I just thought—

A courtesy call it is. Well, have fun with Ian and I'll let you know when the contract's on the way. Hate to imagine you panting at the mailman.

He hates it too, I said. *Talk soon, Colin.*

Click.

I wiped my hand over my mouth down to my chin. I eyed the dregs of my coffee. I picked up my phone and walked out to the espresso machine in the kitchen, where I called Franny. She didn't pick up, but just as I slid my phone back in my pocket it rang.

She started to speak, though I couldn't make her out over the espresso machine. When it finished I told her I hadn't heard a thing. She was annoyed at me, she *ugh*'ed into the phone. *Birdie's at Brooklyn Methodist.*

A church?

Herschel, the hospital.

In Brooklyn?

Please come. Something terrible has happened. She's— She took a moment to reset, she hated being emotional. *She's in a coma, the doctor said it's induced, or maybe it's not induced, I can't—*
Again. *We're in the ICU. Room 2019. Will, her husband—or, you know, her soon-to-be ex—he's flying out now. I just can't leave her here alone.*

Of course, I said. *But tell me what's wrong.*

She had a terrible fall last night. The Uber driver found her on the sidewalk, brought her straight here. God, I wish he'd made the trip to Manhattan, I can already tell the staff is . . . Sorry, they're around. She's been here all night. They tracked down Will this morning, he got in touch an hour ago.

She fell? How do they know she wasn't attacked?

They know. I mean, they can tell by the abrasion—the, you know, appearance of her head.

I see, I said. *Well, she was quite tired. And it had rained, hadn't it?*

What?

I'm just— Right, I said, glancing at the finished espresso. *I'll come now.*

In retrospect it's hard to believe that my first sight of her brought peace of mind, but it did. She looked serene, even with the bruising: deep shades of green, gray, and purple that covered half of her face. If it didn't quite seem like she was resting, then she at least appeared to be in some sort of very deep, rest-like state, a restorative mode, one that was required by severe circumstances but also had an end: a return to her regular self. No, it wasn't until the doctor—a handsome South Asian man with very parted hair—lifted her eyelids to reveal vacant and slightly misaligned pupils that I had to stop deluding myself. It was then that I felt my presence in the room, the weight of my skin and all it contained and the clothes that kept it hidden and carried my phone and wallet, all of it kept aloft by just two legs, each with just one joint—a system that couldn't possibly be sustained for a lifetime let alone a minute more.

I took a seat; Franny followed. This doctor was not the one Franny had already met, though he did have mostly the same questions. He established our relationship to Birdie. He confirmed her age, nationality. He asked, fruitlessly, about her medical history.

Didn't you talk to her husband? I asked.

Unfortunately, I didn't personally, he said, making me aware of my tone. He scrawled something on his pad and looked at Franny, who would receive most of his attention now. *Did she seem off last night? Was she acting, you know, normal?*

Franny looked at me. I was too absorbed in Birdie—the doctor hadn't bothered to reclose her eyelids—to help her answer the question. *She was a bit talkative,* she said. *I think there's a lot going on in her life. She's getting a divorce.*

Do you think she may have been under the influence of anything? he asked.

Drugs? No, Franny said.

Well, I said, *she'd been drinking.*

She had three drinks, Franny said. *For her that's nothing.*

I reached for Franny's hand. She turned and we made eye contact. Why hadn't we talked about the ZzzQuil on the phone? Was it something we absolutely had to mention, medically? I waited for a sign, anything, but she hardly moved. At first I thought she was too overwhelmed to remember. But she didn't seem overwhelmed; she'd been here with Birdie for several hours now. Then I thought she was acting—albeit giving a performance I didn't know she had in her. And then, finally, I entertained the only option left: that I should reexamine my memory of the very end of the night, or rather what preceded the very end, when we had, for the first time together, unprotected sex. *The night's saving elixir,* I'd said, before drinking some myself. I'd even done an impression of Birdie after she took a sip: *My God, it tastes like divorce.* I hadn't been too drunk to remember all this with certainty. But had I misjudged Franny's comprehension of it, even her attention? Now I remembered the scene differently. This time she wasn't quite present—lost in a rare level of arousal, or maybe just blind-sided by my sudden readiness for children. A stark contrast to the face I saw now, which was giving me its undivided at-tention. Her eyes reminded me of the first time I saw them, I still remembered my exact thought: that she couldn't possibly fulfill their promise, no person could be that present, acute, perceptive.

I looked down at the floor and then back at Franny. No, she had no idea what I'd done.

The doctor gave up on getting anything more out of us and set down his pen. *Because you're not kin, I'm really not sup-posed to share a prognosis with you. But based on an MRI and an EEG we performed this morning, I would be very surprised if she emerged.*

Emerged? I asked.

Emerged into a vegetative state. It's possible she may not wake up.

That's terrible, Franny said. *Awful.* Her tone was off; she had no tone. But I understood, I felt the same numbness.

The doctor said something I didn't hear, and then, taking one last look at Birdie, left us. I asked Franny what he'd said but she hadn't paid attention either.

We sat in silence watching her. Slowly her body seemed to absorb his prognosis, the rise and fall of her chest given new meaning. This was the time to do it. We now had enough privacy to talk things through, to strategize if need be. But the words wouldn't come; when I looked at Franny I became too focused on her face, I was trying and failing to imagine her disbelief, her disappointment. I'd never witnessed such an expression on her, not at that magnitude. I had to extrapo-late from what I knew; quickly the image became monstrous, unlifelike, and once it had lodged itself in my head it stayed there, it choked the words as they tried to come out a second time, a third. Her face seemed to be getting bigger, but it was just that the rest of the world had narrowed—a cliché, fine, but I had tunnel vision: when I looked down I saw my pink hands, my thumb, my pants, and the floor, that was it, there were curtains of darkness on either side, and when I looked up to the bright ceiling light the curtains only closed more.

Herschel, she said. I turned toward her, my vision abruptly normal again. *I can't do it. I can't be here when Will arrives. She's already told me so much about him, and I just can't be here for that.* I nodded even though it didn't quite make sense. *The doctor said that there's nothing to do, that these things can take time. Would it be horrible if we left?*

I agreed, I nodded again. I was staring, I realized, at Birdie, her eyes. Did the doctor know he'd left them open? Did it not matter? I thought of her seeing into the room, of her hearing us. I was suddenly aware of my own body again, its mass; this was the same sensation I'd felt the few times I'd smoked marijuana. Back then it had seemed up to me whether I found this awareness disturbing, but this time it didn't feel like a choice. I was disturbed, not just by the intense recognition of my own body, but also by the fact that it somehow displaced all other feeling, it was as if my sensitivity to the world had turned inward. I was, if anything, angry; I didn't *feel* angry but I thought angry thoughts, I resented myself, for being so unemotional, for failing to react physically. Why wasn't I vomiting at such a dreadful sight, and one I myself was responsible for? *Dreadful*, I thought again, but the word was hollow, pronouncing it in my head was like a puff of voiceless air.

You nodded, she said, *but you mean it* wouldn't *be horrible, right?*

I looked at her. *Yes, that's what I meant.*

We spent another minute or so in solemn silence. *Solemn:* another meaningless word. Franny walked up to the bed and squeezed Birdie's hand, she studied the vitals monitor, its beeps only now entering my head. It seemed false, cruel even, for her blood pressure, her heart rate, to be so normal. Finally I heard the last thing the doctor had said. Something about her vitals, and then, *It'll be up to her husband to decide what to do.*

We gathered our things and called an Uber. On the way out Franny used her phone to photograph the vitals monitor, the chart behind Birdie's bed, even Birdie's face. She also took a video, slowly rotating to record a panorama of the room while I stood behind her, swiveling too so I wouldn't be in it.

Outside we waited for the car, her head buried in my shoulder, the light drizzle and distant thunder helping to drown out her sobs. I sensed that she hadn't cried the whole time she was in the room with Birdie by herself; only when she was with someone else, with me, was she overcome. This made me think of when her dad died a couple of years ago. I found her in our old guest bathroom, sitting on the edge of the shower. It was her posture, her expression—I sensed she was hiding from me. She didn't even want to make eye contact, but when she did a great wave of relief passed through her. It seemed like a revelation to her, this relief, as if she was just realizing that someone else could help bear the weight of her pain. It made me wonder about her past relationships— she'd broken off an engagement a few years before we met— and how, if they lacked openness, we could ensure that our relationship didn't. Well, ours didn't, at least from then on; I'd never dreamt of being so vulnerable with another person. Revisiting that memory now, I suddenly questioned why she'd sat where she had, facing the door—instead of on the table beside the toilet, or on the toilet itself. Had she, in some way, wanted me to find her? I visualized the room, putting myself in her shoes, and had another thought: she'd only wanted to avoid the mirror over the sink.

At home we kept the lights off, kept the darkness of the overcast sky. In silence we prepared the leftovers from last night—the escarole, ravioli, and pork—and ate them in front of the family room television. We pulled up the movie at the top of our list, *The Banishment*, or *Izgnanie* in its native Russian. Изгнание. Each of these words seemed more truthful than the last, perhaps because they made less and less sense. The film was slow, beautiful, and depressing. I became bored midway through, bored enough to forget to read a few of the subtitles. I didn't want to ask Franny to rewind, I didn't want to speak at all, and so with the feeling of having missed something small but vital, I stopped paying attention altogether.

By the one-hour mark my restlessness had become impatience, and then a feeling of laziness, an accusation: Why wasn't I using this time better? I allowed the guilt space, I often do; it gives me the motivation I need. I looked to Franny, who was absorbed in the film. I squeezed her hand twice, our way of excusing ourselves, and went up the three flights of stairs to my office, grabbing a brownie and a glass of milk on the way. When I turned on the light it felt like a new day, like I was this small world's God. I thought again of that afternoon's failure of a pitch, of Milosz's sharp shoulder blades as he erased the chalkboard. Then I recalled my brief chat with Colin, which in retrospect seemed more positive than it had initially. After all, there'd been busting of chops. There was even mild flirtation, at least the kind you can achieve with such a straight-presenting man. I sat at my desk. I wrote a nice, unadorned email to Ian, asking him to lunch at the most expensive, most pompous restaurant in the vicinity of the office. I reread it and decided on a closing flourish: *I hope an uptown creature like yourself will deign to dine below Houston. We bohemians must eat too.*

Again I researched him online, using a finer-toothed comb than when his name originally crossed my inbox. I confirmed my hunch that he was unmarried and without kids. He apparently played squash regularly and had, for less than a year, belonged to the board of the Neue Galerie, a museum of twentieth-century German and Austrian art. I was surprised to find that he owned no property, at least not in this country. Given his way of behaving, and the sort of people he associated with, I'd had him pegged for a Jackson Hole guy, maybe Palm Beach. But it appeared he only rented, and just in Manhattan. I shot off an email to our due diligence lawyer, Jonathan Resnick, for his take.

As soon as I hit send I got tired. I hadn't even had my brownie. I brushed my teeth, slid into bed, and fell asleep faster than I knew myself capable of. It felt like I had one long dream, as if such a simple scene could occupy me for eight hours: I was at the beach with Franny and our daughter, who took after me. A seagull began circling us, getting closer and closer until it decided to attack. It seemed to know exactly how to hurt us, how the human body worked, how its own could be made into a weapon. Another seagull came to assault us, and then another, and then crabs appeared at our feet, biting. Soon, other non-beach animals joined in: squirrels, pigs, cats. It wasn't long before, from a distance, you couldn't even see the humans inside the flurry. Despite the animals' intelligence and brutality they never incapacitated us, we were always fresh, full bodies for them to dismantle. And despite all the horror, the feeling that persisted, that lasted even after I woke up, was amazement at my ignorance—that all my life I had never bothered to think about how easy it would be for animals to use themselves against us if they only knew how.

～

Franny was sleeping in. This she communicated by pulling the sheet over her head when I turned on the lights. She only slept in when she really needed it; to avoid waking her I forwent my morning espresso, the news on the television. The house was so silent and dark it seemed heavy; I was aware of the building's mass. If this made me feel cocooned, somehow protected from the outside world, it also made the air inside feel slightly pressurized, as though we had our own, stifled climate. I read the *Financial Times*, without caffeine it took me longer to make my way through it, but the words sank in more. Well, no; they sank in less, they were harder to read, they showed themselves as words. *Talks on the UK's future relationship with the EU boiled over when Britain lashed out at an indication from* . . . Each time I came across one of these physical metaphors—*boiled over, lashed out*—I took it at its primary meaning, I imagined a pot overflowing, one man whipping another. For financial writers to use such language seemed either silly or violent, the two perspectives irreconcilable, the choice of which to take up to me, but as I kept on reading I began to inhabit the latter. In just a few paragraphs I came across *largely fruitless* (a barren vineyard), *talks bogged down* (gods sending storms upon the earth), *points that have dogged the negotiations for months* (ruthless, ravenous hounds), *dealing a blow* (one final, fatal strike)—as if there were, underneath this world of finance and politics, a Greek tragedy, or a biblical parable, an unrelenting battle between good and evil with humanity stuck in the middle.

I took a slow shower. I put on one of my best suits. I called a livery car, gathered my things, and grabbed an orange from the bowl, sending a troop of flies scattering. I nearly fell down the stairs to the family room when I caught sight of Franny sitting on the couch, her face lit by her laptop.

I thought you were asleep, I said. She didn't respond, or even look up. She had on her signature frown, the near grimace that attended her most serious ruminations. *Getting an early start on work?*

Yeah, she said. *No, I mean no.* She shook herself out of it and looked up at me. *I'm researching Birdie's condition. Traumatic brain injuries. Uses of hypothermia, and . . .* She trailed off. I walked over and sat beside her. On the screen was a medical article: "Cooling the Injured Brain: How Does Moderate Hypothermia Influence the Pathophysiology of Traumatic Brain Injury." Beside her computer was a notepad with a list of names and numbers. Beside that was her phone, the image of Birdie's vitals monitor zoomed in.

Her phone would give us timing, she said, looking at me. *I mean, how long the ride took. Brain injuries are a matter of seconds. If they'd done hypothermia right when she arrived, she might already be better.*

Right, I said. *But now, given—*

I really wish the Uber had taken her somewhere else. Really I wish I'd escorted her out or had her stay over. We haven't used that Murphy bed once.

No, I said, rubbing her back. *We couldn't have known.*

She nodded, she admitted as much, but if she couldn't rectify this fact, she still needed to compensate for it. She was hoarding knowledge, practically, as if some blithe lack of it had allowed such a fluke disaster to occur.

Have some coffee, I said, squeezing her hand goodbye.

Outside I waited for the car and peeled the orange, pushing down on the crown until it gave way, my thumb burrowing between the thick skin and the dry, white tufts protecting the fruit. *I'll eat that too*, I thought, *the pith*—such a submissive word. I wondered what it would be like to eat an orange without that word or any other, without *rind* or *pulp* or *juice*, without even the name, its own color, and without any way to pronounce it good or satisfying. Would that not be transcendent? To experience without the urge to simplify, catalog, condense the present into some sort of future— A bird cawed and I looked up. It had no colors or patterns of note but I knew it wasn't a common pigeon. I thought of my dream; in contrast to the attacking gulls this bird appeared remarkably indifferent, of its own world. It settled on a branch of the oak tree in front of our place. Its head twitched a few times and then it was still. It looked young. I'd never before considered the age of birds, that they aged at all, but this one seemed to me an adolescent, newly capable but still somewhat unaware, his face—how did I know it was male?—sharply defined: the fleeting, easy beauty of youth.

The car came and I quickly peeled the rest of the fruit and put the skin in the compost bin. I'd had this driver before. *Cedric, how are you?* He nodded exuberantly but didn't speak. As I buckled my seatbelt I yawned, a yawn that seemed to never end, that nearly hurt my jaw. I rolled down my window and saw, across the street, tied to the railing of a stoop, a beagle. Her fur was white with big black and brown splotches that looked painted on. The dog belonged to the man who lived on the top floor of that building, the one across from ours, a man I didn't like not just because he seemed pretentious and aloof—I'd tried and failed to make conversation twice in our first week here, all I'd gleaned was that he was a book editor and married—but because I suspected he didn't pick up his dog's shit. I had stepped in some during my first stroll around the new neighborhood, it was the kind of shit a medium-sized dog might leave.

The dog had been panting. I wasn't really aware of this until she turned her head to look at me and stopped, she retracted her tongue into her mouth and closed it. Her brow knitted and then settled down again. I sensed sympathy. How? *Wait*, I said to Cedric; he'd put the car in drive. *I might have left something.* I pretended to search my wallet and continued looking at the dog. How did I sense sympathy? How does anyone? It was the ratios of her face, the tension of its muscles, her eyes. I squinted; they were chestnut brown. I tried to swallow but didn't have enough saliva. I sensed Cedric's attention, I'd stopped pretending with my wallet, I heard his head swivel to face the dog. No, it wasn't sympathy I saw, it was simpler than that, but deeper too. It was recognition. She recognized my guilt. Yes, guilt: that word—unlike *dreadful*, unlike *solemn*—wrapped fully around its meaning. It was such a pure, true thing, *guilt*, it was something even a dog could understand. And she did. She not only understood it, she took it from me, we shared it, between us there was this thing, this thing that was *guilt* but it was so much more. Guilt can be many things, but this thing—it was beyond language, it had to be, if even a dog could understand it. Yes, of course—that was why I'd felt nothing in the hospital, why I struggled to feel anything even now: I was trying to put something into words that couldn't be. I was trying to construct a coherent narrative about what happened and why, but there wasn't one. I wanted to laugh, I wanted the dog to see me laughing, she should know how she'd made me feel. I started to smile, I—

Are you okay, Mr. Caine?

My throat was too dry to speak. I coughed out empty words, the harsh air scraping my trachea, and then, inhaling again, filled the car with a screech.

Cedric winced, he turned to face me and repeated his question with more urgency.

I looked his way but stopped short of eye contact. *I'm okay*, I said. *And we can go, I found what I need.*

———

The activists, again. At eight in the morning. This time they only glared at me. They chanted more vigorously than their afternoon counterparts, and they were better dressed, too; maybe they had jobs.

I walked onto the trading floor, saluted Peter, and was stopped in my tracks by the sight of Simo at his desk. Simo was a Serbian researcher who I played at disliking but really was fond of, we all were; he had way too much charm for someone with his kind of brilliance. His focus was computational linguistics, in his past life he had published a well-referenced article on predictive modeling for infant vocalization. (His nickname—which he loved so much he asked for it on his business card—was *G4*, as in *goo goo ga ga*.) In

his final interview with us, Simo had said he had one require-
ment, which was that he never wanted to be in the office before eleven a.m. We allowed it and, up until now, had never
seen him a minute earlier.

I turned to Peter. *He was there when I got in*, he said.

I asked him to check the logs and he did, rotating his laptop so I could see. Simo hadn't left since yesterday, he'd been
here all night. I strode over to his desk, but before I could pronounce the second syllable of his name his hand shot in the air.

No no, he said. *No.*

I walked up behind him and looked at his screen, as if I
could tell what he was doing. Deafening house music wafted
up from his earbuds. How could he even hear me?

I made myself an espresso and went to my office, where I
found a sticky note on my door:

DO NOT DISTURB SIMO.
SIMO

I pulled it off, dropped it in my wastebasket, and sat at my
desk. I was eager to get the day going. That odd moment in
the car had stayed with me, nagged at me. In retrospect it was
ridiculous, the whole thing was, my connection to the dog,
the belief that what had happened with Birdie couldn't be put
into words. On the drive in I had done exactly that, I'd repeated to myself the sequence of events, over and over. We
had a dinner for friends we were trying to impress. We invited
Birdie with the hope of impressing them further. Birdie was
so obnoxious I had the idea to accelerate her jet lag by making her a cocktail with ZzzQuil. It worked, she left, and on
the way home she apparently fell, causing a traumatic brain

injury. Though it was impossible to know for certain, it was likely that the ZzzQuil had contributed to her fall. I was guilty of a terrible mistake of judgment, but only in hindsight. I could just as well have acquiesced to her request for more and more booze, and if the same thing had happened, what then? She was in critical care now, what was done was done, I wished it had never happened and could only pray that she made a speedy recovery. I should have told Franny but I didn't, and if I told her now it would only cause her serious distress; it would be a secret she'd also bear the weight of keeping. Yes, she would come to my same realization, that it would only do more damage to force onto Will or Birdie's family or anyone else the painful knowledge that it all could have been avoided. My own distress was affording them ignorant bliss; all the pain they were spared was passed on to me. And it *was* pain, it *was* distress. Every minute in the car had felt like an hour, all I wanted was to be at work, because then all this extraneous thought would be washed away. And here I was. Except when I pressed my finger onto the keyboard scanner, instead of opening my desktop, the screen showed five red asterisks below my name. I tried again, and then again after wiping my finger clean. I felt my fingertip with my thumb, as if there'd be a discernible difference, as if it were my skin that was the problem and not some system error.

I called Milosz, who picked up immediately. I explained the issue and he said he'd fix it when he got into the office, he was on his way. I asked if there was an extra laptop I could borrow, though I already knew the answer: no, he'd built our entire infrastructure—from our intranet to our email servers to our data servers to our fucking catering system—expressly so that no one could just *borrow an extra laptop*. We could each

access our work only from our office computer, with Milosz's
and my phones and home computers being the exceptions.

But I think I know what's wrong, he said. This was one of
his favorite lines, he wouldn't care much if the world was in
flames as long as he knew why. *Yes, I know now. Simo needed
more space on the server so I—*

Simo was here all last night.

I know.

Why is that?

I heard background noise, he was in Grand Central. Why did
someone who had made more than a million dollars a year for
five straight still take Metro-North? *Listen, Hersh.* He never called
me that, even though I begged him to. *Simo found something
very interesting yesterday. Something that might be, you know, big.*

What's big?

*Our phones aren't as encrypted as they should be, as we've dis-
cussed. And anyway I want to double-check his work myself before we
start larger conversations.* Larger conversations, I loved it. Finally
he was realizing that he had some agency, that he too could be
an entrepreneur. Maybe he'd even buy himself a tailored suit.

Absolutely, I said. *Double-check his work, and when you need
me I'm here.*

He hung up without a word, forgoing the usual *Goodbye,
Herschel.* This made me even more optimistic, it gave me a
great feeling, one strong enough to focus my attention on and
finally cast out all the other loose thoughts.

———

And yet. With access to the internet but none of my email or
work accounts, I couldn't help but spend much of the morning

researching injury liability. It was more curiosity than worry, at this point I had a clear head about it, I just wanted to know what the law said, I often found it surprising, it was like math or computer programming if they weren't undergirded by objective truths or relations but instead by realpolitik compromises between very human preferences. In this case, it seemed liability presupposed negligence, which in turn required proof of all of four distinct elements: duty of care, breach of duty, causation, and damages. Regarding my negligence in what happened to Birdie, these elements were, in my estimation: probably not, probably not, probably, definitely. The jurisdiction and the judge's personality seemed to matter—more proof that law was hardly even a social science. I tried researching the legality of the specific act, but drink spiking was associated with far darker territory; by then I was at the restaurant and didn't need that on my mind.

I didn't want to be impolite and order a drink before Ian arrived, but if I'd known he was going to be twenty-five minutes late I would have had one to relax, tardiness being one of the only traits I cannot abide. Instead I had to play whack-a-mole with the waitstaff: *No, water is fine; Yes, I'm fine for now; Just water, thanks*. It was a new waiter each time, each quite distinct from the last but all in the same disconcerting dress—high-waisted, oversized navy blue pants, the material more cottony than cotton, the texture like overlapping blurs—which matched the art, mostly de Kooning knockoffs and the like, though right in the center there was an authentic flake of art history, an amorphous, grotesque portrait by Frank Auerbach, *Head of J.Y.M.*, apparently on loan from a museum in Madrid. It was the restaurant's focal point, the main attraction of its website, too; I'd read about it when I looked up the menu. The painting was given yards of space on every side, and a dedicated trio of light fixtures; I wondered if the *museo*'s curators would approve of such direct illumination. I sat facing it but, just a minute before Ian arrived, moved to the opposite seat.

He walked in, gave his name to the maître d' and was escorted to our table. As he made his way over I was taken aback. Here was a new man, downcast, his pallor put in stark relief by the warm, golden lighting. I was ready to ask him if everything was all right, if he preferred to reschedule, but as soon as he saw me his face lit up, and he reverted back to the person I'd met two days ago.

We shook hands, exchanged *Good to see you*'s. As we sat down I waited for an apology for his late arrival, even a perfunctory one. Instead I got *Caine's not a Jewish name, is it?* I laughed, I didn't know what else to do. I wanted to ask how he knew I was Jewish, but couldn't. Was that the point? I tried to read him but he seemed absorbed in the décor. I followed his gaze to the painting behind me.

Auerbach, I said, *at least from the looks of it.*

Mm, he said, bringing his eyes down to me; they were alert, expectant. What? Still that first question?

You're right, of course, Caine *was* Cohen. *It was changed during the war, for the obvious reasons.* Why had I said it like that? As if it were some small inconvenience.

Yes, he said. *The war erased so much. Up my mother's side of the family you'd find prominent landowners in Austria, but it all went away during the* Anschluss.

On my own mom's side you'd find most of two generations gassed or starved. *Terrible*, I said, and glanced at the menu. *Will you be indulging this afternoon?*

If you will.

I called after the waiter and ordered two glasses of Gewürztraminer. I'd normally offset the choice with a comment about my sweet tooth, but I suddenly didn't care to.

He took some time to scan the menu. *It all looks great*, he said. *But the cacio e pepe has me at truffle.* Did I sense pride? For favoring something even pigs enjoy? He closed the menu and set it down. We made small talk about the neighborhood until the waiter came with the wine, at which point we put in our order: the cacio e pepe, and a lamb shank for me.

So, he said, picking up his wine glass. *To Colin, our public intellectual nonpareil.* In recent years Colin had begun moving into the Davos phase of his career, booking sundry speaking appearances, expounding on public policy, and democracy, and any other subject he was deemed to be expert in purely due to his net worth. We clinked glasses. *No, the man can get ahead of himself, but he's got more bona fides than he gets credit for. It's not the attention he's after, really, he's just an obsessive at heart. Last month, for example, he dedicated himself entirely to affect theory. He read all the books on it, could talk for days. Did, actually.*

And this month?

Charisma, he said, not missing a beat. He took a sip and I followed. *It's a topic we're researching together. Amazing how we take something like that for granted. It's in every story, at the core of every great man who's ever changed history, and still we don't know much about it. And I mean the real kind of charisma, by the way, not that salesman-y sort.*

I nodded, I looked into my glass. *A bit sweet, no?*

Maybe, he said. *But this is a sweet occasion, after all. Yeah, let's get down to it.* He set both palms on the table. *He's sick of the usual, the Webber crowd and all that. We both are. Every year they seem more and more behind the times, and now, finally, he's warming up to making a move—something I've been hinting at for years, by the way. But it's good timing. I think it was just at the end of your and Milosz's garden leave that he decided we should look around.* Mine, or Milosz's? He must have known they were different, Webber had done a great job of making that public, that I was precluded from working anywhere else (while still receiving my salary) for two years to Milosz's three, the implication being that Milosz would be a greater asset to the competition, the purpose being to make me livid, which it had.

Behind the times, I said. That's putting it mildly. I wouldn't be surprised if they were felled not by obsolete strategy—and their strategies are, definitely, obsolete; I'd sooner put my savings in some fucking robo-advisor—but rather a series of crippling lawsuits.

You think they've played on the inside?

Oh, I'm sure of it. Why else should their biggest coups come from pharma? They just happen to put their chips on all the right drugs pre-approval, hmm. But no, I'm talking about more prosaic legalities. The place is brimming with sexism, homophobia, casual racism, it's basically a time machine to 1985. I ran my thumb down the wine glass, taking off a streak of condensation. *I remember a managing director musing about how to incentivize women to stay home and have children. It wasn't a joke. He and his deputy crunched some numbers, landed on a salary of sixty-five a year. This was in the presence of our whole group, including two women. It's not just sexist, it's demoralizing.*

He shook his head in disbelief but couldn't hide a small trace of amusement. I felt challenged to pull out even more abhorrent examples. I told stories involving sexism and racism as well as terrible investment strategies, even investor deception. There was no question he was more interested in these latter categories, so I leaned in that direction. As the minutes flew by I found I was describing that byzantine, crumbling empire in perhaps too much detail, but I didn't care, my NDA with them didn't cover this sort of nonsense, and even if it did, people shared these things all the time.

It wasn't until the food came that we broached the topic of Atra Arca; in fact his questions began right as the plates hit the table. I was surprised, for someone supposedly *sharp as hell* he mostly asked for info he could have found online: the size of our first fund (besides, hadn't I told Colin?); whether we were using a master-feeder structure (ditto); whether we were an LP, an LLC, or a corporation; plans for satellite offices. I could have answered each of these in just a few words, but I padded my responses, spoke about what the leading quantitative hedge funds were doing, showed that I knew the field, that I'd even acquired privileged information. At some point he looked down at my plate and, seeing I hadn't taken my first bite, put down his fork and spoon. I usually lost my appetite in the thick of work. To appease him I started, I set the tines of my fork on the meat and stuck in my knife, down to the plate. The metal sliding against the ceramic sounded like nails on a chalkboard, I tried to be more careful as I began cutting, but each time a serration severed a hank of protein I felt a disturbing vibration in my hand. It reminded me of when I'd learned the saxophone as a child, the day they had us start to play with our teeth against the mouthpiece. No one else seemed to have a problem, but every time I blew into the instrument the hard rubber would vibrate against my teeth, bringing goosebumps out of my skin. It was an odd sensation, not only for being uncomfortable to me alone, but self-inflicted, too; every second of music was a second of pain. I'd refused to do it, learning to play without using my teeth.

Is there a problem with it?

I looked at the dish. It was magnificently arranged, not clever but well done, the braise a deep, smoky red, the bone dry and sliced impeccably flat, in the middle you could see the marrow, undisturbed. How did they manage to cut it so evenly? A saw, or— I was staring at it, I hadn't answered.

No, I said. I squeezed the utensils harder but that was as much as my hands would do, I couldn't stand to have that feeling again. I lifted the fork off the lamb and, keeping the knife still, gathered a bite of the side dish, charred eggplant and onion. I waited for the strange sensation to return. In its absence something like pleasure shot through my arms and shoulders, like when I'd first sipped the wine. I placed the forkful in my mouth, it was cooked perfectly, some cardamom, something sweet. Ian was looking at me. My skin had gotten clammy, and my own awareness of it didn't help. Could he sense what was going on? What *was* going on? What was this, this all-consuming uncertainty, I hadn't felt anything like it in years, decades, I was like a child who hadn't done his homework. I needed the moment to pass, I looked down at the meat, the braise had already dripped into the cut. I put the fork back on top of it and, using the knife, widened the incision just enough to peek inside. I set my utensils down. *Well, maybe it's a bit undercooked. Not to be picky, but you know, even with this sort of farm-raised blah blah blah you find terrible things. I'm sure they won't mind me sending it back, the last thing they want is a record of food poisoning.* I raised my hand for the waiter.

Well, maybe it was done on purpose, he said, flashing a smirk. *Some plot to stop the rich bastards that run this city. I say eat it anyway. You'll get good money, intentional torts are big business.*

Intentional torts. *Oh, really.*

One semester at Harvard Law. Torts is as far as I made it.

Hello again. The waiter. He gave us a small bow. *May I help with anything?*

I think this is a bit underdone, I said. *But you know, I really love this eggplant, I think I'll just switch to the eggplant tagliatelle.*

Excellent choice, he said, and removed the plate from the table.

Ian began speaking again. I couldn't focus, I only knew he had circled back to business by the way he laid his palm on the table, his other fist casually supporting his jaw. It took the word *Milosz* to make me present again. His head was bobbing to either side. *Two days. Three at most.* He was—what? Suggesting he meet directly with Milosz? Why would he need to do that when he had the CEO right in front of him?

I'm happy to assist in any way I can, I said. *I'm an open book, more to you and Colin than any other—*

But you're not intimate with the algorithm, or the data for that matter. Herschel, you're not a numbers guy.

But neither are you, no?

I'm not a PhD, correct. And anyway, this is just to cover our asses. Legally, I mean. What you're doing, it's uncharted territory, you said it yourself.

But why the need to see—

Herschel, listen. He stared at his plate for a protracted moment, returning to the face he had when he first came into the restaurant. *This isn't a negotiation. This ask, it's not a nice-to-have. We're not investing $220 million in a brand-new quantitative* *fund without knowing that we can access, if need be, every line of code.*

Well, you can't, I said. *We just don't do business that way. And please quote that to Colin.* I needed to digest a lot of this but I didn't need another second for that. Two hundred twenty million dollars was a lot, it was foundational, but we stood to make billions, tens of billions. I'd heard this story before: I compromise, I give in, and then down the road I find that some other firm Colin and this stooge invested in just happened to make the same inroads. I inhaled, I held the air. He leaned back and folded his arms, his hands clutching his biceps.

That's quite a disappointment, he said. The blood had returned to his face, he was his sly self again, the person he was always pretending to be. *But we can still enjoy this meal as friends.*

Your pasta, sir. A new server, this one short and pale with cropped blond hair.

She laid the dish in front of me, the steam rising into my face. I remembered how I'd begun to sweat earlier, and was afraid, for a moment, of pushing my fork into the food. But when I did I felt only the familiar sensation of metal against pasta, that reminder to assume a light touch; without it you'd hardly feel the food at all.

———

I spent the walk back to the office much the same way I'd spent the one to the restaurant: researching law on Wikipedia. I hardly gave myself a second to think about anything else—and that was the point, wasn't it? There wasn't a single thing from that meal I wanted to remember, starting with the lamb. Was I having a fucking stroke? I'd checked my heart rate, I'd recited the alphabet backward. I would talk to Magda about it in our session tomorrow, if it came to that—no, I was sure by then the episode with the lamb would feel like it had never even happened. But it would be impossible to forget the rest, each and every moment after my first bite of tagliatelle had brought some fresh hell.

First I had to endure an endless stretch of silence in which we both ate our food, looked around the restaurant, and avoided eye contact. I contemplated leaving—probably he did, too—but that would have meant burning the bridge for good. In that period of solitary eating I managed to convince myself that the relationship could be salvaged, that a perfect email later in the day would erase the lunch—and, if it couldn't, that maybe his suction with Colin wasn't as strong as he'd led me to believe.

And then, after we finished, while we waited for the opportunity to call for the check, and then as we waited for the check itself, he told me a story, unprompted, his voice like a knife cutting the air between us. It involved a Turkish artist who had been commissioned by an upscale French restaurant in Midtown—*in the same vein as this place*—for a painting that would be the dining room's center of attention; it would even grace their business cards. He took six months to finish it, and then had a handler bring it to the restaurant. The work was similar to Picasso's *Guernica*, too similar: there were the fragments of limb, the bull, the flames, even the light bulb eye overhead, not to mention that the colossal dimensions were almost exactly the same. Perhaps the painter was challenging the restaurant not to accept the work—he'd shown disinterest in the project from the beginning—but they did. Well, once it was hung and featured on their business cards, website, emails, et al., it was leaked to the media that the rich crimson that filled the background was made using the blood of human trafficking victims. Was it really? Who knew, the authorities didn't get involved and certainly the restaurant wasn't going to get a forensics team on it. At first, the incident seemed to prove the old saw about bad press—who wouldn't want to see the painting in person? But it quickly became a symbol of decadence, of the violence inherent in inequality, and who would be caught eating a seven-course meal under that thing? He finished the story, just as the check hit the table, with some derogatory remark about the Turks, how the *ottoman*, the stool, was the perfect word for what it was.

The way he told it—so knowingly, so self-tasting—made me think that I was missing a world of subtext. It was too neat a story, too unbelievable. But I couldn't figure out what the hell it was about, my concentration being spent on the check—rather, on not looking at it, at that point any hope I had for rapprochement was supplanted by my renewed desire to show him I wasn't going to grovel. For multiple minutes we again sat in silence, not even looking at our phones, a game I either won or lost when he said, so suddenly I almost flinched, *Let me get this.* He took out his wallet, smiling as if nothing had happened, and then dropped a heavy, jet-black American Express card on the bill.

By the time I got to the office I'd been able to focus on my phone just enough to confirm that, yes, intentional torts were *big business*, as he'd put it. And the term was quite a misnomer, torts need not be intentional at all, such as in the case of a prank with unintended consequences. It was fine, the potential legal severity of my deed made the whole thing easier. That is: over. There was simply nothing more to do. I regretted the act with all of my heart and that would have to be enough, I was not going to prison for doing something that was the equivalent of serving her two more drinks. I just wasn't.

I shook the thought away. For the past hour I'd been doing nothing but shaking thoughts away, but now I had a proper distraction. As I stepped through the doorway I saw, across the floor, Simo at his computer and Yuri by his side, looking on with a notepad. I made it halfway there before I was intercepted by Milosz, who put his hand on my back—had he ever touched me of his own accord?—and directed me toward my office.

Your computer should work again, he said, handing me a piece of paper. *But I had to change your password to this jumble. You can reset it, just not to your old one.* He opened my door for me, watched me sit down, and then closed it behind us. *How'd the meeting go?*

It was a success, I said. *I mean, I'd prefer to work directly with Colin, but—* He wasn't listening, the question was a formality.

I'm ready to talk, he said. *I've checked the work.* Was this what he'd looked like when his wife had given birth? No, this was more; it was his own gift to the world. *It appears we may not need as much data as we thought. We're getting confidence intervals that— Okay, um. We set a price. It did, the algo, it gave us a stock and a price and a time. It gave us $1.27 at 12:34, exactly. We'd only asked it to choose sometime today. So we waited for 12:34, in the meantime we tried to figure out how it got there, what it was putting together, if there was some industry trend, or maybe a sympathy play, but there was nothing remarkable. The stock started the day* at 1.13, the algo bought some there and along the way, and then, at 12:34, we sold at 1.26. We couldn't believe it, a point away from the prediction, this was miraculous, enough cause for celebration, but then we looked at the order book. There was a single trade for one hundred shares, at 1.27, at 12:34. Ten minutes ago, last I checked, it was back down to 1.15.

What's the stock?

It isn't consequential.

I know. I'm curious.

OBLN. Obalon. They make a balloon that you swallow and then it inflates in your stomach. For weight loss.

What's average volume?

One hundred thousand. It's small, sure. We made about $15,000, it was the max the algo would allow. But this isn't about profit, it's about validation. Simo calculated the odds of it hitting that price at that time, he took into account volatility, he took into account everything. Now he stopped pretending to play it cool, that this wasn't the best day of his life; he was a priest who had been visited by God. Hersh, it was one in fucking seven hundred something. He just— Well, we'll need to give him a raise. We'll need to rethink bonus structure. We prided ourselves on our egalitarianism. Every researcher had two coefficients, based solely on seniority and education, that defined how much they'd profit from the company's success. It was more Milosz's idea than mine.

Let's just stay level for a second, I said.

No, you're right. We'll need to think through some things, legally, I mean. I don't know if the laws even cover—if this would be— We'll need lawyers. Patent attorneys absolutely, and finance attorneys, I'm not sure. This is your side of things, no? Law? Apparently not. But hiring the best people to do our work? Yes, that was my job.

We already have patent attorneys. For the rest I'll talk to Mathis, see who she suggests.

Okay, and I'll— He looked up, moved his hand in a circle; this meant he was trying to convert his thoughts into words I could understand. *We need a new security system. Well, not new*—he knew *new* was a red flag—*just more. More, and—like, bolts, theoretical bolts. Not, I mean— It'll be a day of work, max, and less than the last upgrade.*

The last upgrade was $53,000.

Godspeed, I told him.

Godspeed, he said. He held his fist in the air. He was beaming. He left my office as promptly as he'd brought us in.

I opened my computer and entered the thirty-two-digit password he'd assigned me. I had eighty-three emails. The third most recent was from Resnick, a reply to my inquiry about Ian. *I couldn't find much except for the attached, which is as good a sign as any to keep away from the guy. FYI this settled out of court.* The document was a court filing from three years ago, alleged securities fraud, with Ian one of two codefendants. From the brief it looked like a classic pump and dump— a scheme to artificially boost demand for a stock, these days usually involving networks of message boards and the like— until I noticed that the plaintiff wasn't the SEC, but three hedge funds. He hadn't defrauded some schmucks on Reddit, he'd taken actual traders for a ride. (The filing even referred to Ian as *an experienced quantitative analyst,* which meant that he'd either fooled the funds into thinking so or downplayed his own capabilities to me.) It made sense then, why they'd settled, and why I hadn't found the case online: the hedge funds would have been embarrassed for it to see the light of day. Yes, the lawsuit certainly suggested I should *keep away from the guy*—this wasn't the sort of hijinks Liz Warren was always yelling about; it was abjectly criminal—but it implied much more. I had underestimated him. He'd not only done what he did but, even with that record, managed to get himself into the good graces of a man like Colin.

My inbox chimed, another message from Resnick. *And yes, you were right: He doesn't own property anywhere, not even under a shell co. And no wonder: Just last month he defaulted on a loan of only $225,000 from Deutsche.* Unscrupulous, wily, and (likely) bankrupt. I knew the type, in this industry you met him every once and again: the guy with more than enough cunning to make a decent living, but too much to ever do it the right way.

Just below Resnick's initial email was one from Colin, an empty message, the subject line *Call me when you're back.* Right, *you're back* implied *back from lunch*, he'd already been filled in. It hit me then, what was happening, not with Colin or Ian, but what was unfolding yards from where I sat. I closed my eyes. It wasn't so much what Milosz had said but the way he'd said it—even if I'd watched that scene without volume I would have understood what it meant: This wasn't just the best day in Milosz's life. It was, it could be, the best day in all of ours, everyone in this office and their families, their unborn kids, their kids' kids' kids. My arms filled with goosebumps, it was almost uncomfortable, like my teeth on the mouthpiece, like the lamb. Fuck the lamb. I stood up. I walked to the window, then back to my desk and then back to the window. Across the street I saw into another office, a company I'd always suspected was a design agency based on the spare space, the spare dress, those beanie hats they wore. On the street below I saw the protestors, there were now just four of them. Back up to the office. A woman at a printer, flipping through a pamphlet of oversized pages. It seemed like a scene from the past. It was, I really felt it: What had just happened, what was happening, was a first glimpse into the future of the markets, a paradigm shift that would eventually—not instantly, but over enough time to make enough people profoundly rich— upend the very definitions of public stocks, investing, money itself. Yes, I'd started the firm with ambitions no less than this, we'd sought to build an algorithm that could, without human intervention, systematically harvest profits from the public market. I'd just never let myself believe it was possible.

I went back to my desk; it was hard to sit down but I made myself. I grabbed my phone and called Colin. He picked up on the fourth ring.

Hi, Herschel.

Why hadn't I given this more thought? What exactly was I aiming for? Or rather, what—

Herschel?

Colin, hi, I said. *Sorry, just getting my bearings here.*

But you had only one glass.

Did you install a spy cam on the man? Or is he just one big recording device? I swear, I almost knocked on his head to see if it'd clink.

He laughed, a real one. *He's more warm-blooded than you'd think. But let's, uh— Well, Herschel, I want to be clear that what he said was right. We'll need to reestablish some of the working assumptions on our deal.*

That's why I'm calling, I said.

Oh, he said. *Good.*

For one, we'll need to cap you at 199. We've decided there'll be no majority investors. Also, with some recent news we're only able to offer you a seven percent stake instead of the twelve percent we talked about, which takes into account the downgrade from 220 to 199. And finally, as I believe I conveyed to Ian, we're firm that no investor, including yourself, will have access to any IP or proprietary tech.

A cap? And just seven percent? I can't say I'm not curious, just yesterday—

Things have been accelerating over here, and much faster than we could have anticipated. So I'll send over an updated draft of the contract and invite you to get your paperwork in before they accelerate further.

A cough, a reset. I could imagine his eyes swimming above his well-fed British cheeks. *Well, you've said your piece, then. I'll think, okay? I'm not pleased, but you know that. I'll think.*

He hung up.

Just like that, I could feel that our buyer's market had become the seller's. With this new energy I drafted an email to all those unpromising souls who'd come in yesterday, and everyone else I hadn't counted on making a move: Friday was the deadline. And then I wrote one to those I believed would sign, eventually; I'd done enough deals to know that, with enough heat, *eventually* could be smelted into *tomorrow*. I batched the emails and sent them all at once. I'd be fair. First come, first served. And unlike Colin they could keep the current terms. After all, we still needed to fill the fund. I stood up to go to the window again but on my way I heard a yip—there was no other word for it—from the trading floor.

I left my office and found, huddled around Simo's desk, almost everyone, nine or ten in all, including researchers, two traders, and Peter and Milosz. They were exchanging exaggerated *shhs*, and then, before I could make my presence known, they erupted, fists in the air, high fives, a hug, there could have been a football match on those screens. Peter and probably even the traders couldn't possibly have understood what was happening, but that didn't matter; they knew that whatever it was would likely make each of them millionaires. (Even Peter's relatively negligible equity could, given the new developments, amount to seven figures.) I hardly saw Milosz approach, he grabbed me by the shoulders.

CTHR, he said, shaking his head. *1.81 exactly, and at exactly 1:54. Simo had it at—*he snapped his fingers at Simo—*What was probability?*

One in two hundred forty, Simo said, still facing the computer, the only one who had kept himself together.

OBLN was one in seven hundred, Milosz said. *Together that's a probability of one in one hundred sixty-eight thousand.*

I shook my head, there was nothing else to do. The moment was too large to have any sense of, and so I hardly felt anything at all. Déjà vu—this same sensation had visited me recently, it took me a second: misaligned pupils, mouth agape, Birdie in the hospital.

Herschel, Milosz said, leading me a few feet away from the rest. *When I said we needed more security, I didn't— We need a new system outright. Look, retrofitted—it's going to cost a lot, I mean, as much as we've made today, which is now a hundred and sixty thousand. And we need to make some changes, some internal changes, the open-office policy, something more— Oh, a firewall, a serious firewall.* Firewall. I thought back to the *Financial Times* that morning, my urge to take words literally. *Starting now.* He looked back at the rest of them. *I mean right now.*

Right, I said, and rejoined the group. *Look, this is exciting,* I told them. *More than exciting. But it's not the end of our hard work, it's the beginning. So let's enjoy a bit of a reset. All support staff and traders can take the rest of the day off.* Peter looked disappointed, the traders ditto but they hid it better. *Researchers, please meet us in the conference room in thirty. By then we'd like everyone else gone. Thanks.*

I turned around and walked back to my office. I expected Milosz to follow but he didn't, probably he was feeding every stray paper through the shredder. If this new security spree was how he wanted to celebrate, so be it. I myself preferred to pretend as much as I could that nothing had happened, indulgences were a great way to lose sight of all that needed to be done. And yet, okay—when the idea came to me, I had no choice but to entertain it. No, it was too obvious, really. But the last time Bruce and I spoke, hadn't he said to let him know *how the whole endeavor shakes out?* True-to-form prick-speak— and reason enough to call.

Rebecca picked up, she didn't recognize my voice. She was about to tell me he was *in a meeting* but I said the call was about *a disturbing performance discrepancy.*

That same hold music, hopelessly optimistic.

Bruce Burns here.

Herschel Caine here. He laughed. Before he could say *The prodigal son returns* or something equally unimaginative I said, *I'm calling you as a courtesy. I wanted to let you know, before you hear it elsewhere, that things have picked up over here. To be candid, you may soon find that one of your old reliables has pulled some cash to throw into my endeavor. And before you call legal—yes, I've read the noncompete, inside and out. As have my lawyers.*

His silence lasted a moment, a moment more, long enough that I started looking around my desk, rubbing my hand along the wrinkled leather of my shoe.

You haven't changed, Herschel. You can sell, I'll give you that, but you treat funds like they're cars. God, he loved to hear his own voice. *In finance you sell money, you trade like for like. Sometimes it can be unclear who's selling who.*

He hung up, or at least he thought he did. Through the line came the white noise of his office. I continued to listen, waiting for him to curse me, to call someone and tell them what I said, but all I heard for the next five minutes was the steady rhythm of his typing.

———

We used the meeting with the researchers to reiterate our privacy policies, their NDAs, and the code of conduct around the dissemination of proprietary information (never ever). Milosz also introduced new security measures, including a reinforced VPN, four-factor authentication, security cameras in every section of the office, a new no-bag policy, lockers for electronics including phones, a firewall between researchers and the rest of the team, and standardized hours of 8:30 to 6:30. (Milosz had already talked with Simo about this last point. For this sacrifice—and, more so, his work—he'd been low-key promoted to vice president. *Low-key* meant that we weren't ready to announce this to the team, and *promoted* meant we were sidestepping our merit policies to give him 1.25% of the company up front, and an additional $200,000 in salary, effectively doubling it.)

So as not to let the meeting be a downer, we ended the workday early and Milosz took the team out for the most expensive sushi lower Manhattan had to offer. I was awkward at dinners like this, or maybe I was just the only one who wasn't; I said I couldn't go, that I had to lend a hand at home. When I returned to my office I found that the excuse had been made true: Franny had spent most of the day at the hospital and texted to ask if we could have dinner together. I said I'd order Indian and scheduled a delivery for later. I emptied my inbox and caught up on the market. I gathered my things and left, clocking out at what was probably a career best (except for holidays and the like): 5:45.

It wasn't until I stepped out onto Wooster Street—the May afternoon feeling more like July, the activists looking more like tired loiterers—that it struck me: I'd ordered a completely vegetarian meal. A coincidence, surely. I thought back to when I'd scrolled down the menu. Yes, I had only asked myself, *What would Franny want?* This day was too meaningful—was it not the most significant in my life?—to waste on worrying, and over something so trivial. I felt nothing but the wind at my back, my limbs light and agile, my joints frictionless. I wanted to sprint down the street, run into next week, next year, see all at once what difference I'd make. Earlier in my career I'd dreamt of a press profile, my face in *The Wall Street Journal* or *Bloomberg*; I would have settled for *Forbes*. Now that thought seemed so small, provincial even: to be yesterday's news, to keep a stash of copies in my office—for what? To show people? I felt sympathy for that man, but not empathy, I didn't want to repossess that mentality, let it repossess me. A well-managed career meant never decreasing your ambition (one of the few worthwhile lessons Bruce had taught me).

I'd write a book one day, I decided then. Not a business book, something more philosophical. How to apply the best lessons of finance to life. After all, this spirit I felt moved by, the spirit of forging ahead, it wasn't just about making money, it did not prescribe a one-track mind. Success meant applying yourself equally to all parts of your life, treating every aspect as worthy of your time, consideration, and courage. Like the situation with the meat, a great example. I could keep on ignoring it, this vague angst, or I could confront it head-on, look it in the eyes, acknowledge what I knew, deep down, must have been its source: I was fooling myself into thinking I couldn't eat meat just because of that dog, just because she'd justified, for a moment—through some ludicrous mental gymnastics—my numbness to Birdie's injury. As if it needed to be justified. As if I could go on like this forever.

I walked over to the halal cart at the corner and ordered a lamb shawarma in a pita, with none of the fixings; I wanted to see the meat as I ate it. A cab rolled up just as I paid—more wind at my back—and I got in. Tawfiq was the driver's name, I was about to ask how his day was going when he spoke in what I guessed was Urdu; he was on the phone. As we drove through SoHo and Chinatown I watched the commuters, the delivery bikers starting their night shifts, the street grocers with nearly depleted bins of produce. I didn't normally get to witness this part of the city at this time of the day. On the Brooklyn Bridge I craned my neck to see the tourists taking selfies and panorama shots. I picked up the sandwich, felt the weight of it in my hand, and parted the foil. There was no steam but the smell traveled fast, I couldn't help but visualize the odor. What shocked me was not that the familiar scent was now fetid, but that the particles carrying the putrid aroma were now in my nose, on my face, that even if I wasn't going to eat the meat—and I wasn't, I would vomit before it hit my lips—it was now a part of me, it was inside me, I had already consumed it. I moved it away from my face, my arm as straight as possible. I was conscious of the driver, that he might wonder what I was doing, I thought to just throw it out the window but then, making eye contact with him in the rearview mirror, reconsidered.

I'm not sure it's good, I said. *Does it smell weird to you?* He said something into the phone, checked the road and then flashed me his eyes. *Do you not eat meat?* I asked, but he didn't answer, just reached his hand back and held it open. I gave him the sandwich, he brought it to his face and then gave it back.

It smells fine to me, he said, and continued speaking in Urdu. Again I felt its weight. Now that I wasn't going to eat it I was curious, it was intriguing in the same way any ambiguous, terrible stench was. I gave it a brief sniff and then a longer one. It seemed obvious now that it would be so repugnant, after all it was a dead animal, one that had been killed, allowed to rest, and then heated, the fire annealing its cells, making waste of the bacteria and pathogens that had been otherwise thriving. I'd had enough. I rolled down the window. The wind muted the odor, fresh oxygen cleansed my passageways. I looked back at the sandwich, remembering the feeling of the knife going through the lamb. I held my hand over the meat, I extended a finger, but before I could do anything more I tossed it out.

I spent the rest of the ride listening to Tawfiq talk into his earpiece, half expecting the chatter to coagulate into something more than noise. If at first I felt like an infant, waiting to acquire speech, by the end I realized I was more like a dog; even as I became familiar with the sound of the language—the cadences, stresses, intonations—not one jot of meaning materialized. We could have driven like that for the rest of our lives and still I'd never cross the invisible boundary between us.

When we got to the house I gave him a tip as big as the fare. As if to make up for my behavior, as if I had to apologize—no, I wouldn't even be the weirdest passenger he had today. As he drove away I felt funny, as if I were, some-how, still in the car. It was déjà vu, again: I'd been in this exact same spot before, this morning, when I'd seen the dog. All of this nonsense had started then, when I sensed that the dog could sense me, sense my guilt. Of course it was all just my conscience, compensation for my inability to face Birdie's ac-cident and my part in it, I'd deluded myself as a punishment, to atone. There was nothing special about the dog, a fact so obvious I almost laughed. I only needed to see it again, to come face-to-face with it, then I'd see it as it was—a dog. And then I'd understand how much of this was all in my head, could be done away with, but properly: through careful intro-spection, coming to terms. I'd wake up early tomorrow, be on the lookout; its owner, Ben, walked it every morning. I looked up to my office window, and then to all of the other windows of our house. Was Franny home? It didn't seem like it, but she would be soon. I imagined us in the dining room, eating, her telling me about her day. No, tomorrow morning wasn't good enough, between now and then was tonight, and I couldn't deal with more of this, another moment like the lamb, not in the presence of Franny, she knew me as well as I knew myself, she'd pull the thread as I had, see what a tremendous ball it was part of.

I looked from the windows of our place to those of the top floor of the building across the street. I walked over, opened the black metal gate and hopped up the stoop. I buzzed num-ber 3: *Ben & Hadley John.* I waited a moment, looked back at our place. The intercom: *Leave packages in the foyer, thanks.* The door unlocked. I waited, buzzed again. When the intercom clicked I said, *Hi there, is this Ben?*

Yes?

Hi, it's Herschel, from across the street. I hope you don't mind the impromptu visit, but I wanted to talk about something, if you're free, of course. It's about a book idea, actually.

Silence, a long one, well past polite. *Sure, you can come up.* The door buzzed again.

The stairwell was musty, dark, carpeted. He met me at his door, his brow furrowed until I was a few feet away, and then his face melted into genuine friendliness. *Herschel, good to see you.*

Likewise.

He stepped aside and I came into the apartment, where I saw no dog, not even a trace of one. There were rugs everywhere, books on every wall, dark wood furniture and a couple of mid-century-modern statement pieces. It was exactly how a book editor might live, but there was another gestalt at work that I couldn't quite put my finger on. Then I saw a Chagall print, and then another. *The Essential Leonard Cohen* facing outward on a shelf. A framed illustration of an everything bagel. Yes, it seemed to be a Jewish household. He wasn't, I was sure, his nose and—he just wasn't. His wife, maybe, that would explain the décor, but now I spotted one more object of that order: his hair. Yes, he had a Jew-fro. And the facial expressions too, the way of being. Perhaps I shouldn't have been so sure. I recalled our past encounters, yes, he wasn't just neurotic but the exact right valence: aloof, vigilant but distracted, quick to laugh, to demur.

You've disproven a theory of mine, I said.

Oh?

It's that Brooklyn Jews don't own dogs.

Oh, I'm not— He laughed. *We're not.* Yes, my comment had given him some small pleasure. And now that I knew for sure,

I saw the sliver of daylight between him and my people; his wasn't disposition but affectation—permanent by now, sure, but it was fundamentally contrived. It wasn't the only thing that now seemed like a performance, it was like his whole personality was; he presented himself as some serious man, a man attuned to meaning, as if he'd tapped into a deeper stratum of life. He was the type to look down on a businessman, as if the world didn't show itself to me the way it did him. I'd read Whitman, Austen. I took an entire class on Barthes in college. Sure, it was good with a few glasses of wine, but in the morning it didn't mean anything.

He invited me to sit down and I did, on a couch, across from him. I was about to mention the dog, a comment meant to make him call it into the room, or tell me its whereabouts if it wasn't here, but then he said, *Remind me what you do. For work, I mean.*

Right. So, I run a hedge fund built around algorithmic trading.

I've read about that. He seemed to be putting two and two together, or failing to. *Have you been in the neighborhood long?* Ah, so he didn't think a certified Finance Guy could appreciate the modest charm of Cobble Hill.

Since February. So, no, I laughed. I readjusted in my seat, taking the opportunity to again look for the dog. *Co-op, I assume?*

We rent.

Right, much easier that way. The second you buy you find a million little things wrong.

He gave a slight smile. *So what's this book idea?*

Of course. So, it's—it's really about how to apply the best lessons of finance to life. His face fell; the pitch was dead on arrival. *Treating yourself as a business, one run by the finest—*

Ah, I should have made it more clear, I really only do fiction.

These days, anyway. He glanced around, surely looking for the words to kick me out.

And I should have gone with my gut. I just thought self-help sold well. No, I've got something much better. It's not fiction, exactly. Stranger than. What my firm aims to do, it's— Well, if we're successful—and trust me, it's just a matter of time before we or one of our competitors are—there will be no such thing as a stock market. Bingo. *You see, people buy and s—* My consonant continued, starting before and ending after the interrupting noise: a ragged tear that ripped the air and made my steady *s* seem as artificial as a computer sound. I swallowed, I felt the air against my neck, my wrists.

Lucy? Ben shouted, his expression both grimace and frown. The noise again, now so obviously a bark, and then the scampering of feet and the chime of a collar. She jumped on his lap, he ran his hands up and down her neck, saying *Okay okay okay.* He was trying to take her interruption in stride but he seemed annoyed; probably the dog was his wife's idea. He looked at me, felt my glare, performed enjoyment. The dog had gotten what she wanted, she barked again and then hopped off him. She made a half-turn, facing no one, and then snapped her head in my direction. She cantered over and lifted her front legs onto the couch, her paws right next to my thighs. I flipped my palms up and she answered by placing her paws on top. The motion was inelegant, like she'd forgotten about gravity, to stop herself from slipping off she had to dig her paws into my hands. It was pleasantly strange, her claws were made of such lifeless material—the pads underneath, too, like a baseball scuffed by pavement—and yet it was through these dead cells that she felt the world. I peered into her eyes, my body tight. I expected the same look as before, the recognition of my guilt, but the transmission of emotion had reversed. Now *she* was open to *me*, the expression on her face naked, like a human in a play or a bad movie. I was embarrassed by her sincerity, and then in awe, nearly jealous of her guilelessness. I saw sadness, and loneliness, but I didn't, really; those two words needed to be added to the list, after *solemn* and *dreadful*, more examples of the hubris of language. Words and logic could not help me describe to myself the kind of pain she felt in this world, a world mostly confined to an apartment filled with things that meant nothing to her, supervised by a man and woman who lived a life she couldn't make sense of and never would, and when her day finally brought her into contact with a like mind, in a park or on the street, and she erupted in emotion—in all emotions at once, after all she'd finally met another being who could recognize the full spectrum of what she felt—she was scolded, her collar pulled, the intensity of her passion matched by the discipline imposed to smother it. But stop. I was still clutching language, clinging to it as I would to a ladder over a too-cold pool. If I was afraid the water would be painful, still I knew it wouldn't hurt me, really, and when would I ever have the chance to feel something like this again? I let go, and the second I was immersed I knew it would be just as cold getting out as it was getting in. I was already acclimated, the world had shrunk, it had become muffled, pale, all the colors were still there but they were severely diminished versions of themselves. Still underwater, I lifted my hands from under hers, ran them up her arms to her shoulders and back, to her neck, I ran my fingers through her hair, feeling her skin and the pounding life beneath. It took a lot to force me up to air: my name, now being practically shouted, *Herschel. Herschel!* I looked up to see Ben across the room, his hands on the seat of his chair, ready to push himself off if necessary. Colors refilled; sounds were crisp again, no longer that oceanic rumble.

What are you doing?

I couldn't help but let his words infect me, force me to think through language, too. What *was* I doing? I was holding his dog. I was crying. I wiped the wetness from my cheeks, I could feel my face tighten in consternation. He gave a brief laugh, so contrived, so obviously meant to release the moment from its gravity, that it disgusted me. He snapped his fingers twice, ordering the dog to return to him, and dutifully it did.

It's been a day, I said. For a fleeting moment I was aware that I was debasing myself, matching his deception—and then I didn't care. *I'm sorry, I've just been under a lot of pressure at work. I guess it was bound to come out somehow.*

He nodded, and then again, more reassured, happy that we'd found an explanation.

No, he said, *I get it. I mean I think I do. I imagine that kind of workplace doesn't allow for much show of emotion.*

It doesn't, I said, looking at the floor, the whimsical patterns in the Tabriz-style rug. Back at our place we had the real thing: $12,000, another $1,000 to ship it back. *Though I don't imagine you bawl your eyes out in front of colleagues.*

Not every day, he said. I laughed, but he wasn't kidding. *Really, I'm often moved by my work. When I find a manuscript that I love— Well, actually, it's not when I'm reading it myself, but communicating my love of it to my peers.* He nodded to himself. *It's interesting.*

Indeed, I said, glancing at him before scouring the rug again. Finally, he snapped his fingers and pointed to the door.

The dog barked, bowed its head, and with its collar jingling scuttled out. I leaned back on the couch and resumed eye contact.

So, he said, *there will be no such thing as a stock market.*

That's my take, at least. But actually, I think I ought to call it a day thinking about work. So let's pick this up some other time.

He sucked in his lips, nodded, and stood. I got up, too. As we walked to the door I watched his face, worried what it would show, but he seemed, if anything, amused.

I trotted down the stairs and out to the street, which had already darkened and dropped a few degrees. Franny had arrived home while I was at Ben's, or had only now turned on the lights. The warm glow of the living room and kitchen made it seem like a home; if I were a stranger walking by I might feel envious of those inside. The wind blew in from the piers, making me aware of the wetness still around my eyes. I wiped them dry and then again, the cotton of my sleeves too abrasive for that thin skin. I breathed in, and out. If I could still access that moment, just a few minutes ago, it was only as an echo. I was happy it was over, I felt at home in my body again. I imagined being in the house with Franny, between the thick walls of our relationship, her gaze reaffirming exactly who I was.

I crossed the street and stopped at our steps. I was surprised to find that I was looking forward to hearing about her time at the hospital, as if I was about to be updated on some national issue. It gave me pause, this new peace, it was detached enough from reality that I feared she would notice the space between, stick her hand in, tear it open. I needed to get my head right, think critically. Yes, and this started with catching a blind spot I'd failed to see before: the color of the drink

I'd served Birdie. It had been a deep crimson unlike anything we had on our liquor cart. What if Franny asked? Thoughts like these came to her all the time, it was like her brain was constantly being dredged, minutiae surfacing for no reason at all. I turned and started down the street, east, to the liquor store.

Yes, she had a genius for loose ends—not that she was scatterbrained; no, I believed it was the very order of her mind that made uncategorized thoughts so noticeable. I was the opposite, it seemed all of my thoughts lived in one big space with only gossamer organizing principles between them. This I hadn't realized until I'd met her, known her long enough to grade my mind against hers. We did this often, set ourselves side by side, by this point it was practically a reflex. In fact, even before I first saw her face, we were, in some way, competing. It was a Sunday morning. The eastern leg of the Prospect Park loop. She appeared at my left, a vague figure, her pace quicker than mine, but I was at a jog. I increased my speed until it was just above hers; she was obviously keeping up with me. I slowly accelerated, so she wouldn't notice, and when she finally did, when she gave up and peeled off to the grass, I stopped and turned around. Grudgingly she met my eyes; she was a poor loser, this I'd learn over and over. But the attraction was obvious, we talked for a bit, she told me her number, without giving me the chance to write it down, and then sprinted ahead. I chanted it to myself for the thirty minutes it took to get home. When I texted her later that night, she responded with a shamelessly cheesy riddle: *Tuesday at 7 works. Meet in the middle of Tennis Court.* This took me some time to decipher, as there was a large tennis facility adjacent to the park, but she didn't seem the type for errant capitalization.

Sure enough there was a *Tennis Ct*, a short road south of the park. It was a bit precious, out of a fairy tale, nothing I was used to—she either, I'd learn. But it made sense in retrospect, she had a side to her that was so childish, so unguarded, she was the kind of person to search Google for *bagels near moi*. And this trait was put into sharp relief by the rest of her: she was brutally honest, profoundly self-sufficient, and unyielding in her professional life. She was well aware of the distance she set others at; she owed it, she said, to her upbringing, which she described on our first date as *joyless*. When I told her she had an interesting laugh she just nodded, she knew. She believed it was because she had rarely heard anyone in her family laugh, and so she'd had to invent her own. This laugh she deployed mostly in the face of life's biggest tragedies; or maybe it was just that her laugh expressed exactly this, that life was tragic.

I walked into Ruben's Liquors, nodded at the cashier, and, making my way to the back, spotted the exact color I needed: red apple schnapps. At the counter I asked for a bottle of Laphroaig 16, too—what we drank at the end of our first date.

We were ecstatic together, bewildered by one another. In the beginning it felt like it was us two against the world, a feeling we were guilty of indulging. In the first nine months we went on three trips to six different foreign cities (this was at the beginning of my garden leave), and in each we faked a proposal in the middle of the city square: in Plaza Hidalgo, Trafalgar Square, Östermalmstorg, Campo Santa Margherita, Piazza Navona—even in the crammed grand Bazaar of Tabriz. We never told anyone we did this, it was obnoxious, and besides, we were, in a way, superstitious. It seemed to us that out of the couples we knew, the ones proudest of their relationship in the

beginning—those who were the most conspicuously happy—
were the ones falling apart. The couples going through the
slow drudge of divorce (or headed in that direction, anyway)
were the ones who never appeared to disagree, who were always polite to each other. In retrospect it was obvious: po-
liteness implies distance. Franny and I disagreed frequently,
openly, perpetually we played each other's devil's advocate.
Likewise, we often discussed the attractiveness of strangers, I
felt free to check out women, and she men—often she'd point
them out to me. In some unspoken way we were ashamed of
this even though we knew we shouldn't be; when with friends
I wouldn't dare let my eyes wander. And it seemed to be the
couples I feared would be the most judgmental who were now
fundamentally unhappy. It was no small irony that their problem appeared to be, at its core, a crisis of morality. Sometimes
it seemed as if they treated virtue the way previous generations had treated wealth: not just as a precondition for social
acceptance but as something with only one number attached
to it. They fetishized morality, practically, they forgot the very
thing it was, that it was not about scale but priorities, that its
power came from compromise, that two people might both
strive to be *good* while having irreconcilable definitions of the
term. It was as if, after having spent years not coming to terms
with who their spouses actually were, these couples were suddenly realizing there was a foundational discrepancy between
them. Years ago, when most of my friends were more or less
single, they looked for partners with certain traits—charms,
talents, kindred deficits or proclivities; and maybe morality
was on the list, too, but it was at most a minor box that could
be checked off with just a few evident acts of probity: donat-
ing, volunteering, palpable displays of empathy. They now

hated each other, these couples, hated even the other's laugh; it seemed that once someone stopped being *good* in your eyes, it was only a matter of time before they'd earn your disgust.

I saw Franny now, through the window. She was lifting our dinner from a large paper bag. Her movements appeared languid, but perhaps I was only projecting, given the day she'd had. Either way, I felt ready to hear about it, I was bracing myself: the proper emotional state for what was to come.

I opened the door and walked up to the kitchen. When Franny saw me she stopped what she was doing and came over, slowly, her head and limbs limp. Her arms wrapped under mine and around my back, she squeezed me harder than usual; through the pressure of her clasp I felt my own muscle, fat, ribs. We lasted like this for a minute or more, I let her be the one to end it and when she released me I saw her eyes were wet. It was unlike her, I thought it was proof of her difficult day, but then she said, *I'm so happy we're trying.* That word, *trying*, repeated in my head, each time attaching to a new meaning. Inside of me bloomed an unexpected joy, but it seemed unearned, premature, we were so far away, after all we were only trying. The feeling was familiar; I'd felt it earlier, at work. Sure, if it wasn't full-on kismet it at least felt right that the firm was in a similar stage of inception. Yes, the algorithm doing its job was wonderful, a miracle even, but that was just the first step of Atra Arca as a business. As I'd already learned, and brutally, getting the capital we needed while protecting our intellectual property was not—

What are you thinking about? she asked.

A lot, I said. *New beginnings.* I thought to tell her about the breakthrough at work but wanted to wait until I'd heard about the hospital.

She looked down to the bag in my hand. *Something good?*

Not really, I said, which I thought, incorrectly, would decrease her interest in it. She watched as I walked over to the liquor cart and, with my back to her, crouched in front of it. I placed the red apple schnapps behind an oversized Svedka bottle, and the Laphroaig in front.

What do you think of the door? she asked. I didn't understand. I stood and she nodded down to the foyer: in place of the painted gray front door was a dark walnut slab. *I'm sick of feeling like we live in someone else's home. It's one of the few things you don't need a permit for.*

I'm sorry, I said. *I hadn't even noticed*. I walked down the stairs, ran my hand over the smooth finish, admired the pattern in the grain. My eyes went to the distortions where there'd been knots, the nested ovals like rings around planets. I imagined being the first to discover that this was what was in trees, that our universe hid such beauty, and the power I'd feel from that. I thought of being on Wooster after I left work, wanting to sprint down the street.

I felt her stare. Even from a distance she could tell my mind had wandered. I couldn't help it, I hopped up the stairs and let it spill out of me, I told her what happened as I'd lived it, starting from when I got back from lunch and ending when I left the office. She was excited, proud, curious—all of the things she should have been, except their intensity continually lagged behind what I myself felt, what I was hoping for from her. We both felt this gap, just as we both knew its cause: the guilt of having this conversation instead of the other one. She asked the right questions, I expounded with the requisite enthusiasm, we shook our heads in wonder. And then, to allow for a proper reset, we didn't speak at all. I set the table, she apportioned the meal, I opened a bottle of Malbec. After we'd each tried the food, taken a few sips of wine, and felt fully in the room, at the table, she told me about her day.

She didn't know where to begin, she started and stopped multiple times and then left to get her notepad from the other room. Even before she went to the hospital she'd tried calling over two dozen doctors, nurses, and administrators, at Methodist and elsewhere, first to find out precisely what had transpired when Birdie arrived, then to determine if it was medically safe to move her to another hospital (it wasn't), and finally to see if she herself could be designated as Birdie's health care surrogate (that would be up to Will, though transnational laws complicated things). She now had a grasp on traumatic brain injuries, phases of consciousness, diagnostic imaging, standard neurological exams, and the overwhelmingly wide range of prognoses. (*No two brain injuries are the same*, she said. *I must have read that or heard it fifty times today.*) She filled me in with the expediency of someone who only needed to deliver herself of her burden, her words came too fast to carry tone, sentiment, emotion; that seemed, in some way, to be the point. It was only when she'd reiterated everything she'd learned, or at least everything she could remember to say, that she returned to herself, the same woman who'd sat next to me in the hospital, just as dumbstruck as I. And then, with a slow, weary voice, she spoke to me not as a case manager but as someone who'd just visited a friend afflicted by tragedy.

The biggest change since yesterday was probably the presence of Will. He hadn't slept since he'd heard the news; mostly he stared blankly at Birdie while Franny tried to find encouraging things to say or else just talked about her own life, asked about his. They were strangers united by something that affected them at a severely disproportionate scale, and Franny confided to me that she felt nervous about outdoing him in grief, about even showing emotion if he wasn't.

· The only good news was that Birdie might have temporarily *emerged* from her coma into a vegetative state; this was exactly what yesterday's doctor had said wouldn't happen. Franny hung on to this error, as if it might mean that his entire summary of her condition could not be trusted. But today's doctor was actually much worse, he seemed to have an affinity for disabusing Franny of her optimism. She preferred to listen to the nurses, who repeated that her condition was *stable*. Being the only positive word that could describe Birdie's state, it bore the weight of all their encouragement to her, and, in turn, of her encouragement to Will, and to Birdie, whom she often spoke to, even if—as today's doctor repeatedly reminded her in his blunt tone—Birdie couldn't understand her. This was easy to forget, or choose not to believe, because for a few minutes Birdie spoke. Maybe it wasn't *speaking*, but that was the word Franny used with Will, with me, too. The noises that Birdie produced, which didn't seem to be in response to external stimuli, were too unusual to explain in words. Franny tried. *Primal moans*, and *Down syndrome-esque*, and *brassy brays*. After every attempt I nodded as if I got it, not just because I was desperate for her to stop, but because I feared exactly what happened next. She prefaced it by saying she didn't want to do it, only that she wanted me to understand. And then she did the impression.

My anticipatory dread had been inadequate. The sound filled my head, I was aware of the depth of my skull just as her earlier hug had made me feel the dimensions of my torso.

It was more than noise, I saw it in me as smoke, it left a trace of moisture that occasionally collected into a drop and fell, causing me to hear again an echo of the original imitation. Each new time I experienced the sound, it seemed more and more like a caricature, something grotesquely humorous, it was cruel of her to do, disrespectful even. I was being unfair, but still I now wanted to get the meal over with as soon as I could, I couldn't stand hearing those echoes in her presence, couldn't stand to blame her any more for putting them into my head. I ate as fast as I could without being obvious about it, and when I'd finished my plate I excused myself, saying I needed to go upstairs and catch up on work. To make up for it I told her I would clean up, and when she went to the bedroom to call her mom I came back down and washed the dinner dishes along with all of those in the sink; we had a dishwasher but it felt good to do it myself, to feel the grease come off, at least the running water helped muffle the echoes, which had become less frequent but more—what? They had become something else, louder and more pixelated, a noise I could no longer imagine coming from Franny's throat. As we went about our evening I found that their infrequency was its own curse, I could no longer anticipate them, feel the condensation gathering on the ceiling of my mind. After Franny went to bed, early even for her, I tried reading in the living room. The book was about the history of debt, it was repetitive and left-leaning, I hardly read two full paragraphs before I surrendered. The echo sounded again as I closed the book, and then again as I put it out on our stoop for the taking. It happened as I opened the fridge, and as I checked the thermostat, and it would happen again and again, follow me to bed and into my dreams, if it let me dream, if I could fall asleep. I turned on music, *The Four Seasons*, Max Richter's recomposition. I knew every movement, it was stabilizing, already I sensed that the echoes would stop. I needed it louder just to be sure, but I didn't want to disturb Franny, so I put on my noise-canceling headphones and set the volume so high I couldn't even hear the liquor bottles jangle as I fished out the red apple schnapps. I loved *The Four Seasons*, it made me feel like a boy, especially the first movement of "Spring," which was genius in art, it was truth, this was what spring would sound like forever: rebirth, renewal, reawakening—concepts that were around long before we were, you could play *The Four Seasons* to a pig or an elephant and they would have to feel, somewhere, what it was all about, what Vivaldi and Richter had captured, truncated, transmuted to fit our conception of beauty. No, maybe it would only repulse them, serve as just another example of our need to abstract everything away from what it actually is. I emptied out a quarter of the schnapps into the sink, and then poured myself a glass. As I took my first sip my finger brushed against my eye and I realized I'd cried. Past tense. So it had been brief, surely just the rapture of the music. I sat down and listened more, but by the end of the third movement of "Spring" I felt nothing, it was maudlin and contrived, the soundtrack of some romantic melodrama. The moment I thought this thought, *I feel nothing*, the echoes returned, louder and longer and more warped, one elongated vowel that hardened into a consonant. I stood up. I finished my glass. This was the power of my imagination, I reminded myself, this was only a punishment inflicted by one part of me on the rest. But if I was acting this irrationally, volunteering myself for some bogus moral retribution—well, what else hadn't I thought through? Wasn't it also possible, for example, that I'd failed to properly investigate the supposed offense? Was I taking my own involvement for granted? NyQuil put me fast to sleep, sure, once I was already in bed, usually late at night. But what was the effect when you were trying to stay awake? When you were outside with the cool night air on your face?

Birdie had started with a glass of wine, just as I had tonight. Then she'd had that black currant cocktail with barely a splash of vodka, the alcohol content far less than that of my glass of schnapps. Then she'd had the ZzzQuil, with another splash of vodka. I went to the liquor cart and picked up the Laphroaig, I filled my glass a quarter of the way and shot it. I listened for Franny, there was only silence. I went up the stairs to the bathroom, retrieved the open bottle of ZzzQuil, and came back down and into the kitchen, where I emptied it into my glass, filling it almost to the top. This would make up for the difference in weight between Birdie and me, if there was one, and my presumed short-term tolerance, given I'd had ZzzQuil two nights ago and NyQuil three nights before that.

I sat down and looked at my phone. 9:52. I'd give myself half an hour, that was about how long Birdie had stayed after drinking the ZzzQuil cocktail. I'd forgotten about the music; I was now on the second movement of "Summer." I listened impatiently, taking the echoes in stride. I tried to hear them as part of the composition, evaluating the new work as a whole. By the end of "Winter" it was 10:16, which was good enough. I grabbed the empty ZzzQuil bottle, put on my jacket and shoes, and stepped outside. The air was like it was two nights ago, same temperature, same humidity. There was even the residue of a light drizzle. How had I forgotten about that? It was so important. I walked down the street in the same direction she had. I threw the ZzzQuil bottle into the trash can of an apartment halfway down the block. I felt a bit woozy, tired—like I'd had a few drinks and a lot of ZzzQuil. At the end of the block I stopped, stood still, and then began walking slowly. I watched my feet, deciding which exact spot on the pavement I wanted to plant each step on. I walked forward and in reverse; I was, for the most part, precise. The investigation was complete, it should have been at least, but then I remembered there was something else I could try—an idea I'd dismissed when it first came to me as I left the house. I walked toward the street and then, without looking at my feet, stepped off of the curb. The movement felt natural enough, but when I brought my other foot down it surprised me, it touched the ground a moment sooner than I expected. No, I hadn't slipped, I hadn't misjudged where it would land, but before I could put those facts to work the echo came, and not as some monstrous version of itself but as Franny had initially done it; I remembered her face, too, which wasn't meant to mimic Birdie's but, without her even trying, showed me how she herself had looked when she heard the noises. I felt I was inside her, Franny, looking at Will looking at Birdie, those whines filling the room, how empty they were, it wasn't even communication, it was one-way, the emanations of a mind that could no longer latch on to the world.

I was sprinting now, the wind against my face negating what I'd drunk, it even seemed to turn it in my favor, like I had a new reserve of energy, I could tell how fast I was going but it felt sustainable, as if I could go like this forever. I thought of earlier, my urge to run down Wooster and into the future, and how different this was, I was running only to stay present, the faster I went the more I felt in place, in my own body. The echoes had stopped, I heard only the wind whipping in my ears, the sounds of cars. I hit Court Street, a commercial strip, there was hardly anyone out but I wanted to be completely alone, I turned onto Wyckoff and picked my pace back up, I ran past the projects and down more blocks of brownstones. Soon I felt my body start to resist, not some sudden warning but a continuous reminder, a gentle plea. My lungs were fine, my legs were fine, my arms and core were barely straining, my body only asked how much longer. I wondered if I could actually hurt myself, if it was possible to kill yourself from the inside, to exert yourself past some limit, if the body had a backup plan besides the doling out of more and more pain. We could slit our wrists, take ourselves to the top of a building and jump off, pull a belt around our neck and kick the stool, but in the absence of sharp objects, multistory structures, and cords, what was to be done? My impulse wasn't to kill myself, it was to kill my body, take myself elsewhere, a thought that wouldn't have come to me even yesterday but I now knew it was possible, you could feel not in your own body, it was what I felt at Ben's, with Lucy, her paws on my hands, her sadness in my head. I needed that now, right now, that exact feeling, I slowed my pace to think. I could be there in five minutes, I'd say I wanted to talk about the book, that I'd just had an epiphany. But it was too late, of course it was; he'd suggest I come to his office tomorrow, or that we talk on the phone. That was fine, it would have to be. I thought of seeing Lucy this morning, tied to the stoop railing, and moments before, the bird on the branch, the adolescent. I knew then intuitively that the bird could have given me what Lucy had, if only I could have looked into its eyes.

I was running again, as quickly as before, and in another few minutes I came to Third Avenue. A bodega on the corner lit the street, its sign refracted in the windows of parked cars. I walked over and went inside, the door chiming above me. There were only four aisles, I went down each one and then each one again, I was about to leave but thought to ask the cashier: *Do you have a cat here?*

No, we don't have a cat, he said. His tone was antagonistic, he seemed to want to hurt me emotionally. But it was thin, a performance, he'd only wanted to say, *I'm not going to be friendly with you.* It made me sad that he kept himself at a distance, but I was happy to feel the sadness, it was a way to connect to him whether he liked it or not.

I appreciate your help, I said, making myself vulnerable, hoping he too would show himself. *And I like your beard.*

Yo, get the fuck out, he said. He leaned forward over the counter so that he could shout to the other clerk, a man stocking shelves: *Danny, get this fucking weirdo out.*

Danny turned, assessing the situation. I couldn't handle more aggression, I hurried out onto the street, where I looked back into the store and then, as another echo came, continued running east.

At Fourth Avenue I tried another bodega, but there was no cat and I didn't ask. At Fifth Avenue again the same result. By the time I got to Flatbush I didn't want to try again, I knew that even if I found a cat my behavior with it would not be tolerated. I fully understood I was in a different state of mind, one that would be categorized as that of a *fucking weirdo*, but knowing this didn't make me feel what I felt any less; still the echoes came, more frequently, unpredictably, louder.

Flatbush was more crowded than I would have guessed. Even though I didn't want to interact with more people, I thought that their presence might increase my chances of finding an animal. But there weren't any, in the nearly two miles I'd covered there wasn't a single dog or cat, how could there be miles of space without animals? It was night, they were all in apartments, in cages or designated spaces, alone, bearing witness to their owners' freedoms, freedoms spent mostly staring at screens that might have seemed magical or miraculous if it hadn't been for their owners' apparent disinterest, their expressions of laziness, apathy, inertia.

Another echo. It wasn't loud but it came from nowhere, it pulled a yelp out of me; a group waiting in front of a bar looked my way, laughed. And then another echo, and another. I was now sprinting again, looking at telephone wires for birds, at piles of garbage for rats, but I knew better, I needed to look an animal in the eyes, yes, and it was only when I said that to myself that the answer became obvious.

I ran straight through Grand Army Plaza, past the head of Prospect Park, and continued down Flatbush. The sprinting was becoming too much, as if the ZzzQuil was finally working as it should, but I was almost there, and in just a few minutes I arrived. It didn't seem right, it was too nondescript, just a banner on a pole and a small sign above a plain gate: PROSPECT PARK ZOO, A WILDLIFE CONSERVATION SOCIETY PARK. Plants in terra-cotta pots guarded the entrance; they made the gate seem even less effective. I walked up to it, looked around, and lifted my foot onto the horizontal bar midway through. I pulled myself up so I could grab the top bar, and then, pushing my foot against the crown of one of the shrubs, reached the sign above the gate. I hoisted myself on top of it, caught my breath, and then jumped down, crumpling to the ground. I stood, waiting for my body to notify me of some damaged limb, a twisted ligament, but I heard only a resentful silence.

Looking out of the gate I briefly felt like I was in a cage, but as I stepped back, giving myself more space, it seemed that it was the rest of the world that was enclosed. I turned around to find a large pool with a cluster of rocks in the middle: the sea lions. I went over to it and, leaning over the railing, saw only black, tranquil water. They must have been hiding somewhere, asleep or left to their own devices. This was the only time of the day their lives weren't entertainment, when they didn't have to perform for us, trade their presence for food; such is our power that we can impose our workday on other species. I walked around the pool once and then went down a path that led to the DISCOVERY TRAIL. Guarding it were just two linked gates I could step over. I wandered around, there were no lights and I could hardly see, if there were animals in these netted enclosures they were out of view. I'd come all this way, I didn't know if I could run anymore—I was wearing my brogues, already I felt the blisters forming. I was suddenly afraid of what might happen, being so alone, I was afraid of myself, there was no one here to call for if it came to that, if I wanted to admit that what was happening to me was beyond my control, if I needed medical intervention. I felt watched, someone else's presence, I pivoted to look behind me but stopped halfway—something had moved. I turned back. Its tail jerked, once. It was staring at me. I lifted a foot to see if the creature would flinch. It didn't. Slowly I walked up to it, past it, to a placard. STYAN'S RED PANDA. It didn't look like a panda. It had the face and tail of a raccoon, it was that size, too, but its legs were the black stumps of a much larger animal, and the fur was copper, the color of a penny, except for the ears and patches around the eyes and nose, which were pure white. I looked back at the sign. Why was my instinct to read a description of him? Why did I even care what name he'd been given?

I walked up to the animal. He lurched to his left but then turned back. I stopped, my eyes adjusted, I saw every inch of his face. He was nothing like Lucy, no, there was hardly any sadness here, he didn't even have a grasp on his own life, what was wrong with it, what humans were using him for. This made me even sadder than Lucy had. I hardly even felt like crying before the tears came. They sounded natural, my sobs, it was like hearing my own voice. It *was* a voice, a way to communicate, surely he could sense the tears, my sadness, that I was sad for him. I thought of my own life, what I didn't know about it, what was too obvious for me even to realize, and then I thought of our algorithm, how it would, eventually, see us the way we saw animals: our movements predetermined, our freedom a nice lie. The thought was oddly calming; the more I felt and believed in the algorithm's omniscience the closer I felt to Lucy, to the animal in front of me.

Suddenly he seemed naked, that one simple difference between us now glaring. I saw his bare legs, his stomach. I felt the cotton on my thighs, the polyester on my chest. I looked around, and then, as slowly as I could, I took off my jacket and shirt, my pants and briefs. I placed the clothes in a neat pile behind me, and then turned around. There I stood in front of him as he'd never seen a human before. I felt vulnerable, honest, more myself, even, and yet, when I looked down I was struck by a pang of shame: my penis was circumcised; it looked like a penis that had had something done to it. For the first time in my life I was ashamed of it, ashamed that we did such a thing. *Shame.* I'd never considered how the word contradicted itself: it was both the feeling of having done something shameful and the trait that helped us avoid the shameful act. I looked back at him, searching his face for judgment. No, he couldn't sense my shame, he wouldn't even know what it was. If anything he looked worried, as if my abruptly bizarre appearance might portend danger. This was calming, too, calming like the thought of the algorithm. I was happy to be a predator, I sat in the feeling, it meant I was no longer a spectator, some untouchable god. He flinched to the side, paused, and then ran away.

I stood there, watching the dark patch of air he disappeared into. I knew he wouldn't return but I wanted to hold on to the feeling he'd given me. When finally it left, when I felt alone again, when I felt naked, I put my clothes back on and made my way home.

———

I dreamed nothing, nothing I could recall. I awoke feeling well rested, I had a clear head. In fact I felt unusually myself, as if I hadn't felt like myself in years; I had none of the low-level anxiety I always had to bat away upon waking. I lifted myself up and planted my feet on the floor, the blisters on the sides of my toes proof that last night hadn't been a dream. Even though Franny was still asleep I turned off the white noise machine it was for me, anyway; I was the one who always woke from the chirping. I heard them now, those noises I'd cursed every sleepless morning. *Trill*, *warble*, *quaver*, *tweet*, if I was aware of the words I had no idea what they meant, I'd never cared to differentiate them before, I'd never even heard them as language.

I grabbed my robe and walked to the bathroom. Standing in front of the mirror I put my fingers in my ears, listening for the echo, but I knew it wouldn't come. I couldn't even really remember what it sounded like. I closed the door, turned on the vent fan, and tried making the noise myself. What I produced could have passed for a tribal chant. When I closed my mouth my jaw ached. My dentist had warned me about clenching while I slept, every dentist since I was twenty had. I pushed my tongue forward and to the right—a pang of pain, but not from my jaw. I closed my mouth, recirculated the saliva, and reopened it. I pulled down my lip and saw, at the bottom of a bicuspid, right at the gumline, a chunk of tooth missing, as if it had been chiseled away. *Abfraction*, that was the term my dentist had used. *What I'd be worried about are abfractions.* The word sounded too industrial, too modern to refer to something that must have been with us for as long as we've had teeth. The thought of making an appointment made me clammy. My teeth had always been something—one of the only things—I felt deep and irrational shame about. Starting in college I had habitually, without much effort, regurgitated my food shortly after swallowing it, only to chew it more and swallow again. It was hard to explain how exactly it happened, I just tightened some passageway and brought it back up. It was a recognized disorder called rumination syndrome, but it didn't feel like a syndrome, if everyone did it I would think it was as normal as sneezing. It is quite rare, obviously, and especially for someone like me; it's usually only infants and the mentally ill who ruminate. The food is undigested, it hasn't passed from the esophagus to the stomach, so it tastes just the way it did when it first went down. This should preclude the acidic erosion of teeth normally associated with bulimia, but still I frequently wondered—and hated to think about—what effect it might have. (Occasionally, I was able to quit—in fact I hadn't done it for the past week or so—but it always came back.) It was such a sensitive issue for me that I hadn't even told Franny about it until three months ago. She'd reacted well, better than my ex. It wasn't until I made a joke of it, mentioning that only animals who ruminate are kosher—goats, sheep, cows—and so I too could be eaten, that she'd seemed a little disturbed.

I went back to the bedroom. She was waiting for me, her underwear on the floor, her hair already tied back. On the smart thermostat console hung a T-shirt; she didn't trust that it couldn't hear us, let alone see us. Morning sex had always been my preference, not hers—was she ovulating now? I took off my robe and went to the bed. As soon as I kissed her she grabbed me, nearly forced me inside of her. Entering her felt more, what? Sensual? Bodily? It was the absence of a condom, of course—but had I felt this way on Monday night? I found myself less attuned to how she was feeling, I anticipated my own climax more than hers. That sex now had an objective, something at which we could succeed or fail, made me horny, astonishingly so. I pulled out of her, put my nose to her stomach and pushed it down through her hair. As soon as I started licking her I only wanted to be inside her again, but when I pulled away I wanted to be back, closer to her scent. It wasn't enough to breathe her in all at once, it was gratifying only when I wasn't paying attention, when I let it come in with the air I breathed. Again and again I considered reentering her, she asked me to, her fingers grasping at my shoulders, but I couldn't, instead I placed my fingers on either side of her, making her wider, making it easier—

Whoa, she said, sliding up the bed, away from me. *What are you doing?*

Going down on you, I said. *Eating you out.* I made the rock-and-roll gesture. *Not literally.* She laughed but it faded fast. As she searched my face I became aware of my own expression. *Did I do something wrong?*

No, she said. *I mean*—she glanced at my hand, now lying on her thigh—*let's just stick to the script.*

I laughed, but it didn't sound like me. I ignored the feeling, ignored everything and climbed up the bed. I reentered her, I was hard but no longer horny, at least not the way I'd been before.

We went through the motions, after a few minutes she came, and I did too. She smiled at me, got out of bed and, while getting changed, made her daily call to the Department of Buildings. *Hi*, she said, *this is— Yes, Francesca Olsen. Yes. Correct. Yes.* On these calls she spoke as she never did, enunciating every syllable, like a diligent pupil asking for a hall pass.

I listened to her walk down the stairs and then replayed what had just happened. Except I couldn't, really. No, and this had now become a familiar feeling: a frost that lay right across my memories. Like last night, at the zoo. When I thought of it I saw myself in the third person, blurry, the colors drained from the image. It was easier to relive it through words. *I'd gone to the zoo to see an animal, any animal, hoping the connection I felt with it would relieve me of the echoes. I found that red panda, its ignorance made me sad. I took off my clothes and scared it, which felt good, to feel our relationship was that of animals.* Yes, it was a strange experience. I felt the air leave my nose, I breathed it back in. No: it wasn't strange at all. In fact it was the most natural thing. I'd said *It was a strange experience* to myself but I hadn't thought that, really, it was just what I felt I should think, what I expected of myself. It reminded me of being in temple as a kid, saying the Shema. I could say *The Lord is our God, the Lord is One*, even though I had no belief in or conception of the words I was saying.

I got up. I went to take a shower. The water pressure was thin, I made a mental note to call the plumber. I put on pants and a shirt, I shaved and combed my hair. Downstairs on the kitchen table was a dismantled *New York Times*, a crisp *FT*. I opened the latter, the feature story was about Ethereum. Why did they continually debase themselves with this crypto analysis? Their readership thought even omakase was risky. Just beyond the paper I noticed, still out of focus, an unfamiliar cluster of color: a bouquet. A dusty black rose drooped in my direction, its color camouflaging a fly skittering across its petals. The fly moved as if in stop motion, its life just a series of images. The flowers weren't Franny's style, too recherché— had Birdie brought them? I didn't want to ask. It was certainly possible; they were wilting. I looked away and then back. I couldn't stop staring, the beauty and apparent rarity of the selection seemed cruel, the flowers were exotic not just to me but to each other, never in nature would they have sprouted from the same soil, and now in such strange company they each grasped for life, feeding off the same urn of cloudy tap water.

Franny brought me a latte and the fly flew away. By the flower she had drawn in the coffee's foam I knew it was Thursday. This same day each week she plunged herself into work, was productive from when she woke up to when she fell asleep, a mindset she'd invented in college. I liked to tease her that after her chairs were in every dining room in America she'd write her entrepreneurial self-help book. But actually she'd already started, it was titled *The Opposite of Cheat*

Day. When we moved in together I learned that this ethos extended past her work life—to lattes, for example. And now, apparently, procreation. I took a sip and told her it was lovely. I set the cup down and picked up the paper. There was a photo of the new Goldman chief. God, the way he smiled, the way all these guys did. There was a feeling in my stomach, or higher. A warm wave traveled up my neck, my hunger abandoned me. I lowered the paper and looked at the coffee, the foam flower, the small white bubbles hardened in the froth. I stood up, kept myself still for a moment, and then ran to the sink, the news still in my hand. With my palm on the faucet I unloaded what little remained in my stomach, it was really just acid. Even in the mucousy gunk I could make out the froth—the offending substance, I knew, because when I saw it I started to gag. I lifted the faucet handle but then brought it down, I wanted another look at the stuff: it was proof. I hadn't even thought, *This is milk, this comes from a cow*; it was beyond logic or intent. But then, what about last night's meal? Franny had had saag paneer and I'd tried some. This didn't undo any of what I felt, it only made it worse. I thought of my stomach acids breaking down the curds, the animal protein absorbed into my body, the animal fat burned for energy.

Are you okay?

Yeah, I'm fine.

God, was it the picture?

What?

She picked up her phone to show me but then decided against it. *It's— Well, I couldn't sleep last night. I was just— I kept thinking about her, what happened. I mean, what actually happened, just down the block. It must have been four a.m. or so, I went and found it, the spot, there was still blood on the curb. I took a photo, just in case.*

You found the spot? In the middle of the night you were able to find it?

Well, yeah, she said, peering down. Her face tightened for a moment and then she looked back at me. *I went on her phone yesterday, when I visited her. I wanted to see how long it was before she got to the hospital. And it showed where exactly she'd been picked up.* This made sense, and yet, having started the confession she couldn't help but finish it. *It was just lying there, along with the rest of her stuff. It was locked, actually. I brought it over to her, I pressed her thumb against the sensor. That's how I did it.*

Jeez. She looked down. *I mean, that's okay.*

So it wasn't the photo, she said, changing the subject.

No, I said. I turned to the sink and, seeing the vomit, washed it away.

Well, I'd guess it was the Indian but I think I know better. I turned around. She nodded toward the liquor cart. *Not like you to leave a mess. Apple schnapps, really?*

I smiled. *No reason to turn your nose up. Give it a try.*

A bit early for me. But if you take a seat I've got you a better hangover cure.

To my left was the cast iron. I leaned toward it and saw four eggs, sunny-side up.

No, I said. *Thank you, but I can't eat anything.* She looked disappointed. This was meant to make me change my mind. If she disdained her upbringing, still she never shook her rural roots; to miss a morning meal was practically impious. *I'll sit with you, though. And I'll be as quiet as I would be eating.*

She went to make herself a plate and I sat back at the table.

But when she joined me she had a plate for us both. One of my yolks had broken, it ran onto the piece of toast below. I knew that eggs weren't stillborns, but still the word surfaced, twisted, showed itself both poetic and sterile: *born, still; born still.* The sight of it sapped me of any hunger I'd reclaimed, I didn't even want to look down.

Please eat, Herschel. You're going to have a big day, I know it. Deadlines make dominoes. Dead lines. That's what you say, right?

Ah, but it's best to stay hungry.

Now she was annoyed; irony wasn't the move. She cut an egg in half, cut off a piece of toast, and speared them together. She lifted it and opened her mouth. I saw her molars, her pink tongue, her pink palate, it was briefly erotic until she closed her mouth and I imagined the taste, the flavors of another being. I lifted the paper in front of my face. The peace lasted a moment until I realized I could hear her chewing. She did it slowly and with her mouth closed—she always had impeccable manners—but still there was noise, the muted transfer of liquid, the pharynx and larynx working in concert to usher the bolus down into her body.

I'm thinking of going vegan.

Finally, the chewing stopped.

Really? Why?

Did everything need a reason? The environment, animal cruelty, my own health—she would have been satisfied with any of these but none was right.

It's hard to say, I said. *It's just a feeling I have.*

I lowered the paper.

Confused. Her entire face could be summed up in a word. But emotions aren't so simple unless we want them to be. She was trying to be confused, she was defensive, as if my wanting to be vegan without a concrete reason was an attack of some sort. She did a kind of head tilt and looked at her food through the side of her eyes, as if her eggs could help her figure me out. As she prepared herself another bite the eroticism returned, this time for long enough that I realized it wasn't lust at all but a distant cousin, another remorseless passion, a different craving. In some small but definite way I had hate for her.

She was now taking a bite every few seconds, not waiting to swallow before filling her mouth again. It wasn't like her, I figured she just wanted to end the meal, avoid the conversation about me being vegan, but when I told her I liked having breakfast together, that we should do it more often, she looked up at me with kind eyes.

Honey, I do too, she said. *I'm sorry, I should have checked the time. I promise I'll be out in ten.*

Out in ten. I looked at the microwave clock: 8:17. Thursday, therapy, right. *Okay, great*, I said. *I'm just going to go clear my head.* I brought my plate to the sink, pushing the food off into the disposal. I ran it and then made myself an espresso. I took the coffee along with an orange up to my office, where I sat at my computer and listened to her shuffling around, getting her day in order against the clock. I loved her, I did. If the debris of hate was still in me it was just like the pancer: already incorporated into my body, but soon enough it would be recycled, discarded.

I tried checking my email but the page wouldn't load. I went to call Milosz but saw I had a text from him, something about needing to reconnect the intranet. To pass the time I paced around the room, I looked out onto the street, the courtyard. I saw Clara there, reading a paperback and drinking coffee, her outfit more stylish than the hour required. There was something about the way she was sitting, or twirling her hand—both struck me as a bit self-aware—that annoyed me. It was the artifice of it, and the fact she was alone, that even without an audience she seemed to need to perform.

The front door closed at 8:28. I typed in the address of Magda's telemedicine portal. That same banner: SIMPLE. FREE. SECURE. I would have traded the first two for more of the third. I entered in the name I used, *Cohen*, and waited. When her face showed on my screen—always it looked the same; her hair, too—I realized I had started peeling the orange. I didn't know what the etiquette was, I asked if it was okay and she said, *Of course*, but still I set the orange down once it was naked. I started talking about work, I said I couldn't go into too much detail. She nodded graciously and said, *Of course*, and then asked me to describe how I was feeling. I told her about leaving the office yesterday, wanting to run down the street, that I couldn't wait for our recent developments to unfold, that I'd never before felt there could be such a thing as infinite potential. She laughed. I liked when she laughed, it made me feel like I was succeeding, her laughter was never belittling, always joyous. But then she said it was important to stay in the moment, no matter how excited we are for tomorrow, and I said, *Of course*. We went through a few of our normal topics, starting with what we now referred to as *the finding of Lisa*. Sometimes therapy seemed like a song, there were basically four or five dominant chords and each could color a given digression or verse, but in the song between Magda and me the one chord that every musical phrase had to be played in was Lisa. She had been my babysitter, a college dropout with platinum blond hair who, at least in memory, was the most engaging person I'd ever known. She committed suicide in my bedroom while I went to get a soda at the 7-Eleven. Yes, I was the one to discover the body, but that scene wasn't what Magda and I usually focused on. Lisa probably sexually abused me, a term I didn't think was accurate but felt compelled to use with Magda. (Although Magda generally allowed for evasion—hence that oblique handle, *the finding of Lisa*—she refused to call Lisa's transgression anything but sexual abuse.) Lisa never touched me, only had me, at age eleven, undress and watch her masturbate. It happened four times, no more. What I had regretted most, up until I started with Magda, was the narrative shape Lisa always threatened to give my life, that anything special or meaningful might always be traced back to her. I preferred to see those events in isolation, to see the version of me who experienced them as having very little to do with who I was today. I understood that this wasn't the *healthy* way to get past trauma, but it suited me just fine. I considered it a skill, even, this ability to cleave cause and effect, to chop up the emotional ingredients of my life and use them as I wished. At her best, Magda made me appreciate that this was my prerogative—that narratives were contrived, a manipulation of history, and thus we each had the freedom to plot our own. At her worst, she seemed to tie every loose mood or recurring deficit to this thing that might well be entirely distinct.

With Lisa in mind we discussed a recent visit to my father, who has inoperable lung cancer; although he is likely to survive the next year, he may not make it another three. Under Magda's guidance I drew a connection between the unfair, seemingly arbitrary failing of his physical health and Lisa's mental deterioration. We then moved on to my recent discussions with Franny about circumcision, whether our children, should they be boys, would be initiated. Franny saw my preference as a *reflexive genuflection to Judaism*; these were the same words she used to describe my automatic support of Israel. On both accounts she may have been right—of course she was—but I felt that she was overlooking her own knee-jerk aversion to all things religious. This was the first fundamental, intractable argument we'd ever had, and it nagged at me in a way that was both abstract and agonizing. At the end of the day, I just wanted my boy's penis to look like mine. By this point in the session Magda and I had begun to find our groove, where radical honesty no longer seemed radical. I spoke about the shortcomings of my parents, my concept of money and ambition, my feelings of inferiority at work, and Franny's and my decision to start trying to conceive. We had a ways to go on this last topic, I really wanted to dig in but saw we only had ten minutes left. If my instinct was to not bring up what was happening, it was a self-defeating one, the point of therapy being to mine the very things you are consciously hiding.

I started with my new perception of words, my experience reading the *Financial Times*. And then I mentioned the other glitches of speech: *firewall* and *I'm so happy we're trying* and *stillborn* and *deadline* and everything else.

She nodded thoughtfully, she seemed to catch herself in boredom and said, *That's very interesting. It's exciting when everyday occurrences appear to us differently.*

Right, I said, nodding. *On that note, I had an odd experience yesterday. A few experiences, actually.* I picked up the naked orange and jammed my thumb into the orifice at the top, splitting the segments. *Yesterday morning on my way to work I saw my neighbor's dog on the street. Looking at her I began to feel something strange, a sort of intense connection, a kinship, even. I couldn't shake the feeling, it made me feel kind of crazy, actually. Well, I felt that if I saw her again I would realize that it was all in my head, and so when I got home I made up an excuse to visit my neighbor in his apartment, just so I could see her, the dog. And when I did, when I was in his apartment, I really felt how sad she was. It made me quite sad, actually. I cried.*

She was nodding at a rhythm slower than I'd seen before. Her head settled at the lowest point, her pupils at the tops of her eyes.

You cried? Even she had hardly seen me cry. She took hold of herself, twisted her disbelief into encouraging curiosity. *Herschel, tell me about what you were feeling when you cried.*

It was simple, really. I was just sad for the dog. I—I— No. That's it. I felt I should say more, make it all make more sense to her, but I knew that every inch in that direction would be an inch away from the truth. What had happened was ineffable; that was the point.

She wore the same face I'd seen on Franny an hour ago. Confusion, unalloyed—that is, performed.

You look skeptical, I said. *Do you not think dogs feel sadness, or do you not think I'm capable of having empathy for a dog?*

Well. Neither. It's been well documented that animals have emotions similar to ours. And I myself know your empathic capacity. But, to be honest, Herschel, I do question the sudden change in behavior. It makes me wonder why you didn't experience such a strong connection to dogs before yesterday, and what might have happened to make you so susceptible.

Yeah, I said. *It's been a long week. There's a lot going on at work. And, you know, we've just decided to start a family.* I stopped speaking but she continued to stare. *Hmm. Actually, a friend of mine, or really an acquaintance, she was in a terrible accident involving brain damage. Although I had no way to anticipate it, of course, and of course I had no intent of it happening, I'm worried that I am, in a way, blameworthy.*

She nodded solemnly. That was it. Had she heard me? Did she think I was exaggerating my involvement? I retrieved my words, listened to them again.

I do feel responsible, actually.

I can sense that, Herschel. And that's such a good, strong word. Responsible. *Responsibility can take so many forms. So maybe you feel responsible for this dog's sadness, but maybe it's really some other responsibility you're carrying with you, and applying to the experience with the dog. A responsibility coming from the future, perhaps?*

Hmm. I'm not sure. The incident with the dog sort of feels detached from the rest of my life. She looked skeptical again. She needed a cause, a source—as if everything could be explained away, as if life was held together by such airtight logic. What was I paying her for? *Can I ask what you'd say if I told you that I'd found God? What if I was on my way to work and had an epiphany, and now I wanted to go to temple and keep kosher and all of that? Would you try to figure out why, exactly, that had happened?*

Yes. Absolutely. Ah, but of course she would; in fact she'd love to. When we'd first started, about a year ago, she'd constantly brought the conversation back to my Jewishness, from my distant relatives killed in the Holocaust—she was projecting, obviously, given that her parents' generation had so effectively purged their nation's Jewry—to the shame I felt for not being as religious as my parents had hoped. This last one had been a potent subject: I had, until we talked it through,

pretended to be kosher in their presence; I'd even gone so far
as to tell them Franny was considering converting. But after
Magda and I put the issue to bed I'd gently asked that we focus on other things—and then, when she replied that *to forget
history would be to forget the ground we stand on*, I'd asked less
gently.

Right, I said. *Okay.* I was annoyed but didn't want to say so.
Instead I made it obvious by looking at the time in the corner
of my screen.

She sighed and sat back in her seat. *It's a miracle, Herschel.
It's a revelation to you, obviously. But it's my job to help you explore
what's behind it, so that you can understand it and even experience it at a higher level.* I nodded without making eye contact.
I regretted being so immature with the clock. *You know, often
when someone is about to experience a change as big as the birth of
a child, they start to feel differently about the world. And when your
child comes, believe me, the world will never be the same.*

We continued down that path. We discussed my hopes for
a family, my fears. And when it was over, when she concluded
our session with her usual courtly nod, I felt nothing.

I stared at the screen long enough that I grew accustomed
to the graphics and could see my face in the reflection. I stood
up, I felt light, not just from not eating but altogether, it was
easy to move my body through the room. I wouldn't talk to her
about it again, her very mode of thinking—her profession—
was irreconcilable with what this was. The thought made me
happy, elated actually, like I'd been released from some burden. It was exactly how I'd felt when I ended my relationship
with my ex, uttered the words that would be the last of a long,
drawn-out breakup. But as I began ambling around the room,

my habit after therapy, I felt, well, also the way I had after I broke up with Kay: alone, on my own, like there was nothing to hold me accountable.

I turned on my phone. A text from Franny: *At the hospital. No progress.* I started to draft a reply—*I'm sorry, I wish*—but deleted it. I called a car, brushed my teeth, and put on socks. I went downstairs, leafed through the *Financial Times*, and then packed it away for the road. My shoes were in the foyer, still out from last night. They'd taken a beating, the leather bearing new, unexpected creases. The leather. I went into the walk-in closet and scanned every pair, if any were made of synthetic material I wouldn't know. My running shoes were, though; they would have to do for now. There was a store just up Wooster.

Outside, just as I locked the door, I felt the pressure on my hips. I took off my belt and set it on our steps, right beside the history of debt book. Philip was on his stoop next door, his hands on his waist, staring up at his place. He waved. *We had a great time on Monday, really.* It seemed such a stock phrase, a conversational set piece.

Well, it was good company, I said. I almost flinched, my words were even more contrived. Had I gone so far as to mimic his tone? *And we'll do it again soon.*

I saluted him and went down to the street. The car wasn't here yet. I turned back around. From this angle I couldn't help but question whether the oak tree in front of our house did, in fact, breach the property line. When we bought the place we'd filed an application to cut it down—ostensibly out of concern that the roots were a risk to the building's structural integrity, though really I hoped it would reduce the morning chirping—but Philip and Clara had protested on the grounds that the tree was theirs and ours both. Their objection had come through the Department of Buildings, which I thought was odd, cowardly perhaps, and for a week or two I had resented them—until we met in person and their charm washed away any lingering ill will.

Philip? He lifted his chin. *If you don't mind me asking, why did you become a vegetarian?*

The question had, somehow, polluted his smile. *You know, I just saw one too many of those films. You witness how they prepare the animals, what their life is like, and you just lose your hunger for it. And it's not just factory farms. It's the organic stuff, too.*

I nodded thoughtfully. *Sounds interesting. Can you send me some? The videos I mean.*

Sure, he said; still something sour there.

I waved and looked down the street, the SUV was approaching. It wasn't Cedric this time, but someone new. When I got in he said, *It's a pleasure to drive you, sir.* I knew he was just doing his job, being cordial, but still the words sounded ugly to me, a lie I was complicit in. I glanced over at Ben's stoop; Lucy wasn't there. I thought to look up at their apartment—had she heard the car?—but restrained myself. Already I was letting my work self take over, I needed to, needed to pare down distractions and wring the most out of the day, which promised to be a big one. It was true: deadlines make dominoes.

———

The new shoes were comfortable, or would be once I'd spent a few days in them.

I walked into the office, nodded to Peter, and was immediately accosted by Milosz, who paced over from Simo's desk.

Herschel, he said, *where've you been?* I was no longer *Hersh*. And he was no longer in awe of the world, or even happy.

Is everything okay? How are the trials?

The new buys? They're spot-on, exact, by now we can confidently iterate. But we're wasting time, I need your signature on new data orders, I needed it two hours ago. I thought we agreed on eight thirty?

He was artless, he'd never been anything but. I had always thought of this as some defect, his inability to cater to others, but now it showed itself as an honesty I myself could rarely achieve.

It's Thursday, I said. *I had therapy.*

Therapy, he repeated. As if I'd said *handball*. I nodded. *Okay*, he said. *I think we need to rethink some things. I already have, I mean.* I saw past his shoulder to the windowsill, which no longer featured our very expensive plants. *It would be too easy to hide a camera there, a listening device, anything. And from now on there are no electronics allowed past that line.* He pointed to a strip of blue electrical tape two feet behind me. *So, your phone.* He put out his hand. This gave me a brief, unexpected glimpse into him as a father, something I always struggled to imagine. Actually, it often felt like he kept that part of his life completely insulated from the part I inhabited. A few months ago he'd set a photo of his wife and kids on his desk. I was mesmerized by it, by his smile, which was more tender than I'd known him capable of. He seemed unsettled by my interest in it, and the next day the picture was gone.

Milosz.

We agreed on this. You yourself announced it to the team. I took out my phone, turned it off, and gave it to him. In return he reached into his pocket and handed me a large set of keys. *The one marked with your*—he stopped, noticing Peter next to us, and led me away. *The one with your height in inches accesses the server room. The rest do nothing.* He pulled out the right key, as if I couldn't calculate it myself: number 70. He walked past me, nodding for me to follow.

As we walked across the trading floor I noticed that Simo was now closely flanked by four other researchers, their computers pushed screen-to-screen. On the floor, enclosing them, was a three-sided box made of that same blue electrical tape. Their backs were parallel, their spines at nearly the same angle, they looked like they were servicing something more hands-on, a car, or maybe it was the opposite, that they themselves were being serviced, cows to be milked.

We came to the server room. On the door, in addition to the new keylock and the old padlock—I had that combination memorized better than my Social Security number—I saw another combination lock. *It's the eight digits of your birthday in the order of last digit, first digit, second-to-last digit, second digit, et cetera. But please, do not go into this room unless I'm present. There are wires everywhere, it needs to be organized, I've already ordered bins.* He looked at me, waiting for my nod, and when he got it he turned to walk away. *The data orders and VPN invoices are waiting on your desk.*

When I could no longer hear his footsteps I exhaled; I hadn't even noticed I was holding my breath. I rested my hands on the industrial metal cage that made up the outside wall and door; even that felt like a small defiance. The room emanated a subtle warmth, like breath almost assimilated into air, but this heat was different, it was dry. All over the room red and yellow-green dots blinked and disappeared into black metal or matte plastic. I listened to the hum, which was oddly diffuse, the chorus coming from every section: the soft whir of fans fighting the heat. I concentrated on a few of the blinking dots, capturing their rhythm; most kept a steady pulse but some were random. I focused on one in particular, trying to discern a pattern in the sporadic flickers, but I couldn't, not even after a minute. It was frustrating, I knew there was one; despite the complexity of the algorithm that controlled it, despite the sheer number of calculations these machines performed each second, there was no essence, there was nothing that couldn't be explained, eventually. The algorithm's victory was only quantitative, like ours over animals; a dog can understand human language—it understands its name—but at such a small scale. That was who we were to the algorithm: dogs. We understood it bit by bit but were lost in its orders of magnitude.

I felt hungry, suddenly. Ravenous. It was almost eleven and I'd only had an orange and an espresso. I went to the kitchen and grabbed two eggplant sandwiches from the refrigerator. I stood there for a moment. Something was bothering me, had been since I'd first got in. It was like it was right in front of me, I looked around and then closed my eyes: The noises. The alerts. They were gone. Of course—another of Milosz's precautions.

I took the food back to my office and sat at my desk. I unwrapped the cellophane and ate one of the sandwiches in just a few bites. I signed in to my computer and checked the market. The S&P was up 0.71%, the Dow 0.63%, the NASDAQ 0.66%. This was no longer relevant to my work but it was an old habit, a score I checked like the Knicks'. And like a basketball game, the day's trading was just one point in a much larger arc. For the past year the narrative had seemed to be, at least among the "experts," that of Icarus: a downturn was imminent, and it was hubris to think otherwise. This doomsday story seemed to exist only to placate those who had missed out on the recent upswing; year to date the S&P was already up 12%. It wasn't just that the prediction was specious, it blinded analysts to something much more interesting: the detachment of price from value. Interest rates were impossibly low, people were practically forced to invest, as long as they had savings and weren't ready to buy a home, or already had one and didn't care to buy another. And so, with all this money permanently parked in the market, prices were squeezed upward, and upward, and upward, far, far beyond the true worth of the companies they supposedly represented. It was a violation of the basic tenets of the stock exchange, but that didn't mean the trend wouldn't continue. No, the opposite: the more inflated prices became, the more everyday investors expected them to inflate more, the public market—any market, really—being one big, airtight self fulfilling prophecy. This was all just another reason our conception of finance was ready to be torn to shreds.

Not that I don't love the market. There's truth in those sharp, jagged lines. The market's past is never changed or rewritten. Stocks move in unpredictable fits and spurts of success and failure, and just when they start to make sense they defy logic, just as reality defies logic. A price moving through time is a sound not like a song, not like the call of a bird; it's a single note but a cacophonous one, it's a million people speaking at once. No, it isn't such a coincidence that some of the original thinkers in quant trading started in speech recognition. Quant analysis is a science co-opted, the discipline haunted by its original subject. Stare at stock charts long enough, imagine where they'll be in three months, one year, five years, fifty, and yet another property of speech emerges: its brevity. Sound preordains silence. If every voice behind a stock stopped, if we all looked away at the same time, the price would drop to the ground, dead. Companies are mortal, they are. Like us they guarantee so much action but with a guaranteed end, and there is peace in that.

Continuing my sign-in ritual I checked my bank accounts—$2.8 million, all combined. It was a lot of money, I never thought I'd make that much, at least not when I first entered the working world. But it never stopped seeming insubstantial, or tenuous, it was just a number, I could spend an hour on my computer and get rid of it all. I opened my email, reaching for a notepad and pen before I read a single word. One by one I would tally the new commitments, I would circle the total and deliver the good news to Milosz. But my eyes jumped to the words *Eubanks, Colin* first. I clicked on his message. *It's a lot of pounds, need to think more.* Pounds; pounds of flesh. I went through the rest of the emails. About half of our potential investors hadn't responded to my deadline message; most of the rest had bowed out with good wishes (*We'll be watching from the sidelines.* Fuck you.), a handful had punted like Colin, and two of them had committed. One for 3.3, the other for 2. I wrote *5.3* and circled it. Not a number to take to Milosz. No, a deadline and a tone conveying my confidence were, apparently, not enough. People needed more: results.

I wolfed down the other eggplant sandwich and went out to the trading floor. There I found Milosz, just inside the blue box, watching over Simo and his gang. I stood by his side, squinting at the computers. Simo's was the most active, boxes appeared and vanished so quickly they hardly could have registered. He was now leaning back in his chair, rolling an unbitten apple between his hands. He was often this way while in the thick of concentration—childlike, almost. Maybe it was only that he was enjoying a state unavailable to most other adults. People like him—those whose work consisted of being curious, who could simply sit and think and know that their thoughts mattered—seemed to be afforded a certain wellness that could not be gained any other way. Not that having such a privileged vocation (and mind) guaranteed access to that peace; Milosz too had made a life out of thinking, but that may have been the bane of his existence. In his hands potential was a burden, something that had to be made good on, but which he never could, fully.

Milosz, I said, startling him. *You mentioned the new buys were* spot-on. *What exactly does that mean?*

All I got was a nod, his stare steady on the screens.

I think we should start putting real money into this.

Now he looked at me, his gray eyes wide open. *We have. We've put in what we can. Since yesterday morning we've made $270,000.* It was as if he'd said lunch had been successfully delivered.

That's great, I said.

He nodded and turned back.

I scanned the screens, searching for some conspicuous number or indication. It would be very like them to have the most crucial metrics look no different than the rest; it all seemed to be in ten-point type. I moved to the side so I could follow their eyes, as if they were interested in the same things I was—alpha, beta, standard deviation, value at risk, kurtosis. No, and anyway they seemed to be taking it in all at once, like pigs at a trough, greedy for any bit of information they could extract something from. *Greedy.* As if what they were doing was wrong. It's such a dirty word, *greed*, and for something so natural. We don't blame pigs for acting greedy but for us it's a sin. And pigs are hardly as tempted as we are; how would they act if in front of them weren't just their calories for the day but something they could take and keep and use to buy enough feed to last them their whole lives, and those of their kin, and buy shelter, too, buy protection from other pigs, and still have so much left over they could pay to be entertained, they could forge new modes of leisure, they could buy themselves happiness, well-being, and self-esteem. No, the word alone, *greed*, could not be trusted—it came with a morality that was false from the start.

Keep me informed, I said. *Please.*

I walked to the kitchen and got a can of seltzer. On my way back to my office I noticed that Yuri was finally wearing shoes: a beat-up pair of Adidas, but still.

I sat down at my desk, opened a text file, and spent a good thirty minutes finding the best language to describe what we'd just accomplished. It had to be sent as soon as possible; instead of running it by Milosz I wrote it with his feedback playing in my head. (Was it a coincidence that two of the words his Polish accent distorted most were *nothing* and *proprietary*?) When I was done editing I sent it to every potential investor who hadn't outright rejected us, and then went back to my inbox. There I found, along with another rejection, a message from the address Head_of_JYM@yahoo.com. There was no subject line. I opened it.

Please keep in mind that my endgame is to work together, really.

There was an image attached. I hovered over it, I savored not knowing, and clicked. The picture was so familiar it took me a few seconds to understand the severity of its arrival in my inbox. It was me, straight-on, in my home office, head tilted to the side, a slight smile on my face. In a square in the corner was Magda.

I stood up and sat down. I stood back up. It was from today, I was wearing that shirt and— I just knew it was from today. I focused on the annoying email address, the obnoxious tone of the message—it made me think of men who think they can pull off a fedora—so I wouldn't have to reckon with everything else. I closed the image and opened it again. Still I needed to delay thought, so I Googled *Head of J.Y.M.* Apparently Auerbach had painted many works by that name, each with the same essence: a face cut into pieces, or maybe collapsed inward, the thick lines that might normally form its perimeter broken into slabs that intruded on the subject's eyes, ears, mouth. Each work was immediately disturbing—the subject looked as though they had been hacked at, disfigured by the artist—but what lingered was a more muted terror. It was the lack of a barrier between the subject and the rest of the world, the sense that they might start to leak out of themselves, lose their shape, slowly fade into the background. I closed the browser and saw the image of my own, unmutilated face.

The session this morning: Simo's breakthrough but not in detail; my excitement over our progress, how I wanted to run down the street; Lisa, how she acted the last time I saw her alive; my father's recent reticence; Franny's and my arguments about circumcision; my mother's guilt and the projection of it onto the rest of the family; how I compared my worth to the firm with Milosz's; Franny's and my decision to try to conceive; language glitches and my connection to Lucy, which Magda had decided, or at least implied, was caused by the specter of parenthood. I felt the clothes on my skin, my white shirt, I imagined my sweat yellowing it. I was calm, at least I'd convinced myself I was, until I thought of all the words I'd said in that hour—words I could no longer access, but he could, probably he'd recorded the session. My fists pushed up against the underside of the desk, I gnashed my teeth, I imagined another abfraction. If I felt naked or exposed, defiled even, I also sensed that I shouldn't, that I was being too sensitive. I knew this wasn't about me, my life, my most personal information. Yes, this was obviously a better way to think about it, a way to keep my head, to deal with this strategically and summarily. It was, after all, nothing but a scare tactic, one that was meant to say: *Look, I can hack. Now give me what I want before I take it myself.* As if phishing his way into some unencrypted WordPress site was anywhere near as difficult as laying a finger on the firm's internal systems.

I picked up my phone and called Colin. I hung up, I needed to get level. I walked around my office. I opened my door and called for Milosz. While I waited for him I looked at more Auerbach, but really I was thinking about Ian reacting to the story of Lucy. Seeing it through his perspective I had the urge to laugh, I felt giddy, it was amazing that Magda had held it together; she was, after all, a professional. Milosz walked in and I waved him over, turning my screen so he could see.

From this morning, I said. *This was taken from my therapy session.* I told him about Ian, about our lunch, what the references meant. I promised him over and over that I hadn't given Magda any specifics about our progress, that she wouldn't even know the word *alpha*. I knew he was convinced only when the vertical line between his eyebrows finally disappeared, and then he seemed suddenly content, amused even.

He repeated, with evident glee, the obvious: it was Magda who had been hacked. Yes, this whole thing only underscored how imperative security was, that his paranoia was justified.

This is just the beginning, he said, shaking his head at my screen. *Can you imagine what they'll try once our returns are out there?*

I can't.

Well, he said, *you could try using a different teletherapy provider, but I'd—*

I'll stop completely, I said.

He nodded, still staring at the screenshot.

I clicked away and looked up at him. *Thanks,* I said.

I watched him leave and then walked over to close the door. I sat back at my desk, put my feet up, cracked my knuckles. I grabbed my phone and dialed Colin.

Colin Eubanks's office.

A secretary? I thought this was his cell.

Is Colin there?

Who's speaking?

Herschel Caine.

Mr. Eubanks is currently in a meeting.

This is very, very, very important.

I'll be sure to tell him you called. Anything else?

I hung up. I found Ian's number. I played a hypothetical conversation in my head. I refreshed my memory of who exactly he was, the kind of reptilian, arrogant, tedious— It didn't matter, just as it didn't matter that he knew I'd been sexually abused as a child, or even that I'd cried for a dog's pain. He still didn't have what he wanted; I did. I had all the power.

I dialed.

Herschel?

Already I relaxed. It was wobbly, that word, he could hardly say my name.

It's illegal, Ian. It's a federal crime.

What is?

Didn't Harvard teach blackmail before torts?

Ah, nice callback. You have a good memory. Mine's not so great, but I do recall all the privileged info you shared about Webber. You know, it's also illegal to—

To break my NDA? Who the fuck cares. I paused. If he'd recorded the therapy session, why wouldn't he record this, too? *I said nothing you can't find in public filings.*

You did, you said—

I said nothing.

I waited five seconds, ten. All he had was some personal dirt, some loose comments I'd said at a lunch, if he thought that was worth— I heard paper rustling, a cough.

Here we are, he said. *Tell me if these ring a bell. OBLN at 1.27. CTHR at 1.81. STAF at—* I took out a notepad. I put myself on mute so he wouldn't hear me, and wrote down the stocks. *And SPCB at .94.*

Good luck, I said, and hung up.

I grabbed a new notepad and left my office. Milosz was at the blackboard with Yuri, gesturing with a piece of chalk. He saw me, finished his thought, and joined me by the espresso machine. I asked for our recent successes, I promised it wasn't for investors. He gave me a look I had no idea what to do with, either he wasn't used to nonverbal communication or I wasn't used to him deploying it. And then he named them, I wrote them down even though I didn't need to; it was the exact same list Ian had read out in the exact same order. I thanked him.

Again he was staring at me. What would happen if I told him? No. No, no. He would go mad, he was already losing it, he'd move the business to a remote base in Nevada. I looked at Simo and co, the blue tape surrounding them. How long before there was a literal wall between them and everyone else? And how long before I was considered *everyone else*? Sure, I would have to tell Milosz eventually, I would. But only if I couldn't fix it myself.

There were ten ducks, or twelve, more. Each time I tallied them I sensed I was counting the same one twice. They didn't like to be looked at, not by me, not by their own kind. And yet I could tell by their movements that each knew exactly where the others were. They were mallards, most of them male, their heads that opalescent green, their necks marked by a neat white collar; below that was a brown so unremarkable as to accentuate the uncanny palette above. The females took the effect further, they were entirely mundane but for a brief banner at their sides, a folded flag that, when they flew, unraveled into a lustrous indigo band bordered by black strips bordered by white ones.

It made more sense then, why they pivoted so often: they were showing themselves off. And that was why they never looked at each other, refusing to give in to another's beauty. My gawking must have seemed gauche to them, a capitulation even, given I was not exquisite like they were, my greatest physical traits were a strong jawline, high cheekbones, pectoral muscles I had developed by repeatedly pushing myself away from the floor of my office; if they knew I'd spent all that time only to make my chest bigger and more tightly bound they would feel, at most, pity. Perhaps they already pitied me, surely they could see I was the same breed as the gaggle of girls next to me, who were currently enacting a scene the ducks must have witnessed a thousand times: the pose practiced and graceless, the arm jutting out, the chin lifted, the smile feigned, as if a smile could be feigned—no, all it said was that something more authentic was not on hand.

Obviously I was in a terrible mood, I didn't want to be here, didn't want to see him or speak to him ever again, every time I did some new bad thing glommed on to my life. And now he was twenty minutes late, of course he was, he'd done the same thing at our lunch. *2 pm, on the dot*, he'd written. Or was *on the dot* just another lame reference, this time to the pin he'd dropped me, showing where we'd meet? (It was in the water itself, at the southern end of the Central Park Reservoir, I was now at the closest spot on land.) I had almost been late myself, Milosz had forgotten the code to my locker, but thank God I wasn't, I would have missed out on nearly ten minutes of these girls photographing each other, encouraging each other with words that seemed to have no use but to annoy me—*I'm not mad about it*, and *I'm here for it*, and *all of the things*, and *I love this human*—language without substance, verbal memes that meant nothing, that did nothing but reference themselves. *Yeah?* they would say after declarative statements, a rhetorical device that only created voids between them, it was more important to mimic each other in sound than to exchange genuine, intimate information.

I'm so sorry, Ian said, appearing by my side, shaking his head at his own misdeed. I looked at my watch, made my irritation obvious. *Well, yes, for being late. But much more so for the whole, you know. I didn't listen, I swear. And I already deleted the file. I didn't want to be so aggressive, but I figured you wouldn't agree to see me again unless— Well, here we are.*

Right, I said, looking beyond him to the girls.

Let's find someplace more private. He walked past me, I heard the sound of our jackets chafing but didn't feel it. *It's so exciting, what you've already accomplished.* He turned his head so I could hear him, he slowed so I could catch up. *And if my understanding of what you're doing is correct, I think we're just a few small tweaks away from really opening the lid on this. We may need a week or so—*

We? No, Ian. This has nothing to do with you; it never will. Not that I believe you have any fucking idea what you're talking about, and even if I did I wouldn't give you one byte of our algorithm. So enough, please. I'll forget this morning, forget whatever else you've done, but if you try to intimidate us one more time I'll go straight to the authorities.

He stopped walking. He smiled at me. Why could I never make contact with him? It was like he had no center, like he was made of only disparate, shiny, borrowed traits: a person like terrazzo.

Brass tacks, he said, his voice deepened in caricature. *Okay, fine. Everything on the table. So I did listen a bit, mostly to the part about your friend, the one with brain damage. What the hell was that about?*

I kept my face still. I didn't react, even inside. How could I have forgotten about that? But even now it felt like it hadn't happened—that my confession, having failed to be correctly interpreted by Magda, had vanished. I breathed in and when the air came out his image appeared to tilt. His head dipped slightly, he was trying to look concerned, trying to hide his pleasure, but really he was trying to look like he was trying to hide his pleasure, his entire being seemed one infinite recursion, everything was about something else, I couldn't stand it anymore, all I wanted was to shake him until something real fell out. I imagined putting my hands on him, on his jacket, and then, before I could even think to do it, they were there, the nylon balled into my fists. It felt too easy, like I'd hardly done anything, and yet I'd breached a serious boundary, I could tell by his eyes, which were finally honest, he was startled, nervous, I wanted more of it, wanted to wring out whatever truth was inside him, I pushed my knuckles into his chest, I slapped my hand against his neck, dug my fingers into the thin skin, around a thick, tender cord. He had closed his eyes, he was squeezing them shut, waiting for me to hit him, I waited too, waited to surprise myself, but all I could think about was a distant beat, a rhythm, coming from my left, my hand, his neck, his pulse, not a *thump-thump* but a *thump*, steady, shallow— could he himself feel it? I was too calm now, too rational, I was aware people were watching. It wasn't a second after I released him before he was his usual self again, his shock gone, already pretending to find the whole thing funny. He pulled his jacket straight and took a step back. I almost apologized, the words were on my lips. To say anything else I reminded him that we'd offered him a stake, that he could have made money the right way.

The right way, he repeated, and then chortled, a sound I could tell was genuinely his by how repulsive I found it. *You have no idea, do you?*

A gust of wind came, lighting a small pain in my hand. I looked down to see a thin line of blood trailing off my thumb.

The stocks you're playing with, he said, *they're all low cap, low volume, low float. No? Still nothing? Well, I'm sure Milosz can explain it to you himself.*

I meant what I said. Never contact me again.

As I walked away his face stayed with me, a more natural smile than I'd seen on him before. I couldn't believe I hadn't hit him. I turned back around. *I'm sorry Hitler took your family's farm, but I had relatives they didn't even waste bullets on.*

He nodded, he seemed to appreciate the reference. *Of course, Herschel. Moral victory is always the victim's.*

———

I dropped a cricket in. It padded around the mulch, it could hardly find purchase. Once it did it stopped, it was completely still before starting again, its legs moving too fast to see. The lizard was the same in that he never betrayed his next step, but always seemed to be in motion, his lungs continually pumping oxygen, his tail painting shapes in the air. Except now. He paused for a suspended moment, he was unusually inert. And then he darted across the cage, the bug in his mouth before my eyes could find it.

Anoles, the clerk had called them. *It's a weird word but you can name them what you want.* What had initially caught my eye was a pair of gerbils in the window, when I walked past they stopped to watch, displacing their own worries with mine. They always worried, it was like breathing, this I realized when I came inside to see them up close: they had already moved on to something else. I needed a steadier counterpart, I walked past the rodents and the rabbits, the birds and the fish, I found the anoles in the back of the store, practically hidden beneath a row of spiders. Their bright green skin was reptilian but supple, scaly and thick but with plenty of give; it felt as though I was touching them with my eyes. At first they seemed oblivious to their surroundings, to their condition even, like the red panda, but it wasn't obliviousness, really. They simply didn't care what happened outside their tank, what was inside was enough; they had consciously chosen a smaller world.

I asked to buy the first one I saw, and then one much smaller, from another tank. He wasn't even half the size, about the length of my pinky, not including his tail; when he exhaled, the absence of air left large notches in his sides. The clerk, a dead-eyed young man who probably wished he worked at GameStop, told me I should pair the adult male with another adult, as that would increase the chances he would deploy his dewlap. This was a flap of skin under the neck that, to intimidate or seduce, extended into a bold, strawberry-colored semicircle. He pulled the dewlap out so I could see, even though I asked him not to. He interpreted my distaste at his violating the animal as a sign I didn't get it, he said the dewlap was really the only reason people bought anoles. When I asked him how he would feel if a greater being pointed out his erection as his most noteworthy feature he gave a brief laugh and then told me about their ability to camouflage. I nodded, I repeated that I'd like to buy the two anoles, I now wanted to leave the store as soon as I could, the squawks of the birds were filling my ears, and even the parrots' speech— *Thank you, have a nice day; Thank you, have a nice day*—seemed to be cries of pain.

They'd yet to change color or use their dewlaps; I didn't think the younger was even of age. Either way, I took this as a sign that they found my office comfortable. I was worried, I'd bought the largest tank I could carry—including mulch, branches, hiding spots, and a heater—but it seemed hardly big enough. They appeared calm, though, and more so now that they were digesting. Watching them like this—the crickets in their mouths, their eyes barely moving—helped me cultivate my own patience, which I needed now more than ever; I'd asked Milosz to my office forty-five minutes ago and he still wasn't here. The anoles were a reminder that life could be lived slowly, that you could spend it just sensing and interpreting what was around you. Mostly they looked out my window. At their angle they could see the planes coming from LaGuardia, I watched them myself, the flight paths satisfyingly simple, a single line, its empty perfection accentuating the rhythms of the birds, which now appeared as wild but taut balances between liberty and obligation.

Milosz appeared in my doorway. I motioned him in and he took a seat.

I caught him glancing at the tank, before I could explain it he said, *Simo wants more money. Up front, I mean. He wants half his raise now.*

A hundred thousand? Up front? He nodded. *I don't like that.*

But considering what he's worth to us.

Okay, I would just rather incentivize. Let's increase his stake.

I think he— He really means up front. He said something about his family. Simo was from Serbia, the southernmost region. From what he said about his home I got the feeling they lived as if Tito were still around. *He wants the money today.*

I rolled my eyes. Simo was smart to send Milosz. *I'll wire it later. But say you had to wring it out of me.*

Good. His shoulders dropped. *And the round is filling out?*

We got 5.2 this morning, and 2 more this afternoon. That puts us at about 150, uncommitted and without Colin.

Great. And when will he close?

That's what I want to discuss. I told him about my call with Ian, and only the call, that that was why I'd wanted to know which stocks the algorithm had fed us. Then I asked him what he thought our biggest security weaknesses were, I knew that the question would exhaust him, so that when I asked my other question he would give me his simplest, most honest answer.

He spoke about advanced encryption standards, our no logs policy, and something called a *kill switch.* Then he stated what he seemed to think was already obvious: that Ian was still nowhere near the code itself. *If he was, we'd probably never hear from him again. No, I'm sure his access point isn't the network but something more physical. A video camera, or a person.* I looked to the door and he obliged, getting up to close it. *Really,* he said. *The stocks, the prices—these are just purchase orders.* He squinted up at the ceiling. *It's like he's trying to get us to give him our credit card number just by showing that he already knows our date of birth, our middle name.*

I see, I said, looking out the window. *You know, he brought up something else, too, something interesting. He pointed out that all the stocks we've had success with, they're all low cap and low volume. Low float, too.* It took all of a second for his face to confirm what I'd feared most. *Why is that?*

Well, it could be reduced complexity, it's easier to map and all that. With black boxes you really don't—

Milosz.

He nodded and looked away, at the tank. *Okay. So, it seems, as of now, that we will only be able to capture stocks that fit that profile. Reduced complexity* does *make them— Well, okay. I'll put it like this. If we predict a price for a given stock but then don't let the algorithm buy along the way, that prediction, I have realized, will be false. And that would, by all measures, seem to suggest manipulation.* I held up my hand but it was too late, *manipulation* was the one word I didn't want to hear. Did he himself understand the implications of what he said? He looked as though he'd found a small wrinkle in our strategy, and not recast the entire business as a borderline criminal enterprise. The algorithm wasn't just predicting prices; it was, somehow, manipulating the market to make those predictions a reality.

When were you planning to tell me this? Why am I the last to know everything?

You're not. In fact I don't think anyone knows, certainly no one has said anything. This isn't— They don't think along those lines. He gauged my reaction, he looked down. His face brightened for a moment but he extinguished the thought.

What?

He shook his head in amusement. He looked back up at me. He couldn't help himself. *It just didn't add up, how it worked. We were obviously building a ladder, establishing some price, then one a bit higher, and so on. But it made too much sense, I didn't think retail investors were that logical. Well, they're not. No, our algorithm had only figured out the trigger points of other algorithms, and then triggered them at the exact right times, even causing them to trigger each other, if that makes sense. We're fundamentally lining up other quant funds, all in a row, and then with one bullet—*

It's illegal.

It's not, actually. Not yet at least, not if we don't know what's happening. And we don't, that's the whole point, isn't it? It's a legal gray zone, it has to be. Like traffic laws and self-driving cars. But not even. People see cars every day, they care about traffic safety.

Mathis suggested a lawyer at Baker McKenzie. We'll see what she says.

Please, he said. *We know what she'll say. She won't condone it, that's her job, to not condone things.* I shook my head. *Hersh, please. There's a reason why there aren't laws for this. We've built something the world hasn't even anticipated.* The glint in his eye. His pinched cheeks. It made more sense to me now, why he chose finance over a more august career. What did any mathematician want more than to construct something the world hasn't even anticipated?

I looked at the tank, at the younger anole. There was now direct sun and he was hiding under a branch, his breathing still, his mind elsewhere. Milosz was saying something about money, he was changing tack, appealing to my greed. Of course we wouldn't lose what we earned, not most of it, if it was made illegal it would be years from now, only after it became some public issue, after there was enough outrage, after Congress figured out how the hell the market worked—at least how it's worked for the past decade. By then we would have turned our profits into real estate, or reinvested it elsewhere, or just created an offshore fund. If need be we'd work with the government, help them understand what would then be an industry-wide phenomenon, we'd work something out.

It's a big accomplishment, I said.

It's bigger than us, he said, not without hesitancy; he was finally discovering abstract speech. *I've never felt so small in my life. Really. I saw a twenty-dollar bill on my desk. It looked primitive, like a relic.* I caught myself smiling, his own smile was infectious. *What we've invented, it's like fire, it's going to spread no matter what, so we might as well make it as big as we can. We need Colin, Hersh, no other way, even if it means Ian. I don't care, give him— Let him buy a stake in the firm, anything less than the board threshold. Give him four percent, five percent, give him last year's terms, whatever it takes to get him on our side and out of the way.*

Not last year's terms.

Of course not, but that's your job. You fill the fund, I don't care how. I'm ready to go all in as soon as we have the capital.

I brought my tongue over the abfraction. *I'd love to never speak to Ian again.*

Take his money, Hersh. He stood up, he put his hands on his head and then dropped them to his side. *You can do it, Hersh. Okay?*

I nodded. He waited for my eyes, and when he got them he shook his head, again in amusement, and left, closing the door harder than I would have liked.

I looked out my window—no planes, no birds—and then at the tank. Both anoles were hiding now. I peered in from above and still couldn't find them, so I tapped hard on the glass. The elder stuck his head out, and then ran to the highest point in the tank, atop a branch. He was panting, he was scared, but it suited him. He was more present than usual.

I leaned back in my chair. I put my hand on my face and pushed it around, dragging my mouth down and to the side. I went to my email, found Ian's message from this morning. *Please keep in mind that my endgame is to work together, really.* I opened the attached image but closed it before I felt anything.

Two minutes. Two minutes more of him. That could be all it took, and then I would finally be able to concentrate on what mattered. I gathered my thoughts, recalled all our past interactions and imagined every pose he might assume, and then called.

That was fast, he said.

Do you have a minute?

So Milosz set you straight.

You think it's manipulation. It's not, end of story. Low caps are just easier to map, and they have greater upside, obviously. But we're moving to large caps this afternoon. And speaking of. I'm calling because we're ready to start playing with real money. It's full now, the fund, but that's if we take some Saudi capital, which I'm reluctant to do, given, you know. So I'm calling for Colin's share, which I understand you have some say in. And in return for your good favor, I'd like to offer you some stake in Atra Arca itself, at a reduced valuation. Fifty percent reduced. Milosz said the most he'll approve is a two percent stake, but I'll convince him to raise it to four. That assumes Colin signs, and that you quit this le Carré shit.

Interesting. Two hours ago you were at my throat.

Right, literally. I'm just ready to move on. I listened. Silence. *I need the money, Ian. It's that simple.*

Okay. So, to make me go away, you're trying to sell me something. He probably didn't have cash enough to buy a bip.

Well, I'm offering you—

You know what I want.

We can't give you access to anything proprietary, we can't. Even if I was okay with it—which I'm not—Milosz would sooner die than give his approval.

Which is why I was hoping to make an offer with you, not Atra Arca.

What does that mean? Silence again, this time absolute; he was on mute. *Ian?*

Give me a second. Was he annoyed? He breathed out of his

nose. Yes, he was. Another ten seconds passed. *Herschel. Does your wife know about this brain damage situation?*

Now I put myself on mute, even though I wouldn't make a sound, even though my breath was stuck in my lungs. I knew the answer, the correct one, I just didn't know how to say it. I double-checked that the phone was on mute and then tried: *Yes*, confident. *Yes*, exasperated. *Yes*, simple.

Hello?

Yes, I said. *She knows everything. She's devastated, it's a terrible situation.*

So it would be no problem to call her and offer my condolences?

Do not contact my wife.

He breathed out again. Whatever came next would only deepen the threat, give me yet another chance to fuck up. I ended the call and put my phone down. I watched it, waiting for it to ring, but it didn't. Fuck. I looked at the elder anole. Fuck. He hadn't moved from his branch but his breathing had settled. He was thinking slowly again, lost in himself.

He wouldn't do it, no, not right now. If he really thought the threat had value the last thing he'd do was squander it. But still I couldn't get the image out of my head: Franny, caught in the middle of something, the phone cradled between her jaw and shoulder, his voice in her ear, her eyes narrowing, her eyebrows knitting. The scene abstracted itself, I saw a foul pink spirit wafting over her silver silhouette.

What would he say? That I'd told my therapist I was responsible for a friend's brain injury? Franny wouldn't believe him, no, but even so, she would tell me the story, she would watch my reaction. And then what? I couldn't even lie about her to Ian—*She knows everything*, I'd told him; why did I have to say *everything*?—how could I lie about Ian to her? It would unravel right then, right in front of us, the truth and all of the other deceits rolled up in it. It wouldn't make sense to her, that I hadn't told her before. It *didn't* make sense, except everything does, the discrepancy would fall on me, or my nature, I would be someone who could have hid such a thing.

I wanted to see the younger anole. I ducked low, in the glass of the tank I saw my reflection. I looked away, to the window, I couldn't stand it, not because I couldn't look at myself but because I could.

Why didn't I care?

I felt nothing for Birdie. Even when I thought of Will it was just with pity, really, the type I might feel for anyone visited by tragedy. If I had intense regret for my actions it was only because of how I felt right at this moment, for the sweat on my forehead and in my palms, for another rein around my neck that led back to Ian's hand. The more I searched for remorse the more it seemed nothing but a word, one that matched no genuine human experience, it was far too rhapsodic. *Remorse*, it didn't even make sense, it had no internal syntax, *to morse again*, you could pull off the pieces and there would be nothing left, there was no center. But I was curious, I looked it up on my computer: from the Latin *remordere—to bite back*, or *to bite again*.

The younger anole appeared in the corner closest to me, his front feet on one pane, his back feet on another. I imagined petting him with my thumb, the pressure and rhythm of his breathing against my skin, its steady tempo passing me composure. I stood up, maneuvered myself over the tank, and slid the top over, just a bit. I lowered my hand in, careful not to touch the glass, and held it there, a few inches above his body. He knew I was there, he must have, but he didn't move.

I dragged the back of my ring and middle fingers across his torso, it was a wonderful sensation but only in retrospect, the moment didn't last long enough for me to feel anything; suddenly he was clutching my thumb, scurrying up my hand and arm, stopping only when he came to the top of my shoulder, where I could see him, barely, out of the corner of my eye. Slowly I stood up straight, I was afraid to move more. How had I been so careless? Why didn't I think things through? I felt light, goosebumps rose out of my skin, I worried he would feel them through my shirt and run. In one steady motion I brought my other hand up and over him and snatched his tail. As I lifted him off me he writhed through the air. I thought he might squirm free and had to pinch him tightly until he was safely in the tank, at which point I closed the lid and held my hands on top of it. I didn't want to look inside, I felt in my fingers how hard I'd squeezed him, that I'd momentarily disregarded the fact he was another being in order to remedy my use of his body. When I finally sat back down, instead of peering through the glass, I fixated on my own reflection. I refocused, seeing with terrible clarity the mark of my own hand. Yes, his tail was crimped, the clean curve horribly interrupted, what pain he must have felt, and all because of my impulsiveness. I needed him to do something, confirm he was okay, again I tapped on the glass and immediately regretted it—why had I done that before? I'd made the elder feel he was about to be killed just so he would grace me with his presence. He must have believed I was some monster—and he was right, in his world I *was* a monster, when in fact I could have been a benevolent god, how easy would it have been to make their lives as good as possible? How had I not thought of this? Why did I refuse to acknowledge my privilege? Really, how long had I watched the ducks at the reservoir and not thought to help? It would have taken five minutes and fifty dollars to bring them a week's worth of world-class semolina. I had taken them for granted, all of them, all my life, their beauty and inspiration and entertainment and grace, I had thought it was some moral accomplishment not to *eat* them, not to *wear* them.

The younger's head twitched up, down, and up once more. Slowly the skin beneath his neck extended, it was about halfway open before it snapped back again. But then, with a bit more effort, it fanned out fully. It was of a lighter shade than the elder's dewlap, but still the hue was marvelous, nearly lurid, it *was* lurid; instinctively I knew that this was the first time it had happened: this was his sexual awakening, a premature leap into adulthood brought on by trauma. How had I compared it to an erection when it so clearly resembled the dropping of testicles? It even had the same pattern of dots found on a stretched scrotal sac.

For five seconds he kept it open, and when it closed he dipped his head down. But then, in a last juvenile flourish, he lifted his jaw as high as it would go, flaunting himself once more for all to see.

I couldn't believe I was going to leave them here all night.

———

I set the tank down on the bench beside the bay window in the dining room. It was starting to get dark, I hoped they understood they were looking outside, I'd given them as much nature as I could. The dining room walls occasionally thrummed, mechanical noises, the cooling system, I believe, it was why I'd planned to keep them in the family room, but Franny was in there, watching television, and I thought the dining room would be quieter. The anoles were quite sensitive to sound. At the office, when I'd finally forced the damaged tail out of my mind and begun to work, I'd noticed that they tensed as I typed. I'd switched back to my laptop's built-in keyboard, which wasn't as loud. I'd had a lot of typing to do, I was now willing to be even more specific with our results, including exact profits and a full risk analysis of the week's trades. This time I wrote without keeping Milosz's feedback in mind. I sent it to everyone, even those who had given us hard no's.

Left alone with his injury and the newfound ability to express his masculinity, the younger anole came quickly into adulthood. He only really showed his age during the ride back to the house. Whereas the elder went to the highest branch to see what the noise and shaking was about, the younger took cover; he was out of sight until I brought them into the house.

I went down to the family room, which was lit only by the TV. Franny was absorbed in a movie—something new starring Tom Hanks—her legs heavy on the ottoman, her hand resting on the remote. This wasn't *opposite of cheat day* behavior. I sat down on the couch next to her. The Hanks character was at a bank, failing to get a loan. He was demonstrating his defeat in every twitch of his face, in his coltish arms. I found it embarrassing, his performance, if he were really a man failing to get a loan he would be more self-aware, he would try to suppress his emotions, he would use his body to hide the ball of shame that lay at its center.

Can we turn it off? I asked.

She didn't hear me. I reached under her hand for the remote and paused it.

Oh, yeah, she said. She wiped her mouth with her palm. *On!* she yelled. I was too close, my shoulders lifted. The lights lit up. She looked at me and smiled, for a moment her expression seemed as exaggerated as Hanks's. Her cheeks were covered in makeup, her lips too red, her eyelids a false shade of pink.

What? she said, wiping her face again.

How was your day?

Fine? He hadn't called her. Obviously. She was squinting at me, I became aware of my own face. *Actually, Birdie made a bit of progress.*

Oh?

She seems to be responding to music. Not that the doctor would admit it, that she was reacting—*probably because he was the one who said it wouldn't do anything, that she couldn't hear. Fuck him.* I laughed, she didn't. *I read it everywhere, even comatose patients hear what's going on around them. They might even be able to feel things, too, that's why I put my phone on her stomach while it played, so she could feel the vibrations. We listened to Joni Mitchell, "Both Sides Now," we used to play it all the time in college, we'd bonded over it, the fact that both our moms loved it. They told me I was playing it too loud, the nurse did. I could have sworn she let a smile creep in.* She cackled so suddenly I flinched. *Like, I fucking get it, okay? Possibly the saddest song in history being played to a woman with tubes keeping her alive.* Her face fell again. She picked up the remote and then tossed it away. *But show some compassion, for her or for me, I don't care. Maybe they've seen too much to have empathy, maybe it's a vocational hazard, but how hard is it to treat patients like humans? Well, I was right, when we came to the chorus she started moving, and in rhythm with the song. I immediately asked for the doctor, I demanded that he come so he could see it himself. And you know, when he did he just nodded, he said it was* interesting, *that's it. I asked if he was going to write it somewhere, like on her chart. He said he could if I wanted him to. As if I'm a child. Meanwhile, right in front of us, here's a woman who has shown barely any signs of life, and she's, well, her arms kind of—* She started to mimic Birdie, lifting her limp wrists and moving them up and down. I grabbed the cushion beside my leg, bracing myself; the last time she'd done an impression of Birdie the echoes began. But it had no effect on me now, it seemed so far from reality, cartoonish even.

She calmed herself, she reset. She told me about Birdie's medications, the nurses, the screaming man next door, and Will. While Franny was there he continually fielded calls from clients; he was a psychotherapist of some prestige, at least that was what Franny had gathered from Birdie, long ago. These calls mostly consisted of him putting on a soft, compassionate voice and repeating the same line, nearly verbatim: *Things are still scary here, but I hope to be back in due course. And trust that we'll pick up right where we left off.* It bothered her, this easy, transactional sympathy, especially given the fact he showed no real emotion in the face of a catastrophe in his own life. She reminded herself that people grieved in different ways— and, it had to be said, he and Birdie were all but divorced. (She used this opportunity to tell me that he'd cheated on Birdie, and not just a few times. This was another obstacle to her taking him in good faith.) She hated to wonder what would happen if Birdie were here for weeks—months, even. If he went back to London she would be here all alone, except for Franny and a few other every-now-and-again friends. (She had no close, immediate family; her parents were dead and her brother estranged.) Yes, they were, legally, husband and wife.

And yes, he was the person in the world who knew her best. But the two must have, up until a few days ago, despised each other. That was what divorce did, especially when you were relatively young and there were no kids involved. *Tastes like divorce*, that was what Birdie had said about my drink. What she'd meant was that it was bitter but relieving.

And how is the destruction of modern finance? she asked, desperate now to change the subject.

Tricky. Our whale is threatening to back out.

That's odd. Does he know what you've been capable of?

I believe so. It's just that he wants too much.

Tomorrow's another day, she said, standing. *But tonight is tonight. The food should be ready now.*

Oh, great. But you know, I think I'll—

It's vegan, Herschel, she said, and then adjusted her tone. *No, I'm happy you're trying this. And I should have been more thoughtful this morning, too.*

It's fine, I said. *Really.*

As I followed her up the stairs and into the kitchen she told me about her day. Visiting Birdie and preparing dinner were just the bookends, in between she had finished a scale model of her newest chair, finalized a prototype with her mill, and even begun sketching out something new. If talking about the doctor and Will had rankled her, she found calm again in revisiting the day's progress, its unexpected flashes of inspiration. In fact, compared to all her undertakings involving Birdie, her job now seemed, if anything, a diversion.

We plated the food—vegan mac and cheese, charred broccolini, roasted cauliflower with ramps and raisins—poured ourselves wine, and put on music. Just as we were about to enter the dining room, when she pointed out that *we've been living with those German fucks' design choices for exactly three months now*, it occurred to me that I hadn't mentioned the anoles.

There are lizards there, I said, a moment before she'd have come to the same conclusion.

She stopped in the doorway. *There are*, she said, not looking back at me.

We continued setting the table. We sat, we tried the food and the wine.

Is the dining room their permanent home?

Well, I'd bought them for the office.

But they're here now.

A fly buzzed past my face. *I didn't want to leave them alone*, I said, swatting it away.

She nodded. *Does this have to do with you being vegan?* Again this obsession with motive, rationale. Yet if I told her I wanted to keep kosher, would she not readily accept it? She never questioned my parents' adherence to *kashrut*, in fact she took pains to prepare strictly kosher meals whenever we had them over; we even had a second set of plates. But that was okay because, what—it was their faith? So it didn't matter that Jewish law was arbitrary, outdated, and bizarre, so long as it had an explanation you could put into words: God said so.

It would appear that way.

You said you wouldn't want a dog. Even with kids. But now we have lizards.

Well, I don't want dogs. They're a lot of work, as I said. And they're too emotionally taxing. You're always letting them down, telling them what not to do. Anoles are different, they're self-sufficient. I glanced up at her, she was peering at the tank. *I plan to get more, so they feel like they're in a real social environment.*

More lizards?

Something beyond her shoulder caught my eye: a piece of fabric featuring every conceivable color, resting on a chair in the living room. It was garish, jarring, vaguely familiar. Birdie's shawl. It must have dropped off her before she left—but why was it up here, in the middle of our home?

Anoles, yes.

In that tank?

A bigger one.

And will this new tank be in our dining room or at work?

I looked over at the tank. From this angle it blocked the bottom half of our Matisse cut-out print, which she loved. When we moved in, I'd wanted to hang my Simon & Garfunkel poster there, but she had, not so subtly, suggested I put it in my home office.

I'd like to set up two tanks, and then get some sort of smaller device to transport them.

She put down her fork and knife. *I want you to be happy. And I will always support you. If this all makes you happy, being vegan, and the lizards, then of course I have no problem with it. But I think at this point I deserve an explanation.*

I nodded, but this was a lie, already I was lying just with the movement of my head. *I don't have a reason. I can't offer you an explanation. I stopped eating animals because the thought repulses me. And I bought the anoles because I find them inspiring and I feel a connection to them.*

But just a few days ago you didn't think eating meat was wrong. And you've never wanted pets, not dogs, not cats, not lizards.

Sure, and thirty years ago I thought girls were gross. I regretted the regression to humor, it was an excuse not to be forthright.

I've changed, sure. I'm changing. That happens. I've realized that something I believed was wrong. People are allowed to vacillate.

She looked confused. *Vacillate means go back and forth.*

Did it? How many times had I used that word in my life? How many of my words were wrong, defective, misrepresentations of who I was and what I felt? And what if it wasn't just nouns and verbs but prepositions and whatever else, the connective tissue, without which we would only have loose parts, could only hand one another a bag of bones?

Okay, I said. *That's the opposite of what I meant. What I meant was that this isn't some thing I'm trying out. It's not some cause. It's physical, actually. It's permanent.*

She nodded, she repeated the last word. It was the one she'd used so many times to describe her ideal home. *I feel like you're about to tell me that you've seen the light, that you've been born again.*

Another fly darted by. Where were they coming from? We kept the windows closed, we had screens on everything, we threw out expired fruit. Was it just the warm weather—would they be with us through summer?

Right, I said. *So you think I'm some kind of cliché. Well, I'm sorry if I can't express how I feel in novel, new language. In fact I don't care to express myself at all, you're the one who demands a reason for everything, you ask me to show my math on basic moral decisions like not eating other living beings. Can you explain why you can't kick a cat but you can kill a goat in front of its kids? Can you explain why you don't eat horse? Or just tell me why you wouldn't eat a human. Explain that.*

Fucking Christ, she said. *Can we just eat?*

No, I couldn't. I'd lost all appetite, I could hardly look at my food, the plates used to serve countless meals of cows and pigs and chickens. But she had no problem eating. No, and to see her lift the food to her mouth—it disgusted me, the chomping and disintegrating performed with such practiced grace, the pink tongue and gums and white teeth, this obsession with the whiteness of teeth, the purity of our mouths, the need to be free of evidence that food passed through us, we were like deranged soldiers who frantically cleaned their guns each night, who made them shine and cherished the luster.

I think we should reconsider whether we're ready, I said. *For children, I mean.*

She made a quick, guttural noise. Her eyes blurred, she went elsewhere. She set her fork down but held her knife. With her free hand she picked up her plate, raising it slowly, and then slammed it down onto the table, the ceramic suddenly everywhere, in every corner of the room. The noise was surprisingly simple, a clean break, not like the screeching of her chair, which rattled the glasses on the shelves as she backed away from the table. I listened to her climb the stairs, slam the bedroom door. I turned to the window, to the anoles; from where I sat the tank appeared empty. I looked back at her chair, far from the table and turned to the side. It struck me that in her absence I did not love her more, as was usually the case after a fight. I had hate for her. Yes, *hate* was actually a good word, it served its purpose—not like *love*, which did too much: without the word I might not know the thing itself.

I stood up, brought my dishes to the sink, and washed them. I went up to my office and signed in to my computer. I wrote a brief email to Magda, thanking her for everything, and terminated our relationship. Philip had sent me a message, links to the videos that had turned him vegetarian. I clicked on one, I couldn't watch more than five seconds of it, I wondered what person could. To wash away those images I selected one of the suggested videos on the sidebar. It featured two storks celebrating after laying an egg, performing a choreographed dance they must have practiced or witnessed before, or maybe it was always there, dormant inside them. I clicked on another suggested video, I watched rats laughing, and then I watched one of squirrels planting trees, I watched chimpanzees trading bananas and seahorses giving birth, and snails sleeping for years at a time, and elephants jumping, frogs vomiting, bats waking up, cows ruminating, prairie dogs kissing, pigs nursing, octopuses trying new food, dolphins speaking, sloths digesting, otters swimming, the facial expressions of horses, the loneliness of crocodiles. I watched two minutes of an interview with a writer named David Abram called "Language and the Perception of Nature," and then I downloaded the audio version of his most popular book, *The Spell of the Sensuous*. I started listening to it and then clicked on the trailer for a movie called *Gunda*. I bought the movie, which was without a voiceover or any words at all, and so I was able to watch it while listening to the book. It was in black and white, long scenes of a mother pig and her newborns, and a few other farm animals. We saw the piglets suckling, walking through nature, growing up; after about an hour they were adolescents and then they were loaded into a truck and then we saw only the sow, bereft, searching, attempting to understand what could not be understood, that her children were gone and would never return, her udder now a heavy reminder of their absence, and all of the previous scenes depicting her indifference as they grabbed at her, fought over her nipples, were suddenly recast as memories of hers—memories that would fade, were already fading.

When the credits came I felt my chest expand and contract, I was close to hyperventilating, I wished I could cry and get it over with but I knew I wouldn't. I switched to my noise-canceling headphones and went downstairs, through the now completely dark house, to the kitchen, where I laid out garbage bags and put in all the meat and fish, all the cheese and eggs and milk. I did the same with the pantry, and then the backup freezer we kept in the basement. I took the bags outside, three in all, and stuffed them in the trash.

I grabbed a seltzer from the fridge and went back upstairs. By this point, Abram was discussing the ways in which humans have integrated with the natural world: how our senses were originally developed to abet a reciprocal relationship with the earth, but are now spent on mastering it. As he spoke of the magic of plants and animals, wind and soil—"we find ourselves in an expressive, gesturing landscape, in a world that *speaks*"—I began to feel trapped in my office, the lacquered oak and pulped wood, the bulb shining through the frosted globe, the computer screen soaking me in blue. With my attention freed up I put the book on 1.5x speed, and then went downstairs again, this time to the dining room, and the anoles. As I entered I stepped on a ceramic shard. I bent down to pick it up and held it in front of my face. It reminded me of something, the rectangular shape, the way it reflected light: Birdie's glass as she'd shaken it at me, asking for another drink. I put the shard in the tank and lay down on the floor beside it.

I had more concentration than I knew myself capable of. In fact, the more the night progressed the less tired I became.

The feeling was familiar, it was like the withdrawal I felt after I used a sleep aid too frequently. And yes, I'd done just that, but this was more, I couldn't stand to stop listening, Abram's sentences were mesmerizing, the writing spectacular, it was whimsical but fully committed to truth. He at once justified my new mistrust of language and made me see those feelings as unformed, a hunk of metal that could, with enough thought, be hammered and tamped down into a tool that could actually *do* something.

He painted a clear arc leading from the beginning of man to today. His history was not one of tides, or shifts in power, it was not decided by individuals or even armies, it was a tale of relentless human progression and our resulting departure from nature. He spoke about how words had once bound us to the land, how we borrowed from it sounds and expressions. Then we wrote them down, at first as symbols that mirrored the natural world, but soon the Hebrews, my own people, devised letters as loops and lines that referenced only themselves. But the Hebrews retained reverence for a higher power, the spirit, the wind of the soul, and so omitted breath, vowels, from their writing. The Greeks pushed us further still, adding symbols for the air between the consonants, giving us the power we once reserved for God or for nature.

At around five a.m. the book ended. I was surprised, the story clearly wasn't over. I checked the publication date: 1996; this seemed its only flaw. Since then we had only further adulterated language, irreparably so, we had discovered how to extricate information even from words, we could build systems and tools without the flamboyance of serifs and glottal stops, the grammar of today and tomorrow had nothing to do with the way the human mouth moved, it cared only for the most efficient way to transmit information from one machine to another—that was, after all, how value was created.

Language had always helped us extract value from nature, but over time it had completely severed itself from it, ceasing to echo what had once been its inspiration. And now, just over the horizon, was a world where we too would be a part of nature language did not need. And it would be the old story told anew: language becomes detached from something, and thus is free, finally, to eat that thing alive.

I only noticed the morning's first light because the anoles did. They scampered awake and then settled in their usual territories: the elder on top of his branch, the younger in his corner. I fed them, watching as they caught the crickets, and then as they maneuvered the meal down into their bodies. Staring at the gut of the elder, seeing his breathing rate settle, I had an odd feeling, a sensation I couldn't quite grasp. It wasn't until I thought of yesterday, how I'd held the younger by his tail, and imagined the scene from his point of view that I found it, something so simple and obvious and yet it had never occurred to me before. Even if the anoles saw themselves reflected in a window, or in water, or in an actual mirror, they would never know what they looked like, really. They could never see themselves as a predator could. Their own being, so small, so fathomable, would forever be their blind spot.

—◡—

I awoke to the sound of the espresso machine. I was still in the dining room, on the floor, the end of the rug curled into a pillow. I was relieved, somehow, to see that the shattered plate still hadn't been cleared, that Franny hadn't been in the room while I was asleep. I stood up. The sun blinded me, it flooded the room. In the harsh light I remembered myself, who exactly I was, the day awaiting me. However mundane my morning routine had always seemed, it was now imbued with the significance of a last lap. Perhaps this wouldn't be my final day at Atra Arca, but it would be the last time my coming to work had a purpose. Yes, today we would decide to shut down operations, we had to. If this happened to be a good, prudent, lawful business decision, well, that was useful insofar as I wouldn't be the only one making the decision. Milosz, the board—I appreciated that they didn't know what I knew. They didn't feel what I felt. Even the thought of the office, the servers alone in that room, the algorithm silently shifting the market—it was, all of it, repulsive.

When I walked into the kitchen Franny made sure to turn her back to me. I went up to my office, took out my toolkit, and measured the dimensions of the free space against the back wall. This was where I had, until now, planned to put a bookshelf. I signed in to my computer, still on the screen was *Gunda*. I went to PetSmart's website and searched for tanks, I added two 120-gallon aquariums to my cart, as well as bedding, hiding spots, plants, branches, high-quality crickets, and a vitamin supplement to dust the crickets with. I found transport bags for my exact purpose, I added one and checked out with express, same-day delivery.

I took a shower. The water pressure was fine again, I could wait to call the plumber. I dried off, shaved, combed my hair, and got dressed. I ordered a car and brought the anole tank down to the foyer. In the kitchen I grabbed an orange as well as the *Financial Times*. I had no desire to speak with Franny or kiss her goodbye but felt I should, it was an essential part of my morning ritual. I walked up behind her, when I put my hand on her side she swatted it away. She shook her head, she was upset with me and needed to communicate it, but still I knew that she wanted affection, she wanted to know that we were, foundationally, okay. I stepped forward, my chest against her back, I let her lean into me, we stayed like this long enough for the familiar feeling to return. Such extended close contact always made me feel that we were, for a moment, one person, that anything one of us felt would soon drift into the other. But today the feeling was muted, I couldn't forget myself, forget that I was in my own, distinct body. After all, there was something in me that could not pass between us, that would not even survive in her. She had rejected my arguments about meat, how could she accept a belief much greater, one I myself couldn't even explain, one I knew not through words, not even through thought; it was, by this point, faith. I kissed her neck, and then I left her.

I brought the tank outside and saw Lucy across the street, tied to her stoop railing. My presence ignited her; she began barking nonstop. It wasn't until I walked down the steps that I realized what was going on: the meat and dairy had been there, in our trash, for hours. I didn't want to look her in the eyes, she was being tortured and I alone could fix it. The car should have been here already, I set down the tank and took out my phone but this seemed to make her bark all the more, so I put it away and unfolded the paper, the salmon-pink sheet I'd always thought of as a quirk but now I wondered, for the first time, how they made it that color. I glanced at the door, our new walnut door, and then back at the paper, I looked the cover up and down, I was holding my breath, nervous for something I hadn't yet become conscious of: besides the title, which I knew to be *Financial Times*, I couldn't make sense of any of the text, it was as if I had absolute dyslexia, I could stare at individual letters and see a *b*, a *G*, but the spaces between words were elusive, the ordering of letters arbitrary, they changed every time I blinked or refocused. This was confusing, it was funny, a laugh choked my throat, it shook my chest and tensed my stomach. Lucy could tell, she stopped barking, but when I lowered the paper to check for the car she started again. I briefly despised her for her rashness, her stupidity, and then regretted it; she was only desperate. I folded the paper and went over to the trash. I lifted the top from a can and flies dispersed. The thought of reaching my hand in, fishing out a steak—I couldn't. I looked up to the windows of Ben's apartment and then back at Lucy, her eyes; that was enough. As I walked across the street she knew to be quiet—no, she wasn't stupid. Her collar was complicated, the blue nylon was both frayed and slippery, I had no idea how it worked, but why was I concerning myself with this end? The other was tied to the gate in a simple knot, I unraveled it in seconds. Lucy darted forward but I held the leash, the tug pulling even my heart. She turned around and stared at me, pleading. *Hey!* Her mouth hadn't moved, no, the sound came from the back of my head. *Hey!* I turned around and saw Ben bounding down the stoop. *What are you doing?*

I was just letting her— I put out some meat last night. One of the bags has frozen steak in it, I'm sure it's good.

Okay, well just, like, don't untie someone else's dog.

I know that, I said. *I would have asked, but you weren't here.*

He was baffled, he was trying to show me that my actions

baffled him, his face said: *This doesn't make any sense.* He walked over to me, grabbed the leash from my hand and then tied it back around the gate.

He wasn't going to let her have the meat? Because I tried to help her myself?

You're free to take her there on your own, I said. *It's good stuff and it will just go to waste.*

She's well fed.

I looked at Lucy but she didn't notice my gaze, she was still staring at the trash cans. Ben and I made eye contact; his eyes flicked away but then came back to me.

It's hard to see her like that, I said. *She's desperate.* Again he squinted at me, performing his worry. *I'm about to leave for work, once I do you can feel free—*

What's the problem here? A new voice, from across the street. I turned to see Philip trotting over, waving at us. As he got closer I saw that his face mirrored Ben's, even though he had no idea what was going on, what there even was to be disturbed by. His hands found his hips, his chin lifted. God, he wanted to arbitrate.

He tried to untie my dog, Ben said. *And now he's trying to tell me I have to feed her his trash.*

Philip placed his hand on my shoulder and looked at me. *I'm sure it's just a misunderstanding.*

Ben started to speak but stopped. His face refreshed, he was no longer confused. *Philip Guggenheim? I had no idea you lived around here. I have to say, we loved* The Phoenicians.

Oh, thanks, he said, looking down.

You know, Ben said, *it was just— It's this superlative display of realism, nested in a sort of—*he twisted his hands like he was solving a Rubik's Cube—*almost magical conceit. And it was effective, too. I swear, for days I couldn't eat meat.*

Why did everyone say that? Like it was some accomplishment to change people's minds for a week. I lifted my shoulder so Philip would remove his hand.

But you eat meat now? I asked Ben. *You eat animals as intelligent as Lucy?*

Philip looked at Ben's nonresponse and then said, *Awareness can be action in itself.*

It can be whatever you say it is, but still it doesn't do anything. Do you think the Uighurs are grateful for our awareness? Or the victims of the Holocaust? I'm not sure they appreciated the rest of the world looking on, aware. No, I don't think awareness is action, I think that's just something you can tell yourself to pretend art is powerful, to make our obsession with entertainment seem noble. I paused, my instinct was to gather myself, but I was already gathered, I knew that what I was saying was true just as I knew how it was being taken. *Real art should change people, for good. A clever exploration of vegetarianism is not art, we'd do better to put out more of the pornography you sent over yesterday.*

Philip looked to Ben, *I sent him some videos from PETA*, and then back to me. *I think what you're saying is that art has to be political. But it can be more, it can be human.*

I agree completely, I said. *What's more human than creating more and more bullshit without thinking about the consequences?*

Got it, Ben said. *This has been stimulating, but I'm going to—*

I know how I sound, I said. *I'm passionate, but that's only because I know change is possible. If you let yourself believe in something it will change you, it will make you want to change the world.*

My car was here. It had been for some time. I looked at

Lucy, conveying my sympathy, and then at Ben and Philip, each in the eyes, I wanted them to know that even if I was zealous I was still sane, that my words were worth considering. I went back to my stoop to get the anole tank and brought it into the car. I looked ahead, I didn't want to see them now, I knew they'd be trading eyes, drenched in defensiveness, focusing on my display of emotion to avoid thinking about the contradictions baked into their arbitrary morals. How could I have expected otherwise? Denial was comfortable, ignorance a luxury I no longer had. No, I'd seen into the future. I'd even helped build it.

⁓

The server room was cooler in the morning. I didn't even feel warm air wafting out. The machines were just getting started, waking up from the night. Like the sea lions at the zoo they were bound to our workday, except we believed that processing our data was their God-given purpose, that they owed us their lives. Even the name, *servers*, made it easy to ignore what was now nearly inevitable. It was a failure of our own imagination, sci-fi gave us images of metallic humanoids that slashed our throats and fucked our spouses and turned off the life support of astronauts. But the future we risked wouldn't make for a movie poster. There would be no explosions, no screams for help, in fact we wouldn't scream at all. Like dogs and pigs, trees and streams, our speech would be reduced to sound, noise in a world of information.

I know, it's a mess. Milosz. How long had he been there? *I didn't mean to scare you.*

It's okay, I said. I turned and saw Simo, too.

Can we talk? Milosz asked. *In private?*

Right, I said. *Sure.* We went down the hall and into my office. Once we sat down, Milosz looked at Simo and held out his palm, inviting him to speak.

So, Simo said, mostly to Milosz. *Last night I was approached, just outside the office. I'm sure you know who I'm talking about.*

I'm sure I do, I said.

Well, he asked me to dinner.

Why did he say it like that? *You went?*

I did, yes, but only because I thought it could be useful to us. And I believe it was. I played along with him, I pretended to be interested. He made me an offer to start something new, together I mean, he said he'd buy me out of my contract. He talked and talked, he went on forever about his ideas, which are pretty much our ideas, which he apparently knows in great depth.

Great depth.

I was also surprised. I thought he was like you, a businessman. But he has a much deeper understanding. The way he talked, and even the terms he used—he looked at Milosz—*well, they were very similar to the terms we use here. Eventually I asked, in so many words, how he knew what he knew. He told me that I wasn't the first person here he spoke to. He referred to a* source, *that was the word he used. He said he had a* source *inside the company.*

So it was. All this goddamn hand-wringing over VPNs and lockers for our phones and it probably took, what—a hundred thousand? Less? Maybe nothing, I doubted Ian had money to throw around, and I supposed his excuse for charm could have won over one of our junior traders. Tim, if I had to guess; his ego was an unlikely size, given that his last job had been doing municipal bonds at some family office.

Okay, I said, looking at Milosz. *So our work is compromised*—

all of it, probably. *At this point I have no choice but to tell investors what's going on, and to be honest I can't imagine they'll—*

Herschel, Milosz said, *why don't we have this conversation—*

If I were an investor of ours, I said, my voice raised just enough, leaving plenty of room for more, *and I knew what we know now, I would demand my money back. In fact I think we have a fiduciary—*

Okay, please, Milosz said. *Let's keep our heads.*

I exhaled. I gathered myself. I was starting to feel like I'd only gotten two hours of sleep. *Perhaps instead of building a fortress around ourselves we should have paid more attention to the people walking out the door every day.* I stood up. *But it's too late. No, Simo, you shouldn't have gone to dinner with him. It'll be a great anecdote to drop while he's poaching our investors, he won't say he bribed some junior researcher but that he worked directly with the VP. Yes, I know the NDAs are a formality, but—*I raised my voice higher*—fucking read the thing. You violated it by going out with him. You both have created so many fucking breaches of trust and contract we hardly have a business anymore. This isn't a fucking math department, this isn't a thought experiment, we're creating something in the real world. We were. No, given what we know now, given everything—*I glared at Milosz*—I don't see any other option but to wind things down.*

What are you saying? Milosz's voice now matched mine. *You don't say "It's time to wind things down" like there's some switch only you have access to. In fact you control seventeen percent.* He glanced at Simo, he wished we were alone but couldn't stop now. *We've talked about this. If there are small legal hurdles they're in the future, okay. There's a leak, okay, but think. Why would Ian stalk our building unless he was desperate, he doesn't have anything but stocks and prices, maybe some strategy. Just— I need until the end of the day. No, lunch. I'll get the team together, we both will, me and you, the problem will be resolved.* He stood up. I always forgot he was taller than me. *We've gone too far for this.*

There was nothing I could say, in fact it was best I said nothing at all. I reminded myself I wanted him to find the leak, I wanted the problem to be resolved.

Let's do it off-premises, I said. *I wouldn't trust a single inch of this place.*

Sure, Milosz said. He paused, looking down at my desk. He reached over it, took my phone and put it in his pocket. He looked at Simo, who stood too, and without another word they left. Well, I thought they did. After a moment I realized Simo was still there, staring at my bookshelf. He picked up a book, Piketty, and examined it.

It's trash, I said, but he didn't seem to hear. For a few seconds he just stood there. And then he put the book back, closed the door, and retook his seat.

I smiled at him. I waited for him to say what he needed but he only stared at the anoles.

Don't worry about the NDA, I said. *I'll forget it happened.*

He pushed the air out of his throat. Had I ever seen him without his sense of irony?

You look tired, he said.

It's been a week.

I'm sorry, he said. *About the money.* I nodded, I pretended to know what he was talking about. *Milosz said you had to make some sacrifices.*

His up-front cash, right. *You deserve it*, I said. *We wouldn't have said yes if you didn't.*

He nodded, he lowered his brow. *So I didn't tell Milosz everything. Actually, I first spoke to Ian yesterday morning.* He looked at me, gauging my reaction. *He called me. He made it clear how much he knew, the stocks we'd targeted, the prices. And he told me it was illegal, that he was ready to go to some guy in the Southern District. Polk, he said, an old friend. Not that I didn't already have an idea about, you know, what was happening. I just didn't think that much about it, it's really not my domain. But it became so obvious then, how short-lived this would be.*

So you wanted your money now.

It's a lot, I know. It's even more in dinars. It was a thud, the phrase, he'd practiced it too many times. I trusted that he believed what he was about to say, but still I couldn't hear the words as anything but tools of persuasion. *It's enough to change my parents' lives. To let them go somewhere else if they want. Really it's giving them the chance they gave me. You know, it's a miracle I'm here. My younger brother is twice as smart, but I was the one my parents sent to university. They can't believe I have three laptops, that I eat dinner out most nights. Sometimes it feels like I'm living in the future, but then I remember it's just that they're stuck in the past.*

It sounds like you had reason enough to do what you did.

Even so, the money came from somewhere.

Yes, the algorithm you built. I looked at the tank. Both anoles were now on the top branch. Still he was staring at me. *Simo, you're forgiven.* I tapped lightly on the glass but neither moved. They were remarkably motionless aside from their breathing, which was as rapid as I'd seen. I leaned back in my chair. *You made a good decision. A savvy one. No, we can't continue what we're doing. It's not right, and it's illegal.* I looked up at him, his arms were now folded. *But look on the bright side. This whole thing probably would have made a couple of people unreasonably wealthy while putting a lot of great thinkers out of work. Today you're an accomplished quant, tomorrow you're as good as cavalry in the nuclear age.*

Well, tell that to Milosz.

Try telling anything to Milosz.

He laughed; we both did.

But really, I said, *the metaphor holds. Oppenheimer didn't let the idea of a massacre stop him. Would he have let the SEC?* Now only he laughed. *To Milosz this is all just an idea. He can't see the reality of things. He's not the one who's going to have to call our investors, who's going to have to wring every last cent out of the business.*

Simo raised his eyebrows at me, and then he—what? Smiled?

What?

Well, you tell me. No, I had no idea, I expressed as much. *Just now, when you were outside the server room, you were—* I wondered if, you know. *They're insured, aren't they?*

He held his smile, but now there was nothing behind it.

For a PhD you think a lot about money. You should start your own firm.

He chuckled, so much so his shoulders bounced, perhaps it was only relief.

What exactly did you think I had in mind?

His laugh was tight again. *Well*—he forced a new smile, trying to reclaim some of his irony. *I think we both know it's a mess in there. I told him to get a specialist in, the way they are now they could overheat.* He nodded to himself. *It's fathomable that they could overheat.*

I see. I looked back at the anoles. I put my arms over my head, grabbing one hand with the other. *Well, you can take the*

Piketty. Maybe you'll get more out of it than I did. He nodded, he didn't catch on that he should leave. *And I'll start wading through my inbox, which is practically quicksand.*

He nodded and stood, grabbing the book on his way out.

I looked at his now empty chair. What had he said? *Fathomable.* Fathom, the measurement. I looked it up, six feet exactly, the height of a man, as if anything bigger were unfathomable.

I opened my desk drawer. There was the matchbook from The Dutch, from a dinner late last summer; it was Milosz and I, and Dominic, who had just agreed to loan us $2.2 million. He had wanted to discuss European soccer, for nearly an hour we pretended to care. We'd yet to return the sum, in a few months we'd owe him another $200,000. Whether we would be able to pay him back or not I didn't care, didn't really care, not beyond losing him as an investor for something new. You couldn't. He'd known the risks, they all did.

I struck a match, I waited for it to burn my fingers and then shook the fire away. The insurance money wasn't important, but it did do something, it helped convince a part of me that was, though no longer relevant, still present. A minority stakeholder. Such a corny thought, I still had my sense of humor, that was how you knew you were still yourself, still centered, despite how others made you feel.

I stood up, I walked out of my office. In the kitchen I found Milosz alone, at a table, eating something from a bowl. It was just how he looked when we first met. I made an espresso and took the seat across from him.

You'll need to talk to the team yourself, I said. *I've got too much work to do.* He knew this was bullshit, it didn't matter, he wasn't going to put up a fight. *I'll need my phone back, too.*

Without a word he got up and walked away. I followed

him to the lockers, waited as he put in the code. He handed me my phone and went back to the kitchen. I had three missed calls from Franny, and two texts: *Are you okay?* and then *Philip stopped by. He was worried about you.* I started to type but stopped, Milosz was making a speech: All researchers were to be ready to leave in five minutes, they would be back in the office by 10:30—forty-five minutes from now. I wrote Franny back: *I'm fine. No need to worry.* I walked down the hallway, past the servers, I didn't look inside but I did slow down, enough to feel that their warm exhales had resumed.

I went into my office and, standing in the center, took inventory. There was valuable equipment, hundreds of books, there were objects of sentimental value, photos of my family, of Franny and me, souvenirs from London and Venice, my father's baseball mitt, my grandfather's yarmulke, a football signed by Brett Favre. It was hard to think of it all together, but still that sum couldn't hold a candle to the $1.3 million I'd personally lent Atra Arca. Yes, the insurance policy could yield $1.5 million, but that would be used to pay off the rest of our lease, and then any outstanding invoices—hardware, software, Milosz's worthless security system—and if there was anything left it would go to our preferred lenders, and who exactly was *preferred* would be up to the lawyers; right, the lawyers needed paying, too. I wouldn't recoup a cent, no, I wasn't fucking over just lenders and investors but myself as well.

Herschel?

I turned around to find Peter waiting in my doorway. He told me someone from PetSmart was here, he said it like a question. I had him send them in, and a few minutes later a tall, thin man with a protruding Adam's apple rolled in a hand truck bearing two boxes, one of which was massive: the tank.

He then went out and returned with another hand truck—the other tank? I was about to say there'd been a mistake but realized I was the one who'd made it. Why hadn't I shipped one tank to the house? I heard Milosz and the researchers gathering their things. I told him to unpack only one of the tanks. He looked worried, he said he didn't know it was a tank, he couldn't move it himself. I said I would help, he said I couldn't, that he needed to call his coworker, they were waiting in the truck just around the corner. I checked the time, I told him to leave it, leave everything, I offered to buy the hand truck and then got out my wallet, which offended him, he didn't look at me as he repeated that he needed to call his coworker. I looked into my wallet, all I had was three twenties. When I held them out he paused, like he wasn't going to accept it, and when he did he averted his eyes, as if he didn't want to see me see his misconduct, as if I weren't complicit. He reached into his coat, pulled out an invoice and pen, and placed them on my desk. I leaned over the page, it was just lines and dots scattered at random, I took the pen to the middle, as soon as I started I forgot what letter I was on, I drew three loops in a row and handed the invoice back to him. He pushed it into his jacket and then, finally, left.

I went to PetSmart's website; again I couldn't read a thing. I pinged Peter and told him to come to my office. When he arrived I pretended to be on the phone and asked him to go to my computer, duplicate my last order—minus a tank—and send it to my home, same-day delivery. I walked around my office while he did this, nodding, looking concerned.

Once he left I opened my desk drawer and took out the matches and keys. Again I surveyed the room, but before I could think of losing this, losing that, I walked out to the hallway and pulled the fire alarm just outside my door. It was the sound I expected but still I was startled, it rang so loud I could hardly think, my shoulders rose high and my head dipped down. I forced my chin up, my arms down, and I walked out to the trading floor. Peter was standing, already calling 911, competent as usual. I told him to leave immediately, he nodded and hung up. Oren was walking to the door, I asked him where Gina and Tim were, our other traders, he said he didn't know. I watched as they exited into the stairwell, and then jogged back to the server room.

Inside and just above the door was the camera Milosz had installed. I didn't doubt that the footage would be kept on one of the very servers it monitored, but still I lit a match, reached my arm through the cage, and lifted the flame up to the lens. I counted to five, for good measure I lit another and held it under the belly of the camera. It started to smoke, white wisps that creeped up the device. It was so suddenly absurd, that something as simple as fire could ruin a device that had taken us hundreds of thousands of years to invent. I felt it then, the reality of what I was doing, that I was *doing*, taking action and not just passively existing in a world that continued to lose its soul. I put in the combination for the old padlock, opened it, and took out the keys. I found the one labeled 70 and unlocked the door, but when I pushed it just shook. At chest level was another lock, the new combination—my birthday, that permutation of it. I tried something but knew it wasn't right, I tried again three more times, it was impossible to think with the alarm blaring. I closed my eyes, I shook the cage, I let myself scream because no one would hear me. I calmed myself, really I pretended I was calm, and then failed twice more. I ran to my office and scanned the walls: behind my desk, on a shelf, was my Louisville Slugger. There was hardly enough room in the hallway to swing, but still the lock cracked on my second try. I picked it up, put it in my pocket, and went inside. Two steps in it was already warmer, the air thicker, I unbuttoned the top of my shirt as I found my way to the back of the room, there you couldn't even see the hallway over the towers. On the floor was a tangle of yellow and black cords, most leading into the column of servers it abutted. I lit a match, got down on my knees, and held it under the thickest wire I could find. Ten seconds passed and nothing happened, I stood up and tossed the match, there were only four left, I lit another and stuck it through a hole in the back of a server. I waited, I smelled something blunt, sour, I looked at the floor and saw a thin trail of smoke. As I bent down to get a better look the server above made a crinkling noise and then popped, and then again, louder, loud not like the alarm, which was basically a song, it had rhythm, this was chillingly spontaneous and almost too loud to hear, it entered my ears not as sound but as pain. It happened again, twice in a row, I might have fallen but caught myself on the wall. Already the smoke was crawling across the ceiling, and by the time I made it out into the hallway it was seeping out of the room. The pops came from all over now, the crinkling noise, too. The smoke was pouring upward, flowing into itself unnaturally fast, it was so dense and opaque it almost hid the fire at its center, which was such a light shade of yellow I worried it wasn't hot enough, I was about to step inside to light another match when a wave of heat slapped me on the forehead. As I covered my face I heard a hiss, it was soft but steady, I removed my hands from my eyes and found the room entirely aflame, light flaring from every corner, already the fire had jumped from box to box, through wires, it had found every piece of plastic that could be burned, it had only needed a spark, an iota of life. I let myself stand there for a few moments. And then another few. What I saw felt like an extension of myself, a seemingly small truth that had been given air enough to breathe, had showed itself to be greater and more dazzling than I'd ever believed.

I put back the padlock, picked up the bat, and ran to my office. The elder was on his branch, I removed the top from the tank and lifted the stick into the carrier bag, shaking him off. The younger was in the corner, I held my breath, grabbed him as gently as I could, and dropped him in, too. Against the zipper I felt the sweat on my fingers, already the room was warm. With the bag on my back I went out to the trading floor, I wanted to take one last look around but the sprinklers went off.

The street was full and getting fuller. People were coming to watch, filming the scene on their phones. If some of them were worried—crying, consoling each other—most were excited, they were intoxicated, no small part of them wanted to see the whole thing burnt to the ground. I scanned the crowd for the activists, I suspected no one would cheer destruction more than those who had defined themselves by opposition to institutions, but I couldn't find a single one. No, and come to think of it they hadn't been there that morning either, they'd already given up, they'd accepted failure, if that was even what it was, perhaps they'd already gotten what they came for: a sense of purpose, however fleeting. I saw Oren and Gina, I shook my head in disbelief and looked up at the building, watching as the smoke escaped from our floor. I heard sirens in the distance, and walked away, up Wooster.

If I felt a sense of accomplishment standing outside the server room, watching what I'd done, it had already dissipated. Thinking of it now only made me more energized, more inspired, more awake to the work that lay ahead. Yes, if I'd achieved anything it was to suppress a single outgrowth of something more systemic. Of course the problem wasn't Atra Arca, it was the strain of thought that gave it life, it was the collision of greed and ingenuity with our eternal myopia, our blind faith in progress. We now built things that exceeded even our imagination, by the time we understood the consequences it was far too late. Yes, I'd been given a rare glimpse into the future, a blip of horrible insight, and it was a gift I wouldn't waste.

I took out my phone and pulled up the website of the United States Attorney for the Southern District of New York. Ian wasn't bullshitting: David J. Polk. I called the number listed on the page but no one answered, it wasn't even a personalized voicemail, no, I'd reached some report line for the public. I left a message, detailing who I was, what Atra Arca was, where we'd gone wrong, where the law had: failing to foresee how machine learning-based algorithms could take intent out of the equation, absolve its creators, enable people to profit while freeing them from responsibility for their actions. I urged him to consider the integrity of the market, to look into this as soon as he could, it was only a matter of time before someone less principled built what we did. I hung up and then put my phone on silent.

By this point I was north of Houston, NYU territory, this was obvious from the number of children I saw. Maybe they were old enough to drink but they were children, they were innocent, unserious, they gave themselves to their phones.

And what a banal thought, how trite, we knew this already, young people loved their phones, we all did, even to say it out loud was silly, that was how bad it had become, it was an idea too big to comprehend yet too obvious even to state: we had forsaken the world in front of us for one we created. We were now a culture of narcissism—yes, of course, again this had been said with such frequency it was meant to be ignored—but we were more: we were a species of it. Each and every one of our greatest breakthroughs put just another mirror between us and nature. Language let us forget the sights and sounds of the world, the wheel let us transcend our bodies, artificial light let us control night and day, photography let us outsource and manipulate our memories, books and phones and the internet reduced distances to a point, denied Earth its immensity. And with every upgrade the human race wrought we saw more and more of ourselves, we saw less and less of the world we'd opted out of, we grew only in confidence, we became bold in our ignorance, we became deranged, obsessed not with who we were but who we weren't.

Did we always walk with our mouths open? These students, they were slack-jawed, literally, they'd been infantilized, debilitated by their own comfort, spoiled by safety, we all were, so few of us knew hardship, brutality, violence. No, of course we should be safe, we should never make war, but for thousands of years we'd been forged through nothing but, we were built for it, we had the imagination to make do with any set of constraints, but more and more we had no constraints, our imaginations were hammers without nails, and we grew anxious without nails, we became depressed, so we pretended to need what we didn't, we sought to acquire more and more, and when there was nothing left to acquire we sought just the *ability* to acquire, we yearned for money, value itself, the last resource whose finitude we respected. We created a zero-sum game, emphasis on *zero-sum*, emphasis on *game*, we were willing to take from others just to put our imaginations to work, we were willing to make a science out of profit. It was the final frontier, value, the last opening to reality that our own contrivance would soon close for good.

God, it was great to be outside, the breeze on my face, the wind in my ears. It was this block, it created a wind tunnel, you never got this much breeze in Manhattan. I stopped the next person I saw and asked him what street we were on. *Mercer*, he said, which seemed funny, like *one who gives mercy*. I said the thought out loud so he wouldn't think it was him I found funny, as he looked unique, like someone who wouldn't use traditional pronouns. Franny's cousin was like that. They always struck me as slightly from the future, they were, people like them helped us imagine an undoing of the lies inherent in language, revealed it as a sclerotic system that would always lag behind current modes of thought by, at best, decades. I was white, heterosexual, and wealthy. But really I was Jewish, I wouldn't have been considered white a hundred years ago. Though I'd never slept with or kissed a man, I did notice male beauty. And weren't we all rich compared to someone else? This was just the sorites paradox: Take a grain of sand and add another, and another—when exactly does it become a heap?

Soon I came to Union Square. The sun was now high in the sky, it was hotter than it had been all year and everyone had prepared, wearing their best new summer outfits. It seemed that cinnamon brown was in for women, and pants were higher waisted for everyone. As I passed a home goods store

I glanced at my reflection, I took in my slacks and button-down, the shirt folded up around my forearms, the way the wind lifted tufts of my curly hair. It wasn't a solid image but it served its purpose, the person I saw then would play me in my memories, when I thought of my interaction with that nonbinary soul he was there, transparent like the rest of the scene. As I walked up Broadway I saw him with his hands in his pockets, the bag hanging from his shoulder. I saw him as others did, as a black box, and then I looked inside, I saw his thoughts, how lost humanity seemed to him, how misguided, how our delusions had wrought havoc on other species, on the planet, on our own destiny. I liked seeing me as a *he*, it gave me a new perspective, one that was a bit elevated and set at a distance. It gave me something else, too, something that I couldn't quite put a finger on but that carried with it relief, it was the sort of calm that comes prior to the administration of general anesthetic.

He lived the day in reverse: walking uptown, setting fire to the servers, the PetSmart delivery, talking with Simo, and then with Milosz there too, getting to work, that awful conversation with Ben and Philip, waking up after just a couple hours of sleep. In each scene he imagined everything he could, he scraped his memory for every last detail. By the time he was done he was at Fiftieth Street. He was surrounded by sky-scrapers now, the phrase *concrete jungle* came to mind, carrying with it a sense of irony. All his life he had leaned on irony, a defense mechanism meant to preempt embarrassment or humiliation, but it had an upside, he could see that now: it forced him to be his own cynic. Yes, and that was exactly what he needed here—a counterargument to all of this, something to make the case for humanity, for progress, he squinted and thought of the neighborhood. Not two blocks away was the Museum of Modern Art.

It was lunchtime on a Friday but the lobby was packed. He went over to the membership table and gave the woman his card; he and Franny were members though they hadn't visited since last summer. In the elevator was an old woman, she clutched her purse like he might try to steal it. She got off at the fifth floor, he waited and then got off, too. He walked into a nearly empty room, there was a young Asian couple, a man his age. To his left was a work—Hopper, he was sure—depicting a man at a gas station. He couldn't see what the man was doing, but he was alone, that was the message, *This man is alone.* Hopper was always pointing out the alienation of the modern world, but really he was consecrating it, his paintings excused solitude, for him it was natural to feel apart from society. He was craven, a coward whose work only calcified the status quo.

He came to a column of disconnected teal metal prisms set against a wall. The placard was a brief jumble of letters. He breathed in and held it, he looked away and then, quickly, back at the placard, he did this again and again; he could read it without reading. Donald Judd. And of course it was *Untitled*, an irony given works like this required so many words by so many critics just to mean anything at all, and still all that writing summed up to nothing. He was ready to leave, he turned to the exit but something caught his eye, the bottom left corner of an otherwise unremarkable canvas, he saw half a tomato painted in such a way that it didn't look like a tomato so much as it represented how we conceive of tomatoes, it admitted the falseness of our own perception. His arms filled with goosebumps, he walked up to it, again the trick with the quick glances. *The Carbide Lamp* by Joan Miró. He took a picture with his phone, he turned away and looked back, he felt a flash of joy. With this new energy he walked deeper into the galleries, to a new room, where he saw, on a wall by itself, a painting much larger than he was. It featured a giant red horse, a few other horses, at the periphery were men working, carried away by the momentum of the central stallion, with wisps of white and streams of light implying many moments at once; there was too much action for a single frame. He recognized the artist, not by name but he knew the movement, he and Franny had seen an exhibit on Italian Futurism when they'd just started dating. Ever since, when the topic of modernism would come up in conversation, he would dutifully note that he liked most of all the Italian Futurists, he would parrot the curator's words he'd read years ago, that the Futurists *celebrated transformation and glorified revolt*, they *sought to revitalize a decaying culture*. But now he felt, if not those thoughts exactly, then at least the presence of some wild truth—a truth not constructed by well-articulated arguments but one that could exist without words. What he saw was a cry for the natural, and not some Thoreau bullshit, which was just a lament for the past, but a way to live in the future, to wield conflict, to actively work against the order crystallizing around us. In front of him was art that said no thought mattered unless it led to action. It was true, of course it was, this was a philosophy so obvious even children knew it, intuitively. He touched his arm expecting goosebumps again but the skin was flat. No, the idea wasn't new to him, he'd felt it just an hour ago, as he stood outside the server room, watching his flames engulf something that was never meant to be. He took a photo of the work, and then the placard. *The City Rises*, Umberto Boccioni.

Retracing his steps he found the elevators. He called a car, and by the time he made it downstairs and through the lobby it was waiting for him, a black SUV that smelled of upholstery and cheap fragrance. Franny never used perfume, which even the old him had appreciated. He lowered the windows and asked the driver to turn the music down.

She was a good starting point, Franny, there was no better option, she trusted him and he her. She would listen to him, help him hone his ideas, she'd even play a firm devil's advocate. He took out his phone, he had four missed calls from Milosz. He thought to call her but worried he'd have to start the conversation right then, instead he sent her a text with the help of Siri: *Are you working from home?*

But she was more than someone he trusted. She was the love of his life. It had been a rough week, she'd yet to become acclimated to who he'd become, but yes, he loved her, of course he did. If anything it was the old him that had taken their love for granted, had defined it, had defaulted to a too-easy composite of other concepts: fondness, attraction, mutual respect, and admiration. He had defined her, too; she was intelligent, empathetic, playful, stimulating—adjectives that could be written down and applied to millions of other people, they were senseless, literally, they distracted him from all of what he felt in her presence but could never describe, not without deforming it, reducing it, making it into something it wasn't.

This was a new beginning. From now on they would submit themselves to that other love, the one even animals feel. That weekend they would not utter a word to each other, they would only be present, understand each other through intu-ition. And then, after two days of silence, they would make love, what a beautiful way to conceive, through a dedication to something not even words could capture. The thought of having sex without language aroused him, so much so that he felt real pleasure as his pants began vibrating. He reached into his pocket and pulled out his phone: Milosz. Outside he saw the East River, they were on the FDR. He rolled up the window.

Hello?

Where are you? Milosz said, his voice cut by wind. *Why don't you answer your phone?*

I'm on my way home.

What happened? The fire was on our floor?

Yes, in the server room. There was nothing—

In the server room?

Yes. I saw it myself. He waited for Milosz to respond but heard only the pixelated breeze. *In fact I was the one to pull the alarm.* He looked at the screen of his phone. *Milosz?*

Right, he said, and then something else that was too soft to hear.

Did you find the leak?

This is a setback, that's all it is.

Milosz, I think at this point—

He started yelling. Herschel pulled the phone away from his ear. When finally there was silence again he said, *Right, I know. But let's talk about it later.* Again no response. *So you didn't find the leak.*

No, Herschel. I have no idea.

Okay, talk soon.

He hung up and put the phone down. He tried to resume

thinking about Franny, their coming weekend together, but it was like trying to return to a dream in the morning. They drove past StuyTown, the Lower East Side, the Financial District. They went through the Battery Tunnel and came off the highway into Carroll Gardens. Clinton Street had never seemed so placid, poised. He thought of the Boccioni painting, he pulled up the image on his phone, there was more action there than these streets saw in a year. But he was being foolish, he was too literal. Revolution was a matter of perception. The painting was a work of art because it showed what could not be seen. He himself knew that catalysts of radical change didn't need to look the part, those servers were just black boxes with wires in between. Yes, even those who had to program the things found it tedious, painstaking, prosaic. It was only a select few with enough acquired intuition who could get a sense for the scale of outcomes, who understood that success meant chaos, that we could be a trading day away from a kind of anarchy history had yet to imagine.

But then what about Milosz? His view into the future was far more precise, it must have been, and still he forged ahead. Perhaps that was the problem, to Milosz it was just a vision, he didn't have to consider the reality of it, no, that was Herschel's job, to infect the world with Milosz's idea; without Herschel an idea was all it would be. But it wasn't Herschel whom Milosz needed, really, it was just someone like him— and didn't he already have exactly that? Yes, he had the perfect proxy waiting for him, Herschel's understudy, practically. Ian would love nothing more than to fill the void he'd left. Okay, it had been a good idea to call the Southern District, but this couldn't wait months, years—those two could make something happen in days.

He picked up his phone. He had a text from Franny, which he asked Siri to read aloud: *Yes I'm home. Also dryer broke again.* He opened his conversation with Ian and dictated a message: *The firm's had a bit of a setback. I'm desperate for capital and willing to talk access. Let's set up an in-person.* He sent the text and looked out his window. It was pacifying, this neighborhood, all the sturdy brownstones and empty sidewalks. The car came to a red light and he told the driver to let him off.

It was cooler here than in Manhattan. Maybe it was just the breeze, or how you could hear it through the trees. They were flowering now, soon the wind would be louder still, when all those pretty petals formed circles on the ground. He thought of a time-lapse video of plants he'd seen a few weeks ago: vines reaching for metal poles, their arms tottering like Dr. Seuss characters. What had struck him was their intent, they appeared to make plans and execute them, like animals living on a different time scale. He thought of Milosz's obsession with teraflops, how many operations our computers performed each second. A given machine could accomplish more work in a minute than we could in our entire lives. If they could see us, if they cared at all, our movements would hardly even register.

He began the walk home, thinking of Ian, the practicalities. He envisioned himself in the park again, or just outside, by the Met. He'd offer to get coffees, he'd go early and have them ready, Ian's cup in his right hand, that was how he'd remember. But that was the easy part. Right, acquiring what was needed, that was the problem. He knew you could find poisonous substances on the dark web but he'd never been on it before and suspected it was all one big FBI honeypot. His friend Rafa took drugs, weed and molly, he had a dealer, maybe the dealer knew someone. No, that idea was much worse. He put his hand on his forehead and pushed the skin up, it looked ridiculous but it helped him think, feeling the random corrugations. Botox, it was toxic, that was the point, it caused paralysis. There was the story of the woman in Maine who'd died from botulism, acquired the drug on her own and self-injected. And what about that guy from the squash team in college, Nick something, Nick Bowers, he was a dermatologist now—didn't he have a practice in Murray Hill? He could stop by, tell Bowers that he was researching a skin care corporation, a major acquisition, the company was public, too. He couldn't say which one but with his tone, his smile, he'd imply he might as well. *I'm doing some competitive research. Botox-related. You don't— Do you have some with you? I'd love to see the packaging.* And then a distraction, some gossip, his phone would ring and he'd take it outside, he'd have to run, it would happen so fast he'd forget to give the Botox back. *Nick Bowers*, he wrote the name in his memo app.

He was at the house. Fridays were nice because it was garbage collection day, for a few hours their block was spotless. The place was still so new to him that he could stand outside and bask in it: their ownership of something so stately, well-appointed, imposing, even. That was why it had bothered him so much, that brief squabble over the oak tree. Philip and Clara were right, of course, it was dreadful to think of excising one of the block's last vestiges of nature—but had that been their rationale? No, their objection had cited only their own loss of property value. That was how far we'd come: the best way to protect nature was by attaching a dollar value to it. As if people could own trees. It all seemed so decadent now—such an embarrassing, bourgeois tiff—but really it had nothing to do with class, country, culture. What was more timeless than two groups of people arguing over control of the natural world?

He climbed the stoop. As he slid the key into the lock he heard the kinetic pulsing of violin. He pushed the door open: *Flight of the Bumblebee*. This was a welcome surprise, and auspicious, all that jubilant energy; she never listened to those Hollywood classics on her own. He hadn't thought of music, whether that would be part of their silence. Up the stairs he found her in the living room, drawing, her back to him, couch pillows on the floor and an orange peel by her side. She hadn't heard him come in and he didn't want to disturb her, she scared easily and was probably in her flow. He thought to go downstairs and close the door again, harder, but then she stopped drawing, she sensed something, she turned around. Her instinctive delight in seeing him was quickly replaced by apprehension, but it was thin, obligatory, necessary to maintain continuity with their earlier conflict. To hell with the narrative arc, he thought, and smiled at her, warmly, naturally; it grated so confidently against expectation, and even against the music, that it proved itself. She seemed relieved—hesitant but relieved. He set down the carrier bag, she stood up, and they embraced. He rocked them back and forth, alternating which foot bore his weight, and, glancing into the dining room, saw that she had cleaned up the plate. They came undone and looked at each other, his serenity was contagious, it bloomed on her, too—and that was the point at which she questioned its source.

She looked away, stepped to the side. *You were right about not being ready*, she said. *For kids, I mean.*

No, no, he said. *Please, I didn't mean it. We're both ready, I know we are. Actually, I wanted to talk about exactly that.*

She noticed the bag on the floor, her vague doubt resurfacing. But when he told her what was inside she simply nodded and said, *You can keep them here. You can keep them wherever you want.* To show she meant what she said she picked up the bag and brought it into the dining room. He followed her, but was stopped in his tracks at the doorway: the new tank had been delivered, and she'd already set it up for him, it was full of all the accessories he'd ordered. On top, neatly stacked, were the containers of crickets. *I love you*, he said. He did. God, she was thoughtful, she was too humble even to connect eyes as he expressed his gratitude. He walked up to her and they hugged again. In her arms he told her that he'd had quite a day, he laughed at the understatement. *Jesus fucking Christ, Franny, the office burned down.* They came apart and he laughed again, he covered his face with his hand, and then he told her what had happened, as he would tell it to Milosz, to anyone else. It was good practice, she didn't know as many details, he could make more mistakes. At each new kink in the story her head shook in disbelief, and when he said that their work was lost, that he was sure they'd need to close down, she took a seat. After he finished—telling her that he'd walked for hours, thinking—she stood and they hugged once more, they kissed, she contorted her face to convey optimism. Her eyes ticked to the bag on the floor, she picked it up and brought it to the tank. She only wanted to make him happy, show him that she cared, again he said that he loved her. She held the bag over the transfer window of the tank and unzipped it. One of the anoles, the elder, leaped down. She peered inside the bag, tilting it one way and then the other.

Oh, she said. *I thought there were two.*

The younger must have been caught in some fold, unless

he'd packed away just one. No, he hadn't, and before he could let the thought run its course he went over to the bag and looked himself, he turned it upside down and shook. Out fell a stick, hardly even a twig. It seemed to be made of dark green canvas. It was a tail.

He handed her the bag and crouched down. He picked it up, it was hard, already lifeless, though he could still make out the crimped segment. He looked at the tank, where the tail belonged, he thought to put it inside, but when he saw the elder, his body distended, he fell to the floor. Cold air came under his shirt, came against the skin of his stomach, his neck, he was sobbing, softly, he didn't want her to hear, though the sound was so much more horrendous muted.

He needed to breathe, the air came in all at once, through his desiccated throat it became a screech, one that lifted Franny's shoulders. She came down to the floor, put her hand on his side, but her empathy was wasted, he wasn't worth consoling: it was all his fault, if he didn't know why exactly it had happened he at least knew that. He hadn't fed them since early that morning, had he? Of course not, he hadn't even checked in on them once he'd left the office, for hours they'd tumbled around in that bag like clothes in a dryer, without light, they must have been terrified, even humans resorted to cannibalism in desperate circumstances. That wasn't far off, they were basically stranded on an island together, they had been from the very beginning, it was all his doing, against the advice of the salesman he'd paired an adult with an adolescent, he'd had the hubris to build a social environment on a whim.

He sat up and wiped his eyes. He breathed in, and out, he believed he had himself under control. He stood and walked to the tank. The elder was on a branch, looking out the window. His torso was bulging, it was asymmetric, the terrible fact of it took shape as some cold, spatial curiosity. Herschel tilted his head, he tried imagining it—but why was he just standing there? Maybe it wasn't too late, maybe the younger was still alive, still— He opened the lid with one hand and plunged the other inside. The elder darted away, out of sight, and that brief bit of action was enough to bring him to his senses. Again his own thoughtlessness surrounded him, buzzing, warming his cheeks. He had almost doubled his sin by not fucking *thinking*. Just fucking *think*. He was ready to shove his fingers down another's throat just to, what? Relieve himself of his own guilt? He looked through the other end of the tank, found the elder in the corner, he was in discomfort, having had to scramble with his body full, he just wanted peace enough to digest. Herschel glanced at Franny, who stood facing him, her arms loose at her sides. She was wearing makeup, he realized, she was wearing the black blouse she knew he loved. He wanted privacy, he wished she weren't there, her presence made him feel trapped in himself, in his own humanity, with her in front of him he could not deny how different he was from the anole, how hopeless communication between them was, but if he were alone with him, if there were just two beings in the room, he could let go of his doubt, he could make what seemed then like a magical leap. But of course animals could recognize our emotions, and that was all he wanted, he didn't need to speak and be heard, he just needed the elder to identify *sorrow*, he needed him to understand he was being asked for *forgiveness*, concepts that existed in any social environment, how could they not?

He told himself Franny was not there, he closed his eyes

and believed it. He used his face to transmit remorse, he made himself a mime, expressing the emotions as much as he physically could. He opened his eyes to see that the elder was staring at him, and now that Herschel had his full attention he asked, silently, for forgiveness, his eyes wide with hope, his hands out, his palms up.

Herschel.

He kept his concentration, he was almost there.

Herschel, she said, louder.

He glanced up at her, when he looked back the elder's mind was elsewhere. He stood up straight and faced her, her arms were now crossed. He found her expression oddly satisfying, it gave him a bit of joy, even; this was exactly what the elder felt but couldn't communicate: disappointment, anger, confusion.

Franny, he said, approaching her. *It was my fault. I didn't feed them, and then I stuffed them in that bag.*

Do you think this has anything to do with the rest of the day?

No, I don't.

Okay, well, you didn't mean to do it, right? It was an accident.

That makes it better?

Of course.

So you would rather be accidentally killed than murdered?

Jesus.

Think about it.

Sure. I mean, I'd be dead regardless.

What about me? What if I was murdered? Would you rather it have been an accident?

I don't know. It would depend.

On?

On a lot of things, she said, her face pleading—for what? For him to have some sense? He was asking her for the opposite: that she abandon herself for just a moment.

If I died in a car crash, and the driver had tried to kill me, would that be worse than if he was just drunk?

She looked away, shook her head to herself. To her it was still just some thought experiment.

Look, he said, *is it really any better that what happened to Birdie was an accident?*

Her face dropped, finally. *That's not funny.*

Exactly.

Yes, Herschel, it is better.

Why?

Why? she repeated. Her eyes narrowed. And then, when his face didn't change, they opened again. She may have despised him then, briefly, she couldn't even look at him as she said it. *We don't have to feel angry. There's no one to blame.*

There wasn't, he reminded himself.

Her face was still. Her eyes flicked to the side, narrowed again. She was thinking, replaying the last few seconds. When they made eye contact again she looked unsure, dumb even, it was a rare sight. Desperately he wanted the moment to pass, he felt his desperation and shoved it down, he shoved everything down.

A plane sounded in the distance. When it petered out he heard silence, but as a faint, high-pitched ring. He laughed, at least it felt like he did, his stomach contracted but there was no noise. She looked more confident now, now that he wasn't, if she didn't know what she didn't know she at least knew the answer existed, it was in the room, in him. Her shoulders relaxed and her head ticked to the side. Challenges suited her, put her mind to use; she felt let down whenever she finished a crossword puzzle.

Was there any other way? Would she settle for anything but what she knew was the truth? He wanted to sit down. There was a chair in front of him, the thought of pulling it from the table, putting his weight on it—the room seemed crowded, dense, hot, the air from his lungs dragged against his throat and came out as white noise. He put his hand out but there was nothing there, he stepped forward and grabbed the chair. It was uncomfortable, sitting, the wood was too hard, his legs too long, he leaned forward until his cheek found his palm. He didn't hear her sit but there she was, pulling his hand away from his head, forcing him to hold it up himself.

Can I have a few moments? Alone?

She sat back in her chair, her arms folded. No, there was no other way. She wouldn't accept anything but what she knew was the truth.

I had no idea, he said. He felt relief already, just for making the decision, for taking the first, irrevocable step. *Of course I didn't. I just wanted her to leave.*

Suddenly he was on his feet, unsure if he could balance, a toddler amazed at his own uprightness. He walked into the living room, over to the couch, and sat on the floor before it. In front of him was the drawing she'd been working on, it was the leg of a chair, as soon as he picked it up she took it from his hands. She was sitting now, too, angled as before, not beside him and not across.

I gave her a fairly large dose of a sleep aid. I put it in her drink. It sounded much worse than it was, *sleep aid*, like he'd bought it for that purpose. He hadn't wanted to say the brand name, with it came the original tone of the decision, which was that of humor, spontaneity, inspiration even. *It was ZzzQuil. I found it in the medicine cabinet.*

He leaned forward, over his knees. It felt good to fall like that, with his spine carrying his weight. He bent down more, and to the side, he found her lap, the crease between her thigh and calf. When her hand began caressing his head he felt that he could touch her leg; he brushed her, caressed her, soon he was kneading her skin. He smelled the detergent on her clothes, he felt the air from the ceiling fan. She was crying. He knew it from how her stomach lurched. In those random contractions he tried to decipher what he couldn't ask: what she was thinking; for whom, exactly, she was crying. He himself cried, he ached, he yearned, he longed to be anywhere else, anyone else, himself just a week ago.

He hadn't expected to feel humiliated. But he was, he was a disgrace, a fraud exposed, he had pretended to be someone he wasn't. But now it was obvious, he was hopelessly himself, someone who would do what he'd done, would hide it from her, hide it from even himself, and in the most wretched ways. It was against this humiliation that he felt the other thing, the sensation shame barely allows. No, he hadn't expected gratitude, either. Disbelief, really. That she held him, that she bore his presence, that she didn't leave him alone. She didn't yell at him. She didn't ask him questions. Still her hand stroked his hair, the motion so familiar but had she ever done it before? It was wrong for him to receive so much love, any love at all, but to refuse it would be to refuse her, it would be to ignore her sacrifice, which was not some noble gesture but the corruption of something all her own. Yes, in her tears—still she was stifling them, swallowing them into the sharp spasms of her gut—was a promise. She was crying for Birdie, and she was crying for him. But her tears flowed for no one more than herself.

His head fell further into her lap, his body became slack. And with his knees together, his legs bent, he closed his eyes for good.

———

It all felt so distant it might have been a dream. My actual dream was of our hotel room in Stockholm, years ago. Over and over I watched Franny receive and prepare our room service breakfast: stirring coffee, spreading jam on toast, deshelling eggs.

I reached for my phone but it wasn't on the bedside table. I sat up to see the clock on the other side of Franny. 5:51 a.m. I'd slept for what, sixteen hours?

I swung my feet off the mattress and stood up. Something unusual; I was already dressed. If I had the urge to question whether yesterday had happened at all, I couldn't once my hand found my pants. I lifted from my pocket the broken combination lock, the loose numerical discs.

I couldn't think of any of it—smashing the lock, guiding the match into the server, *The City Rises*—except through something like disassociation, I saw someone who wasn't me, who looked like me but acted on his own, I couldn't remember being in his body. Yes, to relive any bit of it was embarrassing, but it was the embarrassment of another's humiliation. To think I had almost asked Franny to be together, in silence, for a whole weekend—and then try to conceive. It was comedic, sure, it was too absurd not to be, but what lingered was horror. It wasn't just that I'd thought those thoughts, but that I might think them again—the possibility that my current sanity might only be a brief reprieve, the eye of the storm.

I walked out of the bedroom and into the bathroom. I turned on the light and, seeing myself in the mirror, flinched. But it was encouraging, the sight of myself afraid; fear had been so foreign to that other person. Yes, I was fearful, I've always been. Just as I was ambitious and practical and vain. I, Herschel. Me.

I closed my eyes, remembering more, and opened them again. Temporary insanity or not, I couldn't deny that those actions were mine, I owned them now. Yes, I'd set fire to the servers. Yes, we'd lost all of our proprietary code. But okay, well, it was actually the right thing to do. Even if it meant leaving a lot of money on the table, even if my stake would have been worth tens of millions of dollars. Hundreds of millions. More. That would take some time to absorb. But still, I'd helped maintain the integrity of the financial system. And that wasn't hokum, I was the last person to suffer righteous regulation bullshit; no, what I'd done was necessary to preserve the market—not to mention my own career. It was what Bruce always said, *Anyone can trade in their integrity for a quick mil. But it'll be their last.*

I tugged my lip down and saw the abfraction, I touched it but it didn't hurt. I started brushing my teeth.

Bruce. Yes, I regretted calling him Wednesday, rubbing our success in his face. Surely it would make the closure of the firm that much sweeter for him. But it was okay, thinking of that regret, it was such a different thing from thinking about yesterday, which didn't surface regret so much as disorientation. No, there was no through line between that person yesterday and me now, whereas I could be ashamed of calling Bruce because that *was me*—I could recall exactly how I'd felt in that moment.

I set the toothbrush back and washed out my mouth. I took off my pants and shirt, my briefs. I looked at the shape of my legs, I'd always liked my thin ankles. In the mirror I inspected my collarbone, my disheveled hair, I was proud of my body, I enjoyed my face, it made sense in the most fundamental way that I looked like me. I stepped on the scale. One hundred sixty-five pounds. Pounds: *It's a lot of pounds*, that was what Colin had written in his email. He'd be happy he hadn't sent us a penny.

I stepped off the scale. Wasn't that my first memory, being weighed? As a baby, on that cold metal basin. Our building had caught on fire. That was news. Investors would need to hear from us, need to hear that everything was okay, that we would be working out of a temporary office, et cetera. And then, in a few months, we would deliver the unfortunate news: things hadn't panned out, the idea was there, it was possible, but not with our resources, and we couldn't responsibly ask for more. It would be easier that way, insurance-wise, lawsuit-wise.

Fucking shit. Hundreds of millions of dollars. That was fuck-you money; I would have called Bruce and literally told him to go fuck himself. I felt it in my stomach, a pang that carried with it something else, too: there was no place to go on Monday. I was, for all intents and purposes, unemployed, at least I would be, soon, after I'd spent a couple of months shoveling dogshit into the furnace. And then what? If I ran into an old colleague, someone from business school, I would have no answer to the golden question. Years ago I worked at Webber, and then I failed at starting my own fund, and now I was trying to conceive with my successful, working wife.

These thoughts pushed me out into the hallway and up to my office. As I waited for my computer to boot up I did push-ups, which felt great, I could really tell I hadn't done them in days. I signed in and went to the business bank accounts; yes, Simo's bonus had already been withdrawn. I opened my email, there were 113 new messages. I scrolled through, only about 30 were real: 10 potential investor rejections, 3 invoices, 2 notes regarding a new hire, and around 15 lenders and investors asking about the fire. I Googled *wooster fire* and found just two articles, one from a CBS affiliate and the other from a very local publication; apparently a fire isn't news anymore. Both articles were short, a couple of hundred words, if that, just long captions for the same video of black smoke rising into the sky. There was no mention of foul play or anything like it. But if there were some suspicion, would it really end up in an article like this? How careless had I been? I had no idea, I'd burned the lens of the video camera—did that even do anything? There was Ian, he could call the police, an anonymous tip, even, an investigation would surely— No, Ian didn't know what had happened, why would I think that? I needed to get my head straight. I coughed, swallowed, closed my eyes. Once I'd emptied my inbox I'd feel better. I went back to my email but the thought of him stayed with me, as I began reading an invoice I saw his face, every wrinkle of it. I closed my eyes again. Ian. My plan. I could now retrace those thoughts exactly: I was going to poison him, with Botox, that I stole from Nick Bowers. *Do you have some with you?* That was what I was going to say. *I'd love to see the packaging.*

The room was too cold. I went into the hallway and adjusted the thermostat. I walked back into the office, I sat down, I reminded myself that I'd done nothing wrong.

I had been temporarily insane.

Yes, but then why did I still feel it? If I didn't feel the desire to kill him, still I knew that desire's shape, its color.

The thermostat still hadn't kicked on. The water pressure, the dryer, the heat—why was everything in this house broken? I thought to do more push-ups to warm myself, that was a good, healthy way to channel my angst. Yes, but I needed something more sustained.

I left the office and went downstairs, back to the bedroom. Quietly I grabbed my running clothes and took them to the bathroom to change. In the kitchen I had a bowl of dry cereal and cashews and drank two double shots of espresso.

Outside the sun was up, the streets empty, even for a Saturday. I ran through Gowanus, South Slope, and Sunset Park to Bay Ridge, where I jogged along the water. It was wonderful to feel my body, to feel that I was slightly more out of shape than I'd like to be, that I was no longer so young, that the funny feeling in my knee still nagged. I watched the seagulls fly against the wind, fighting just to stay in place; they were an aerodynamic curiosity, nothing more. When I hit the Verrazzano Bridge I turned back, by then my muscles and joints were demanding more and more of my attention. This was exactly why I loved running. With less headspace to spend on actual thoughts things began to clarify, my analyses became more efficient.

There were four distinct problems: the fire leading back to me, my temporary insanity, the firm closing, and Franny's knowledge of my involvement in Birdie's accident—

specifically, what this would do to our relationship. The four were so brilliantly unalike that I could vacillate between them and continually refresh my perspective. The problem of the firm's closing consisted of mourning lost wealth and questioning what to do with my life, both would take a significant amount of time. That was also true for the issue with Franny, this was not something that would simply go away, it would sit in the corner of every room of our house, we'd notice it day and night, it could take years before it blended in with the rest of the furniture. The problem of my temporary insanity contained vague questions I could entertain if I wanted to— Why did it happen? What should I make of it?—and one quite concrete: Would it happen again? No, it wouldn't, I now knew that instinctually, knew it as I knew when I was dreaming. I was myself again now and forever, the Herschel I'd been for thirty-eight years, and each new mile I felt it more, I did, that it was all in the past—no, on another timeline altogether.

By the time I got back, sprinting down the block and then walking the last bit, I had only made theoretical progress on the first problem, reducing it to a question of the missing lock and the security footage. There were unknown unknowns— was there something inherent in the fire's spread that implied arson?—but my hesitation to leave a trail of Google searches like *how to know if it was arson*—even on a VPN, even on DuckDuckGo—allowed me to avoid unnecessary worrying. There was Simo, too. He was under the impression I wanted the insurance money, but it wouldn't be like him to do anything with that knowledge, and not after that fat bonus—not to mention that the fire was, after all, his idea. But the lock, the footage, for these questions I'd need to extract some information from Milosz's brain, really they were but two of the million things we needed to discuss. And sure enough, when I entered the foyer I saw I had five missed calls from him, as well as two texts: *We need to talk ASAP* and then *Meet you at your place, leaving now.* This last had been sent at 7:02 a.m., forty-five minutes ago; the trip took just short of an hour.

As soon as I walked up the stairs I knew I was in the thick of Franny's morning routine: I was hit simultaneously by the smell of fried eggs and the sound of the shower. She liked to let the eggs finish on the pan while she washed and dressed. One of the first times I knew I was in love with her was when I discovered this habit, how irrationally efficient it was. In the kitchen I listened to her shower, waiting for her hums, but they didn't come. I heard a brief torrent of water and then it stopped altogether.

On the pan were two eggs, sunny-side up, a piece of brioche was waiting in the toaster. The scents mixed wonderfully, I took it as an act of ill intent that she had made only one portion until I remembered I was vegan, at least I had been yesterday. But I wasn't now, why would I be? My feelings toward animals, language, humanity—they all belonged to that person I wasn't, that person who'd only, up until I came clean to Franny, occupied my body. The seagulls looked like seagulls, why would an egg not be edible? I took a fork and lifted off the pan a sliver of cooked egg white. I brought it to my nose, it smelled fine, good, the way an egg should. I split my lips and moved the fork down, but I couldn't do it. No, I didn't want to. *Want* to, yes, this was a decision, not like the lamb or the shawarma or the milk in the latte, each of those had induced a physical sensation—discomfort, disgust. But why didn't I want to? If the feeling was elusive it was also, somehow, familiar. Distantly familiar. Was it years ago? I walked into the living room, to the spot on the floor where I'd confessed to Franny, where she'd held me until I fell asleep. How had I gotten upstairs? I found it then, the feeling I was looking for. Yes, it was years ago, many years ago, I must have been twelve. We were in a hot tub, me and my friend Joel and two girls a few years older than us; he was an assistant at the sports camp where the girls worked. I was nervous, excited, the night had a purpose, Joel's doing: the girls had previously agreed to let us touch their breasts. When the time came, when he asked them if we could do it and they said yes, I left the hot tub, went inside, got dressed, and called my dad to pick me up. I was a good kid, it was a moral instinct—albeit one likely inherited from shows like *7th Heaven*. But it was more, this would have been my first sexual experience beyond kissing a girl on the lips, and watching Lisa masturbate. It would have been an initiation into a new understanding of life, one that would utterly replace my old one.

I walked through the kitchen and into the dining room, where I saw the anoles. The anole. I remembered the scene, myself on the floor, sobbing. The pain of reliving it was progress, already I could do so for more than a few seconds and without clenching my teeth. But still, I didn't need the reminder, nor did I need to have to remember to feed it crickets, or do whatever else. I made a mental note to put the tank out on the stoop and walked out of the room, through the kitchen and up the stairs, to the bedroom, where I found Franny, a towel around her body and one tied on her head. She looked at me and smiled, it was slanted, self-conscious, but still she held it for my sake. She didn't know what to do with the sight of me, but she was doing her best, she was a marvelous woman, I couldn't believe how lucky I was to have found her.

The permits were approved, she said, her tone so even it took me a moment to grasp the sentence. *I called the contractor. Work can start next week.*

Wow, I said. *Amazing news.*

I invited Philip and Clara over to celebrate, she said, breaking eye contact. *Yesterday, before you came home.* She undid the towel around her hair and set it on the dresser. *I understand if you're not up to it.*

I nodded and, turning away from her, began to undress.

It would be casual, she said. *I told them noon.* She coughed. *I'd just pick up some pastries.*

I turned around and held out my hand. She threw me the towel and I covered myself.

I don't know what you said to him, she said, *but I thought it would be nice to smooth things over.*

No, I wasn't up for the get-together. But it was what she wanted, and I owed her so much. *Sure*, I said, *that sounds good.*

I went to the bathroom and started the shower. Looking at my face in the mirror, it hit me: the permits, the contractor, the gut renovation. What was the estimate? It wasn't seven figures, but close. Given the state of the firm, my $1.3 million loan now all but gone—no, maybe the renovation wasn't such a good idea, not until we talked with our accountant. *Work can start next week*, she'd said. God.

Just as the water got warm I heard the doorbell—Milosz— followed by Franny scrambling to get dressed. I got in and began washing myself as fast as I could. Even Franny's social dexterity was no match for Milosz's inability to make small talk, mostly he stammered observations of his interlocutor; I imagined him telling her that her hair was drier than he remembered. But there was something else, too, the vague sense that it was against my interest to let them talk. I soaped just my head and hair, letting the lather trickle down, as soon as it rinsed away I got out and toweled off.

I found them in the family room, him on the couch, her in a chair. She was nodding sympathetically; she seemed, if anything, sad.

Herschel, he said. His voice was so soft I wouldn't have understood if I hadn't been looking at him.

Franny stood and excused herself, I didn't hear her exact words because I was caught by Milosz's posture, I'd never seen him sit like that, one leg draped over the other, his hands resting on his knees, so mannered. When I sat down, taking Franny's place, he waved at me, only once, his hand tracing a rainbow.

I'm sorry for the visit. I just really needed to talk.

No, I said. *Of course.*

But can we have some privacy?

Franny was still within earshot, I knew because the clanking of plates stopped abruptly. We could have gone up to my office, but I had an instinct against bringing him through the house.

Franny, I said, raising my voice, *do you mind going out to get those pastries?*

We listened as she finished what she was doing, she came down the stairs to the foyer, put on her shoes and jacket. All that time Milosz and I basically looked at each other, we weren't capable of chitchat, we knew each other too well but in such a narrow way.

She closed the door. He nodded graciously. He seemed so suddenly small, well-behaved, a boy waiting patiently.

Would you describe the fire? he asked.

You haven't checked the footage?

It was kept on the servers.

So nothing saved to the camera itself.

No, they're not— Herschel, *the floor basically collapsed. They wouldn't even let me in.*

I didn't see much, I said. *It happened so fast.*

But tell me what you saw. Anything.

I described the crinkling noises, the pops, the smoke and the light-yellow fire below, the hiss, the wall of heat, the flames scattering as I left. It was hard to look at him while I spoke, each new detail seemed to cause him even more discomfort, seemed to tug his mouth even more askew. In some way it felt like I was breaking up with him, that despite the distress my words inflicted, they brought closure, too.

The fire started in the back of the room? he asked, looking at his shoe.

It seemed that way, I said.

He nodded. *At the back.*

It happened so fast I almost missed it, if I hadn't been looking right at him I might have. His hand and head had already reset. I had to say it to myself to prove it really happened: he punched himself, just above the ear. He seemed to have forgotten it himself, perhaps I should have pretended, too, but I couldn't, so I laughed, I tried to catch his eyes, let him know this could be a joke if we wanted it to be. But he didn't look at me, he only gazed at the piano.

You can sue me, he said. *If it helps at all, then sue me.*

Milosz.

Or report it as negligence. That's what it was, I was negligent, absolutely, even a fucking idiot would have realized it was too hot.

It's nobody's fault. It was an accident.

He laughed, this gave him real pleasure, too much, suddenly it seemed more plausible that he'd punched himself. *So accidents are nobody's fault? What a world, Herschel.*

What was I supposed to do, really? Even if I could take away his guilt—as if I could explain what I did, or why I did it—it wasn't as though it would just disappear. It would only be converted into hatred, one that would never resolve. Yes, Franny was right, it was better when things were accidental; with blame came anger—as if grief alone weren't enough. No, the two together could make you go insane.

Forgive yourself, Milosz. He nodded, but then shook his head. I squeezed the cushion of my seat, I feared he would hit himself again, or worse. *You won't be able to move on until you've done that.*

I'm ready to move on. Why do you think I'm here?

I nodded. Right, of course, already he wanted to start something new, he didn't know how things worked, that you needed money, that even getting our seed funding had been a miracle, one that could not be repeated because those bridges were now burned, quite literally. No, and for all of our work we had nothing to show, because we'd kept everything on servers we could see and touch, instead of on a remote network like everyone else, because he was paranoid, he confused the emotional security that came from physical proximity with actual security, so much so he overlooked the fact he was shoving hundreds of hot servers into what should have been a conference room. Yes, it was, actually, his fault. Not to mention that what we had been doing was illegal, or as good as illegal, another detail he had the privilege of casually ignoring, he lived in a world of theoretical delight, he got to spend his working life thinking about things that didn't exist because people like me sold our souls to try to make use of them, we looked people in the eyes and made false promises, we were forever optimistic in the face of the fact that we were trying to sell things that hadn't been built just so we could buy the resources to see if they could be built at all.

Well, you know I wish you luck.

Herschel.

No, the money's not there. People want to know what they're investing in, and, frankly, I can't tell them, because it's illegal. You're brilliant, Milosz, your work is brilliant, but this idea isn't meant for the world.

You're limited by your imagination. Now he wanted to look me in the eyes. I let him, I nodded. *You can't imagine what doesn't exist. This idea is just too big for you.*

Perhaps, I said. *Either way, I know you'll find someone who feels differently.*

He stood up, still staring at me. I forced my arms slack, my neck loose, only in my head did I prepare to defend myself. He inhaled, lifting his shoulders, and walked out of our house.

I sat there, thankful to be alone, thankful that I'd never have to see him again. I wouldn't, I'd make sure of it. I had handled it well, all things considered, I'd explained my reasoning, I'd given him the freedom to go on without me. *Well, you know I wish you luck.* That was gracious, even if we both knew it was a lie; no, I'd hate to see him take this idea to someone else. So why say it at all? It was gratuitous, he knew me well enough, he wasn't dumb. Saying such pablum was effortless; how easily I left myself, gave him just an empty husk. I thought of the last time I'd sat in this chair, Monday night, after Birdie left, when it was just the four of us. I saw Clara in front of me, bent at the waist, her phone in my face, a picture from their ultrasound. *Isn't that marvelous*, I'd said. Was it? It looked like every other ultrasound. It was something you said, just something you said, we say things that are just things to say. By that point Birdie was in the hospital, or on the way, unconscious and bleeding from the head in the back of a stranger's car. If I'd known— Well, what? I knew now, and I was just sitting here, for days I had lived my life without ever asking for an update on her. But I had been that other person, and— I'd incapacitated someone, I had taken from her the capacity to be herself, to communicate with her friends and family, to laugh, be hungover, write plays, feel the joy of shitting. Never again would she misplace her keys or fall in love or be annoying or boorish or self-involved or talk over anyone, I would have given anything for her to be in this room, to ignore me and casually insult others, to be given back her freedom. I could feel the wood inside the cushions of the arms of the chair, it was rectangular, which seemed inelegant, but what else would it be? I wanted to punch myself the way Milosz had, immediately and with no reaction, no indulgence, just the pain. I brought my fist up, I closed my eyes—I couldn't do it, I was a coward, I was actively deciding not to, just as when I'd failed to eat the egg. Instead I pushed my fist into my forehead—if anything it felt good, moving it around, wrinkling the skin. The Botox, Ian, yes, I'd planned to poison him with a drink. My tongue hurt, it ached, my fingers dug into the chair, feeling for the edges of the hidden wood. Birdie again, Ian now—a drink over and new excuse, an act but, I'd decided against, yes, yes, where was Franny, she should be home, her hair like always and me in her arms. I took out my phone and called her but she didn't pick up. I went to the window, she was crossing the street, a nice white cardboard box in her hands. I sat on the couch, where Milosz had been, and soon she came into the room.

He's gone?

He left, I said.

She set the box down and then pushed her hair away from her forehead, briefly forgetting I was there. She turned to face me. *Will's staying through May. He booked an Airbnb.*

That's great. I'm glad to hear that.

She nodded. *Have you spoken to Magda about what happened?*

No, I said. *Not really. And I'm not sure it would be a good idea. Legally, I mean.*

She opened the pastry box, an excuse to look away. I shouldn't have said it like that, shouldn't have even brought up legality. And I'd lied to her too, by omission; I'd fired Magda—not that I couldn't take it back, of course I could, I would just tell Magda that I'd made the decision under—

My phone was buzzing. I reached into my pocket, a 917 number. I looked up at Franny but she'd already left.

Hello?

Hi, is this Herschel Caine?

Speaking.

This is David Poke.

Not sure I know that name.

I got your message. Message. *I'm with the Southern District.* Poke. Polk. My message. *Is now a good time?*

I have a minute.

Okay, well, I'd like to start by setting some ground rules, as—

Sorry, David, really, I meant that I have a minute.

I just need to confirm and clarify some things. Starting with your exact role, and how you—

I've given you a head start, and anonymously. That much was promised on your website. So don't contact me again.

Yes, but—

And isn't this the SEC's domain? No, really, don't call me again.

I heard him inhale, I hung up.

What the hell had I said in that voicemail? I scoured my memory but could hardly find purchase, it didn't matter anyway—what more was there to lose? If it had been a mistake to call it was only because it could bring more attention to the fire, but even that was a stretch, people gave the Southern District far too much credit, the SEC, too. There were criminals managing pension funds, market manipulation was rampant, people spoofed prices for fun. A fire? No, they wouldn't get their suits dirty. The important thing was that I wouldn't have anything to do with any investigation into algorithmic trading, if I got one smudge of cooperation on me I might as well become an accountant.

It felt good to exert myself like that, it made me use my brain in the right way. Proficient, effective, strategic. And there was so much more to do, by now I'd have dozens of emails to answer, and many more to send, there were relationships to salvage, losses to cut, lawyers to whip into gear. I ran up to the kitchen, where Franny was eating her eggs and reading the paper. I grabbed the *Financial Times* and peeled an orange. When I threw out the rind I saw, in the garbage, stapled sheets of paper. I squinted: a medical article, marked up with pen and highlighter. I went up to my office, where I did four more sets of push-ups while listening to *Flight of the Bumblebee* on repeat. I logged on and browsed my email while eating the orange. I started small: invoices that would need to be punted, such as this VPN bullshit Milosz had ordered in his paranoid lunacy. Vendors were easy, at the end of the day they would get nothing. Next were lenders and investors, the same gist would work for each—a terrible accident, to be sure; we've already made progress on a sublease—but they needed to be individually tailored. This was time-consuming and tedious, in fact when I was finally ready to move on to the lawyers I was relieved, at least with them I could use shit grammar, I had to if I had any chance of getting this done, I'd lost count of them all, who was who, I had an Excel sheet for just this purpose. It had made more sense to file as an LLC but *Atra Arca Capital Management Inc.* sounded better. I'd pay for that now. I sent call invites for tomorrow, from 8 to noon and 12:30 to 3; I'd keep office hours for investors from 3 to 7—as if they'd ever stop calling.

I'd saved the worst for last: employees. To steel myself I went downstairs for another coffee and more food. I was starving now—what the hell did vegans eat? I made a large bowl of spinach, chickpeas, strawberries, walnuts, and canned beans, and packed a container of hummus under my arm. In my office I ate without pause while the words came to me. I had to fundamentally fire them all, without severance. And they'd need to be reminded of their NDA, the relevant portions. It couldn't be an apology; there was nothing to apologize for, this was due to the fire—but that could only be implied, not even: the inference had to be theirs. And anyway we'd given them good jobs for some time, an interesting story for their next round of interviews. By the end of the meal I had a nice paragraph in my head, I wrote it down, tweaked it, and sent it out with some personal touches. The last on my list was Peter, last in terms of salary but also ease; I knew he'd be crushed, I remembered him saying that the job would be the first time he had health care. I thought to call him but feared the lies he would force out of me, and anyway it would be too much to hear him feign courage, to hear him thank me. His was the only email in which I wrote *I'm sorry*; they were my last words to him.

God, it felt great to be done. I reclined in my chair, allowed myself to appreciate the give, the lumbar support. Something in my chest, a familiar feeling. Without thinking about it I brought back up the salad, which was as flavorful as when it first went down. Having broken my weeklong streak, I now let myself ruminate at will, and for the next few minutes I sat there chewing, swallowing, and regurgitating—starting the process over again.

My email to Peter was still on the screen. *I'm sorry.* It was too easy to say, but it mattered. When you told someone you were sorry you were siding with them, against your former self. You were drawing a line between you now and you then. That was what this whole noon get-together was, wasn't it? *Smooth things over,* she'd said. That was fine, I looked forward to it, even; like these emails, my apology to Philip would put things even more in the past. I stood up, puttered around, looked out the window. The stoop of Ben's building. Yesterday morning. That insufferable conversation. I thought back, heard myself—*Art should change people, for good*—and cringed. No, a basic apology wasn't enough, I needed something that truly demonstrated my remorse, something that could repay the immense social debt I'd created for myself. I looked again at

Ben's place. He was owed an apology, too, the same apology in fact, yes, but with much lower stakes. A practice run.

I closed my email; already I was getting replies, follow-up questions. I checked the time, 11:46, and went downstairs. Franny was tidying up, which was normally my job, I made a mental note to make it up to her.

Outside it felt like the first day of summer, but then, as I crossed the street, I remembered that yesterday had been just as nice; already that day, that person, had been expunged from my memory. I went up their stoop and pushed the buzzer. A few moments later a new voice answered. *Hello?* She sounded suspicious. *Hi*, I said. *I was hoping to talk to Ben. It's your neighbor, Herschel.* A pause, a long pause, she never even answered me. The door buzzed.

The stairwell smelled mustier than I remembered, and it was much darker, too. I expected him to be waiting by his door but he wasn't. I knocked, I heard someone take a couple of steps—he was just waiting there?—and then the door opened. *Hi there*, Ben said, his face glazed with an unlikely bonhomie. He waved me inside, where I saw a woman I assumed was his wife, Hadley, rearranging pillows. It was a fine excuse to be in the room, surely she just wanted to see who I was; she knew everything, of course. Possibly even my first time here, when I'd cried over Lucy, had been recast as what it was: the behavior of a madman.

Thanks for having me, I said. *I won't be long.* I waved to Hadley. *I'm Herschel, I live just across the way.*

Pleasure, she said. That was it? Did people say just the one word?

I looked to Ben, I needed him to invite me fully inside, to take a seat, but he didn't. Instead he glanced at Hadley, right, he was negotiating the urge to show me he was game, that yesterday's incident didn't faze him, with his need to prove himself to his wife.

I just wanted to say that I acted out of line. Yesterday morning, I mean. I looked at Hadley; if she was going to leave this was the time to do it. She didn't. *I don't know what got into me, lecturing you and Philip about art. Of all people.*

You're passionate, obviously. And that's great, you can't write that bestseller without passion. He'd found a good balance: the forgiver, the encouraging authority. And it was the perfect test for me, such a patronizing tone.

Well, I appreciate that. I made a face: breezy contrition, a new expression I'd practice on the way back.

We'll see you around then. At the dog park, I'm sure. I showed my confusion. *Oh, there's one just on Hicks, at Amity.*

Lucy came into the room—had she heard the word *dog*?—and perched on the couch.

We don't have a dog, I said.

Really? I just assumed. You're such a natural with her. A natural. I looked at Lucy, she was inspecting the rug, the pink and red Persian. I remembered it well, it was the background to her image when I'd been lost in it, when I'd felt her sadness. No, that hadn't been such a crazy thought, not one to cry over, of course, but yes, dogs could be sad, she looked sad to me now. This was an odd, simple thought. They were staring at me. I asked for a glass of water, they couldn't deny me that. Ben said, *Of course*, and Hadley left to fetch it.

I asked him what he was working on and pretended to listen. I looked back at Lucy, I waited for her attention, I coughed and she turned. I braced myself; last time it had felt like jumping into a pool, the cold had been all-consuming, so much so that I'd lost my bearings; no, that couldn't happen again. I glanced at Ben and said, *Oh, hmm*, and turned back to Lucy. She was now staring at me, and I at her, I waited, I made myself open, vulnerable, receptive, empathetic, I was now willing to lose myself, make a fool of myself—who cared what these two thought?—I was willing to do anything, I would cry again if that was what it took but I couldn't cry, I couldn't pass through whatever it was between us, no, it was like willing an erection; the more I tried the less it might happen.

Here, Hadley said. She handed me the glass and I took a sip, the cold water tracing the walls of my esophagus.

Maybe she wasn't sad at all, maybe I was only projecting. Of course I was. A dog can't yearn for a freedom it never knew in the first place. But if we took away something more tangible, if we let her feel the fresh air on her body, the wind in her ears, and then led her inside for good, if she knew that from then on she would only experience the breeze in the muted flickering leaves and—

A loud voice, in the distance. It was enthusiastic, performative. Clara was at our door. I turned to see Hadley glaring at me, I drank half the glass and set it down.

I'll get out of your way, I said. *But thank you for listening.* I collected their nods and let myself out, walking one story and careening down the rest, by the time I got outside Philip and Clara had already been let in. I took out my phone, 12:07, and jogged across the street, where I found, at the bottom of our stoop, our old blue laundry bag—right, the broken dryer, Franny had done drop-off. I lifted it into my arms and walked up and inside, where I found the three of them in the family room, Philip and Clara on the couch, Franny setting out the pastries, looking up at me, silently asking where the hell I'd been. I said I'd be right down and then hurried upstairs to the bedroom, where I loosened the bag and dumped the clothes on the floor. I was about to leave when I saw, out of the corner of my eye, a bright yellow women's swimsuit. I'd never seen Franny wear such a thing, no, none of these items were ours, some stranger's clothes were lying in the middle of our bedroom. It was both men's and women's, kids' too. I picked up a brown knit cardigan from the pile and put it on, it seemed such a breach but Franny would get a kick out of it, and I went downstairs.

They were laughing, but it was polite laughter, tenuous, when I came into the room it stopped altogether. I took a seat and eyed the pastries.

The smaller cakes are vegan, Franny said.

I leaned forward, grabbed one, and took a bite. They were watching me, as if I were some hired entertainer. No, but I did have something to prove, that I was no longer socially problematic.

I didn't know they made vegan financiers, I said. *And yet, here I am.* Only Clara laughed. Philip gave a pinched smile and then said, almost to himself, *So you're vegan now.* It would be like this until I did what I had to. *Okay*, I said. *Let's cut to it. I was an asshole to you, Philip.* He looked away, forced his eyes back. *When I saw you yesterday morning, I'd been up all night, for work. I was afraid that things were coming to a close. Actually, I was right. But that's no excuse.*

I set the pastry on my leg and buttoned the cardigan. I turned to Franny, waiting for her to notice, but she didn't.

I'm sorry to hear that, he said. *But yes, you were an asshole.* He smiled, finally, his honor restored. *And you know, I'd still take your company over that god-awful Brit's.*

I glanced at Franny. No, she hadn't told them, and she couldn't now.

Well, she said, standing, *now that the boys have made nice, let's all fatten ourselves up.* She picked up the platter and held it out to our guests.

I love cannoli, Clara said. *But are those croissants almond? Maybe I'll have both. I am eating for two.*

Philip gave a short laugh meant to dissuade his wife, which apparently only I noticed. She took both pastries, and then bit into the croissant.

Darling, you're three months pregnant, he said. *Our child could fit into that cannoli.* We all laughed, but his was nervous; he'd caught himself telling his wife what to eat. He lifted the cannoli from her napkin and took a bite.

Franny went around and poured us coffee. When she got to me we didn't make eye contact—the residue of the *godawful Brit* comment. But our collective cowardice sounded in the coffee splashing into my mug, it appeared in the brief steam, with it came the sudden realization that Birdie was still in the world, and just a couple of miles from our home. I took a sip, I needed to move on. I looked back at the pastries. I'd had barely anything to eat and I'd run fifteen miles. The cannoli, the croissants, I could eat the entire platter. There were two more financiers and I took them both.

Oh, Philip, Clara said, *do you want to tell them what you found last night?*

Again his short laugh; how had I not noticed it before? No, he didn't want to tell us what he'd found, he looked at Clara, and then at Franny and me. Was Clara oblivious? Or did she just enjoy throwing him wrenches? I would. She was a bit impish, actually, it was hard to notice because of the way she held herself; she reminded me of that new senator from Vermont.

Well, Philip said, *I found the Airbnb listing of our neighbor, Ben.* Clara laughed, how naughty of him, she held her hands to her face as if trying to hide her mirth. She was more than impish, it wasn't an act; she was, in some way, unresolved. For a split second I saw Milosz in her place, it had been only a few hours since he'd sat in that exact spot. *He told me that they traveled quite a bit. And given that his wife doesn't work, and he's got an editor's salary—I just had a feeling, and I was right. Two hundred seventy-five dollars a night.* Through various grunts we agreed this was high. *And by the way: classic goy taste,* he said, turning to Clara. *No offense.*

This was funny until we remembered that Franny wasn't Jewish, either. No one was going to say it, though, and how ridiculous, to not say something everyone was thinking. Still, when I opened my mouth all that came out was *I'm sure it's more charming in person.* It was too positive, against the grain of the conversation; to make up for it I said, *It's hard to get past the language on some of these listings. "Make our beautiful home yours" and "We love our house and you will too." Isn't it all a bit . . . wife-share-y?*

They all laughed, Clara the loudest, her laugh was mean, we were being mean, the word stayed in the air, stayed with me even after they moved on. As they talked about their pregnancy I imagined myself palming Birdie's head and cracking it against a curb, I saw my own face looking on in disgust as blood exited her nose and ears.

Vitamin A, Philip said, *Vitamin whatever, it's better to get it through food.*

The thought carried with it its reciprocal: Birdie cracking

my head. Claret goop running down my face. I saw her in the hospital, but as a visitor, watching me, the patient, in a vegetative state. I saw her here, sitting where I was, eating pastries and drinking coffee while I was someplace else, forgotten, kept alive by machines.

Prices of doulas. The absurdity of home births.

What did she look like then, right at that moment? The urge to know inflated at once, it filled me, it pushed against my throat from below.

Franny was looking at me, her eyebrows raised, she was trying to communicate something. She seemed hopeful, excited: she wanted to know if she could tell them we were trying. I nodded, I went to grab another financier but I'd already eaten them all.

So, she said, and then told them, I couldn't listen because of her teeth, they were so white, she was so beautiful and put together, she could run a room, her grace was infectious. I felt like I was watching a movie, it wasn't just the way they acted— just the way they should, I too acted just as I should—it was like there was a screen between us, one I was on both sides of, I was the viewer and an actor, too. But this screen was more like a membrane; with great effort it could be overcome, it would vanish—a hymen, yes, why not, the passage required something magical, a will to freedom I didn't have.

Wonderful, Philip said. *So happy for you.* Beyond his head, through the window, I saw the oak tree, its branches moving with the wind. Such a delicate balance, to be able to bend so much and not break.

Really, Clara said. I imagined Milosz there, saying it the way she did, with such charm. It was funny and I laughed.

Franny turned my way: Why had I laughed?

It will be wonderful, I said, and then they were talking about something else, they were taking turns, allowing for interruptions and spontaneity but within such rigid, unforgiving bounds. Even Clara had great regard for the rules, if she seemed especially alive in some way it was only because she flouted etiquette, but just enough to draw attention to it, she was the worst offender, she was obsessed with convention.

They talked and talked. The less I took part the less I had to see myself as an actor. But the relief didn't last long, the more I was just the viewer the more I felt the screen in front of me, and there was nothing to do but watch, and it was a meaningless show, there was no central concept or conceit, it didn't explore anything at all. Not to say that there wasn't conflict, that they weren't charismatic; they were, Franny most of all, with her white teeth, those white teeth I'd seen go through an egg, which had made me hate her a bit, just a bit, sure, I had hated her then, but now I felt nothing, and now I wanted to feel that hate. I wanted to feel anything.

I pulled out my phone, 12:27. I had a text, from Ian: *How does tomorrow work?* I closed out of the app, the next most recent was my photos. There was *The City Rises. The Carbide Lamp.* I felt Franny looking at me; I was being rude. I put the phone away and tracked the conversation, which was about the Hudson Valley, a house they were looking to buy, I said I'd heard Newburgh was the new best bet, investment-wise.

Again I thought of Ian, and yesterday, and again my fingers pushed into the arm of the chair, to the wood below, but now I was calm, more than calm, the thought was nothing more than a fact—*I'd planned to poison him*—it floated above me, unattached to anything else. How to make Birdie's accident a fact, how to get it far enough away to see; that was the problem, she was inside of me, drifting like wax in a lava lamp, the metaphor was absurd but the ratio might have been exact, in my head she was now the size of those creeping boluses, if she didn't take up most of the space still you couldn't move without bumping into her, any thought held long enough would soon be encroached upon, engulfed.

So I just told her, okay, enough—Clara, talking about her therapist—*My parents are just old, they're not racists.*

Again, me hitting her head against the curb, then her doing it to me, the need to know what she looked like at that exact moment, thoughts that were now so well-trodden they didn't even need to be thought, it was like checking the time, except checking the time was inexhaustible, for the rest of my life I'd be checking the time, as opposed to these thoughts, which were supposed to accumulate, they were little punishments that added up to something, a sum I needed to repay. But how much was one of these thoughts worth, really? Nothing, next to nothing, if I thought these thoughts for the rest of my life still my debt would be unpaid.

Well, there's no use in talking to Franny about therapists. Already they laughed, they were relieved I was speaking at all. Like a good sport I told the story: Franny showing me an email exchange with a client, and then, by way of the timestamps, me realizing it had transpired while she was in teletherapy, the story's purpose being to show that she never stopped working. I'd told it too many times and couldn't muster a performance but still it landed enough that I could parlay it into *Speaking of which, I really must be getting back to my own work.*

It was far too early to end the get-together but they pretended it wasn't, Philip even looked at his watch just to say, *Oh, yes.* We stood, we shook hands and hugged, we begged them to take the pastries and they did, and as Franny saw them out the thoughts returned again.

Well, that was a terrible idea, she said, standing outside of the room. *You could have just said you weren't ready to see them.*

I'm sorry, I said. I was, though she could tell my mind was elsewhere, and before we could get into a fight I let it spill out of me, I described the thoughts I was having as fast as I could, and then in as much detail as I could, except as I did they expanded, they became even more fleshed out, they became an even bigger burden, one I could handle only because I knew she'd carry it with me, she'd think those thoughts, too, but when I finished I saw on her face only disgust. It was hidden, well hidden, though I knew her too well, her expression might have looked neutral, frozen, but still it reflected those horrid thoughts back to me, I saw them anew, as she did, how awful and creepy they were, how contaminated my mind had become.

When had I become this way? Not on Monday, when I'd done what I did. And not on Tuesday, when I'd realized the consequences. Even just a day ago the world had felt enormous, more open than it had ever been. But I was alone now, surrounded by my own failings, my own stench, my world was the size of a cage. It had happened overnight, while I was sleeping, after I'd fallen into Franny's lap. After I'd told her what I'd done.

Can you believe I think these things?

Her lips split, but she didn't speak.

Franny, I'm a monster.

You're punishing yourself, she said.

I deserve it. I deserve much worse for what I did.

Herschel, you made a—

How can you stand me? How can you look me in the eyes? She didn't, her gaze now stuck to a spot on the floor between us. *For days I didn't tell you it was my fault. And it was. If not for me your friend would be back in London, she'd be back in her own life.* She shook her head. Her eyes were glazed. *At least admit that. Admit it was my fault.*

Even if it was your fault, it wasn't because—

But I'm a monster, Franny. You know that now. So just say it.

You're not.

I am, so please, please please please just fucking say it.

She looked back at me. Her hand found the jamb of the archway. *You're a monster*, she said, her voice loud and plain. She turned away, she disappeared up the stairs, up another flight. I listened to her footsteps, waiting to feel—what, exactly? No, nothing had changed, already the thoughts were coming back. *You're a monster*, she'd said, but it was nothing more than words.

I took out my phone. *The City Rises*. The charging stallion, the men strewn, an exciting painting and nothing more. It had meant so much to me before, given meaning to what I'd done, as if setting fire to a roomful of servers made me a visionary. No, but it was a thought, the servers, a fire in a crowded building—had I even bothered to check? Another tragedy born of my own neglect. If something had happened, if I were responsible—

Again I Googled *wooster fire*. There were the two articles I'd already seen. I contemplated emailing the journalists but then I saw one more, also from that CBS affiliate, an interview with a firefighter. He had gray eyes and a soft voice, for almost a minute he spoke about the importance of updating the fire safety code, and then he said, almost as an afterthought, *This building, and in the middle of a workday? It's a miracle no one was hurt.*

I closed my eyes and the thoughts returned, the new details seamless with the rest: her hair stuck together with blood, an empty bag of potato chips on the ground, her dead eyes. Now my face instead of hers, my skin waxen, a leaf lifting with the wind. Her in the hospital, me here, the urge to see her face.

The playground on Fifth Avenue and Third Street, not far from where I lived when I was just out of college, living in that studio. On Sunday mornings I'd come here to think and drink coffee, I'd watch children play tag and on the swings. The idea of having my own had seemed wholly conceptual.

There were more teenagers here than I remembered; had they always been so, what? Flawed? Awkward? Each was either entirely overconfident or disarmingly shy. And the way they walked, like they'd woken up with different legs. It was almost cruel to witness them like this, like works in progress. But maybe I was being cynical, maybe they were now their most natural selves, their edges unpolished and their colors undulled. Isn't that why the teenage years are so embarrassing? We're so vulnerable then, we give the world our naked selves, we've yet to learn how to hedge, conceal, blur.

Just to my left were two young boys, playing in front of their fathers, who seemed to be grinding through small talk. The shorter of the two was more active, he ran circles around his friend. When finally he got tired he stopped and stuck out his tongue, wagging it back and forth. His friend stepped forward and covered the shorter boy's mouth, who then bulged his eyes, flicking his pupils left and right. When the taller boy covered the shorter boy's eyes, the shorter boy started stomping his feet up and down. The taller boy tried to stop him by stepping on his shoes, but instead got his own foot stomped on, and then the fun was over. The taller boy looked to his dad but then decided to exact justice himself: he made a mean face at his friend.

You're the dumbest person I've ever met, the shorter boy said. *But have you met yourself?*

The shorter boy was stumped, outdueled. They stayed still for a moment, staring at each other, and then continued to play.

I stood, drank the last of my coffee, and walked out of the park.

The hospital was four blocks away and I cherished each one. No, I didn't want to go, I didn't want to see her face or Will's or be given an update by some dour doctor or too-hopeful nurse. But it wasn't being there I was afraid of, really, it was leaving, it was success. I was there to undo what my confession had done, to witness my own monstrosity, to wash myself with guilt and be thrust out of this purgatory, even if it meant becoming that other person again—but what then? To lose my grip like that, to be so overwhelmed—like those teenagers in the park. I'd been just as impulsive, just as impressionable, I'd listened to that book and convinced myself I couldn't read. It was embarrassing, ridiculous, as ridiculous as a weekend-long silence with Franny.

And yet, I sensed that I wasn't being fair, that I was not only neglecting something significant but doing so for the worst of reasons: fear. I had so quickly and so willfully scorned that other person, I'd refused to acknowledge what

I'd experienced: I had been connected to the world around me, truly connected, I'd tapped into something sublime, supernatural even; I knew guys from business school who went to India only to feel something like it. It was a talent, actually, just one I'd need to hone. Again I was like a teenager, a gifted guitar player who couldn't help but write insufferable lyrics. I had found a melody, a level of emotion worth sharing, but still I needed to mature into myself.

I came to the hospital. I'd lived five blocks away but had never been inside; it was said there were better places to go. I walked through crowds of people, the hallways were narrow, I finally found the receptionist after retracing my steps back to the entrance.

I'm here to see Bertie Barnes, in the ICU, I said. *Or maybe she's been moved.*

Relationship to the patient?

Friend, I said.

ID.

I handed her my driver's license. She took it without looking up at me, and then tapped on her keyboard. *Still ICU.* She rotated a small camera on the desk, and then, without warning, took my photo. Had they done that the first time we were here? A name tag printed out, she gave it to me and said, *Second floor, room 2008.*

I had as much trouble finding the elevators. Mine was packed. For some reason we all looked up at the ceiling though the light was harsh and bright. I got out, her room wasn't far, a different one than before. Just outside was a nurse on a computer.

I'm here to see Bertie Barnes, I said. *She's in that room.*

The woman turned her head but kept her eyes on her

computer, she finished typing and then looked at me, flashing her teeth.

Sorry, hon, you're welcome to go in.

I peered inside the room. *Her husband's not here?*

Will went home to sleep. Bless his soul.

Right. And how is she doing?

She's calm, she said, nodding. *She's stable.*

I approached the room but stopped in the doorway; her face was full of tubes. I asked the nurse what happened.

She was intubated, she said.

When?

Well, when she got here. She seemed to suddenly question who I was, and stopped just short of asking. *It's what's keeping her with us.*

I nodded and walked inside, I took a seat before I could think of leaving. Still I couldn't look at her, not at her face, just the lump of her body under the sheets, the whiteboard above her bed, the TV hanging from a long arm attached to the wall. It was turned away from her, toward me, Will's seat. An infomercial on low volume.

I forced my eyes on her but saw only the tubes, the slow swell of her chest. No, she hadn't already been intubated when we'd visited on Tuesday, I was sure of it. I'd ask Franny when I got home, or maybe I could speak to someone now, ask to see her records, if something fishy was going on, if I was being lied to, if the nurse outside was, then there was a reason, perhaps it was their own medical care that had led to her current state.

I stood up, I sat down. I was spineless. Craven. Wasn't this the exact purpose of my visit, to look directly at what I'd done, to accept responsibility? It was just that I wasn't ready, I hadn't sufficiently prepared myself—why hadn't I written something down? I took out my phone and opened the memo app. *Nick Bowers*. I deleted the note and started a new one, I wrote as quickly as I could, all those thoughts I'd had on the playground and on my way here. I didn't reread any of it, when I was done I put away my phone, stood up, and pushed myself over to the bed. I placed my hand on the side rail and looked down at her, inspecting first her cheeks and forehead—the bruising was nearly gone, a faint green shadow—and then her nose and eyes. I waited, I held my breath, but still I felt the same, still I was precisely me. It was the TV, the muffled babble was too distracting to think, to digest what I was seeing. Was there no remote? Over and over I pressed the hardly functional volume button on the screen. But then, once it was finally muted, I began to hear everything else, the beeping, the buzzing, the intercom. Was it always so loud? Again I thought of Tuesday, seeing her for the first time, I'd been nearly unable to stand. That was after the doctor had pushed open her eyelids, had so casually revealed such a dreadful sight, as if he were peeking through blinds. I looked to the hallway and then leaned over her. I set my fingers on her lids, my pointer on one and my thumb on the other, and then, gently, I lifted them. Her eyes were vacant, yes, they were horrifically misaligned, but now I was, somehow, numb to it, as though I'd seen the image a thousand times before. It was only after I looked away, to the hallway, and back that something new emerged, a difference between Tuesday and today. Yes, it was still the left eye that strayed, but now it seemed that neither was fixed, that both would tilt if her body did. It was as if the basic grasp of life had become unclenched.

As I took a step back she began to look different, her body

more of an object, a mass, and yet she seemed more diffuse, too. As inert as she was—*calm*, as the nurse had said, *stable*— I felt that she was actively expanding, that, lacking some unifying force, she was starting to drift apart. She was disintegrating, there was no better word, she wasn't just dispersing but reducing, each second that passed there was less and less of her. If she was here, at my side, alive, it was only because of the tubes in her, it was because we allowed loved ones to make the choice. No, if I needed someone to reflect back all that I'd done, to make me feel my sin as if it existed outside myself, I'd come too late. I was now the only person in the room.

I was sitting again, my hands on the seat of the chair, I held them there so they wouldn't come to my face, couldn't wipe away the tears. I sobbed, once, I wanted more, I thought of Birdie, her eyes, the tubes, I thought of Will, I thought of anything I could, even Lucy, even nature, our departure from it, our abuse of it, all those thoughts I'd had yesterday, they were hardly outlines but they too helped cut the shape of my sorrow, which seemed so simple now, a fact so plain it could hardly be thought. No, nothing can be undone, I said it to myself and in every possible way, even the tropes, the clichés, each new formulation brought me closer to feeling it, brought more tears—just another example, *Crying doesn't change a thing*, it was true, for years I could cry and still I'd be here, with this thing in me I couldn't touch or see.

Oh, dear. The nurse was shaking her head at Birdie, frowning. *Yes, it's very sad.*

They came all at once now, the sobs, they overlapped, so much so that I no longer heard the incessant beeping, the rhythmic vibrations of the bed. When finally I managed to stop I assumed that the nurse had left, that I could gather myself alone, but she was only readjusting Birdie's pillows.

I'm sorry, I said.

Darling, of course.

She turned to Birdie, giving her a kind smile, as if Birdie was looking back at her.

My wife told me she was making noises? Vocalizations, I mean.

She was, but not any longer.

I swallowed. I folded my arms. *I can hear my own heartbeat,* I said. *In my ears.*

She nodded, as if she heard it too. *Pulsatile tinnitus.*

Is that temporary?

It could be temporary, yes. It could be permanent.

I nodded and looked back at Birdie. Still the nurse just stood there.

You're welcome to stay for as long as you like, she said, *but she needs to be cleaned. Normally we ask that only next of kin—*

Oh, sure, I said, standing. She smiled at me as I walked out.

I ambled around the hallways, peering into other rooms. I sat on a bench near the nursing station and listened to their small talk. When I went back to Birdie's room the door was still closed. I waited five more minutes, ten, fifteen, I wondered if Will would return before I was let back in, and before either happened I left.

Outside it was hotter still. There was a thickness in the air, that sense of coiled freedom; it was now fully summer. I didn't want to go back home, I wasn't ready to. I walked up the street and went into the first restaurant I saw, Purity Diner. At first I thought it was called *Established 1929*, as that was bigger on the awning; perhaps they were proud to have risen out of the crash.

It was nearly empty, I took a seat in a booth. I wasn't hungry but knew I should eat, I ordered coffee and the daily special. On the TV was CNBC, the NASDAQ. I took out my phone to look at my portfolio and the memo app opened. I saw the phrase *action is not the only* and deleted the note. When I closed the app my photos came up. I deleted the ones of *The City Rises*, the Miró. I checked my portfolio and then my email. The lawyers had responded, all of them. Already they were asking more than they should. Did anyone still believe in client confidentiality? How else did the rumor mill churn?

The coffee came and I drank it immediately. As the caffeine hit I let myself imagine the coming weeks, the endless calls, the meticulously worded emails and hunting down of signatures. A careful undoing. In those hours debts would be repaid or nullified, the measure of our work taken and distributed, and, once all parties had accepted their fate, Atra Arca Capital Management Inc. would cease to exist. How clean, how seamless. How unlike anything at all.

I thought of Franny. She was probably doing yoga, or working—anything to take her mind off me. *You're a monster*, I'd forced her to say. That was the very least of it. If Birdie was my sin, still our silence about it was shared, and it would lurk in every silence we shared; we'd no longer be able to look at each other and be sure of what exactly we'd see.

I looked into my coffee mug and flagged the waiter for more. I picked up my phone and went to my texts, my conversation with Milosz. He'd written last: *Meet you at your place, leaving now.* I looked up at the TV. A bald man talking angrily. Interest rates were set to rise on Monday, the market expected to dip. Nothing that couldn't be undone. I wrote, *We need to talk about yesterday. In person is best.* I hit send and put my phone down.

The waiter came with the coffee, and soon after he brought the food: steak frites, mostly frites. I poured out ketchup, dunked a fry, and ate it. I heard a police siren in the distance, and then another. As if they'd send patrolmen. No, if they suspected foul play they wouldn't arrest me; they'd call, invite me to some well-appointed government building. I thought of my brief chat with Polk, my voicemail to him, the fire itself. Had I remembered to lock the door to the server room? God, I had to tell Franny.

I picked up my fork and knife and set them on the meat. I let the tip of the knife enter, slowly, and then I carved a piece. I looked at it, smelled it, and placed it in my mouth, on the back of my tongue. I chewed slowly, and then, as the juices dripped down my throat, at a normal speed.

I swallowed. I took a sip of water.

It tasted fine.

ACKNOWLEDGMENTS

I'm incredibly grateful to the quant analysts, traders, and CEOs I interviewed for this book, some of whom chose to remain anonymous. Thank you Howard L. Morgan, Duncan Wilkinson, Rishi K. Narang, Zsolt Pajor-Gyulai, Bryant Angelos, and Jake Ralston.

Gratitude to Soul Eubanks, who spoke to me about his views on veganism.

My agent, Ellen Levine, provided critical feedback, and my editor, Jonathan Galassi, guided this manuscript to where it needed to be. Federico Andornino, as always, kept me thinking about the reader. Thank you to everyone at FSG and W&N: Lettice Franklin, Katie Liptak, Christina "Nichols" Nichols, Cecilia Zhang, Gretchen Achilles, and last but certainly not least, Lauren Roberts, who I didn't get to thank in my first book, so it's only right her name appears here twice: Lauren Roberts.

Gabriel Stutman lent some tight opinions and edits.

My father, Kenneth Lipstein, gave me crucial legal perspective.

ACKNOWLEDGMENTS

This book is dedicated to Joshua Mikutis. A friend like you comes along once in a life, I think.

Without my wife, Mette Lützhøft Jensen, I wouldn't be able to do what I do. Your support is never lost on me, and your belief in me makes me believe in myself.

OTHER BOOKS BY PETER ABRAHAMS
WRITING AS SPENCER QUINN

OTHER PETER ABRAHAMS NOVELS

MRS. PLANSKY'S REVENGE

SPENCER QUINN

TOR PUBLISHING GROUP

New York

MRS. PLANSKY'S REVENGE

Copyright © 2023 by Pas de Deux

All rights reserved.

A Forge Book
Published by Tom Doherty Associates / Tor Publishing Group
120 Broadway
New York, NY 10271

www.torpublishinggroup.com

Forge® is a registered trademark of Macmillan Publishing Group, LLC.

The Library of Congress has cataloged the hardcover edition as follows:

Names: Quinn, Spencer, author.
Title: Mrs. Plansky's revenge / Spencer Quinn.
Description: First edition. | New York : Forge, Tor Publishing Group, 2023.
Identifiers: LCCN 2023007718 (print) | LCCN 2023007719 (ebook) |
ISBN 9781250843333 (hardcover) | ISBN 9781250843340 (ebook)
Subjects: LCSH: Swindlers and swindling—Fiction. | LCGFT: Novels.
Classification: LCC PS3617.U584 M77 2023 (print) |
LCC PS3617.U584 (ebook) | DDC 813'.6—dc23/eng/20230228
LC record available at https://lccn.loc.gov/2023007718
LC ebook record available at https://lccn.loc.gov/2023007719

ISBN 978-1-250-84335-7 (trade paperback)

Our books may be purchased in bulk for promotional, educational, or
business use. Please contact your local bookseller or the Macmillan Corporate and
Premium Sales Department at 1-800-221-7945, extension 5442, or by email at
MacmillanSpecialMarkets@macmillan.com.

First Forge Paperback Edition: 2024

Printed in the United States of America

0 9 8 7 6 5 4 3 2 1

For Ben, Cassie, George, and Owen

MRS.
PLANSKY'S
REVENGE

ONE

"Hello, it is I, your grandson, insert name here," said Dinu.

"Correct," said Professor Bogdan, language teacher at Liceu Teoretic. He leaned back in his chair and lit up a Chesterfield. "But too correct, you know?"

Too correct? Dinu did not know. In addition, he was asthmatic and the mere presence of a cigarette aroused a twitchy feeling in his lungs. No smoking in school, of course, but these private lessons, paid for by Uncle Dragomir, weren't about school.

Professor Bogdan blew out a thin, dense stream of smoke, one little streamlet branching off and heading in Dinu's direction. "There is English, Dinu, and then there is English as she is spoken." He smiled an encouraging smile. His teeth were yellow, shading into brown at the gumline.

"English is she?" Dinu said.

"For God's sake, it's a joke," said Professor Bogdan. "Is there gender in English?"

"I don't think such."

"So. You don't think so. Come, Dinu. You've studied three years of English. Loosen up."

"Loosen up?"

"That's how the young in America talk. Loosen up, chill out, later." He tapped a cylinder of ash into a paper cup on his desk. "Which is in fact what you need to know if I'm not mistaken, the argot of youth." He glanced at Dinu. Their eyes met. Professor

Bogdan looked away. "My point," he went on, "is that no American says 'it is I.' They say 'it's me.' The grammar is wrong but that's how they say it. You must learn the right wrong grammar. That's the secret of sounding American."

"How will I learn?"

"There are ways. For one you could go to YouTube and type in 'Country Music.' Now begin again."

"Hello, it's me, your grandson, insert name here," Dinu said.

"Much better," said Professor Bogdan. "You might even say, 'Yo, it's me.'"

"Yo?"

"On my last trip I heard a lot of yo. Even my brother says it."

"Your brother in New Hampshire?"

"No *P* sound. And 'sher,' not 'shire.' But yes, my brother."

"The brother who is owning a business?"

"Who owns a business. Bogdan Plumbing and Heating." Professor Bogdan opened a drawer, took out a T-shirt, and tossed it to Dinu.

Dinu shook it out, held it up, took a look. On the front was a cartoon-type picture of a skier with tiny icicles in his bushy black mustache, brandishing a toilet plunger over his head. On the back it said: Bogdan Plumbing and Heating, Number 1 in the Granite State.

Dinu made a motion to hand it back.

"Keep it," said Professor Bogdan.

"Thank you."

"You're welcome. New Hampshire is the Granite State. All the states have nicknames."

"What is nicknames?"

"Like pet names. For example, what does your mother call you?"

"Dinu."

Professor Bogdan blinked a couple of times. Like the skier, he had a bushy mustache, except his was mostly white. "Texas is the

Lone Star State, Florida is the Sunshine State, Georgia is the Peach State."

"Georgia?"

"They have a Georgia of their own. They have everything, Dinu, although . . ." He leaned across the desk and pointed at Dinu with his nicotine-stained finger. "Although most of them don't realize it and complain all the time just like us."

"Does your brother complain?" Dinu said.

Professor Bogdan's eyebrows, not quite as bushy as his mustache, rose in surprise. "No, Dinu. He does not complain. My brother grew up here. But his children—do you know what they drive? Teslas! Teslas almost fully paid off! But they complain."

Those state nicknames sounded great to Dinu, even magical in the case of the lone star. He knew one thing for sure: if he ever got to America, Tesla or no Tesla, he would never complain. Just to get out of the flat where he lived with his mother, much better than the one-room walk-up they'd occupied before Uncle Dragomir started helping out, but still a flat too cold in winter, too hot in summer, with strange smells coming up from the sink drain and—

The door opened and Uncle Dragomir, not the knocking type, walked in. Professor Bogdan's office got smaller right away. Bogdan half rose from his chair.

"How's he doing?" Uncle Dragomir said in their native tongue, indicating Dinu with a little chin motion. He had a large, square chin, a nose that matched, large square hands, and a large square body, everything about him large and square, other than his eyes. His eyes were small, round, glinting.

"Oh, fine," said Professor Bogdan. "Coming along nicely. Good. Very well."

"In time," said Uncle Dragomir.

"In time?"

"How much longer. Days? Weeks? Months?"

Professor Bogdan turned to Dinu and switched to English. "Weeks we can do, don't you think?"

"I don't know," Dinu said.

Professor Bogdan turned to Uncle Dragomir, switched back to their language, and smiling as brightly as he could with teeth like his, said, "Weeks, Dragomir."

Uncle Dragomir fastened his glinting gaze on Professor Bogdan. "In my career I've dealt with types who like to stretch out the job. I know you're not like them."

Professor Bogdan put his hand to his chest. "The furthest thing from it. Not many weeks, Dragomir, not many at all."

"*Hmmf,*" said Uncle Dragomir. He took out his money roll, separated some bills without counting, leaned across the desk, and stuffed them in the chest pocket of Professor Bogdan's shirt. Then he turned, possibly on his way out, but that was when he noticed the T-shirt, lying in Dinu's lap. "What's that?"

Professor Bogdan explained—his brother, the Granite State, plumbing and heating.

"Let's see it on," said Uncle Dragomir.

"It's my size," Dinu said.

"Let's see."

Dinu considered putting on the T-shirt over his satin-lined leather jacket. Not real satin or leather although very close. But the T-shirt would probably not fit over the jacket. It was a stupid idea. The problem was that he wore nothing under the jacket, all his shirts dirty, the washer broken and his mother once again dealing with the swollen hands issue. He took off the jacket.

Professor Bogdan's gaze went right to the big bruise over his ribs on the right side, not a fresh bruise—purple and yellow now, kind of like summer sunsets if the wind was coming out of the mountains and blowing the pollution away—but impossible to miss. Uncle Dragomir didn't give it the slightest glance. Instead he helped himself to a Chesterfield from Professor Bogdan's pack, lying on the desk.

Dinu put on the T-shirt.

"The plunger is funny," said Uncle Dragomir, lighting up.

Desfundator was their word for plunger. *Plunger* was better. The smoke from Uncle Dragomir's cigarette reached him. He began to cough. That made his chest hurt, under the bruise.

TWO

Something amazing happened on Court #2 of the New Sunshine Golf and Tennis Club just before lunchtime on the day after New Year's, although it was amazing to only one person, namely Loretta Plansky, a seventy-one-year-old widow of solid build and the only female player in the whole club with a one-handed backhand. She and her partner, a new member Mrs. Plansky had met just before stepping on the court that morning and whose name she had failed to retain even though she'd repeated it several times to herself as they shook hands, were playing in the weekly match between the New Sunshiners and the team from Old Sunshine Country Club, the hoity-toitier of the two, dating all the way back to 1989. Mrs. Plansky had been something of a tomboy as a kid, actually playing Little League baseball and Peewee hockey on boys' teams, but she hadn't taken up tennis until she'd married Norm, so although her strokes were effective they weren't much to look at. Now, up 5-6 in a third set tiebreak, Mrs. Plansky and her partner receiving, the better of the opponents, a tall, blond woman perhaps fifteen years younger than the others, lofted a pretty lob over Mrs. Plansky, a lob with a touch of topspin that was going to land inside the baseline for a clean winner. Mrs. Plansky wheeled around, chased after the ball, and with her back half-turned to the net flicked a backhand down the unguarded alley. Game, set, match. A nice shot, mostly luck, and not the amazing part. The amazing part was that Mrs. Plansky had wheeled around without giving it the slightest thought. She'd simply made a quick thoughtless instinctive move—quick for her, at least—for the first time since her hip replacement, nine months before. Mrs. Plansky wanted badly to tell Norm all about it. He'd say something about how she'd found the fountain of youth, and she'd say let's call it a trickle, and he'd laugh and give her a quick kiss. She could just about feel it now, on her cheek.

"What a get!" said her partner, patting Mrs. Plansky's shoulder.

The partner's name came to her at last, literally late in the game. That bit of mental fun liberated a little burst of happiness inside her. Those little bursts, based on tiny private nothings, had been a feature of her life since childhood. Mrs. Plansky was well aware that she was one lucky woman. "Thanks, Melanie," she said.

They hustled up to the net, touched rackets, then collected their tennis bags and headed to the clubhouse patio for lunch. Mrs. Plansky's phone beeped just as she was pulling out her chair. She dug it out of her bag, checked the number, and stepped away from the table, off the patio, and onto the edge of the putting green.

"Nina?" she said.

"Hi, Mom," said Nina. "How're things? Wait, I'll answer—no complaints, right?"

Mrs. Plansky laughed. "Maybe I should be less predictable."

"Whoa! An out-there version of Loretta Plansky! You'd rule the world."

"Then forget it for sure," said Mrs. Plansky. "How are the kids?"

"Great," Nina said. "Emma's still on winter break—right now she's out in Scottsdale with Zach and Anya." Emma, a junior at UC Santa Barbara, being Nina's daughter from her first marriage, to Zach, and Anya being Zach's second wife, whom Mrs. Plansky had met just once, at Norm's funeral, and very briefly. But in that brief time, she'd said something quite touching. What was it?

"Mom?" said Nina. "You still there?"

"Yes."

"Thought I'd lost you for a second."

"Must . . . must be a bad connection. I'm at the club. The service is iffy." Mrs. Plansky moved to a different spot on the putting green, even though she knew there was nothing wrong with . . . well, never mind.

"The tennis club?" Nina said. "How are you hitting 'em?"

"No one would pay to watch," said Mrs. Plansky. "And Will?"

"Will?"

"Yes. How is he?"

Will being Nina's other child, fathered by Ted, Nina's second husband. There'd been a third husband—called Teddy, kind of confusing—now also by the wayside, which was how Mrs. Plansky pictured all Nina's husbands, Zach, Ted, Teddy, left behind by a fast and shiny car, the hair of the three men—none bald, all in fact with full heads of hair—blowing in Nina's backdraft. Was that—a full head of hair—a criterion of hers when it came to husbands? Were there in fact any other criteria? Why had she never considered this question before? And now came one of those many moments when she wished that Norm was around. Yes, he'd say, it's her only criterion. Or, no, there's one other, and he'd name something that was funny, amazing, and true, something she'd never have imagined. And then: "Now can I go back to being dead?"

Whoa. Mrs. Plansky heard Norm's voice, not in her head—although of course it was—but somehow outside, like he'd come down from heaven—in which Mrs. Plansky did not believe—and onto the putting green at the New Sunshine Golf and Tennis Club. She actually cast a furtive glance around. An errant ball came bouncing over from the ninth fairway.

"Fine as far as I know," said Nina.

"Sorry, what?" Mrs. Plansky, moving away from the still-rolling ball, suddenly felt a little faint.

Nina raised her voice as though speaking to someone hard of hearing, which Mrs. Plansky was not. All systems go, said Dr. Ming at her annual physical. Just keep doing what you're doing.

"Will," Nina went on. "He's fine, far as I know."

Mrs. Plansky gave her head a tiny shake, putting everything right inside. "Is he back in school?"

Over at the table, Melanie caught her eye. The waiter was pouring wine and Melanie pointed to the empty glass at Mrs. Plansky's place, seeing if she wanted some. Mrs. Plansky didn't drink wine at lunch. She nodded yes.

"Not exactly," said Nina. "Will's missed so much time already and it's late in the year. He's planning on staying in Crested Butte."

"Teaching skiing."

"There's been a glitch with that. It looks like he'll be working the lifts."

Working the lifts? She and Norm had done some skiing in Vermont in the early days of Plansky and Company, the southernmost ski hills in the state close enough to their home in Rhode Island for Sunday visits, full weekends impossible because of work. The homeward drive at twilight with the kids, Nina and Jack in the back, Norm in the passenger seat, Mrs. Plansky at the wheel—they did it the other way around on the trip up, Norm's night vision never very good—and everyone exhilarated, exhausted, relaxed to the core: that was Plansky family life at its best. But working the lifts was all about getting through to your day off and hoping it would be powdery, in other words a spinning your wheels type of job, which ski instructor was not. When had she last spoken to him? Probably on his birthday, back in July, although she had sent him a check for Christmas. But to what address? She made a mental note to check on that, and a second mental note to call him soon. The fact that he hadn't thanked her yet for the check didn't mean he hadn't gotten it. For whatever reason, he'd missed out on a thing or two in his upbringing. Mrs. Plansky didn't get judgmental about that sort of thing. Will and a buddy had stayed for a night the week after her hip replacement, on their way to spring vacation at the buddy's parents' house in Lauderdale. She hadn't been able to find her bottle of OxyContin—always at the far right of the top medicine cabinet shelf—after they left. Mrs. Plansky was inclined to be more judgmental about things like that.

"But the reason I called, Mom, is I've got exciting news," Nina said.

"Let's hear it!" What a terrible person she was, making her voice so bright and cheery when she was steeling herself inside. But she knew Nina.

"I've met someone fabulous," Nina said. "His name's Matty but I call him Matthew. It's more serious." Mrs. Plansky felt the fast and shiny car speeding up. "You're going to love him, Mom. Guess how tall he is?"

Mrs. Plansky glanced around, a feeble physical facsimile of getting her mental bearings. What she saw was the pretty side of Florida on a bright and sunny winter day. How lucky to be able to afford retirement in a place like this, and while she'd have preferred Arizona she'd kept that fact to herself, mostly on account of the look on Norm's face when the real estate agent drove them up to the big but not too big house at 3 Pelican Way, the style New England as envisioned by someone who'd never been there, and the inland waterway right out the back door. Norm had been thrilled, and the fact that he totally missed the faux part—in fact was incapable of catching it even if prompted—only made her adore him all the more.

"Tallish, would be my guess," said Mrs. Plansky. Norm had been five foot seven on their wedding day, losing an inch or two over the course of forty years. And his body had gone through many other changes as well. But somehow he'd been physical perfection the whole time. At least until those last months. She couldn't fool herself about that.

"Six foot four, Mom!" Nina said. "And three-quarters."

"Oh, my," said Mrs. Plansky. "Tell me a little more about him."

Nina laughed. Right from childhood she'd had this rippling musical laugh—like a song, as Norm had told her, perhaps too often in retrospect, but only due to the love in his heart. Was there something studied now about that musicality? Maybe she was imagining it. Over at the table the waiter seemed to have finished taking the orders and was looking her way.

"Salad," mouthed Mrs. Plansky. The waiter gave her a thumbs-up.

"I don't even know where to start," Nina was saying. "But guess what? You can see for yourself tomorrow."

"Oh?" said Mrs. Plansky.

"We're flying down for a quick weekend with some friends in Boca and thought we'd stop by on the way tomorrow night and take you out to dinner."

"Wonderful," said Mrs. Plansky. "But I'll make dinner. You can see the new place."

"Are you all settled in?"

"Oh, yes."

"Then that'll be great. Bye, Mom. Love you."

"Love you," said Mrs. Plansky, but Nina had already hung up. She walked over to the patio, sat at the table, took a sip of her wine, and then another. Surprisingly soon her glass was empty. The waiter appeared with the bottle. "No, thank you," said Mrs. Plansky, covering the glass with her hand to make sure.

There were two routes home from the tennis club, home meaning Mrs. Plansky's new residence, a condo on Little Pine Lake. One, the shorter, cut straight through the woods to the lake. The longer route followed the inland waterway for two miles, therefore passing right by 3 Pelican Way. The last time Mrs. Plansky had taken that route was the day before she moved out. Now, after lunch on the club patio, her mind on other things, she found herself taking it again, although the realization didn't strike her until Norm's flamboyant tree came into view. He'd decided that if they were going to live out their days in Florida they were going to do it right, and doing it right meant a flamboyant tree in the front yard, and not just a flamboyant tree but the mother of all flamboyant trees, which he would plant from a cutting—definitely not a seedling!—and nurture like no flamboyant tree had ever been nurtured. No nursery in the entire state had been up to the task when it came to supplying a cutting of the quality he'd demanded, the cutting eventually coming from Madagascar, ancestral home of flamboyant trees. The soil in the front yard had also proved less than first rate—not loamy enough and lacking in organic matter—so Norm had replaced most of it and added organic matter he'd come across at a woodlot deep in a Georgia forest, organic matter that had led to trouble with the HOA. But the result—Big Mama—oh, the result: a flamboyant that not only bloomed in May, like everyone else's flamboyant, but also at Christmas, most of the flowers the brightest red on earth, but also some bursts of the much rarer yellow flowers, both on the same tree! Norm invited a Rollins biology prof to take a look. "Unheard of," he'd said. "This is publishable."

They'd had sex twice that night, a double dip, as Mrs. Plansky had called it—she could be a bit bawdy when it was just the two of them—a feat, if it could be so called, that hadn't happened in at least twenty years. For some time after that she would say "Any new arboreal ideas?" at unexpected moments.

Retiring right also meant getting a metal detector and taking it for long beach walks, Norm wearing headphones and sweeping the detector back and forth with an intent look on his face and Mrs. Plansky taking a peek or two at that intent look. She could see little kid Norm at those moments and in an irrational way enjoy the false feeling of having known him all her life. They'd actually met for the first time on graduation day at college. The point about the metal detector was that after a big storm Norm had found an old Spanish silver coin with it, a four reales piece with a shield on one side and two strange pillars in the other. Mrs. Plansky bought a plaque for displaying the coin in the front hall.

"Which side out?" she asked.

"The pillars, of course."

She slowed the car. Big Mama was in her glory—golden suns shining in a red fire. "When you sell the house," Norm said, pausing to get more air inside him from the nasal tube, "you could always take a cutting."

"Why would I sell the house?"

Pause. Pause. "You know."

"I do not."

Norm reached his hand across the bedcover. He lay on the special invalid bed they'd ended up renting. "Normally I always say buy," Norm had said, "but maybe not in this case." And the hand—so withered and also purplish from getting stuck with IV needles so often. She'd laid her own—so indecently healthy in contrast—on top.

Pause. Pause. "For moving on."

An overwhelming urge to weep, to cry, to sob, rose up in her. Mrs. Plansky mastered it. "I'm not moving on."

Norm gazed at her, his eyes now deep in his skull and getting deeper, but she could still see him way down in there, her Norm. He began to sing "My Funny Valentine." Norm was a terrible singer—although he did a lot of singing during the course of an average day—scratchy, out of tune, unstable in pitch—but this one time, two days from death, as it turned out, and until he'd run out of oxygen, he'd sung like an angel, or, to be more specific, Tony Bennett.

Now, beyond Big Mama, a gardener was at work, planting something in the yard. At first she couldn't make out what it was, and then there seemed to be some mental refusal to accept the optical fact. But the something being planted was one of those plastic jockeys, outfitted in painted racing silks. Mrs. Plansky moved on.

THREE

Norm's smell lingered in corners here and there at 3 Pelican Way for a few months after he died. Not the smells of death and dying—those vanished almost at once—but the smell of healthy, living Norm, a smell she loved. Then one morning it, too, was gone. Three Pelican Way was on the market by lunchtime. Remaining there would have meant living life half dead. Pick one or the other, Norm would have said.

The condos at Little Pine Lake were very nice. For one thing they stood at the top of a rise, rises being hard to come by in the county. Then there was the lake itself, almost a perfect circle, and the water wonderfully refreshing, fed by a spring down below. There were only a dozen condos, all at ground level, backing onto the water and taking advantage of the slope. Mrs. Plansky had number twelve, one of the end units, with a private little patio where she liked to sit and watch the sunsets seeming to set the lake on fire. It wasn't cheap, but she'd paid cash and still had almost $400,000 left over from the sale of 3 Pelican Way.

Mrs. Plansky didn't have to worry about money but she hadn't grown up rich so at least she knew what worrying about money was like. She and Norm had started with nothing—actually less than nothing if you factor in the $10,000 loan from her dad at prime plus four and a half, paid back the very first day they could afford it. The ten thousand and all they could save from their paychecks—Norm working for a small engineering firm in Providence at the time, and

Mrs. Plansky a paralegal at a small law firm in Newport—was sunk into the effort to bring Norm's idea to life.

Actually Mrs. Plansky's idea, but it was such a random out of the blue sort of thought, more or less just passing through her, that she never could see taking credit for it, although Norm disagreed strongly and made sure that everyone knew. He himself had had several ideas before hers came along, none of them viable for one reason or another, from the realization that there wouldn't be sufficient demand to the deflating discovery that the invention he'd had in mind was already out there and doing killer business. Then, in the tent on what turned out to be a rainy weekend camping trip in the Berkshires, Mrs. Plansky—pregnant with Nina, and Jack standing but not quite walking—had been slicing a loaf of rye bread for sandwiches, when she'd suddenly said, "Wouldn't it be nice if the knife could toast the bread while you sliced?"

Norm, still dozing in the two-person sleeping bag, sat right up. "What did you say?"

Mrs. Plansky said it again.

Three years later, they sold their first Plansky Toaster Knife, actually fifty of them, to a start-up kitchen store in Oslo. The name of the product was also Mrs. Plansky's idea—Norm had pushed for Lasers by Loretta—as was the choice of the first client. Mrs. Plansky had met the owners at a trade show in Atlanta, a young, hip, sophisticated couple, very unlike her and Norm, except for the young part, and decided they were a good bet. Their next order, for five thousand knives, came from a chain based in Barcelona, after the CEO stopped by the Oslo kitchen store. And after that, the deluge.

"We're going to make billions!" Norm had said.

"That would be a headache," said Mrs. Plansky.

"How about hundreds of millions?"

"The feeling you get when you know a headache is on the way."

In the end—Norm running manufacturing and distribution, Mrs. Plansky sales and marketing—they'd made a nice amount of millions, some—but not too much to be harmful, they hoped—

given to Jack and Nina along the way, and maybe half, almost five million, to various charities when they sold the company and moved down to Florida, envisioning a nice and long last act. Well. When it turned out to be so short, a line of Shakespeare's had kept popping up uninvited in her mind over and over: *As flies to wanton boys are we to the gods; They kill us for their sport.* Mrs. Plansky hated that line and didn't buy it for one second. Finally it went silent, or went away, possibly to some other grieving mind. She didn't like that thought, either.

Mrs. Plansky, unlocking the door to her condo from an app on her phone—she'd refused to grow fossilized regarding things like that—at least not completely, an inventor's wife, after all—went inside. Yesterday had been the day Maria came to clean so everything was spotless, although it was always spotless, never more so than right before Maria's arrival. But now Mrs. Plansky didn't remember whether Nina had said she was spending the night with . . . with whoever it was, the new paramour. Just in case, she went upstairs to the guest bedroom in the loft and made the bed. Then she checked the guest bathroom, made a quick inspection, switched out the flamingo towels—bought on a post-Christmas sale at All Things Bathroom—for plain white. After that, she brewed herself tea in the kitchen and drank it at the island. There were shortbread cookies in the pantry and she wanted one, but hadn't she just had lunch? Loretta! Get a grip! She finished her tea, washed the cup, put it in the rack, gazed out the window at the lake.

Her phone pinged, meaning a text had come in. Mrs. Plansky found she was standing in the pantry for some reason. She went back to the island, checked her phone. A message from Jack: **You there?**

Mrs. Plansky's index finger hovered over the screen. Yes, Jack, I'm here. Good to hear from you. Too wordy? How about, Hi, Jack, present and accounted for. Good grief. Perhaps a simple Yes. Probably the right call, but wasn't it a bit uncivilized? Was there something uncivilized about machines which forced you yourself into being uncivilized if you wanted them to play nice? Oh, how she wished she could be pouring Norm a small glass of that bourbon he liked—there was still some left—and hearing what he'd say about that, or any other—

The phone—such a busy little device and only half smart, the bad half of smartness—rang, snapping her out of her little reverie or whatever it was. On the screen scrolled the name of the caller: Arcadia Gardens.

"Hello," she said. "Loretta Plansky speaking."

"Hi, Loretta. It's Jeanine. Any way you can swing by here, maybe settle things down?"

"What's the problem?"

"Something about football."

The plaque with the four reales piece now hung in the front hall of the condo. Back at 3 Pelican Way, headed out for Norm's first brain scan, Mrs. Plansky had glanced back and spotted him touching the coin for luck. She hadn't let on. Now, on her way out the condo door, Mrs. Plansky touched the old Spanish coin. Her hand pretty much did it on its own.

Arcadia Gardens, a forty-five minute drive south of Little Pine Lake, had beautiful landscaping—weedless flower beds lined with conch shells, big shady trees, mostly cabbage palm but also some ancient bald cypress—and looked like a well-preserved hotel from prewar Florida days, even though it was not yet ten years old. Jeanine, a trim woman of forty or so wearing a tan business suit, was waiting in the lobby.

"Thanks for coming," she said.

"Of course." They stepped into an elevator and rode to the top floor. "A football problem?" Mrs. Plansky said.

"There was an argument about a penalty call," Jeanine said. "Offensive pass interference, maybe? Is that even a thing?"

"Yes," Mrs. Plansky said. Jack had played in high school. She knew football.

They walked down the hall on the top floor, a sunny hall with nicely framed prints of clipper ships on the walls. The last door was closed.

"He's got something wedged against the doorknob," Jeanine said. "We can't get in."

Mrs. Plansky knocked lightly. "Dad?"

Silence from the other side of the door, and then: "Go away. And I'm not paying a goddamn cent. Don't you, neither." Then came more silence, followed by "Disloyal bitch," spoken in the low, confidential tone some people reserve for talking to themselves.

Mrs. Plansky turned to Jeanine. "Paying for what?"

"The TV in the lounge," Jeanine said, "but I don't know where he got the idea there'd be a charge. No one would have told him that. It's covered by our insurance."

"He broke the TV?"

Jeanine nodded. "With a beer bottle."

"He threw it that hard?"

Jeanine shook her head. "He wheeled right up to the screen and used the bottle like a club. Have you met Mr. Blucher?"

"I don't think so."

"He's new. That's who the argument was with. Naturally a staff member was on scene, serving refreshments and such, but it all happened very quick."

"Dad's ninety-eight. How could it have been quick?"

"I should have said surprisingly quick. Unfortunately Mr. Blucher was struck by a shard of glass and needed a stitch or two."

"My God. Struck where?"

"The arm. We dodged one there."

Mrs. Plansky turned to the door and knocked harder this time. "Dad. Open up."

His voice came from closer, like he was right on the other side. "Why should I?"

"Dad! What kind of question is that?"

More silence. And finally: "A head-scratcher."

Mrs. Plansky and Jeanine exchanged a look. Jeanine called through the door. "Your daughter drove all this way to see you, Mr. Banning. Please open the door."

"It's only thirty-two miles," her dad said. "And I'm not moving. This is my room and that's final. Finito. End of story. Full stop."

Mrs. Plansky plucked Jeanine's sleeve, drew her a step or two down the hall. "What's he talking about?"

"Well," said Jeanine, "it's not just this incident but there have been a few other things, too. We're recommending a move down to the third floor. The room will be just as nice but we can give him more assistance there."

"You think he needs more assistance?"

"Not just me, the whole team," Jeanine said. "Including Dr. Albert."

"If more assistance is necessary, why can't he stay here and have it?"

"Procedure. The third floor is where we provide the next level of assistance." Jeanine touched Mrs. Plansky's hand. "Our concern is self-harm."

"Self-harm?"

"Not intentional. But with the temperamental side of him maybe getting the upper hand a little more often these days . . ." Her voice trailed off.

Mrs. Plansky went back to the door, and this time didn't knock. "Why are you making this so hard?"

"This is all about the shekels, that's why."

"What are you talking about?"

"The so-called move. The third floor's another ten grand a month." Mrs. Plansky could feel a tiny breeze as Jeanine shook her head. "Any notion what this place costs?" he said.

Since she'd been footing the bill, Mrs. Plansky had a precise notion. What would happen if she voiced that thought aloud? Mrs. Plansky wasn't sure, but she'd shut down any such experiments on her father long ago. She took a deep breath and played her last card, the only one in the deck with any chance of working.

"Nina's coming for dinner," she said. "Do you want to join us?"

"At that condo of yours?"

"It's where I live, Dad."

"I like the old place better. With the tree. Why the hell did you move?"

"We've been through this."

"Not your best decision. Also not your worst."

That last part was code for marrying Norm. He knew and she knew but anyone else would have had trouble believing it for so many reasons, such as after all this time, and how long and happy the marriage was, and most of all the fact of the specialness of Norm. He'd never been good enough for her, but not in the ancient no one could be good enough for my daughter way. That, Mrs. Plansky understood—suddenly and parenthetically—was more like the way he thought about Nina. No, in her case there was another reason. *Shekels* was the clue. She came close to saying forget it. Damn it, yes. The words were on the way. But before they got out in the world, her father spoke again.

"All right, all right, the itty-bitty condo it is," he said. "I better poop first." Scraping and bumping went on behind the door and then it opened. There he was—slumped sideways, but somehow aggressively, in his wheelchair, her dad, once a good-looking man in a *Mad Men* sort of way, and now much reduced, even a bit orc-like. He raised his voice. "Julio! Julio!"

"Who's Julio?" Mrs. Plansky said.

"The attendant who helps him with his sanitary needs," said Jeanine.

"The other guy was better," Mrs. Plansky's dad said.

"Marcus is no longer here," Jeanine said, and Mrs. Plansky knew at once how come.

FOUR

Julio wheeled Mrs. Plansky's dad across the Arcadia Gardens parking lot. Mrs. Plansky opened the passenger door. Julio helped her dad to his feet.

"I can get there myself," her dad said, batting Julio's hands away in a movement that was meant to be forceful. And it was true that on their last outing a month before—ostensibly for milkshakes although they'd detoured into a bar he liked the look of, where he'd been a big hit, downing two shots of bourbon and entertaining the barflies with his age, saving the puking part for the ride back—he'd managed to get into the car by himself. But not this time. He took one step, stopped, and teetered. Julio gathered him up smoothly and got him sitting comfortably on the front seat.

"Give him a tip, Loretta."

"You know there's no tipping, sir," Julio said.

"Yeah? How about at Christmas?"

"That's different," Julio told him.

"I win," said her dad.

Mrs. Plansky drove out of the parking lot to the main road and headed north.

"Some music, Dad?"

"Nosireebob."

A few miles passed in silence and then they hit the section with all the strip malls, auto body shops, and car washes, including the one where you could have your car washed by sudsy young and not so young women in bikinis. Her dad turned his head to watch, then sat back, folded his gnarled and veiny hands, and said, "Seeing anybody?"

Mrs. Plansky glanced over at him. He was gazing straight ahead.

"Lots of people," she said. She came close to itemizing them for him but in a deus ex machina way her phone, sitting in the cup holder, pinged the incoming text, saving her from a really bad move. Mrs. Plansky, whose vision after cataract surgery two years before—"I've found the best guy for this," Norm had said. "No random bozo gets to mess with those eyes"—was very good, had no need to bring the phone closer. The text was from Jack and it was just this: ? She realized she hadn't gotten back to him. Mrs. Plansky did not send texts while driving and even if she did she wouldn't have now.

"Did I hear something?" her dad said. "Like one of those pings?"

"No," said Mrs. Plansky.

"You know what I meant."

"Excuse me?"

"Seeing anyone like a man. An XY to squeeze into your XX."

"For God's sake!"

"After all, you're still reasonably attractive."

"Thanks."

"Matter of fact I have a candidate, if you don't mind the type with lots of chins. I'm talking about Ernie Oberst's kid brother. Bruno, I think it was. Came to visit a while back. His girlfriend walked out on him."

Mrs. Plansky made no comment.

"Meaning he's available," her dad explained. "Based in Tampa. Lives in one of those developments with lots of swingers."

She wanted to throw up, or at the very least turn around and deposit him back at Arcadia Gardens. But she did neither of those things, just drove on in silence. That side of her, the sexual side—but for certain not swinging, physically, mentally, or spiritually, and how could swinging be in any way spiritual? Surely it was the total absence of. But not the point, which was about the sexual side: now gone. And if not gone, then in a coma of some sort. She knew comas up close. The last time she'd held Norm he'd been in one. Her eyes welled up and a tear or two got free and slid down her cheek. She glanced over to see if her dad was watching. He was asleep. She could let those tears flow to her heart's discontent. But she did not.

Six foot four and three-quarters could look like an NBA player but it didn't have to, and Matthew DeVore, Nina's new beau, was the proof. Narrow-shouldered, knock-kneed, splayfooted, chinless: Mrs. Plansky silenced that judgmental part of her mind and gave him a friendly smile as they shook hands. She'd left out wet-palmed, and also paunchy. But he did have a full head of hair, the rusty-colored kind you see on men too old not to be graying, and that was another issue, although in disguise: he was a lot older than Nina. She would soon turn forty-six and this gentleman had certainly crossed the sixty barrier, making him closer in age to the mom, meaning her. Mrs. Plansky re-silenced the judgmental part of her mind.

"Nina's told me so much about you," he said during the slightly damp handshake. "And call me Matty."

Ah. Didn't Nina prefer Matthew? More serious, wasn't it? Mrs. Plansky didn't quite remember, but she pushed past that little roadblock and said, "And I'm Loretta."

"Yeah?" said Matty. "I had a Loretta."

"Excuse me?" said Mrs. Plansky. She glanced at Nina, still smiling her introduction smile, seemingly unaware, although of exactly what Mrs. Plansky was not sure. Maybe the fault was hers, imagining nonexistent shortcomings. It hit her at that moment that some part of her mind might benefit from the brain equivalent of a hip replacement.

"My first high school girlfriend was Loretta," Matty explained.

"Perhaps a more common name back in the old days," said Mrs. Plansky. Maybe postreplacement she would have gone with something nicer.

Matty's own smile seemed to stiffen a bit. Nina took him by the hand and led him toward her grandfather, sitting in his wheelchair by the little bar in one corner of the living room, drumming his fingers on the armrest.

"Hi, Pops," she said, leaning down to kiss his forehead. He reached up, did his best to wrap his arms around her.

"Hello, beautiful." He clung to her. She patted his shoulder, kissed his forehead again, and straightened.

"Pops, I want you to meet Matthew. Matthew, this is Pops, a legend in the family."

They shook hands. Mrs. Plansky caught a change of expression on her dad's face, which had to have been when he grew aware of the dampness of the handshake.

"Nice to meet you, Pops," Matty said. "And call me Matty."

"Or Matthew," said Nina.

"Which is it?" said Mrs. Plansky's dad.

"You pick, Pops," said Matty.

"Am I your grandfather?"

"No, sir. What would you like me to—"

"What do you call your own grandfather?"

"Well, they're both passed."

"There you go."

"But what would you like me to call you?"

Mrs. Plansky's dad opened his mouth but no words came out. Instead he licked his dry lips with his dry tongue and closed his mouth. Nina and Matty gazed down at him, Nina worried, Matty confused and somewhat put off. Mrs. Plansky came over.

"How about calling him Chandler?" she said. "That's his given name."

Her dad nodded and returned from wherever he'd been. "Chandler Wills Banning," he said. "Princeton, '46."

"Chandler it is," said Matty.

"Where'd you go to school?" her dad said.

"You're lookin' at a Fightin' Blue Hen."

"Huh?"

"University of Delaware."

"Who wants a drink?" said Mrs. Plansky.

Nina, Matty, and Mrs. Plansky's dad had drinks at the bar—white wine for Nina, JD on the rocks for Matty, the smallest scotch Mrs. Plansky thought she could get away with for her dad. She turned on the Golf Channel, her dad's favorite and which had his full attention at once. Nina and Matty sat on the barstools. She leaned against him. Mrs. Plansky went into the kitchen to make sure she caught the crab soufflé at the exact right moment.

She was a bit nervous about the crab soufflé. Mrs. Plansky liked to cook and the crab soufflé was one of her specialties, but she hadn't done any cooking in quite some time, her diet now consisting of toast and fruit for breakfast, a salad—often at the club—for lunch, and whatever happened to be in the pantry, tuna, for example, or even sardines, for dinner, unless she was going out with friends, of which they—she—didn't have many in Florida, and none of them close. She'd never felt the need for a lot of friends, at least not since her wedding day. When Norm was alive she'd cooked up a storm, a storm that had weakened with his loss of appetite and died with him.

So in the kitchen she kept squatting down and gazing through the oven window. Why wasn't the darn thing rising? She was checking her watch when Nina came in.

"Here's some wine, Mom."

"Thanks." Mrs. Plansky rose, one of her knees grinding in pain—in an uncomfortable manner—which she hoped was inaudible.

"Oh my God," Nina said. "Are you going to need a knee replacement, too?"

"Of course not." She took her glass. "And if I do it's not a big deal."

Nina thought about that. Mrs. Plansky read the thought, all about Norm and what a big deal actually was, medically. The inward look on Nina's face at that moment, deep and dark: it had never been in evidence when she'd had Nina under her roof, appearing for the first time around the time she'd left Zach, and showing up more often early in her marriage to Ted the first, a marriage that took her to L.A. for ten years or so, Mrs. Plansky losing track of Nina's inner journey during that time. But what a beauty she'd always been and still was, with fine features and shining hazel eyes, both coming from Norm. Her body was more like her mom's, shapely in a sturdy way, Mrs. Plansky's shapeliness no longer what it was, although she seemed to be hanging on to the sturdiness.

"I like the place, Mom. Is it expensive?"

"I'd call it affordable," said Mrs. Plansky.

Nina laughed her musical laugh. "Otherwise you wouldn't be here. I know my mom." She gave Mrs. Plansky a hug. Mrs. Plansky hugged her back. She hadn't hugged Nina—or Jack—in months, and didn't want to let go. At the same time, she felt tension inside her daughter, and plenty of it. They stepped away from each other, sipped their wine.

"I'll set the table," Nina said.

"Done," said Mrs. Plansky. "But you could make that vinaigrette of yours."

"Sure thing."

Nina got busy with oil, vinegar, Dijon mustard, a touch of maple syrup. Mrs. Plansky took another peek in the oven. Still no action.

"So what do you think of him?" Nina said. "Matthew, I mean."

"He seems very nice, but I've only just met him."

"And now you want a thumbnail."

Mrs. Plansky laughed. "Shoot."

Some people were capable of telling stories in an organized way, but not Nina.

"Wow, I don't even know where to start."

"Where he's from, for example."

"Originally? West Hartford. His father had a small law practice that Matthew joined and eventually took over. He retired early and we met on one of those sunset cruises. After, he came down to Hilton Head. For retirement, if you're following this."

Which Mrs. Plansky was. "You went on a sunset cruise?" she said. When Nina married Ted the second, she left L.A. and moved into his house on Hilton Head, a house she ended up with when that marriage fell apart, although that was all she got. The point was she was a Hilton Head resident and Mrs. Plansky had never heard of locals going on sunset cruises in their own harbors.

"I know," Nina said. "Total impulse. I was out power walking, saw the boat, and hopped on board, if you can believe it."

Mrs. Plansky could.

"And now," said Nina, "we're remodeling."

"Your place or his?"

"Oh, mine. Matthew's renting at the moment. Way too soon to be telling you this, but we're contemplating marriage."

"Ah."

"I know, I know. Numero quatro. But—call me conservative if you like—I've come around to thinking these arrangements should be formalized."

What arrangements exactly? Were they in love? Those were the questions Mrs. Plansky kept to herself. Instead she said, "Does he have any formalized arrangements in his past?"

"Ha-ha. The iron fist in the velvet glove!"

"Really?"

"No, of course not. Sorry, Mom. And yes, he was married once and had a relationship after that. What else? There's a son in the Bay Area but they're not close. And yes, he's a little older, if that's what's coming next. But he's super energetic and witty in a quiet way, and aren't you as old as you feel?"

The answer to that was no, and so far Matthew's quiet wit was pitched at a decibel level beneath her hearing range. She was about to say something about how nice it was that Matthew felt energetic when the soufflé rose, rose quite abruptly, almost popping up like . . . well, you know. Would a bolder mom have now said, "And how is he in the sack?" Mrs. Plansky was not that mom. She donned oven mitts and pulled this tumescent wonder—certainly the best-looking soufflé she'd ever made—out of the oven.

"Wow!" said Nina. "You go, Mom!"

Mrs. Plansky set the soufflé on the counter. The scent of the shore spread through the kitchen.

"By the way," Nina said, "I'm shutting down the gallery."

"Oh?"

Nina had owned a few art galleries in her life, this latest one on Hilton Head specializing in landscape and seascape photography. She had a wonderful eye, in the opinion of Mrs. Plansky, who'd gone with Norm to opening night and bought a strange close-up of a moray eel caught in a moment that seemed to be contemplative, which had hung in Norm's study back at 3 Pelican Way and had not yet been unpacked.

"Business has been slow with the economy and all," Nina said, "but it's not just that. Matthew and I have this fabulous idea. In fact, we'd like to talk to you about it."

"I'm listening," said Mrs. Plansky.

"How about at dinner?" Nina said. "When we're all together."

FIVE

The Americans had a Georgia of their own. Their Georgia was a state. There turned out to be fifty of them. So many, and they all had nicknames. Dinu—his back to the radiator in his seven square meters' bedroom, with part of that space taken by an old, jutting-out, unusable, coal fireplace, the radiator working sometimes although not today—had his laptop on his lap and was supposed to be solving ten trigonometry problems for class tomorrow at 9 a.m. Dinu gazed at the first problem. *If the shadow of a building increases by 10 meters when the angle of elevation of the sun rays decreases from 70 degrees to 60 degrees, what is the height of the building?* The first answer that came into his mind was this: the builder cheated and the building fell down, therefore zero height. There were ways of working this out, of course, probably beginning with a diagram. A notepad and pencil were visible under his bed, partly concealed by the socks he'd worn yesterday and maybe for a few days before, just about in reach if he leaned forward as far as he could. But Dinu decided to put that off for the moment, and instead check out those state nicknames.

Dinu found a list almost at once and opened a second window on the screen showing a map of the whole country. He had super-good Wi-Fi in his bedroom—far faster than at school—thanks to Romeo, a computer genius actually slightly younger than Dinu, who had piggybacked Dinu's Wi-Fi, as he'd put it, using one of those cool American expressions their own language lacked, off the Wi-Fi from the private clinic two blocks away. Alaska was a state? Way up there with this other country—so that was Canada!—in between? Did that make Alaska something like Transnistria? He checked out a few photos of Alaska and decided the answer had to be no. But if the whole continent was like some sort of animal, then Alaska was the head and Florida was the tail. He glanced at the nicknames of both. Alaska: the Last Frontier. Florida: the Sunshine State. Ah, yes, sunshine. Frontiers, as he had good reason to know, meant problems. Dinu spent some very pleasant time viewing photos and videos of the Sunshine State. He found a rather long account of its history and read it carefully from beginning to end. Dinu had a very good memory if he switched it on, which he did now. Seminoles! The Fountain of Youth! Key Largo! He had it all in his mind forever, and was researching luxury car dealerships in Miami Beach when Aunt Ilinca laughed her harsh, smoky, boozy laugh in the kitchen, just on the other side of the wall with the radiator. A thin, uninsulated wall—there was no insulation in the whole apartment block—and Aunt Ilinca's laugh seemed to be originating a few centimeters from his ear. Aunt Ilinca lived in the apartment block across the street and came visiting once a week or so, always with a bottle of Stalinskaya vodka, his mama contributing little squares of dark bread spread with the cottage cheese they called zamatise to these get-togethers.

"All men are useless," Aunt Ilinca was saying, "but why do I end up always with the most useless?"

"Is he really so bad?" Mama said.

"I could tell you some of his habits but we're eating."

"Habits?" said Mama.

Dinu did not want to know about the habits of Aunt Ilinca's new boyfriend, or maybe an old boyfriend recycled. And luckily at that moment a text came in from Romeo: **We need you.**

Dinu got his socks from under the bed—cheap thin socks patterned with little circles featuring the face of Megan Thee Stallion—pulled on a hoodie, stuffed his phone in his jeans pocket, grabbed Professor Bogdan's script, and went into the kitchen. They were sitting at the table, Mama in her old woolen housecoat, Aunt Ilinca in an unzipped puffy coat with what might have been a nightie underneath, drinking from dainty little cups, hardly bigger than thimbles.

"There he is," said Aunt Ilinca.

"Salut, Auntie."

She gave him a look, quick but rather close, from head to feet and back again. "My, my, could this one still be growing?"

"You think so?" said Mama. There was brightness in her pale green eyes—the same color as Dinu's—meaning she and Aunt Ilinca were just getting started with the dainty little cups.

"Oh, yes," said Aunt Ilinca. "He will grow to be a strapping fellow like—"

She left it right there, although perhaps not soon enough, Mama's eyes dimming a bit. Dinu went to the door, slid his feet into his sneakers, put on his almost-leather jacket.

"Going somewhere?" Mama said.

"Work."

Mama opened her mouth to say something, closed it, then decided to go ahead with whatever it was. "Maybe this is a good time to discuss a raise?"

Dinu didn't answer. He slid the bolt to the side and opened the door.

"Or how about a commission?" said Aunt Ilinca, blowing smoke through her nostrils like some sort of dragon. "In business there are commissions."

Dinu went out and closed the door, maybe a little harder than necessary.

Dinu's workplace was the Club Presto in the nicer part of the nightlife section of the old town. He went inside.

"Hey, kid," said Marius the bouncer, in English.

"Hey," said Dinu. Marius was a huge guy who spoke a lot of English. Well, not quite true. He spoke a little bit of English often, for

example, "Hey, kid." Or "Even my muscles have muscles," a phrase
that came up whenever pretty girls were around, which was often.
One of the pretty girls was Tassa, a classmate of Dinu's who worked
behind the bar a few nights a week. Too young for that, strictly
speaking, but strictly speaking did not apply at Club Presto. They'd
been in the same class for many years, which was how the system
worked, but he was just noticing her lately.

"Yo," he said as he went by.

"Yo?" said Tassa.

"That's hello in Miami Beach," Dinu told her.

Tassa spread her arms like she was an airplane and waggled them.

He stopped in front of her. Tassa had very beautiful ears. She
must have had them all this time—not the ears, of course, but their
beauty—the endless hours they'd sat at their desks in those cold,
drab rooms. Why had he never noticed? In fact, all of her was beautiful. Not just the ears, but the face and surely the breasts, partly
visible in her tank top, and . . . and . . . was this a good time for a
fist bump? He made a fist and sort of poked it at her.

"What are you doing?"

"Fist bump. Also Miami Beach."

Tassa nodded like . . . like that made sense! Then she raised her
hand like she was about to give him a fist bump but just then a guy
down the bar rapped his glass with the thick bejeweled ring he wore
on his finger and she went off to serve him.

At the back of Club Presto, up and down some stairs and along a
narrow corridor lit with a few red bulbs, stood a steel door with a sign
saying CAMBIO, meaning foreign exchange, and below it a pasted-
on cartoon of the Ceauşecus standing on a balcony addressing an
unseen crowd. They were both wearing furry Russian ushankas and
nothing else. Elena, in the word balloon above her head, was saying
to Nicolae, "Talk to them." It was a famous scene and true, except
for the nudity part. They would soon be shot.

Dinu raised his hand to knock but the door was already opening. Thanks to Romeo, surveillance at Club Presto was world-class. Dinu entered the room that Romeo called mission control, after the place where the Americans had run their flights to the moon, although it was nothing like that, very small, smoky, and the keyboards stained by oily fingers, like in a mechanic's garage.

"Hey," Dinu said.

"Hey," said Romeo.

There were three people in the room: Romeo, who'd opened the door; Timbo, the other bouncer, cigarette in his mouth, headphones on, eyes closed, foot tapping; and Uncle Dragomir, sitting in front of one of the screens, a cigar in one hand and a glass of whiskey on the desk.

"Hello, Uncle," Dinu said.

"Ready to go?" said Uncle Dragomir, not turning from the screen.

"I hope so," said Dinu.

Now Uncle Dragomir looked at him. "Hope?"

Timbo took off his headphones and opened his eyes. He was a wiry little guy with a very full handlebar mustache and a quiet voice, not at all like Marius, although while the occasional drunk or group of drunks might try something with Marius—never with a good result—everyone behaved like a gentleman around Timbo.

"I meant yes," Dinu said. "I am ready."

"Do the briefing," Uncle Dragomir told Romeo.

Dinu and Romeo went to a table at the back of the room. Timbo put his headphones back on, Uncle Dragomir sipped his whiskey and returned to the screen. He was watching footage shot at a firing range. Sometimes, although not tonight, Uncle Dragomir monitored these events through a one-way mirror in a tiny room on the floor above. Both methods made Dinu uncomfortable, but in different ways.

Romeo opened a bottle of Miranda orange drink and filled two paper cups.

"Salut."

"Salut."

Romeo was a chubby kid with acne and wild hair and certainly not good-looking in any way Dinu could see, and also he came from a poor family rumored to be part Jewish but some girls—and not just a few—were interested in him. He was already making lots of money—he wore a gold chain around his neck and had two real leather jackets, one black and one red—but it wasn't just that. Romeo was a genius—the whole invisible structure behind computers, the internet, all that, was transparent to him, out in the open.

"Teach me, Romeo." Dinu had heard more than one girl say that, even an older girl from the university. Girls liked geniuses. It made sense, but of course Dinu had known for a long time that he himself would have to find another way.

Romeo unfolded a printout of his research, but before he could get going, Dinu said, "Do you know about survival of the fittest?"

"Sure. That's what we do."

"What do you mean?"

He waved the printout. "They're soft. We're hard."

"Who is they?"

"The Americans. Brits, French, all of them."

"The Russians?"

"Very funny. They're hard but clumsy. We are subtle."

"Oh?"

"Romance languages make you subtle. But none of the others are hard, just us. There are huge forces at play. It's a dynamic situation, Dinu."

"I don't get you."

"A dynamic situation is a chance for the poor to get rich and the rich to get poor. But it doesn't happen automatically. You have to work. So let's work." They bent over the printouts. "This is the grandpa, eighty-six, widower, lives alone in Texas."

"The Lone Star State," said Dinu.

Romeo looked puzzled for a moment and then continued. "And

this is the grandson—Tucker. Almost three thousand kilometers to the northeast of Texas—a university student at Penn State."

"The Keystone State," Dinu said.

"What are you talking about?"

"All the states have nicknames. Also flowers and songs."

Romeo sat back. "The states have songs?"

"Like 'You Are My Sunshine' for Louisiana."

"How does that one go?"

Dinu had looked up several of the state songs on YouTube, including "You Are My Sunshine." He opened his mouth to sing the beginning, at the same time noticing that Timbo was watching. No singing happened. Dinu and Romeo got busy with Romeo's research, Romeo pointing out details from time to time and Dinu filling in the blanks in his script.

"Hi, Grandpa, it's me, Tucker."

"Huh?"

Grandpa's voice, whispery and wavery and all the way from Texas, came in very clear, but Dinu knew Grandpa was hearing what sounded like a bad connection, all due to a special box with lots of switches and dials that Romeo had made, a box Dinu's headset was plugged into. Also plugged into the box were all their headphones, the kind for just listening—Romeo's, Timbo's, Uncle Dragomir's. They all sat close together, listening with an intensity Dinu could feel. He could also smell them: Romeo smelled like he needed a shower; Timbo smelled of cologne; Uncle Dragomir smelled of garlic, whiskey, cigars.

"It is I, Grandpa. Me. Tucker. Yo." Dinu, who'd already been a bit nervous, got more so. His hands were so sweaty they were dampening the script. "I am in—I'm in a bad situation, Grandpa. I need your help."

"My grandson Tommy?"

"No, Grandpa. Tucker. Your grandson Tucker. I am in—I'm in a bad situation."

"What kind of bad situation?"

Dinu squinted at the script, now smeared in places. "A dwee, Grandpa."

"Huh?"

Romeo kicked him under the table. "I beg pardon, a DUI. I am sorry, Grandpa. I'm sorry. But the police have seized my car and for getting it back and for bail I need nine thousand seven hundred and twenty-six dollars and eighteen cents."

"You need nine thousand dollars?"

"Plus seven hundred and twenty-six dollars and eighteen cents."

There was a long pause. Then Grandpa said, "How am I supposed to get you that?"

"It's easy, Grandpa. Have you got a pen?"

"Hang on."

Silence. It went on for some time. Dinu exchanged looks with the others. Romeo's eyes were excited, Timbo's thoughtful, Uncle Dragomir's unreadable. Finally, a voice came back on the line. At first Dinu thought that Grandpa had somehow gotten stronger during the break, had maybe downed a quick drink.

"Hey, who the hell is this?"

No, not Grandpa, but a much younger man. Dinu shot a quick glance at Romeo, Timbo, Uncle Dragomir. No help was forthcoming.

"BJ? Is that you? It's not very funny."

"Oh, no, not BJ," Dinu said. "It is I, Tucker."

"I'm Tucker, you stupid son of a bitch."

Click.

Romeo rose, put his hands to his face. "Oh my God!" If there was any fault, it was probably his, although it was maybe just one of those things and no one could be called at fault. But certainly not Dinu, who had only been following the script prepared by others. In fact, hadn't he improvised pretty well in a tricky situation? Still, Romeo was not replaceable and Dinu was, which was why Dinu got backhanded across the face twice, first by Uncle Dragomir, which didn't really hurt a lot, no more than that punch to the ribs awhile back, and second by Timbo. He'd never been struck by Timbo before and Timbo didn't seem to put much effort into it, did not even look at him, but the blow hurt him very much. A tooth flew from his mouth and clattered softly on the floor. Dinu did not pick it up. Neither did he raise the issue of commissions or discuss a raise.

At home, a rat—or a weirdly huge mouse—was on the kitchen table, busy with the remains of the little dark bread squares spread with zamaste. His mother lay sleeping on the couch, Stalinskaya on her breath, her housecoat in disarray. Dinu covered her with a blanket, hurled a dishcloth at the rat or mouse, and went to bed.

SIX

When Mrs. Plansky went into the bar to summon her father and prospective new son-in-law to dinner, she found they'd moved outside to the patio, leaving the slider open. They were gazing at the lake and smoking cigars. Mrs. Plansky had never seen her dad smoke a cigar, not once in her life. Was he taking it up now, at ninety-eight? What harm could it do? Still the sight made her pause before calling out, "Dinner is served." And in that pause, she heard them talking.

"Met the kid yet?" her dad said, tapping a cylinder of ash onto one of the wheelchair arms.

"You mean Emma?" Matthew said.

Her dad turned to him. "Matty, is it?"

"Yes."

"Or Matthew? What the hell's going on?"

"Nina prefers Matthew."

"Why?"

"Good question." Matthew tossed back the rest of his JD on the rocks, or possibly a second one, which Mrs. Plansky deduced from the fact the whiskey level in her dad's glass was above that of her original pour. "We all have our quirks."

"Tell me about it. There's some that are nothing but quirks. Head to toe. Name any one of my girlfriends."

"You have girlfriends, Chandler?"

"Had a boatload. This was after Alice died. Breast cancer and so goddamn young." He wagged his finger at Matthew. "Trust doctors and you deserve everything you get."

"Alice being Loretta's mom?" Matthew said.

"Old news," said her dad. "You haven't answered my question."

"About Emma?"

"Why would I be asking about her? Got no problems with Emma. She calls me on the first Sunday of every month, like clockwork. I'm talking about her brother."

"Will?"

"Is there another brother?"

Matthew laughed. "Were you a lawyer, Chandler?"

"Never practiced."

Which was true as far as it went. Going a little further would have meant reaching the full truth: no, I was not a lawyer. Her dad had been first a reckless waster of his inheritance, followed by various jobs in the finance industry, the family living higher and higher above its means, like an untethered balloon. Mrs. Plansky's mother's last words to her—before they put her on the ventilator for what turned out to be the final time—were "I just don't understand." Mrs. Plansky had assumed her mother had been referring to the cancer and dying so young, forty-nine to be exact, but she'd come to realize it was actually about Chandler. Her husband had ended up bewildering her.

"But," Mrs. Plansky's dad went on, "are you ducking my question?"

"About Will?" Matthew said. "I've met him."

"And?"

"He seems like a nice kid."

Her dad turned to Matthew, meaning that instead of the back of his head, Mrs. Plansky now saw him in profile. His visible eye was glaring. "You didn't sell that very well, Matty."

Matthew turned so that he, too, was now in profile, and also glaring. "All right," he said. "The kid's a selfish pothead, a leech, and a born loser. But Nina can't see it."

"I like the way you think," said her dad.

"Dinner," Mrs. Plansky said, and walked away.

"Three Michelin stars," said Matthew, dabbing the corners of his mouth with one of Mrs. Plansky's seagull-patterned napkins, her favorite, but missing a tiny lump of crab on his upper lip. "I knew you were an astute businesswoman but I had no idea you were a fabulous cook as well."

"Well, thanks," Mrs. Plansky said.

"Astute businesswoman?" her dad said.

Before dinner, he'd guided his wheelchair swiftly to what he'd probably assumed was the head of the table because of its proximity to the wine bottle. Mrs. Plansky sat at the other end, and Nina and Matthew were on opposite sides, Nina shifting the candelabra slightly so she could see him better.

"Plansky and Company," Matthew said. "Nina's told me the whole wonderful story. It should be a book, one of those case studies on how to get filthy—how to build a successful business from nothing."

"From nothing?" said Mrs. Plansky's dad. "Did Miss Nina mention the part about me lending ten grand?"

"I—I don't recall. Did you, Nina?"

"I honestly don't remember. But of course it was very good of you, Pops." Nina gave him a big smile.

It was not returned. "And also"—he slapped his hand on the table, a dessert fork taking flight—"besides quote, very good, doesn't that make me pretty goddamn astute as well?"

He looked from one to another. For a few moments it looked like the bait would go untaken—Mrs. Plansky's preference—but then Matthew took a gulp of wine and said, "I suppose, strictly speaking, it depends on your return."

"My return? My return on what?"

"Your investment." Matthew started to say more but then caught a look Nina was sending his way, and stopped himself. Mrs. Plansky also caught the look but couldn't interpret it. All she knew was that she felt like she was watching a tennis match featuring no players she wanted to root for. Not a very nice thought, and she sent it packing at once.

"What investment?" said her dad, batting the ball back at Matthew.

In tennis, most players were attackers to the best of their ability, but there was an unpopular subgroup of pushers, content to merely pitty-pat the ball back until the opponent made a mistake, and almost in contradiction, some were very aggressive about it. That was her dad: an aggressive pusher. After all these years—decades!—she had, at last, the scouting report on him.

"It was a loan, my young friend," her dad said.

"Oh," said Matthew.

There was a silence. With pushers you could try to outpush them, leading to a long and miserable dead zone in your day that ended with making you want to hang up your racket for good, or you decided you'd had enough and you went after them with a deep drive to one corner which you followed to the net, taking the angle and putting away whatever pushy-wushy bullshit came back. Excuse the language, Mrs. Plansky said to herself. To her dad she said, "Which was so nice of you, Dad. Remind me of the interest rate."

His mouth opened but no sound came out. The look on his face was the look of a pusher who realizes that pushy-wushy will no longer get it done. By this time, Mrs. Plansky was at the net. She glanced Matthew's way. "I'm sure the number will come to him. He has a wonderful memory."

Oh, dear. Too much. Mrs. Plansky wanted that one back in the silo. The silo was where, in Norm's blueprint for making a Loretta—his image, not hers—she kept her heavy artillery, which she hardly ever rolled out and remained a secret from almost everyone they knew, with the exception of the occasional enemy. You couldn't be in any sort of business for long without making enemies, a fact that would have undone Norm if he was on his own, which he very much was not. Meanwhile all eyes were on her dad.

"Prime plus four and a half," her dad said, his tone sharp, all in on showing off his memory.

"More wine, anyone?" said Mrs. Plansky, trying to move onto something else.

But no use. Matthew—and now they were leaving tennis and entering pro wrestling territory—stepped in, two against one. "And what was prime back then, Chandler?" he said.

"We could switch to red," Mrs. Plansky said. "There's a nice Pinot."

"I don't recall," her dad said. He wagged his arthritic finger at Matthew. "But something low. Prime, right? Low by definition."

Matthew didn't respond, not directly. Instead he slipped his phone from the inner pocket of his powder-blue blazer and said, "What year are we talking about specifically?"

Her dad wrinkled up his already deeply lined forehead. He actually had artillery of his own, but not heavy, just loud. If Nina had heavy artillery, Mrs. Plansky had never seen it. Perhaps, in the privacy of a bedroom, some men had. Mrs. Plansky had no desire to pursue that idea one inch further. But she was pretty sure Matthew had heavy artillery. Just because you were unsuccessful—although what right did she have to assume that about him?—didn't mean your silo was empty. She smiled at Matthew and looked him right in the eye, using mental telepathy to plant the next utterance in his mind: the Pinot sounds great.

Instead he looked her right in the eye, smiled back, and said, "I'd bet anything you know not just the year but the exact date."

Nina gave him an adoring look, meaning she was pleased that Matthew was flattering her mother. Why, Mrs. Plansky wondered, would that be? In fact, she was pretty close to knowing already, lacking only the details of the ask. She told Matthew the year, the least cumbersome of any responses she could think of.

Matthew tapped at his phone and looked up. "The prime rate in that twelve month period fluctuated between ten and ten point five. So plus four point five would be . . ." He left that sentence unfinished, sliding the phone back inside the powder-blue blazer.

"Usury!" Mrs. Plansky had told Norm, bringing him the news. He'd laughed, hugged her, and said, "It won't even be a blip in the long run." That was Norm. Meanwhile, her dad had now gone pale and looked his age and more. Mrs. Plansky rose. "I hope everyone left room for dessert."

For dessert Mrs. Plansky had thawed one of the pecan pies she'd baked around Thanksgiving, using a recipe she'd learned in Miss Terrance's ninth grade home economics class. "Now don't you girls be cloying," she'd said, brandishing a spatula. Miss Terrance had looked ancient at the time but had probably been around Nina's present age. "Not with people and not with this pie. Less sugar! More pecans! And if your parents are okay with it, two ounces of bourbon. But we won't be doing that part this morning."

"Wow," said Matthew. He had two slices, Mrs. Plansky one, her dad just a sliver and then another sliver, and Nina a bite or two. After that, Mrs. Plansky poured coffee. Matthew took a sip, sat back in his chair, shot Nina a look.

"So, Mom," Nina said, "ready to hear our idea?"

"What about me?" said her dad. "Do I get to hear it?"

"Of course, Pops," Nina said. "I'd appreciate your input."

Mrs. Plansky's dad beamed at his granddaughter. He was smitten by her and always had been. Anything she asked for he would have given. The problem was he had nothing to give—or rather nothing of what Mrs. Plansky was pretty sure Nina was looking for. But she could be wrong, and hoped she was.

"Matthew?" Nina said.

"Oh, no, you go, hon," said Matthew. "I'll jump in as needed."

Nina rubbed her hands together. She wore a ring on each, the lovely little emerald in a platinum setting from Zach and the bloated ruby in a twisted golden rope setting from Ted the first. There'd been a largish diamond from Ted the second but when Nina had taken it to Tiffany's for a sizing adjustment they'd discovered an authenticity issue. That had opened the door to other authenticity issues with Ted the second—of which Mrs. Plansky had no details—the marriage ending soon after, the divorce itself authentic and rock solid. But she was over-dwelling on the rings. What about the fact that Nina's fingernails were bitten to the quick? That was new.

"Well, Mom," Nina said, "you can fight for market share or you can make a brand-new market, right?"

"That seems . . . logical," said Mrs. Plansky.

"Great. So hold that thought. Meanwhile what's the most important human emotion there is?"

"Stupidity," said Mrs. Plansky's dad.

Matthew folded his arms across his chest and pursed his lips. Once, on the way to a meeting with a potential distributor, Norm had said, "There are always two conversations going on, the verbal and the bodily." "Oh, yeah?" Mrs. Plansky had replied, mussing his hair at the same time. The meeting was a disaster but a much bigger distributor had called out of the blue the very next day.

"Isn't stupidity more of a state of mind, Dad?" Mrs. Plansky said. "I think Nina means something else, like love, for example."

"Wow, Mom, exactly!" said Nina. "Love. That's our whole concept."

Matthew unfolded his arms, unpursed his lips, shook his head. "My, my," he said. "Astute, as advertised, and more so, Loretta, if I may call you that. Or would you prefer Mom?"

"Loretta," said Mrs. Plansky.

"Our concept," Matthew said, Mrs. Plansky realizing he was jumping in as needed, "was born in love and is also about love. That probably sounds touchy-feely but did anyone ever go broke selling touchy-feely? As for the nuts and bolts, both of us, me and Nina, feel so lucky to have found real love after one or two unsuccessful attempts."

"Or more!" said Nina.

"But," Matthew went on, "we know many others of the post-spring-chicken—" here he inserted air quotes—"generations who have given up. The existing social media structure has failed them. Yes, they can meet anyone from anywhere, but then what? It's all too unfocused. That's where our concept comes in. It's called 'Love and . . .' with three dots after the 'and.' Dot dot dot."

"Is this about the goddamn internet?" said Mrs. Plansky's dad.

"I hear you, Pops," Matthew told him. "But it's about the internet only in the way that . . ." Matthew paused. Searching for an idea? Or just trying to remember where he was in the pitch? Mrs. Plansky hadn't figured that out before Nina spoke up.

"Only in the way that Columbus was about the ships."

"Beautiful, sweetheart!" Matthew reached across the table to touch Nina's hand, a somewhat awkward gesture given the width of the table and the fact Matthew's arms were on the short side for a man of six foot four and three-quarters. "What comes after the 'and' can be just about anything, as long as it narrows the love pool down to genuine prospects. For example—" Matthew glanced around the table, his gaze falling, perhaps a little too dramatically, on the remains of the pecan pie. "Pecan pie," he went on. "Not something on our list, but why not? Love and Pecan Pie."

Nina whipped out her phone. "I'm adding it this second."

"So this is about pie?" said Mrs. Plansky's dad.

"Yes, in the sense of everyone getting their slice," said Matthew. "But broadly speaking it's about finding love in all the right places. The plan is to start with Love and the Caribbean, a place for lovers of the Caribbean who are looking for love."

"The Caribbean's one big slum when the sun don't shine," said Mrs. Plansky's dad.

Matthew blinked.

Nina said, "Pops! What a thing to say!"

Mrs. Plansky said, "Place meaning an internet site?"

"We have a dynamite developer all set to go, Mom," said Nina.

"Pending funding, of course," Matthew said.

"He says it's the best start-up concept he's ever seen," Nina said.

"Naturally he's very expensive," Matthew said. "We're looking for a supplemental two hundred and fifty K. Work starts the day we get it."

All eyes were now on Mrs. Plansky. A list of questions unspooled in her mind, none of them particularly astute to her way of thinking, but simply obvious. What kind of law had Matthew practiced? How successful had he been? How much of his own money was he putting into this? Why had he moved into Nina's house? Had he tried borrowing from a commercial lender? Was he already up to here in debt with nowhere else to go? And what about Nina? Mrs. Plansky had given her—well, no point going into the exact figure, which would have been graceless. But was it all gone? Where?

"If you're wondering about revenue," Matthew said, "it will be subscriber based with an initiation plus a monthly hit, with the prospect of advertising as well, from resorts, for example, in the case of Love and the Caribbean."

Mrs. Plansky had not been wondering about any of that, had assumed something of the kind. As for all her questions? Nah. She could afford it. And this was her daughter, a daughter with fingernails now bitten down to the quick. If you were being exploited knowingly were you actually being exploited? Mrs. Plansky did not feel exploited. She was stepping up. That was all.

"Am I an investor or a lender?" she said.

"Oh, Mom." Nina's eyes moistened.

Matthew's remained nice and dry. "A lender, if you don't mind."

"There'll be interest," Mrs. Plansky said.

"Wouldn't want it any other way," said Matthew, a grin spreading across his face. He appeared to be missing a tooth, lower right, toward the back. "You name it."

Mrs. Plansky fought off a mad impulse to say prime plus ninety-nine, and went with prime plus zero. Her dad looked shocked, but perhaps his mind was elsewhere at that moment, or he'd had a sudden inner pain.

"I love you, Mom." Nina hurried over and gave her a big kiss. Mrs. Plansky buried what she knew well: that the upcoming marriage would be the arranged kind, although not arranged by some old-world parents but by the participants themselves.

Nina was in love with love. Matthew was in love with himself. They were closing in on the last chance café. So why not together? That was the arrangement. Mrs. Plansky buried it a little deeper.

SEVEN

Nina and Matthew cleaned up, wouldn't hear of Mrs. Plansky lifting a finger. She and her dad watched the Golf Channel.

"Men hit the ball sixty percent farther than women," he said. "I bet you didn't know that."

"I did not," said Mrs. Plansky. "It seems a little high."

His voice rose. "You're not entitled to your own facts!"

Mrs. Plansky nodded. "That would be my opinion, too, Dad. All set for the ride home?"

"How about I stay here for the night? Maybe a couple of nights. Three or four. A week wouldn't be out of the question."

"That would be nice, but Nina has the guest bedroom tonight."

"And Matty?"

"Yes."

"Matty sleeps with her?"

"Come on, Dad. Do you have to use the bathroom before you go?"

"You never know."

He rolled into the bathroom, insisted on managing by himself, stayed for not very long, then came rolling out and said, "Nope."

Mrs. Plansky told Nina and Matthew not to wait up. She got her dad in the car and drove south toward Arcadia Gardens. Mrs. Plansky expected he'd fall asleep, like a baby out for a ride at that hour, but his eyes were wide open, greenish in the light from the dashboard. He was silent until the point where the road took an easterly curve and they caught a distant view of the ocean, with a cruise ship all lit up and steaming south.

"Everything's different at night," he said.

"Yes," said Mrs. Plansky.

"I tried Viagra a few times."

Mrs. Plansky made no response.

"This was after your mother passed, of course, when I started with the girlfriends. I never cheated on your mother, not one single time."

Mrs. Plansky nodded.

"Well, if you're going to get all huffy there was actually this one time. Never repeated and it wasn't my fault. A secret I'm taking to my grave."

Mrs. Plansky sped up. The road swung inland, the ocean and the cruise ship disappearing from sight. Her dad was silent all the way to the front door of Arcadia Gardens.

"I want in on the deal."

Mrs. Plansky stopped the car and turned to him. "What deal?"

"What deal? Hells bells! The Caribbean sex deal or whatever it is. The whole thing they were going on and on about."

The door to Acadia Gardens opened and an attendant came out to get him.

"Why not sleep on it?" Mrs. Plansky said. "There's no rush."

"No rush? I'm ninety-eight goddamn years old. I want in."

The attendant opened the car door. "We'll get you right in, sir."

For a moment Mrs. Plansky thought her father would explode, but he slowly deflated instead.

On the way home was an upscale-looking bar called the Green Turtle Club, set in a little clearing off the road and backing onto a canal. Mrs. Plansky had never been inside and couldn't remember the last time she'd walked into any bar alone, but now for a few moments she slowed down. Would she have actually stopped and gone inside? She never found out, because at that moment her phone made that irritating buzz she'd been meaning to change. It was Jack. She still hadn't gotten back to him? Good grief.

"Hey, Mom. Are you hard to reach or what?"

"Sorry, Jack. It's been busy. Nina's here and—" She cut off any further excuses. "But it's good to hear your voice." And that was true. The lights of the Green Turtle Club faded in the rearview mirror. "How's everything?"

"Not too bad. How's Nina?"

"Seems good. I met her new . . . fella."

"Fella, Mom? What century are we in?"

Mrs. Plansky laughed. One thing about her son, through all the ups and downs—he could make her laugh. "His name's Matthew. Or sometimes Matty. He seems very nice."

"That bad, huh?"

"Now now," said Mrs. Plansky. "I see you've been having lovely weather."

"Blue skies and seventy, day after day."

"There must be lots of action at the club."

Then came a silence, and in that silence Mrs. Plansky inferred that there was not lots of action at the club, meaning the Red Desert Tennis Center in Scottsdale, one of the biggest tennis facilities in Arizona, where Jack was director and head pro. He was an excellent tennis player—his gift obvious the very first time she'd had him on a court at the age of three—although not in the sense that Roger Federer was excellent, or any touring pro, for that matter, the top of the tennis pyramid being very steep and narrow. But Jack had been good enough to play number one singles at a D-3 program—in fact, tennis had probably gotten him into Bowdoin, an unlikely result if he'd been relying on academics alone—and it had taken him all over the world as a teaching pro, a tennis journey that had reached, in Mrs. Plansky's understanding, a happy destination where he could finally settle down and . . . and do whatever he wanted, possibly finding some woman with fewer problems than the usual women who appeared in his life and . . . and even raising his own darn family! There! She'd said it. If only to herself. But why was her mind wandering like this? She reined it in. And then all at once couldn't remember . . . couldn't remember . . . And then it came to her: blue skies! Blue skies and seventy, height of the Arizona tourist season, and a lack of action at the club? What was going on? There. She was back on track.

"Well, Mom, life's funny, you know?" Jack said.

Yes and no. Mrs. Plansky saw a safe spot to pull off the road and did so, parking beside a palm tree, its leaves very still although a breeze was blowing in from the ocean.

"I've actually resigned," Jack said. "Effective last Friday."

"Ah."

"It's not that I hated the job or anything. I've always liked working with people, Mom. You know that. But I want more. Do you see what I'm getting at?"

"Not really."

In tennis, having a temper could be good, and a number of champions have been able to channel their tempers and feed off the inner anger in the crucial moments, but most players of the temperamental type ended up letting their tempers get the best of them and falling apart. Jack had always had a temper of the unchannelable type. Mrs. Plansky could feel it awakening now, all the way from the Valley of the Sun.

"What I'm getting at is ownership," he said, speaking perhaps a little too much on the deliberate, extra-clear side. But perhaps that was just the connection. "Like you and Dad had," Jack explained. Nope, not the connection. "And an opportunity's come up. Really exciting, actually. Not tennis related at all, which is kind of refreshing, I admit it. What do you know about the cold chain?"

"Gold chain?" said Mrs. Plansky.

"Cold. Not gold. Cold chain, Mom."

"I've never heard of it."

"Think of the cold chain as a subsection of the supply chain," Jack told her.

"Okay."

"The point is that the failure of just one link on the cold chain means big trouble. And right now the weak link is freezing storage. There just isn't enough capacity. Low supply, high demand—what happens to price?"

"I think I remember," Mrs. Plansky said.

Jack laughed. "Freezing warehouses, Mom. We're going to build a thousand of them every year for the next ten years."

"Who's we?"

"My partners, Ray and Rudy, developers based in Tempe. Two very sharp dudes. You'd love them. I'm one lucky bastard just from the fact they're letting me in."

"In what?"

"This company we're forming, Mom—RJR Inc.—to build freezing warehouses. Sorry if I'm not being clear."

"To build and sell them?" said Mrs. Plansky. "Or own and operate?"

There was a pause. Was it possible the question hadn't occurred to Ray, Rudy, or Jack? Impossible, surely. "That's a real good question, Mom. We've been going back and forth about that and we'll be ironing it out going forward. Um. Speaking of going forward, this is sort of a heads-up."

"What is?"

"This call, Mom."

Another pause, this one longer than the first, which gave her mind time to drift back to a Labor Day weekend in Wellfleet, Nina seven and Jack five, when the two of them had gotten caught in a rip and begun screaming. Norm had frozen—well, not frozen, just hadn't reacted as quickly as she had: dropping the skewer of shrimp and onion rings on the sand and sprinting to the water shouting, "Don't fight it! Ride it out!" Which Nina had done, the rip dissipating about twenty yards out and leaving her bobbing in the swell, but Jack had fought the rip and gone under. Mrs. Plansky had plunged in, grabbed him, yanked him to the surface, and swum him to safety, swimming on her back with Jack facing up on her chest, and one of her hands on his chest. How his little heart had beat! So quick, like a hummingbird's. Her hand could feel it now.

"The thing is," Jack was saying.

Uh-oh. Had she missed something? Mrs. Plansky pressed the phone to her ear.

"I may have . . . what's that British expression? Put my foot wrong. I was trying to line up the ducks, that's all. But I may have done things in the wrong order. If so, my bad."

"I don't understand," Mrs. Plansky said.

"Well, the thing is, I . . . have you heard from Connie Malhouf?"

"Not recently. Why?"

Connie Malhouf, practicing in Rhode Island, was Mrs. Plansky's lawyer.

"Hmm. I kind of thought she might get in touch with you. The thing is, Mom, I got the feeling Connie was a bit pissed at me."

Mrs. Plansky was lost. "I wasn't aware you knew her."

"We met at Fenway Park."

"Fenway—But that was so long ago. Weren't you in high school?"

"College actually. I snagged that foul ball and gave it to Jordan."

"Jordan?"

"Connie's son, Mom. He was about ten."

"I know who Jord—" Mrs. Plansky cut herself off. The point was Jack remembered his name after all these years. He was good with people, no doubt about it. Other than that, there was no surety to be had at the moment.

"Apparently Jordan's in Singapore now, doing something with container ships," Jack said. "Connie mentioned that before our conversation went a bit south, or let's say southerly." He laughed, a little self-congratulatory heh-heh that was new. Oh, how Mrs. Plansky hated to put it in those terms. The phone really was a dangerous invention. We were meant to see the people we were talking to. What if there wasn't a trace of anything self-congratulatory on Jack's face at the moment? She told herself to rein in the judgmental side and pronto. But it balked.

"A bit south?" Mrs. Plansky said.

"Although . . . maybe since she hasn't called you, I—I might be overthinking this."

"Jack? Out with it, if you don't mind."

Then came a big intake of breath. "The rationale being it was a sort of homework call."

"Homework for what assignment?"

"Ah, Christ, Mom. Do you have to be so smart?"

"That won't work," said Mrs. Plansky.

"Oh, do I know that."

"I'm listening."

"Okay, okay. Concerning prospective financing—of the creative type—for RJR Inc., I wanted to sound you out about certain things. In retrospect I take Connie's point. I should have gone directly to you. And never listened to Rudy."

"Rudy?"

"The first *R*, Mom. Some guys have all these subtle moves—Ray's like that—and some have just one, but it's killer. That's Rudy."

Mrs. Plansky took a deep breath of her own. "And what was Rudy's advice?"

"To find out all I could before talking to you."

"About what?"

"Your will, Mom."

Now Mrs. Plansky's heart was the one beating way too fast—maybe not like a hummingbird but enough to remind her of something she actually never thought about, namely her age.

"Ray knows a guy—a lender, a reputable lender—who has a service for borrowing against an eventual inheritance. Uh, well, I know of course what you said after Dad passed, that everything would go equally to your descendants, which is so nice of you. But

Ray pointed out I was operating under this assumption that the descendants were me and Nina, when in fact there's also Emma and Will. Which was how come I wanted to—"

Mrs. Plansky—or rather her voice, operating on its own—interrupted. "I get it."

She was not an interrupter. Neither of them spoke for what might have been a full minute. A car sped by and out an open window came spinning an empty nip, sparkling for a moment in someone's headlights.

"I'm sorry, Mom. Connie wouldn't discuss it anyway. A big mistake on my part. It won't happen again. I mean nothing like it will ever . . ."

What Mrs. Plansky wanted to do now was to sit down at the kitchen table—not the kitchen table in the condo, or even the one at 3 Pelican Way, but the old original one back in Rhode Island—and hash this out with Norm.

"How much money are we talking about?" she said.

Jack's voice brightened right away. "Seven hundred and fifty K would be nice but even half a mil would do."

From out in the swamp—Mrs. Plansky had assumed the open country beyond the palm tree she'd parked under was a golf course, but now realized what it actually was—came a harsh animal cry.

"Why don't you fly out here?" she said. "This isn't a phone conversation."

"Sure, Mom. Thanks." For a not-so-good second or two she thought he was about to ask for the fare. Instead he said, "Love you."

Jack was her son. She could afford what he was asking. But Ray and Rudy were not her sons. Thank God, by the way. And wasn't Jack's call to Connie a sneaky sort of move? She didn't want to put that label on it but she somehow felt Norm nodding yes, sneaky for sure, like he was following along in her thoughts. Therefore, a bit of a conundrum.

"Love you, too," Mrs. Plansky said. Which she did, so much so that just saying the words diminished all her doubts.

Twenty minutes later she was back at her condo. It was quiet, Nina and Matthew upstairs in the guest bedroom. Mrs. Plansky thought about getting a goldfish, even considered a name or two, such as Goldie and Flash. Meanwhile she was on the move from room to room, switching off the lights. At the bar she found herself standing in front of the drink shelf. Why? Because that might be a good home for Goldie's bowl? Plausible enough. She reached for the bottle of Norm's bourbon, untouched since their last evening drink together. Mrs. Plansky opened it, sniffed, and then—not bothering with a glass!—took a way too big swig right from the bottle, like some sorority girl on a night that would not end well.

She went to bed.

EIGHT

Mrs. Plansky had lain in her bed for some time, trying various positions—back, side, front, other side—when it hit her that she hadn't brushed her teeth. Going to bed with teeth unbrushed? When had that last happened, if ever? She entertained herself with a silly thought—the idea of calling out, "Julio! Julio! Teeth brushing assistance!"—but still, this was bad. The proper course of action was obvious. Get up, two minutes of Sonicare, back in the sack with a clear conscience, but her body refused to cooperate, or had simply turned to lead. She lay there, the taste of Norm's favorite bourbon on her tongue. Gradually the bourbon taste began to change, slowly becoming the taste of Norm himself. Night differed from day, all right. Hadn't someone mentioned that, maybe even recently? Mrs. Plansky tried to think who but the answer wouldn't come. Instead she shut down all cogitation and luxuriated in the taste of Norm.

She heard footsteps from upstairs, heavier than Nina's. Then came the sound of the upstairs toilet flushing, followed by return footsteps and silence, all that adding up to one of those night time journeys men of a certain age went on. But why go on about Matthew? Was there something creepy about older men marrying much younger women? There was plenty of it—Aristotle Onassis, Hugh Hefner, Larry King, Clint Eastwood—and no one seemed to mind. But it seemed creepy to Mrs. Plansky, although not in the case of Clint Eastwood.

Annette Franco's husband, Bob—they lived in the condo two over from her—had died six months ago and she was already dating a guy Mrs. Plansky knew vaguely from the tennis club. His service motion was like some Rube Goldberg device. Was he Rube Goldbergy in more intimate activities? Oh, for God's sake! Enough! And as for the six months—so what? The clock was ticking, that was all. Maybe sex made more sense than marriage—or even dating—in old age. Wasn't courtship for the young? Certainly true in nature, with ducks, for example. Mrs. Plansky tried to feel what it would be like to be pregnant, right now, in this present body, and couldn't do it. She went back to the taste of Norm on her tongue. He was gone. Mrs. Plansky turned over, got into the most comfortable position she knew—a sort of twisted *K*—and fell into a sleep that was stormy at first and then quieted down.

Her phone was ringing, and a dream took shape around the sound, a dream in which she was at the club, playing Annette Franco's boyfriend, and beating the crap out of him. Then her conscious mind woke to the fact that her actual unimaginary phone was doing the ringing. Mrs. Plansky reached for it on the bedside table, fumbling and almost knocking it off. The room was very dark, the screen on her phone kind of blurry, or possibly that was the fault of her eyes. She rubbed them with the back of her free hand and now could make out the ID scrolling across the screen: Will.

Will. In the middle of the night.

"Hello?" she said.

"Yo."

A bad connection, static and muffled at the same time. It sounded like he'd said yo, but it might have been the end of hello. Mrs. Plansky pictured one of those Colorado blizzards. It was earlier out there, of course, maybe still party time for the lift line guys and other staff on the mountain. She was pretty good at guessing what might be coming next: he was finally thanking her for the Christmas check.

"Hello?" she said again.

"Yo. It's me, Grandma, Will. Your grandson, Will."

Right away she knew he didn't sound good, his voice higher than normal, maybe nervous about something, although since they hadn't spoken in some time she couldn't be sure.

"I'm aware of the relationship," she said, with a little laugh, hoping to settle the kid down a bit. Maybe this wasn't about Christmas at all, but perhaps some problem. A problem with Nina, for example, with Matthew as the root cause? Ah-ha.

A pause, and then Will said, "Oh, yes, the relationship. Grandparent and grandchild."

This was new: a kind of dry, offbeat, humor. But the connection was still bad. "Will? Try moving a bit."

"Moving? You wish—want me to move?"

"The connection's bad. Maybe stand somewhere else."

"The connection? Right, right. Very good. I will step over here like this. How is—how's the connection now, Grandma?"

"Maybe a little better."

Will lowered his voice. The connection was so bad he hardly sounded like himself. "The truth is, Grandma, I can't move far right now in this situation."

"What situation?"

"A . . . problem. A dw—a DUI. I am in a DUI situation."

Mrs. Plansky sat up. "Are you all right? Are you hurt?"

"Hurt? Oh, no, not hurt, not at all hurt."

"Maybe I should let you speak to your mom. She's here."

"My . . . what?"

"Your mom. She came for dinner and they're staying overnight. She and Matthew. I'll go wake her. Hang on."

"No! I mean no, please. No."

"You don't . . ."

"No, please don't. I—I wish, want to speak to you, Grandma."

Pretty clear what was going on. The mention of Matthew had done it. Will had to know where he stood with the new beau.

"I'm so sorry for this, Grandma, but I have no one else for help. To . . . to turn to. The police have seized my car and for getting it back and for bail I need nine thousand seven hundred and twenty-six dollars and eighteen cents. It's only temporary, Grandma. The money comes right back when I go to the court next month."

Mrs. Plansky found that she was on her feet, her heart beating way too fast. Her mind was in turmoil. She didn't know what to say or do. She didn't feel like her real self.

"I'm sorry, Grandma." Will lowered his voice even more. "There are bad people in this cell. I'm afraid."

"Let me speak to whoever's in charge," Mrs. Plansky said.

"In charge?"

"A policeman, a deputy, someone like that."

"But . . . but they do not know about the phone. They will seize it also. Too. They will seize it, too!"

The poor kid was terrified—although not at all drunk, Colorado possibly having one of those extra-low blood alcohol limits—could barely string a few words together. Some problems were objectively terrifying and maybe not solvable. This was not that kind. It was solvable with money, and not really a lot, most of it even coming back when Will appeared in court, minus a fine and some inevitable surcharges.

"It's going to be all right, Will. Try to stay calm. What was that figure again?"

"Figure?"

"The amount—the car, bail, all that."

"Ah. Yes. For sure. The figure is nine thousand seven hundred and twenty-six dollars and eighteen cents."

At one time—and not so long ago—Mrs. Plansky could hear a number like that—and much more complicated ones—and see them clear in her mind, as though chalked on a blackboard. Those days seemed to be over. "We'll round it off," she said.

"Round it off?"

"To ten thousand. We can sort out the details later. How do I get it to the jail?"

"The jail?"

"Or the police station. How do I get it to you?"

"Oh, not the police station, Grandma. I do not trust these people. It should come to me."

"How?"

"The best system is to send to my Safemo account."

"What's Safemo?"

"Like Venmo or PayPal but better."

Mrs. Plansky had heard those names but knew nothing about them. "Better how?"

"Much. Much better."

"But in what way, Will? That's what I'm asking."

"Oh, I see," said Will. "Safer. Faster. Both of them. Safer and faster. The whole transaction is encrypted and disappears immediately."

"I don't understand."

"Like Snapchat, Grandma. Or WhatsApp, all of them. Totally private for a few seconds and then gone forever."

Mrs. Plansky felt a bit dizzy. She sat on the edge of the bed.

"Grandma?"

"I'm here."

There was a pause and then Will said, "I forgot to mention! Safemo gives one percent of profits to saving the whales!"

Mrs. Plansky's mind—like a dog scenting something it liked—wanted to pull her away to memories of the whale watch she and Norm had gone on, the one where—But she didn't let it, and getting herself back on firmer ground, said, "How do they make a profit?"

"Advertising, Grandma. They take nothing from the . . . the transaction."

Advertising. She should have known. Mrs. Plansky knew all

about it from the other side, having run Plansky and Company's advertising all by herself in the early years. "All right," she said. "What are the details?"

"Details?"

"For sending you the funds."

"Funds?"

"Money, Will."

"Oh, thank you, Grandma, thank you. All you need to do is give me the bank routing number and account number."

Mrs. Plansky rose, felt for her purse on the bedside table, groped inside for her checkbook, took it into the bathroom.

"Grandma?" Will's voice was even quieter now, and sounded shaky.

"It's all right. Hang on." She switched on the overhead light, blinked a few times until her eyes adjusted. Then she said, "Palm Coast Bank and Trust," and read him the numbers. "Are you writing this down?"

"Oh, yes, Grandma. On my phone."

"On your phone?"

"Into my Safemo account. And now it just asks for the password."

"What password?"

"For the account, Grandma. It will encrypt and vanish right away, immediately, tout de suite."

Tout de suite? Yes, he was developing a sense of humor, and somehow, even out of school, getting at least a bit of an education: his French accent sounded pretty darn good. She gave him the password, the same one she used for most things: !NorManConQuest!

"And presto, Grandma. Already vanished forever. Thank you, Grandma!"

"That's it?"

"Finito!"

"Will? Call me as soon as you're out."

"Out?"

"Of jail."

"Oh, yes. The moment I am free. Here . . . here is com . . . here comes the cop."

"Okay, I'll let you go. Love you, Will."

"I . . . I love you, Grandma."

Click.

Looking up, Mrs. Plansky caught her reflection in the mirror. She looked a mess, ancient and distraught. But ten minutes later—Mrs. Plansky back in bed and wide awake—her phone buzzed.

"I am free, Grandma, out on the street, like a bird."

The connection was clearer this time. He really was growing up to be quite funny. Mrs. Plansky felt better at once. "Good news. Stay in touch."

"Yes, for sure."

"And you'd better get a lawyer."

"Oh?"

"To represent you in court."

"Excellent idea, Grandma. Good night."

"Good night."

Mrs. Plansky tossed and turned for a while, then got into the twisted K and fell asleep. When she awoke and drew the curtains midmorning—or even later!—daylight came streaming in. She checked the time: eleven fifteen. Eleven fifteen? When had she last slept in until eleven fifteen, or even past six thirty? Mrs. Plansky showered, dressed, made herself presentable, tried not to look sheepish, opened her bedroom door, and emerged.

But Nina and Matthew were already gone. A note was propped up beside the coffeepot.

Mom, thanks for everything. It was so lovely to see you. You're such a rock for the whole family—like Gibraltar, Matthew says! (We'll be in touch re the loan thingy, no rush.) Lots and lots of love, Nina.

And, in another hand: *and Matty.*

NINE

Uncle Dragomir's pats on the back were more like slaps or even blows, although Dinu did not know what normal back pats felt like, having never before gotten any in his life. All he did know was that these heavy-handed back pats felt great. He felt great in general, couldn't recall ever feeling like this. They sat in the private VIP lounge on the topmost level of Club Presto, where Dinu had never been before: Dinu, Uncle Dragomir, Uncle Dragomir's Polish girlfriend and also his Moldovan girlfriend—but not his wife, Aunt Simone, who often traveled in the West—Romeo, Timbo the bouncer, a Russian businessman who seemed to know Uncle Dragomir quite well, the Russian businessman's bodyguard, and the Russian businessman's date for the evening, a beautiful young woman whose name Dinu didn't know, although he was pretty sure he'd seen her face on the billboard opposite the train station, advertising one of the local brands of toothpaste.

Tassa entered with more champagne on a tray, delicious Carpathian champagne that made Dinu's body tingle. She looked right into his eyes as she filled his glass.

"Have you done your homework?" he said, an inane remark and also making no sense, since they were on vacation. But Tassa seemed to find it very funny.

"Fist bump," she said, raising her free hand. They fist bumped. Was it possible Tassa had made the touching part of the fist bump linger somehow, or was it just his imagination? Even if it was, how nice to have the imagination imagining good things. Until now, Dinu's imagination had mostly worked the other way.

"You see?" Uncle Dragomir said to the Russian businessman. "The little prick has a way with women, young, old, makes no difference."

The Russian businessman said something in Russian. Dinu knew no Russian, and that was fine with him. English—American English—was the only language that interested him, not excepting his own. He did wish that Uncle Dragomir hadn't called him a little prick. Uncle Dragomir had meant no harm. It was just his way, but still. Dinu took a gulp of champagne and forgot all about it.

Marius, the other bouncer, entered the VIP lounge, bringing Professor Bogdan.

"Hello there, Professor," said Uncle Dragomir. "Thanks for joining us. Is this your first time in the VIP lounge?" He snapped his fingers. Tassa hurried over with champagne for the professor.

Professor Bogdan glanced around—spilling a bit of champagne on the lapel of his tweed jacket, a baggy jacket frayed at the cuffs his gaze pausing over the women in their tight party dresses and then moving quickly on. No one smiled or waved. The professor, Dinu realized, didn't have a way with women, or possibly with men, either.

"First time in your club, period," Professor Bogdan said.

"But not the last!" said Uncle Dragomir. "Timbo, a gift card for the professor."

"Ten euros or twenty?" said Timbo.

"Fifty! The professor is a first-class teacher of English and we are a first-class business."

Timbo gave Bogdan a gift card. The professor put on his eyeglasses and studied it. Everyone laughed. The professor's cheeks turned pink.

Uncle Dragomir rose. "And now, Professor, we put you to work, yes?"

"That's why I'm here," Bogdan said.

Uncle Dragomir did not like that remark. His nostrils widened momentarily, like a horse. Dinu knew that sign and several others, but as for exactly what had displeased him he had no clue.

Behind a curtain of gold streamers at the back of the VIP lounge was a small alcove where Uncle Dragomir, Romeo, the professor, and Dinu squeezed together at a round table, all of them wearing earbuds. Romeo did something with his phone and the sound of another phone, a phone with a noisy connection, came through the earbuds.

"Hello?" said an American woman.

And then came Dinu's own voice: "Yo."

Professor Bogdan's eyebrows rose, like he was surprised and maybe even impressed. They all listened for a while. Then Uncle Dragomir, who had very little English, took out his earbuds, sat back, and sipped champagne, his heavy-lidded eyes half closed like he was deep in thought. For some reason, Dinu, too, wanted to remove his earbuds, to stop listening. That happened first around the point in the conversation where Grandma said, "Are you all right? Are you hurt?" and then a few more times. But Dinu kept his earbuds in. Wasn't this an assignment, another part of the job?

Okay, I'll let you go. Love you, Will.

I . . . I love you, Grandma.

That was the end of the recording. The second call—the brief one when he'd reassured Grandma that he was back out on the street— was not in the script and hadn't been recorded. He'd made it on a burner phone Romeo had given him when the two of them were alone in the office. Why? Romeo had asked that very question. Dinu actually hadn't known, but he'd replied, Because I'm not finished being Will. To which Romeo had nodded like that made sense and said, Cool, in English, so maybe that was in fact the reason.

Dinu, Romeo, and Professor Bogdan removed their earbuds. Bogdan gazed at Dinu. Everyone else's eyes were on the professor.

"Well?" Uncle Dragomir said.

Bogdan licked his lips. "I—I would say fascinating. I've never heard anything quite like it."

Uncle Dragomir waved that away with his meaty hand. "I'm not asking for some pussy . . ." He turned to Romeo. "What's the word I'm looking for?"

"Critique," said Romeo.

"I don't want your pussy critique," Uncle Dragomir went on. "I'm asking how he did."

"Dinu?"

"Who else?"

"Dinu, then. In what sense are you asking?"

"In the sense of his English, moron. Why else do I pay you?"

The professor's cheeks pinkened again. "His English was good. Remarkably good." Bogdan looked at Dinu, perhaps not quite in the eye. "You've improved a lot," he said in English.

"Cool," said Dinu.

"What was that?" said Uncle Dragomir. "What did you tell him?"

"Just that he improved."

Uncle Dragomir grunted. He got out a pack of cigarettes, took one for himself, and offered one to Bogdan. Bogdan took it. Uncle Dragomir leaned forward with a light. For a moment their faces were very close. In Dinu's eyes at that moment they were almost like two different species of men.

"Any mistakes?" Uncle Dragomir said, sitting back.

Bogdan took a deep drag, let it out slowly, and seemed to relax a bit. "Sure, but Americans make little mistakes in grammar all the time. They have the Latinate underpinnings like us, but mixed in is a whole other stream of Anglo-Saxon, which is what you hear in everyday—"

"Did I ask for a lecture?" Uncle Dragomir said. "Was he believable?"

"Certainly, just judging from the results alone."

Uncle Dragomir's nostrils widened. Bogdan shrank back. "The

results—of which you know nothing—are not your concern. Understood?"

"Oh, yes."

"Completely understood in all possibilities?"

"One hundred percent."

"Then we have no problems and nothing but smooth roads ahead. Do they have smooth roads in America, Professor?"

"The smoothest, and so many. President Eisenhower built a whole interstate system that . . ." This time he stopped himself. "As for Dinu, he was not only believable but . . ." He glanced at Dinu, again not quite meeting his gaze. "Talented," he went on.

"Talented? The kid has talent?"

"A talent for improvising."

"Explain."

"For quick reactions. For thinking on his feet. There were moments in the conversation, regarded strictly as a narrative without any moral—regarded strictly as a narrative, where the process threatened to take a turn that might have frustrated your—that you might not have liked, but Dinu managed to steer things right. The part about saving the whales? You could almost say brilliant."

Uncle Dragomir gave Dinu a long look. "That is all, Professor."

Bogdan rose. Uncle Dragomir handed him an envelope.

"Thank you," said the professor.

"You will be pleased," said Uncle Dragomir.

"Thank you, thank you."

Bogdan went out through the golden streamers.

"That will be all for you as well, Romeo," Uncle Dragomir said.

"Do I get an envelope?" Romeo said.

Uncle Dragomir laughed a huge happy laugh with no trace of meanness in it. "You get a kick in the ass."

Romeo laughed, too, although his laughter ended abruptly the second he passed through the golden streamers.

Uncle Dragomir took out his cigarettes, held the pack for Dinu to take one.

"No, thanks."

"You don't smoke?"

"No, Uncle."

"What about cannabis? I have some."

"No, thanks."

"Everyone your age smokes cannabis."

"I have asthma."

"Pussy. Drink your champagne."

Dinu sipped his champagne. His asthma hadn't bothered him for a long time, like it had gone to sleep, but all at once he felt it stirring.

"Your father would have been proud," Uncle Dragomir said.

"You think so?"

They'd never discussed Dinu's father, Uncle Dragomir's younger brother who'd died when Dinu was very young.

"Sure," said Uncle Dragomir. "Every father wants a son with talent. He was no different." Uncle Dragomir waved his cigarette at Dinu. "A very strong guy, your dad. A bull. Maybe you'll have a growth spurt." Uncle Dragomir picked up his champagne glass, found it empty, drank from the bottle instead. He wiped his mouth with the back of his hand. "Rule number one in this country, Dinu—don't get involved in politics."

"What about other countries?"

"Same thing. We're all human. There is only one thing to do with politicians. Can you guess what that is?"

Supply them with women. That was Dinu's only idea, based on seeing several politicians ushered into the Playroom, an off-limits part of Club Presto.

"No," he said.

Uncle Dragomir leaned forward. "We pay them to leave us alone. That's it. Finito." He took out an envelope. "Keep this up and there will be more, lots more."

"Lots more . . . ah, um?"

"Money, Mr. Talent. What else is this about? First perform. Then money. Save the whales, you little shit."

Dinu took the envelope.

"And I've set you up with Dr. Vizi. Go see him."

"Who's Dr. Vizi?"

"The dentist. You lost a tooth. Did you forget?"

Dr. Vizi's office turned out to be in the private clinic two blocks from Dinu's flat. They even had their own ambulance with the name of the clinic on it, parked out front. Dinu had never been in a private clinic before, private clinics reserved for rich people and foreigners, but as he rode up in the elevator—a spotless, silent elevator with mirrored walls and a mirrored ceiling, an elevator unlike any he'd ever been in, his mind paused on the fact that, thanks to Romeo, he was secretly sharing their Wi-Fi. Once in English class Professor Bogdan had said, "All the world's a stage," maybe demonstrating something about contractions, and some wiseass student had said, "Then who is directing the play?" To which the professor had answered, "What if no one is?" A remark that had aroused no interest, so he'd returned to the grammar lesson. But now, his mind on the Wi-Fi situation, Dinu thought: *me, I am directing.* At least on this little stage of the Wi-Fi play. But what about on the big stages of life? Were there secret directors? Like Uncle Dragomir, for example?

The elevator door opened and Dinu stepped out, not into a corridor, as he'd expected, but directly into Dr. Vizi's waiting room, large and softly lit, more like a living room in an American movie. There was only one other patient, a man with longish dark hair and a closely trimmed white beard, leafing through a magazine. He glanced up at Dinu, his eyes a very pale blue, and went back to reading. Dinu approached the receptionist, sitting not behind some glass wall, but at a tidy desk in the open.

"Dinu Tiriac," he said.

The woman checked her screen. "Referred by Mr. Dragomir Tiriac?"

"Yes," said Dinu. From the corner of his eye he saw the other patient look up again, this time not so casually, those pale blue eyes intelligent, unreadable.

The woman pressed a button on her desk. A door on the far wall slid open. "Second left," she said.

Dinu went through the doorway. The door closed behind him but somehow he still felt that pale blue gaze on his back.

When he left two hours later with a brand-new state-of-the-art tooth in place—the exact same shade as his other teeth, in the top 10 percent on the whiteness scale, according to Dr. Vizi, and all of this for free!—the man with the closely trimmed white beard was gone. Dr. Vizi had also given him a bottle of pills to take away the pain. Dinu had no pain, but in the elevator going down he swallowed one dry anyway, to enjoy the buzz on his walk home. On the way he noticed a red leather belt in the window of a women's clothing shop. He bought it as a present for his mother—expensive, yes, yet now affordable—but she was asleep on the couch, her breath alcoholic. Dinu flushed Dr. Vizi's pills down the toilet.

TEN

Mrs. Plansky, eating breakfast—toast, hard-boiled egg, coffee—glanced at Nina's note—*like Gibraltar, Matthew says!* She and Norm had actually visited Gibraltar once, on a day trip from Malaga. They'd had lunch at a pub called the Sir Winston. "How many beers do you have to drink before this feels like the real thing?" Norm had asked. "One, we could run an experiment," Mrs. Plansky had said. "Or two, we could zip on back to Spain." They'd flipped a coin. Running an experiment had won. They'd downed a couple of pints each, found the Sir Winston growing more unreal, an unexpected result. Also unexpected was Norm's idea to rent a room right away—at the Admiral Nelson Inn, across the square—just for the afternoon. Mrs. Plansky was drifting into something of a reverie concerning the events of that afternoon at the Admiral Nelson when she got a phone call.

"Loretta? It's Melanie, from the club."

Mrs. Plansky didn't quite let go of the admiral immediately.

"We played the other day," Melanie said.

"Of course. Just . . . just a bit of distraction."

"Is this a bad time?"

"Not at all."

"Sorry for the late notice. Pindar—that's my boyfriend—and I are supposed to be playing mixed at onc with Kev Dinardo—do you know Kev?"

"No."

"He's another new member, like me, has a nice game. Anyway, his cousin from Ponte Vedra was supposed to be the fourth but she can't make it and I was wondering—"

"Sure," said Mrs. Plansky, checking the time. It was what she needed.

Kev Dinardo—about her own age, medium size, in decent shape, still pretty light on his feet—turned out to be one of those players who enjoyed his every minute on the court and did his best to make it enjoyable for everyone else, handing out compliments—

"That one-handed backhand of yours, Loretta! Best I've seen since Steffi Graf."

"Right," said Mrs. Plansky.

—and deprecatory of his own game, but not in the fishing for re-assurance way. On top of that he, like Norm, was a lefty, and Mrs. Plansky liked having a lefty partner. Plus he was a fine player, with a reliable slice serve he seemed to be able to place wherever he wanted, and put-away volleys. And although almost always in mixed the man takes the ad court, he insisted it was Mrs. Plansky's—"your crosscourt backhand will set me up real nice, I'll hardly have to move." In short, they were what you wanted in doubles, a team better than the sum of its parts. They won 6–4, 6–2, even with easing up toward the end.

"The most fun drubbing of my life," said Melanie, although Pindar, even younger than she was, with a big serve and a big forehand, didn't look as happy about it. "Let's do it again."

Kev turned to Mrs. Plansky, an expectant look on his face, a rather nice face, although not so easy to put your finger on why. Maybe she would give some thought to it.

"Sounds good," she said.

"Okay with you if we exchange phone numbers?" he said. "In the interest of logistics?"

"Sure," Mrs. Plansky said.

He took out his phone.

"Mine's . . ." she began, but the darn number, her own darn number, wouldn't come to her.

"Tell me about it," Kev said. "Happens to me all the time. It's because no one has to memorize anything anymore. Not only can't I remember my passwords, I can't even remember where I've written them down."

Mrs. Plansky, rummaging through her tennis bag, laughed. She had no need to write down passwords, having pretty much just the one— !NorManConQuest!—surely unforgettable for the rest of her life. Meanwhile, no phone in her tennis bag. "Must have left it in the car."

He handed her a card. "You can call me and then my phone will do the memorizing and I won't have to lift a mental finger."

"Okay," she said, and headed toward the parking lot. Her number came to her as she opened her car door, but the phone itself was not there. All at once her memory switched on to full power—its former full power—and she pictured it on her bedside table, where she'd put it after talking to Will. She realized it was wrong to keep this secret from Nina. First, she'd have to let Will know. That was the right course of action. But what about the turmoil this was going to cause, even raising the possibility of Nina getting boxed into the position of having to choose between her son and her fiancé or whatever the hell he was. Could the wrong way sometimes be the right way in some grander scheme of things? She considered sleeping on the problem but it wasn't even noon. Mrs. Plansky started the car, only then glancing at the card in her hand.

KEV DINARDO, it read. No photo of him, just a sketch, with only a few lines, suggesting a sailboat. There was also his phone number and this: RETIRED FROM PAYING WORK, BUT NOTHING ELSE. She just sat there in the idling car for a moment, feeling a bit strange, as though in her own house but coming upon a door not previously there.

Mrs. Plansky entered her bedroom, and there on the bedside table lay her phone, just as she'd thought. At that moment she had a realization about Norm. He'd been a lefty not just physically, but in every other way—mentally, emotionally, spiritually. So, despite the fact that he was gone, he seemed to be capable of new self-presentations, the dead taking on a life of their own.

She picked up the phone and saw that Will had left a message: *"Hey, Grandma, it's Will. I've been meaning to say thanks for the Christmas present. So generous of you! And, um, hope you're well. Take care. Bye."*

Mrs. Plansky smiled and shook her head. No mention of last night's drama. How nice to be young—at least young of a certain type—and carefree, and also so quick to revert to the carefree reset position. He sounded so much better than he had less than what—twelve hours ago?—his voice deeper, all tension gone. But listening to the message resurrected the problem of Nina and whether to keep her in the dark. The fact that Will sounded so good seemed to support closing the book and moving on. Except in a big picture way—

The phone buzzed and the caller's name scrolled across the screen: Palm Coast Bank and Trust.

"Loretta Plansky speaking."

"Hi, Mrs. Plansky. Allison Suarez calling. Assistant manager at the bank."

"Yes, of course. Hi, Allison."

"I was just wondering if you wanted me to close out your account. Are you moving or something like that? I hope it's not something about our service."

"No, I'm not moving. Or closing the account. Why would you think I'd want to do that?"

"Sorry if I've gotten ahead of myself. It's just that you drew the account down to zero last night, so I just wondered, you being such an excellent customer and—"

"I what?"

"Drew down the account. To zero, from a balance of . . . let me see . . . um, sixty-eight thousand, three hundred dollars and twenty-one cents."

"Oh, my goodness, no," Mrs. Plansky said. "There's been a mistake—I only withdrew ten thousand. Ten thousand even. Please check again."

Allison Suarez was silent but Mrs. Plansky could hear her fingers tapping on a keyboard. "I don't see anything relating to the figure you mention, ten thousand."

"But that was the amount. I sent it to my grandson and he assured me he'd received it. Ten thousand, even."

"Sent it how?" said Allison.

For a moment the name wouldn't come to her. Why now, of all times? But then something in her mind—call it her old self—rose to the occasion. "Safemo," she said. "We used Safemo."

"Safemo?"

"He said it was the best."

Another silence. "Mrs. Plansky? Can I get back to you on this?"

"Yes, please. I'll be right here."

Throughout her career, Mrs. Plansky—unlike Norm—had been good at waiting, meaning she'd endured the common periods of suspense in business—waiting to hear if you snagged the bank loan, won the big order, avoided a lawsuit from a rival—without getting too wound up inside. But now, pacing back and forth, feeling a bit light-headed, her heart beating too fast, she was wound up, almost the way she'd been while waiting for some of Norm's test results. There'd been no pacing then, or course, no outward sign at all—how would that have helped him? But now there was no one to help. Withdrew the account to zero? That was crazy. How on earth—

"Enough," Mrs. Plansky said aloud. Enough with the passivity. She grabbed the phone and called Will.

"Hey, Grandma."

"Will, I—"

"Did you get my message?"

"Message? Yes, yes, I did. Thanks. I mean you're welcome. But what I actually want to talk about is last night."

"Last night?"

"That whole incident."

"Incident?"

"Will? Did I wake you? Please stop answering questions with questions. Did you receive the money?"

His voice got gentle. "Grandma? Are you all right?" He laughed a very small laugh. "More questions, sorry. But yes, I got the check. That's why I left the message. I'm very grateful. I should have been more timely. Sorry."

"Check?" said Mrs. Plansky. "There was no check."

"Sure there was, Grandma. The Christmas check—five hundred dollars, so generous. And how you wrote 'merry, merry' on the memo line. That was very—"

"Will! This isn't about the Christmas check. I'm talking about the DUI, the arrest, the bail money, the ten thousand dollars, Safemo, all the rest of it."

"Huh?" said Will.

Mrs. Plansky repeated the whole thing, slowly and carefully. There was a slight pause and then: "Grandma? Are you okay?"

"Stop asking me that. Please, Will. Just, just tell me you received the ten-thousand-dollar transfer last night. And if it somehow turned out to be more than that—much more—that's all right. Although why you wouldn't have—but it's all right. It can all be fixed, easily fixed. I just need to know so I can start the ball rolling."

"Jeez, I don't understand. I don't understand what you're saying. It doesn't make any sense. I apologize but it just doesn't."

"Look, Will, are you in some sort of trouble you didn't tell me about last night? Bigger than the DUI? Or . . . or maybe you can't speak freely right now. Ah. Is that it? If that's the case, and you can't speak freely," she lowered her voice, "give some sign—like clearing your throat, for example."

Mrs. Plansky listened, listened hard, for the sound of Will clearing his throat. She heard nothing.

Finally he spoke. "Grandma? Have you talked to Mom recently?"

"Of course. She was here last night when you called. I asked if you wanted to speak to her and you said no."

"Oh, boy," he said. "Oh, boy."

"Will?"

"I didn't call you last night, Grandma."

"But . . . but you most certainly did." Mrs. Plansky sat down on the edge of the bed, sat down hard, her normally sturdy legs failing her.

"No," Will said. "I called this morning to thank you for the check. I left a message. We didn't talk, not then and not last night. This is the first time we've talked in I don't know how long."

Mrs. Plansky's mind was operating at a furious speed but moving in the same circle, over and over.

"Grandma? Is Mom still there? Can I speak to her?"

"Mom?"

"My mom. Nina."

"Nina? No. They left before I got up. I never sleep in but . . ." Mrs. Plansky caught herself rambling. This was ridiculous. There had to be some explanation, like . . . like Will had taken some sort of drug last night. Hadn't she been reading just recently about a new drug, popular with teenagers, that led to a pleasant delirium of some sort but interfered with short-term memory? She didn't want to accuse him, but was there some decent way of approaching the subject? "I'm getting a little worried about you, Will."

"You're worried about me?"

"Are you feeling all right? Your usual normal self?"

"I'm fine. Except for now I'm worried about you."

"I'm fine, too, darn it!" Then, in a calmer tone, Mrs. Plansky added, "Except for this. I don't get what you're up to. I don't get it at all."

"Grandma! I'm not up to anything. I don't know what to tell you. Has, um, have any of your medications changed?"

Medications? She wasn't on any stupid medications. Well, not strictly true, but she definitely wasn't on any medications that would affect her mental—And then she got what he was suggesting, that she was imagining or fantasizing or hallucinating the whole thing—phone call, DUI, money transfer.

"Will? Are you listening?"

"Yes."

"I'm not making this up. I'm telling you exactly what happened. So whatever the slipup is it's happening on your . . ." At that moment the implication of Will asking to speak to Nina just now began to unfold in her mind. How could he do that without revealing the whole story of his arrest, the very thing he'd wanted so badly to keep from her, badly enough to wake his grandmother in the middle of the night? Therefore the very fact that a conversation with Nina was fine with him now meant . . . oh, God. Another furious circle got going in her mind, but just then she saw a way out, a path forward. "What about your friends? Your friends on the mountain?"

"What about them?"

"Is it possible one of them was playing a trick on you? One of those pranks that gets out of hand?"

Will's voice went—not cold, but a little cooler. "My friends aren't like that. And they don't even know about you, Grandma. Maybe you should, I don't know, like talk to somebody."

"I'm talking to you."

"Someone who can help."

"And who would that—" Another call came in, Allison Suarez Palm Coast Bank and Trust scrolling across her screen. "Hold on, Will. I just need to—" Mrs. Plansky tapped at the phone, tapped again—"Hello? Hello?"—and heard nothing but dial tone. She'd somehow lost both calls.

Mrs. Plansky pressed the little round indented button, the name escaping her, and started over, first calling Allison Suarez.

"This is Allison Suarez at Palm Coast Bank and Trust. Please leave a message and I'll get back to you as soon as I can."

"Allison?" Mrs. Plansky took a breath, went on in a lower register. "I seem to have missed your call. I'd appreciate—"

Another call came in, Nina now, and this time Mrs. Plansky didn't lose the connection.

"Mom? Are you all right? I just had a disturbing call from Will."

"What did he tell you?"

"Well, all about what the two of you were discussing."

"Did he mention . . ." Mrs. Plansky hesitated, then charged ahead. ". . . the DUI situation?"

"Mom? There was no DUI situation. Will wasn't arrested or anything like that."

"Well, he didn't want you to know. That's the whole point."

There was a long silence. Then Nina, her voice extra-gentle and annoying at the same time, said, "Are you okay? Are you feeling all right?"

"I'm fine except for this," said Mrs. Plansky. "And I don't need to hear that question again."

"Fair enough," Nina said. "But Will didn't call you last night, and certainly not from a jailhouse. He wasn't even in Crested Butte. He was on the red-eye from JFK to Denver, coming back from a weekend with his dad."

"But . . . but . . . Ted doesn't live in New York. He's on Hilton Head." That little outburst got free before Mrs. Plansky realized how woeful it was.

Actually, she hadn't realized quite how woeful until Nina said, "That's Teddy, Mom. Ted's in Brooklyn."

Mrs. Plansky moved to sit down on the bed and discovered she was already there. She sat and just breathed. Where was her self-control? Her sense of dignity? Her inner strength? "The bank must have made a mistake, Nina." Did that sound better? Maybe a little flat and affectless, but surely better? "I'll get to the bottom of it and call you back."

"Are you sure? Do you want me to come up there?"

"I'll be fine," said Mrs. Plansky.

"You're sure?"

"Positive. Don't worry about me."

"Okay. Love you, Mom."

"Love you. Bye."

Another call came in right away, the caller ID reading: Newport Asset Management. Newport Asset Management was a midsize financial services firm where the Planskys had all their investments, formerly in several accounts but after the sale of the company and Norm's death they'd all been merged into one—the LP account— for tax and estate planning purposes.

Mrs. Plansky held the phone to her ear. "Loretta Plansky speaking."

ELEVEN

"Hi, Loretta. Jerry Levin here."

"Hi, Jerry." Jerry was a friend of Norm's going all the way back to high school in Providence, had later gone to Wharton, and had been their financial advisor from the beginning of Plansky and Company. Back then Jerry was on his own, but his talent was obvious and he'd climbed high on several corporate ladders, the Planskys staying with him. He was now the number-two person at Newport Asset Management, in charge of big-picture things and running only a few of his oldest clients' accounts.

"How's everything—kids, grandkids?"

"Fine. And yours?"

"Same. The reason I'm calling—always good to hear your voice, of course—is something's come up and I'm hoping you can enlighten me."

Norm, not Mrs. Plansky, had always been the mental leaper, at least in her understanding of their marriage and their partnership, with her more as the mental ballast, but now she made a mental leap of her own, knew what was coming. The money—not just the ten thousand but all of it, the exact number or even an approximation momentarily unavailable—had ended up in the LP account at Newport Asset Management. How? She had no idea. But Jerry was a real smart guy. They'd figure it out.

"Summing up, Loretta, I've known you a long time and I'm having trouble believing you'd suddenly close your account without talking to me. In fact, I don't believe it."

"But I didn't close the account. I haven't even looked at it in weeks."

"Then where's the money?"

"The money?"

"The balance. You drew it down to zero last night."

Mrs. Plansky needed to get out of the bedroom. There was no air in it, all silently sucked out in an instant. She hurried across the floor, stubbing her toe on something but not falling, threw open the slider, stepped onto the patio, and sucked in a deep deep breath.

"Loretta? Still there?"

"Yes, yes. Go on."

"Go on?" Jerry said. "I'm waiting to hear something from you."

"But . . . but Jerry!" She took another breath, tried to get a grip. "I don't understand what's happening. Any of it. And I didn't close the account. Or draw it down. Or . . . anything. I didn't touch it."

"Did you authorize anyone else to have access to the account?"

"No."

"Have you shared the password with anyone?"

"No."

"I hear a little hesitation in that no," Jerry said.

Mrs. Plansky hadn't been aware of that, but it was true that last night she'd shared her Palm Coast Bank and Trust password—!NorManConQuest!—with Will. But . . . but not Will. It was looking very much like it hadn't been Will. And then came a revelation of a very bad kind. She used the same password for pretty much everything, including the LP account at Newport Asset Management. But why not? It got a green check mark, meaning highly secure, every time, and it was unforgettable, at least to her.

"Loretta?"

"You sure?" she said. "Sure the account is empty?"

"I checked and double-checked. And so did my assistant."

"But . . . but where did it go?"

"Damn it, Loretta. I was hoping you'd tell me."

"But I don't know, Jerry. I don't—" Another call came in, Allison Suarez from the bank, getting back to her. "The thing is the same problem seems to be happening at my bank. In fact, the assistant manager's calling right now."

"Can I talk to her?"

"Yes. I'm just not sure how to—"

"Press the accept button."

She pressed it.

"Hello?" said Allison.

"Hello," said Mrs. Plansky. "I've got Jerry Levin on the other line. He . . ." Suddenly she was breathless again, almost like this normal sort of business introduction was too much for her.

"With whom am I speaking?" Jerry said.

"Allison Suarez, Palm Coast Bank and Trust."

"Nice meeting you. Jerry Levin, Newport Asset Management. I'm Mrs. Plansky's longtime financial advisor and also a friend. I gather there's been some irregular activity in her account with you."

"It was emptied last night," Allison said. "Apparently without Loretta's knowledge. I'm calling now to ask her—to ask you, Loretta—if you've ever shared your password with anyone."

"No," she said. "Not, that is, till last night."

"Last night?" said Jerry and Allison together, in a sort of frightening harmony. Mrs. Plansky still didn't really understand but at that moment she knew the worst. Not that she believed it. She just knew.

"I gave it to my grandson over the phone. Norman Conquest with two—" She stopped herself. "But . . . but it wasn't him. I get that now. Almost certainly not him."

Silence. Then Jerry said, "Do you use the same password with us?"

"Yes," said Mrs. Plansky, her voice sounding very small, like a four-year-old caught red-handed.

"May I speak to your grandson?" Jerry said. "Will, isn't it?"

"Yes," said Mrs. Plansky, "but don't tell him . . ." She searched

for the best way to put it. "Anything," she explained. "Don't tell
Will anything." She gave Jerry the number.

Another silence. When Jerry spoke again his voice was gentle.
"You don't want the family to know? Or you prefer to tell them
yourself?"

What she wanted was for this—whatever it was—not to be true.
"Both," she said.

"I suppose I don't really need to talk to him at all," Jerry said.
"Water under . . ." He left that part of it unfinished.

"Mr. Levin?" Allison said. "Has Loretta mentioned Safemo yet?"
"What's that?"

"Safemo." Allison spelled it for him. A discussion started up,
a technical and very important discussion with Jerry and Allison
doing the talking and Mrs. Plansky listening. At first. But then
her attention was drawn to some movement in the greenery across
the lake, and an alligator appeared, not particularly big—although
hard to be sure from this distance—and the first one she'd seen
since moving to the condo. The alligator, in no hurry, moved to the
shoreline and slipped into the water, disappearing without a ripple.

Although there was a ripple, an icy one, down her spine.

Jerry caught a flight that afternoon, arriving in time for a six thirty
meeting in a conference room at Palm Coast Bank and Trust, twenty
minutes from Mrs. Plansky's condo. She'd spent the afternoon in a kind
of trance, first indoors, an indoors that now suddenly seemed insub-
stantial to her, like a stage set made of cardboard, and then outdoors,
standing by the lake, eyes on the water. After some time— possibly an
hour or more, a pair of flamingos—unusually far north—flew down
and stood in the shallows, not far from her. In *Casablanca*—a movie
she and Norm had watched a dozen times, maybe two dozen—Rick
tells Ilsa that the problems of three little people don't amount to a hill
of beans in this crazy world, and every time that line rolled around
Norm would shake his head no. Thinking of the alligator lurking

down there somewhere, Mrs. Plansky clapped her hands and called, "Shoo, shoo." The flamingos paid no attention and were still standing there doing nothing, each on one leg, when she left for the bank. Other than that, all she remembered of the afternoon was a call from Nina and several texts, all of which she ignored. Will must have talked to Nina—how had she not foreseen that?—and it was possible that other family members knew. But what? Only that she was caught up in some sort of misunderstanding involving the loss or failure to locate $10,000, possibly somewhat more, but not . . . everything. And wasn't there still a chance that was the bottom line? A misunderstanding, some sort of computer mix-up? Didn't they happen all the time? Just last week, for example, when they'd had to abort a space flight on account of a software glitch? One of the bartenders at the club had taken his kids out of school to go down and watch. So there was still hope, reasonable hope. In the bank parking lot, Mrs. Plansky leaned in toward the rearview mirror to put on her eyeliner, but her hand wasn't steady enough.

Jerry, Allison, and a woman she didn't know were already at the conference table when she walked in. Jerry came right over and gave her a hug. She wasn't important enough as a client for him to have come all this way and at once. This was about friendship, his and hers, but even more than that, his and Norm's. She hugged him back, an imitation of a friendly hug—the realization shamed her—to keep herself from an anxious clinging. Nonsense like that had to be avoided.

"Good to see you, Jerry," she said in a totally normal voice. "And thanks so much for coming."

"Of course," Jerry said. "And I want you to meet Senior Special Agent Rains from the FBI. She flew down with me."

Senior Special Agent Rains, who'd been sitting at the table and going through a folder, rose and shook hands. She was a tall woman, early forties, in a dark pantsuit and with her hair in a tight bun.

"Nice to meet you," said Agent Rains. "Sorry you're going through this."

"Thanks," Mrs. Plansky said, when she wanted to say was, *Does the very fact you're here rule out the computer glitch escape clause?*

"Agent Rains is with the cyber division," Jerry said. "We've worked together before."

"Call me Sheila," Agent Rains said. "And before we get started I'm a big fan of your toaster knives."

"Oh, well, we no longer . . . thanks," said Mrs. Plansky.

They sat at the table. Agent Rains opened her folder, took out a pen. "First I need to confirm something. According to Allison, the mode of transfer was something called Safemo. Is that correct?"

"Yes," Mrs. Plansky said.

Agent Rains made a check mark. "Okay, run me through it— everything you remember from the call."

For a moment Mrs. Plansky couldn't recall one single thing about it. Well, except for Safemo. Like a huge neon sign it flashed in her head: SAFEMO! SAFEMO! SAFEMO! Then she became aware of the gazes, all on her, and all of them smart. And with this in common as well: they were waiting for this elderly person to catch up. Even Jerry, who was the same age, a third grade classmate of Norm's. Then it hit her that whatever was going on, whatever had been done, done to her, had been done to Norm as well. That realization was sickening but it kicked her brain into gear. She owed him her best.

"It was the middle of the night and I was asleep," she said. "A phone call came in from my grandson, Will, in Colorado." She gave them all an angry look. "It said so right on the screen. He told me he'd been arrested on a DUI charge and needed money for bail and getting his car back." And from there, Mrs. Plansky sailed right through it, even maybe dramatizing a little—as though telling a made-up story for entertainment purposes—when she reached the password part: "'And presto, Grandma. Already vanished forever. Thank you, Grandma!'" Mrs. Plansky looked at them one by one— Agent Rains, Allison, Jerry—in a challenging way, half-aware that the heavy artillery was warming up in the silo, for the first time in ages. Challenging—as though the three of them were somehow responsible! Good grief. She amped herself down and came quietly to the end, at which point she realized she'd lowered her head. Mrs. Plansky raised it back up.

The three of them looked from one to the other. Agent Rains spoke first. "What was the phone connection like?"

"Not so clear," said Mrs. Plansky. "But I could hear perfectly well." She stopped herself from adding, *My hearing's good! My eyesight's good! Even my sense of smell!*

Agent Rains nodded. "Prior to this call, when was the last time you spoke to Will?"

"I've been trying to remember," Mrs. Plansky said. Oh, how she wanted that one back! She saw the looks in their eyes, subtle, hidden, but confirmation looks, for sure. Wait—hadn't she actually remembered it already, somewhere along the way? Ah-ha! "And it was—it must have been on his birthday in July."

"July the what?" said Agent Rains.

Every grandmother in America knew the birthdates of all her grandchildren. That was Grammy 101. But all she knew for sure was that it couldn't be the fourth. That would have been impossible to forget. "It's written down at home," she said. "I could get back to you."

"It's not important," Agent Rains said. "Call it eight months, tops. Did it occur to you at any time that it might not be Will on the other end?"

"Of course not! Why would I have . . ." At that point—rather late in the game—Mrs. Plansky's mind flagged a moment from her conversation with—what to call him? The Will impersonator? The moment and suddenly very clear in her mind, like a ray of sunshine had suddenly poked through a thick fog: "Yo. It's me, Grandma, Will. Your grandson Will." That greeting followed by her silent reaction: *Right away she knew he didn't sound good, his voice higher than normal, maybe nervous about something, although since they hadn't spoken in some time she couldn't be sure.* My God. From the very top she'd been suspicious, but she'd rationalized it away. And even more, she'd tried to settle him down a bit, making a little joke: "I'm aware of the relationship." How shameful! Mrs. Plansky felt herself flushing, a sort of bodily heat wave starting at neck level and rising up.

Meanwhile Agent Rains was waiting for an answer. Mrs. Plansky was good at looking people in the eye. It came naturally to her. But now, despite giving it everything she had, Mrs. Plansky couldn't quite do it. At that point Allison—whom Mrs. Plansky didn't know well, ignorant of basic facts like whether she was married or had kids—although today she wore no wedding band and looked tired, so possibly a single mom—spoke up.

"Whatever's going on I think it's important we all acknowledge Loretta is blameless."

"Totally," said Jerry.

Agent Rains nodded the smallest perceptible yes.

Mrs. Plansky's gaze rose the last millimeter or two and met hers. "In retrospect, it might have occurred to me, but not at the time."

Agent Rains made a note. "Let's circle back to Safemo. Had you ever heard of it?"

"No."

"How did he explain it?"

"That it was one of those PayPal things."

"So why not PayPal itself?"

"Safemo was better."

"In what way?"

"The vanishing, as I already mentioned." And something else, something about . . . "Encryption. Before the vanishing the whole thing was encrypted. Plus—plus some percent of their profits went to saving—went to a charity for whales."

Agent Rains' pen, which had been writing busily away, came to a stop. She was looking down, so Mrs. Plansky couldn't be sure she'd caught a flash of amusement in her eyes or imagined it.

"God almighty," Jerry said. "Diabolical."

"Exactly," said Allison.

"So you're saying that's not true?" Mrs. Plansky said. "The whale part?"

Agent Rains looked up, her eyes expressionless. "The whale part? Unlikely but possible, and anything else you can recall about Safemo will be valuable."

"I can't think of anything else," Mrs. Plansky said. "But—" She was struck by an obvious thought she should have had hours ago. "But shouldn't we get in touch with them? Right away?"

Agent Rains seemed a bit surprised. Jerry and Allison exchanged a look that defied Mrs. Plansky's interpretation, but showed no signs of enthusiasm for her idea.

"Get in touch with Safemo?" said Agent Rains.

"Sure," said Mrs. Plansky. "In case the money's still on their books. Or—" She made what she thought was a little joke. "Or do the books vanish, too?"

No one laughed. No one seemed to get it at all. They did that looking at one another routine again, a routine of which Mrs. Plansky had had more than enough.

"I'm afraid it's probably the second one, Loretta," Jerry said.

"What second one?" Mrs. Plansky said.

"The books vanish, too," said Agent Rains.

Ah. She should have known, but so much of the digital world was a mystery to her. There was plenty she could do no problem— linking, attaching, downloading—but whenever she strayed off a known path, usually by accident, it was time to call in IT. Of course in retirement there was no IT. The good news was that the fact of the books vanishing was at least an indication that Safemo was real. A hideous thought to the contrary had been snaking around in her mind.

"Still," she said, "wouldn't it be worthwhile to get in touch with them?"

"With who, again?" said Agent Rains.

"Safemo," Mrs. Plansky said, unable to keep her impatience bottled up. "If this in fact is all a—" She made herself utter the word.

"Scam. If it is all a scam, then shouldn't we—or you, Agent Rains, the FBI, after all—be asking them, or pressuring them, whatever it takes, to tell us who was on the other end? And—and wait! Jerry! Oh my God, Jerry! Are you saying my Newport account got rolled up into the same transaction?"

There was a bit of a silence. Then Jerry said, "I thought you understood."

"But how could that happen?"

"There are a number of ways," Agent Rains said. "A number of known ways, plus unknown ones as well. But the simplest way would be the password. Jerry tells me you used the same password for the Newport account and the Palm Coast account. True?"

Mrs. Plansky nodded, a defeated little motion she thought of repeating more forcefully. But at the moment she lacked the strength. She made herself do it anyway.

"That would be it, then," Agent Rains said. "They got lucky. It happens, actually a lot. Have we come up with a total? For the record?"

"Ours is sixty-eight thousand, three hundred dollars and twenty-one cents," Allison said. Somehow the fact that she didn't need to check any notes, just reeled it right off from memory, made it—made the whole thing—incontrovertible, undeniable, final.

"As for us." Jerry took a sheet of paper from an inside suit jacket pocket and donned reading glasses. "Three million, six hundred and ninety-nine thousand, and . . ." He bit his lip and put the paper away. "And change. The portfolio was approximately sixty-five percent equity, twenty-five bonds, five cash, five miscellaneous."

"Making three million eight, give or take," said Agent Rains. She turned to Mrs. Plansky. "Thinking back, did anything in the call suggest where it was coming from? Did the caller have an accent, for example?"

Mrs. Plansky thought about that. In retrospect, in oh so clever retrospect, he'd sounded like Conrad Veidt or Arnold Schwarzenegger or Maurice Chevalier or . . . She let go of all that, and thought again. "Maybe not an accent, so much. More like he was a bit stilted at times. But I interpreted it as Will growing up, developing a sort of detached, ironic sense of humor. If you see what I mean." One quick glance and she knew they did not.

"Not my area," said Allison, "but re the stocks and bonds, is it possible—"

Agent Rains interrupted. "Same as cash in terms of ease of unloading. I'm sure that's taken place already, through an offshore broker, online broker, crypto broker, dark web broker, or some combo. But it's a nice thought."

Allison made a motion like she was going to reach over and touch Mrs. Plansky's hand. Mrs. Plansky put her hands in her lap, out of sight.

"Where do we go from here?" Jerry said.

"First," Agent Rains said, "I'm of course opening a file on this matter and the bureau will devote its full resources to finding out who did this, bringing them to justice, and recovering what was stolen. But as you know, Jerry, and as I'm sure Allison knows, this particular type of case is very difficult and our record of success at hitting any of the three targets I mentioned is not good."

"What three targets?" said Mrs. Plansky.

There was a silence, and in that silence Mrs. Plansky's flush, which had receded, came flowing back. Quietly, Jerry said, "Finding, punishing, recovering."

"Especially two and three," said Agent Rains. "Most especially three."

Mrs. Plansky got the feeling that Agent Rains was wrapping things up, or had even wrapped them up already, and was about to leave. Agent Rains didn't seem warm or charming but she was strong and tough. Mrs. Plansky didn't want her to go, didn't want to be alone. Her mind thrashed around desperately and came up with something.

"But—" Mrs. Plansky lowered her voice, restarted. "Aren't you forgetting Safemo? Isn't that a . . . a clue at least?"

Agent Rains nodded. "It's all we've got to work with, if it still exists."

"I don't understand."

"Safemo might have been a onetime thing created for this specific purpose and"—Agent Rains made quotation marks with her fingers—"vanishing at completion. But that's where I'll start."

She rose, turning out to be smaller than Mrs. Plansky had first thought, shook hands with everyone, and gave Mrs. Plansky her card. "I'll be in touch. And if you think of anything, or if there's more contact, call right away."

"More contact from the same people?" Mrs. Plansky said. She heard the fear in her voice but could do nothing about it.

"Highly unlikely, unless they're very stupid."

What would that make me? thought Mrs. Plansky.

Jerry walked her to her car. It was a nice evening, a gentle breeze carrying the smell of the sea. Mrs. Plansky again recalled the time she'd overcome the rip tide and pulled Jack to safety. Really? That was the same person as her now?

"Thanks for coming," Mrs. Plansky said. "And for setting all this up so well."

"Please," said Jerry. "And Loretta? I have to ask. How are your finances, other than this? If nothing is recovered, is what I mean. Do you have other holdings of some kind? Other investments? Accounts somewhere else? I won't be offended." He smiled a quick smile. Jerry was a lovely man.

Mrs. Plansky hardened herself—inside, invisibly. "Not to worry," she said.

TWELVE

"It's not a tragedy," Mrs. Plansky said to herself out loud on the drive home from Palm Coast Bank and Trust. No one died. No one even got sick. She owned her condo outright, also her car, the mileage still pretty low. Actually, Mrs. Plansky had no idea what the mileage was. She checked the dashboard display—so very complicated now that she eyed it carefully for the first time—and couldn't find it right away. Ah, that had to be it: 17,842. The car itself was three years old, making annual mileage six thousand, give or take, and with cars these days lasting so long it was conceivable she might never need another. How nice when the numbers were working for you! She and Norm had had many moments like that, for example for a full month after the *Wall Street Journal* included the Plansky Toaster Knife in a feature on kitchen gadgets in its weekend On Duty section.

The Green Turtle Club went by on her left, its sign a neon turtle upright on its hind legs, and raising a glass. She hit the turn signal, pulled off the highway and into the Green Turtle parking lot. "I'm going to go in," she said, again talking to herself aloud, which wasn't her at all. Or was it? Had she been talking to herself lately and simply not noticed? "Never mind. I'll sit down, order a drink, be a normal person being normal." Drinks, of course, cost money. She pictured herself ordering a drink in one of those Belle Epoque spaces on the *Titanic,* after the collision but before the realization. Whoa. She was making herself grandiose and ridiculous. Lucky for her there were no witnesses. But now the numbers that weren't working for her, just discussed in the conference room, came flooding back, and Mrs. Plansky did not go into the Green Turtle Club for a drink, instead merging carefully back onto the highway and heading home.

Mrs. Plansky sat at her kitchen table, a single row of ceiling can lights switched on and the rest of the condo in darkness. She had a pen, a calculator, a sheet of paper, a glass of water. A glass of water at first, and then a very small glass of brandy, as well. She made three columns: *Assets, Liabilities, Income.* Her mind was humming. This was work, and she hadn't worked in some time, possibly too long. Make that obviously too long. Life without work could be so vague. There were vagaries in work, too, but also specifics. She would cling to specifics. Under income she wrote: *Social Security*. And then paused. Mrs. Plansky did not know the amount of her monthly payment, could not even make a rough guess. Didn't that say so much about then, now, and the future? She put her hands to her face. There was a shift in her emotional bedrock and an eruption of tears threatened to get loose. She steeled her inner self, sat up straight, and under Social Security wrote: *TK.*

What else? When she and Norm sold out, the only sticking point in the negotiations was the patent issue, not the patent for the knife itself, which had to be included in any sensible deal, but other patents in Norm's name based on his technology but for other potential devices. Norm had wanted to hang on to them.

"But why?" she'd said. "Are we retiring or not?"

"Maybe someone down the line will be interested."

"What line?"

"Our genetic line."

Which at that time, as now, had consisted of Nina, Jack, Emma, and Will.

"Such as who?"

"TBD."

In the end, the buyer had kicked in a couple hundred thousand or so—the exact figure not coming to her—and Norm had given up the patents. Too bad. Otherwise TBD could have been her, starting tomorrow. She sat back. What would that be like, doing it all over again, and with Norm, now sort of hovering above? Mrs. Plansky felt a slight twinge in her new hip, the first in months. Her phone rang. It was Nina. She let it ring. Tomorrow would be a good time for explaining. Tonight was for figuring out the explanation, a partial explanation, as non-alarming as possible, but wasn't keeping it partial justified by the fact that whatever had happened was not resolved? The FBI was working on it, had just started. There were people, flesh and blood people, who had done this. Safemo was not just ones and zeros in chains of code. It was people. People occupied physical space, somewhere on the globe. They could be found.

Mrs. Plansky picked up her pen and took a long look at the heading marked *Assets*. Beneath it she wrote: *Condo. Car. Jewelry*. She took a sip of brandy, found the glass was empty. She moved onto *Liabilities. Utilities, gas, food*—none of which she had exact figures for. *Condo Fees $1,000/mo. Club membership—$1,200, due in June. Club dining monthly minimum—$300. Gifts, tips, etc*. Mrs. Plansky had no idea what her customary figure would be for that. If you could afford material giving you did lots of it, and not just to family members. What else was the point?

She made a subheading under *Liabilities: Family*. Not that family could ever be a liability—she was using the word strictly in the accounting sense. She stressed that to herself and only then added a sub-sub heading: *Promises:* She began with Nina and the loan thingy: *$250K, matchmaking start-up*. Then came *Jack: $750K*, not exactly promised, but since he's coming all this way to send him back with nothing at all would be . . .

Mrs. Plansky left the Jack entry just like that and moved on to: *Dad*. Oh, boy. She rose, went to her bedroom, opened the desk drawer containing all the files, took out the folder labeled *Dad,* and returned to the kitchen table. Dad's folder included some smaller subfolders, all labeled in Mrs. Plansky's distinctive handwriting. She hadn't known it was distinctive until Norm pointed it out. "No one forms the letters like that. Totally clear but so plump and sexy." Her handwriting was sexy to him. Who had it luckier than her? Mrs. Plansky fell into a brief reverie, or possibly dead zone. She snapped out of it and opened the Arcadia Gardens subfolder. Dad was now receiving tier-two care at $7,500 a month, not including extras like his bar tab, snack tab, excursion tab, and several other tabs unnamed and simply grouped under Tabs—Misc. There'd also been a nonrefundable entrance fee of $100,000. And now there was this talk of moving him down to the third floor where the cost was $10,000 a month more. Surely that couldn't be right. He must have meant the cost was $10,000, not $10,000 more, meaning it was actually only $2,500 more—that "only" applying only in a former time, like yesterday. Mrs. Plansky took another sip of brandy, found the glass still empty. She returned to the bedroom, removed her jewelry box from the safe, brought it into the kitchen, and then just stood there. Did she really want to go through the jewelry box right now in this dark, silent condo? She pictured herself doing that, an old lady bent over a little pile of bright things, speculating.

Mrs. Plansky left the jewelry box unopened, stripped off her clothes, and went to bed. Her body was inert, exhausted. Her mind went round and round, unstoppable, trying out various do-overs. After who knew how long, she realized she hadn't put on her nightie. She always wore a nightie to bed. Right away, she knew that if she didn't wear a nightie tonight she was closing the door—in some cosmic way—to things, specifically this thing, ever being right again. Through sheer mental effort she forced her inert form to rise, don the nightie, and while she was at it brush her teeth, floss, the whole dental shebang, also never neglected before bed. She did all that in the darkness, no way risking the sight of herself in the mirror.

But back in bed, sleep would not come, not even with her in the twisted K position. After what might have been hours she hit rock bottom. Rock bottom was the abrupt realization that in her stupidity, her sloppiness, her vulnerability—and worse, because of her unacknowledged but now so obvious love of the power that came with being the giver—she'd failed Norm. What a pathetically easy mark she'd been! Safemo must have been laughing his or her head off. And now everything she and Norm had built, not just the money but way more important, his trust in her, was—poof. The tears came then. Mrs. Plansky couldn't stop them, didn't even try.

You might think that after a cry like that at least sleep would come at last, but it did not. Instead she just lay there, mind now as inert as body. But not quite. One little idea popped up in her mind, like a creature in a moonscape: the OxyContin, namely the Oxy-Contin left over from the hip replacement. She actually hadn't taken any during her recovery, not even on night one, but wasn't now the time for an Oxy, or two, max, to get her to sleep? Mrs. Plansky was on the point of making herself get up again when she remembered the story of that little bottle, namely how it had disappeared following the spring break night she'd hosted Will and that buddy of his, on their way to the buddy's folks's place in Lauderdale.

The sketchy buddy. Mrs. Plansky couldn't recall his name but somehow she could retrieve a clear image of his face: scruffy beard, weak chin, evasive eyes. And a mumbler. What was more she could picture him texting, his soft, childlike fingers just flying over the screen. A computer adept? He was the type, for sure. Smart enough to come up with Safemo and execute the plan? That remained to be seen, but the moral question was settled. The buddy was already a proven thief.

Mrs. Plansky drifted off.

Someone was knocking on the door. Mrs. Plansky opened her eyes. Her bedroom was full of light. She hadn't closed the curtains before going to bed? That was strange. How could she have neglected to—

And then it all came back to her. She got light-headed and came close to sinking to the floor.

Meanwhile the knocking.

"Coming. Just a minute. Coming."

She hurried out of the bedroom, down the hall, into the kitchen, took in the sight of the kitchen table and everything on it—papers, folders, jewelry box.

Knock knock. "Mom? Are you there? It's me."

Nina. Nina? Wasn't she supposed to be in Boca? Mrs. Plansky took a hesitant step or two toward the front door, then spun around, half-running to the bathroom. Nina was not going to see her like this. Mrs. Plansky raced through the regime of making herself presentable—ending up in a tennis outfit only because it was on the nearest hanger, and at some point dabbing on lipstick in a muted shade, although no other makeup—then tore her quilt off the bed, threw it over all the stuff on the kitchen table, and opened the front door, remembering almost too late to put a smile on her face.

And there was Nina, Nina with a worried look on her face. But not alone. Standing with her was Jack, also with a worried look. Mrs. Plansky had to put a stop to the worry at once. The mere sight of Jack helped with that. She hadn't seen him in months and months—such a handsome man, still young or youngish, and he'd been lovely to look at from birth. Also funny, from a very early age. During toilet training he'd started giving his poops names, depending on their size—Babar, Stuart Little, etcetera. Mrs. Plansky felt her smile turning somewhat real. She opened her arms and hugged Jack tight.

"What a nice surprise!" she said, drawing them both inside. "To what do I owe it?"

"Hey!" Jack said. "Aren't you still my mom?"

"What a question!" said Mrs. Plansky. "Of course you don't need a reason. Come on in. Coffee, anybody?"

"But we do have a bit of a reason," Nina said glancing around as they moved toward the kitchen. "Are you on your way to the club?"

"Not right away," said Mrs. Plansky.

"Oh, good. Because Jack and I are a bit concerned about this situation that came up with Will."

"No need for concern," Mrs. Plansky said. "We're in the midst of sorting it all out now." She got busy with the coffeemaker.

"Sorting what all, exactly?" Jack said.

"That's part of the concern," said Nina. "We're a bit mystified."

"It's just a banking snafu," Mrs. Plansky said. Where was the coffeepot? Had she left it in the dining room, after the dinner with Dad, Nina, and Matthew? She went looking for it, calling over her shoulder, "These things take time."

The coffeepot stood on the sideboard, still partly full. How careless of her to have forgotten it in the cleanup. She picked it up, took it back to the kitchen.

Nina and Jack were standing at the table, now uncovered. Jack was holding the quilt and gazing at her paperwork, folders, jewelry box. Nina had a sheet of paper and was reading what was written on it—in plump, sexy letters—her eyes going back and forth, back and forth, very fast. She looked up.

"Mom? What's all this?"

"Nothing. Nothing important." She made a move to take the quilt from Jack and re-cover everything on the table, but stopped herself in time. "Just some paperwork, that's all."

Nina put down the sheet of paper, opened the jewelry box. "Mom? What's going on?"

"I already explained! Please can we talk about something else?"

Nina and Jack were watching her in a way they never had and that she didn't like one little bit. She got a bit angry at her own children.

"You could help, you know." Oh, God, had those words really come out of her mouth?

They looked stunned.

"Of course," Nina said.

"How?" said Jack.

"How?" And now she was out of control and couldn't stop. "How about giving me the name of Will's friend for starters?"

"What friend?" Nina said.

"The one who stayed here on spring break."

"Luke Easterbrook? But why? Did you want to send a card or something?"

"What are you talking about?"

"His accident."

"What's this?" Jack said.

"A friend of Will's from Hilton Head. He was in a terrible wreck last month. He's still in the hospital—they had to wire his jaw shut, among many other things."

"They wired his jaw shut?" Mrs. Plansky said.

"Just for now until his face heals. It's not that unusual, Mom. And they say he's going to be all right in the end."

But Safemo. Some god above kept that remark unspoken.

"I don't get it, Mom," Jack said. "What sort of help did you want with him?"

"I—" Mrs. Plansky began, but before some new stupidity got loose, there was another knock on the door, as though a stage farce was gathering speed. She answered it.

Another female/male duo stood on the front step. The woman she knew: Agent Sheila Rains. The man was new.

"Hi, Loretta," Agent Rains said. "This is Agent Gatling, one of our technicians. He'd like to examine your phone—the one the call came in on."

Nina and Jack approached from behind.

"Mom?"

Mrs. Plansky stepped aside. Soon Agent Gatling was plugging her phone into some device he'd brought with him and Agent Rains was telling the kids the whole story. Mrs. Plansky sat at the table in her tennis outfit, feeling heavy and dim, and hardly spoke a word.

THIRTEEN

"Do you know what Steve Jobs said?" Uncle Dragomir asked.

They were in the Cambio office at Club Presto, Dinu and Romeo called in early by Uncle Dragomir, Timbo pouring coffee. Neither Romeo nor Dinu offered up an answer. Romeo, so brilliant, may have known and simply opted for caution. As for Dinu, the name Steve Jobs was new to him.

"Look at them, Timbo," Uncle Dragomir said. "Bleg and bleg," *bleg* being their word for *dolt*. "Tell them what Steve Jobs said."

"*A* bosses hire A workers," Timbo said, adding extra cream to Uncle Dragomir's mug. "B bosses hire C workers."

"Exactly," said Uncle Dragomir. "Timbo here is an A worker, a master of his craft." All on its own, Dinu's tongue curled around in his mouth and felt the new tooth. "Am I an A boss?"

"Yes," said Dinu.

"A plus," said Romeo.

"You're an asshole, Romeo. You're both assholes. The moment you slide down from A, the moment I even sniff the first stink of you sliding down, you're out on the street. But not before Timbo and Marius tune you up a little bit. Timbo knows how to tune up. He's a gypsy, don't forget."

"Partly," said Timbo. "One grandmother."

"More than enough to have tuning up in the blood. You getting all this, gentlemen?"

Dinu and Romeo nodded yes.

"Pen," Uncle Dragomir said.

Timbo handed him a gold pen. Uncle Dragomir scratched off a quick note on a pad, tore off the top sheet, handed it to Romeo. "Go see this guy. He's knows you're coming."

"Who's the guy?" Dinu said when they were outside.

"It just says Mircea." Romeo showed the Dinu the note. *Mircea 96 Ion Ghica Road*. Ion Ghica Road was in the industrial part of town, across the river, about two kilometers away. They walked. A cold day but sunny, the river less brown than usual and a swan out in the middle, going with the flow.

"You should ask Tassa on a date," Romeo said.

"Yeah?"

"She likes you."

"How do you know?"

"She told me."

"She said that? 'I like Dinu'?"

"Not in those words."

"What were the words?"

"'He's not so bad.'"

Dinu gave Romeo a push.

"Whoa. I can't swim."

"No?" Dinu was a good swimmer. His father had taught him when Dinu was three. It was just about the only memory of his father he had. "Paddle like a doggie, little guy. Paddle like a doggie!"

"Although from this height," Romeo was saying, "I'd probably be dead as soon as I hit the water."

"You think?"

"Sure. From here the density differential between solid and liquid is immaterial."

Dinu took a sidelong glance at Romeo. He was picking a pimple on his chin, one of those whiteheads. Romeo had an A-plus-type mind, no question about that.

Ninety-six Ion Ghica Road turned out to be a garage, just a few steps past the cement works and not far from the sprawl of the old soot-stained Communist factories. The bay door was open and a car was up on the lift, a man working underneath, his head in shadows, his arms thick and oil-stained. The whole inside of the bay was oil-stained, the walls smoke-blackened, cigarette butts and food wrappers on the floor, but the car on the lift was a Mercedes 500, shiny and new.

The man moved out from under the lift, a stocky guy with short bristly hair on his head and face, and a bristly expression in his gaze.

"We're looking for Mircea," Romeo said.

"Feast your eyes. You Dragomir's boys?"

"Well, uh," Romeo said.

"He sent us," said Dinu, showing off this new improvising skill of his.

"Then you're his boys," Mircea said. "Come."

He led them to the back of the bay, where a tarp lay over something with two big bumps underneath. "Voilà," said Mircea in what sounded to Dinu like good French, not unusual in this part of the country. He whisked away the tarp, revealing two shiny although perhaps not new motorcycles.

"What's this?" Romeo said.

"You blind?" said Mircea. "Yamaha XT660Z, times two. Four stroke, four valve, fuel-injected, rebuilt with these two hands, so better than the original." Mircea held up his hands, gigantic for a man his size. "And brand-new tires, almost." He gave the nearest tire a soft kick. "So who's got seniority?"

"What's that?" Dinu said.

"I do," said Romeo. "I've got seniority."

"Then pick one out," Mircea said. "Red or black?"

"Are they the same price?" Romeo said.

"Huh?"

"The two? Same price for each or is one more than the other?"

Mircea squinted at him. "You making fun of me?"

"No, sir." Romeo put his hand to his chest.

"Then you're slow." Mircea turned to Dinu. "You, pretty boy. Are you also slow?"

"They're gifts?" Dinu said.

"Presto!" said Mircea. "Get it? Presto!"

Dinu and Romeo both got it but they didn't laugh quite as hard as Mircea.

"So?" he said to Romeo. "What'll it be? Red or black?"

"But I don't know how."

"To choose?"

"To ride."

"You don't know how to ride a bike?"

"Not a motorbike."

"What the hell? How old are you?"

"Sixteen."

"Then your buddy here can show you."

"I don't know how, either," Dinu said.

"What the hell?" Mircea said. "What happens when the Russians come?"

"The Russians?" Romeo said.

"What are pussies like you going to do about it?"

"They won't come," said Romeo.

"We'll fight them," Dinu said.

Mircea nodded. "Pick one out, Dinu."

Dinu picked red. Mircea sold them each a used helmet, cheap, and gave them a quick riding lesson. Romeo, on the black 660Z, was very wobbly but Dinu had a feel for it right away, like he'd been born in the saddle. They rode off, across the bridge and back

to the new part of the old town—*new* meaning it dated only from
the defeat of the Ottomans—Romeo in joy mixed with terror and
Dinu in pure joy. As they took the ramp off the bridge and onto
the boulevard, a guy with longish dark hair and a close-cropped
white beard turned to watch. Dinu thought he'd seen him before
but couldn't think where or when.

On Saturday, Dinu took Tassa for a ride on the bike. The word *date*
did not come up. It was just a ride. Dinu picked Tassa up on the
street outside her apartment block, a Soviet-style apartment block
just like his. She was so beautiful standing against the background
of the shabby building that he could hardly look at her. Tassa had
always been nice-looking, but now this? What was going on?

"I've never been on a motorcycle before," she said.

"Just hop up behind me. First put this on." He gave her Romeo's
helmet, borrowed for the day. Romeo hadn't ridden again after the
first time. Dinu rode every chance he got.

Tassa donned the helmet and hopped up. "With this helmet on,
my head will be fine when the rest of me's destroyed."

Dinu laughed and revved the engine. "Nothing's going to happen."

"Where do I put my hands?"

"Do that raising-the-roof motion."

Tassa laughed and put her hands around his waist. They roared
out of town, headed for Tassa's older sister's place, a farm in the
foothills, about forty kilometers away. There was hardly any talking,
just Tassa saying "turn here," or "second right," the route going
from wide two-lane pavement with lots of traffic to narrow two-
lane pavement with less, to gravel and dirt with hardly anyone on
it except for an occasional tractor, horse-drawn carts, and barking
dogs who chased after them. At first, Tassa's hands felt awkward to
him, but she changed the position a bit, maybe simply relaxing, and
after that things felt right, like the three of them—Dinu, Tassa, the
660Z—were one. She hummed to herself.

"What's that song?" Dinu said, raising his voice.

"It's American," Tassa said, practically in his ear. "'Eight Miles High.'"

Tassa's sister and her husband lived in a small, drafty farmhouse and grew grapes to sell to the winemakers. There wasn't much to do at this time of year so they were taking their two small boys to a movie that afternoon. First they had a nice lunch—black bread sandwiches with sausage and cabbage, plus a red wine made from grapes grown on vines they could see through the window, just one small pour each for Dinu and Tassa. Then Dinu took each of the boys for a ride on the bike, their dad holding them.

"You and Tassa are in the same class?" the dad said.

"Only she's at the top and I'm at the bottom."

"Really? The bottom?"

"The middle."

"Any idea what you want to do when you graduate?"

"Not really. Maybe something with English."

"You speak English?"

"A little," Dinu said in English. "But it's starting to come to me."

"Nice bike," said the dad after a little silence.

After the family left for the cinema, Dinu and Tassa took a walk through the silent vineyard, the vines all bare and the ground hard. They came to the guest cottage, a very old, very small structure with a thatched roof and a view across a valley toward the mountains, the most distant ones snow covered, a view that could be easily seen from the lumpy but clean couch by the window. After a while things began to happen on that couch, but fairly far down that road Tassa put a stop to them.

"What?" Dinu said.

"That's enough for now."

"What do you mean?"

"We have time."

"But we have time right now."

"You know that's not what I mean," Tassa said.

"Then what do you mean?"

"What's hard has more value. That's what I mean."

"So then this has value!"

Tassa laughed. "Something to look forward to." She bent her middle finger, pressed the nail against her thumb and then released, a surprisingly forceful and perfectly aimed flick that changed the conversation.

FOURTEEN

"Loretta! So good to see you!" Sylvie Benoit hurried out from behind her desk in her beautiful office, a wonder of contemporary design that had the effect of having been assembled from light alone. She gave Mrs. Plansky a kiss on both cheeks. "You look just great!"

Mrs. Plansky, who'd checked herself in the rearview mirror on the drive down to Fort Lauderdale, knew that wasn't true. "Well," she said, "you sure do."

They sat on a couch by a bay window, Middle River and all the boat traffic far below, the couch insubstantial-looking but perfectly adapted to the human body, at least Mrs. Plansky's. An assistant poured tea, also offering a plate of a kind of French pastries Mrs. Plansky liked, but she found she couldn't remember the name and just said, "They look great but no thanks."

"Oh, try one," Sylvie said, helping herself. "You won't be disappointed. They're from Joel LeMaire—do you know him?"

"No." In fact, Mrs. Plansky had never heard of him.

"Joel's the brains behind Delice Moderne."

Mrs. Plansky knew Delice Moderne, a chain of high-end pastry shops, one of them not far from Arcadia Gardens. She'd taken her dad once. He'd voiced—not in a shy way—his incredulity at the prices, and downed cutting-edge versions of a napoleon, a Florentine, and a mocha éclair before huffily wheeling himself out the door. Now she tried one of the pastries. She somehow knew it was delicious even though she couldn't taste a thing, washing down what felt like a mouthful of dust with the tea.

"Delicious," she said.

Sylvie nodded. "Joel's the real deal, although come to think of it, maybe he started to make it big after you retired. He's a customer, of course. I supply him everything except the butter and the sugar." Sylvie's family owned a worldwide kitchen design business, had sold tens of thousands of units of the Plansky Toaster Knife.

Sylvie was looking at her closely. "I know what you're thinking. You haven't changed a bit! Still with that wicked internal sense of humor ticking away. You're thinking, 'Sylvie, you moron, butter and sugar are the whole bleeping product!'"

Mrs. Plansky hadn't been thinking that. She'd been trying to figure out how to steer the conversation toward what she wanted.

Sylvie gave her a big smile. "I'm so glad you called. I've been meaning to get in touch. When was the last time I saw you?"

"It must have been Norm's funeral," Mrs. Plansky said.

"That I'll never forget," said Sylvia. "Especially when you spoke from the podium. There wasn't a dry eye—except for yours. I don't know how you did it. But oh, what a wonderful man." Sylvie sighed. "So tell me—how are you doing? Still taking no prisoners on the tennis court?"

"Let's just say I'm still playing." Mrs. Plansky put down her teacup. "The fact is I'm thinking of getting back into the working world."

"Really?" said Sylvie. "I know retired folks who get bored, but none of them are resourceful like you."

"I'm not sure I'm—"

"Of course you are! You're still interested in the big wide world out there. Plus there's that rock star family of yours."

"Nevertheless," Mrs. Plansky said, "I miss . . ." What was it she missed about the working world? Actually, nothing. "I miss the problem-solving."

"Take up Sudoku," said Sylvie with a laugh.

Mrs. Plansky laughed, too, just a little. She saw the shadow of a thought pass across Sylvie's eyes. Sylvie was a shrewd operator. She, too, put down her teacup. That was the moment Mrs. Plansky considered making one or two more pleasantries and calling it a day. But she did not.

"Besides," Sylvie said. "What would you do?"

Mrs. Plansky plunged ahead. "Consulting."

"In what sort of business?"

"This sort." Mrs. Plansky made an encompassing gesture with her hands.

"Gee, Loretta, I can't think of any consultants at all in this business. Not successful ones."

"I was thinking more of an in-house setup."

"There are in-house strategizers, of course. I've got a planning committee. But they're department heads, not consultants. And, not to discourage you, but I'm pretty sure all my competitors are much the same."

Well, it was just a thought. That was what Mrs. Plansky should have said, and then made a graceful exit. Instead she went with this: "Are all your department heads, ah, firmly ensconced?"

"Oh, dear," Sylvie said, "you really do have the bug." Her lips turned up in another big smile, although this one wasn't real. Then her expression changed again, and became frank and open. "No reason you'd know this but we have a rule here, meant to encourage the development of young talent. The rule is sixty-five and out. We've stretched that in a few special cases to sixty-six or sixty-seven, but it's universal. I'll be gone in eight years and seven months."

"Oh," said Mrs. Plansky.

"So don't waste time on all this hurly-burly, Loretta. You been there, done that. Now go on and enjoy your life. You deserve it."

"The key fact, the underlying fact, got left out," Mrs. Plansky said to herself, although again out loud, as she merged onto 95 and headed north. She'd sat on other side of the desk for many job interviews, enough to know that the same key fact usually went unspoken. She had a clear memory of one time when it got into the open. This was early in her career and the applicant, a defeated-looking middle-aged woman with no relevant experience and euphemistic recommendations had suddenly blurted, "I'm at my wits end. I just need a job."

Thank God it got left out, Mrs. Plansky said to herself, making sure to keep silent this time. As for the desperate applicant, Mrs. Plansky, not quite so businesslike in the early days, had hired her, the result not good. She glanced in the rearview mirror, checking for signs of desperation and not seeing them. And why all this internal drama? Wasn't it possible that Agent Gatling would unearth something on her phone—about the names behind Safemo, for example—and set the feds in motion? The feds had an amazing history of bringing elusive criminals to justice: drug lords, for example, like that Noriega character, although he might not have been a drug lord. But still, the point was made. She was not alone, had the crime-fighting power of the most powerful nation on earth at her back. Mrs. Plansky was picturing a sunlit upland where this was all in the past, reduced to a surefire anecdote at cocktail parties, when her phone buzzed. She glanced at the screen: Jeanine at Arcadia Gardens. Mrs. Plansky took the next exit, pulled over on a wide, safe verge, and called her back.

"Oh, hi," said Jeanine, "thanks for getting back. I was just wondering if you had any questions about what we were discussing."

What had they been discussing? Mrs. Plansky searched her memory and found something. "The TV thing?" she said.

"I'm not sure I—ah, you mean when the screen got broken? Covered by insurance and not a problem. Sorry if I forgot to mention that. No, what I'm calling about is the underlying situation."

"Don't tell me there's been another incident."

"Well, yes, in fact, a couple, although no damage or injuries. But it's really motivated us to get going on the move ASAP. I just want to make sure you're on board with it and get the paperwork started."

"And this would be for . . . ?"

"The move. I'm afraid it involves a new contract. We're trying to simplify the process—and it will be simplified when the new software's up and running next year—but for now it's like starting over. Without all the financials, credit checks, of course, you already being a member of the Arcadia family."

No financials, no credit checks. That sounded good but where were we going with this? The move, that had to be it. Mrs. Plansky—the best part of her mind not on this but mired in other things despite having her mighty nation on her side —rolled the dice. "You're talking about the move to another floor?"

"Exactly. I should have been more clear. And it is kind of confusing. In terms of care level he moves up but within the building he moves down. Up to level two, down to floor three."

"Right," said Mrs. Plansky. "Gotcha. I think where we got stuck was on whether he couldn't just stay where he was and have level two care. He seems attached to that room."

"That he does. So rather than fight it, here's the plan. We'll have a third floor room of the same dimensions and configuration available five days before the end of the month. That gives us time to repaint and redecorate, make it the identical twin of his current room. At no charge, by the way."

"You do think of everything," Mrs. Plansky said.

"We try," said Jeanine. "So are there any questions?"

"My dad did mention the expense. I wasn't clear on whether he meant it was ten thousand a month or ten thousand more a month. On top of what I'm—what we're already paying."

Jeanine laughed. "He really is a character. The answer is none of the above. My goodness! Ten thousand more a month! What you're paying now is seventy-five hundred a month, although that's being adjusted to nine thousand next fiscal year, which is April for us. And we have a special promotion right now on level two, fifteen percent off for six months, bringing the monthly total down to . . .

let's see—sixteen thousand, even. So it's only seven thousand more, not ten."

Mrs. Plansky had had some business experience with people who could get tricky with numbers. She just hadn't identified Jeanine as the type, until now. But did it matter? All those numbers were impossible until—she corrected herself—unless and until the Safemo problem was sorted out.

"I think for now," she said, "I'll leave Dad where he is."

Silence. "Loretta? I don't seem to be communicating well today. At this stage of your father's case, our protocols, state-approved, mandate a move to level two care, which means a physical move to the third floor. I know he can be stubborn, but you have a way with him. I know you'll bring him around."

"I'll have to get back to you," said Mrs. Plansky, for the second time that morning leaving the underlying fact unspoken.

"Wonderful. And there is a bit of a time issue—his present room is already spoken for by a new client starting the first of the month."

Mrs. Plansky spent the rest of the day checking out—in person or over the phone—much cheaper and then somewhat cheaper, assisted-living places, and imagining introducing them to her dad and him to them. It was grim.

There was a small visitor parking lot at the Little Pine Lake condos that Mrs. Plansky had to pass on the way to her own driveway. As she went by, the driver's side doors of two identical-looking black sedans opened and both drivers got out, Agent Rains and Agent Gatling. Mrs. Plansky hit the brakes. Over the years she and Norm had developed a list of pithy truths—pissy truths, he always called them—that applied to their business. For example: good news travels fast, bad news travels slow. Mrs. Plansky got out of the car—not jumping or hopping out, but quickly for this seventy-one-year-old version of her.

They came toward her, their faces unreadable.

"Hi, there," said Agent Rains.

"Yes?" said Mrs. Plansky, forgetting her manners in her eagerness to hear the speedy news.

"We've developed some information, thanks mostly to Agent Gatling here. Agent Gatling?"

"Well, Mrs. Plansky, it looks like there's been some carelessness on the other end. Safemo has been used before, just the once, but I hadn't expected even that. I assumed it was a one-timer, set up for this little operation and then deep-sixed. Everybody makes mistakes, of course, the good, the bad, and the ugly."

Agent Rains frowned, a quick look that Gatling missed although Mrs. Plansky did not.

"The point being," Gatling went on, "that on the previous case, through a complicated series of events that aren't relevant to yours, the bureau was able to make a geographical hit."

"I don't understand," Mrs. Plansky said. She kept *Am I getting back my money or not* bottled up inside.

"Sorry," Gatling said. "A lot of these scammers are based in Eastern Europe. Also Russia, of course. We're sure—"

"Ninety percent sure," said Rains.

"That the Safemo folks operate out of Romania, specifically a town called—" He fished in his pocket.

"Alba Gemina," said Rains. "And the percentage on that part falls a bit, down to say seventy-five, eighty."

"So we're making progress," Mrs. Plansky said. "What happens next? I assume the first case got solved?"

"What you have to understand," Rains said, "and it's a hard lesson we all learn, is that different countries play by different rules. There's a lot of politics, a lot of quid pro quo, and—"

"But did the people in the first case get their money back?" Mrs. Plansky said.

Rains shook her head. "The embassy—meaning the cyber-crime liaison—was unable, at least so far, to determine the perpetrators."

"But they're whoever's behind Safemo!"

"Possibly. Possibly not."

"But even if not, Safemo will know who they are!"

"That, too, will have to be determined," Rains said. "We've forwarded the complete file to the cybercrime liaison at the embassy. The moment we have any news from them we'll be in touch."

"When will that be?"

"There's no telling."

"That's it?" said Mrs. Plansky.

"For now." Agent Rains stood a little straighter and she was already standing very straight. "The truth is these cases are very challenging, Mrs. Plansky. But don't give up hope."

Agent Rains and Agent Gatling said goodbye and returned to their cars. Mrs. Plansky watched them drive off, except that Gatling did not drive off. Instead he got out of his car and came toward her, loosening his tie.

"This is my last case," he said. "I'm retiring at the end of the week."

"So young for that," said Mrs. Plansky.

"Moving to the private sector, actually. So I feel free to let my hair down a bit. Hate to see folks living under a delusion. Seen too much of it, to be honest. The thing is, at the other end, aside from the obvious corruption, of course, goes without saying, there's also what you might call a demotivating factor."

"Which is?" said Mrs. Plansky. For some reason she was now finding Agent Gatling easy to understand.

"From our point of view the scammers are bad guys, end of story. But to the elite running the show over there the scammers are bad guys who also have a nice little industry going, bringing in the Yankee dollar and lots of 'em. And to the everyday Joe they're punching up, the kind of outlaw people have a soft spot for."

"Like Robin Hood."

"You got it."

They gazed at each other. The message was in his eyes. Mrs. Plansky voiced it.

"You're telling me to lose hope."

"Not in so many words."

FIFTEEN

Mrs. Plansky was up at dawn the next morning. Actually, she'd been awake all night. Dawn was when she got out of bed. She had a plan, the execution of which was going to require inner steeliness. She could do that. To take one example, there was the time, close to the end of Norm's life, when he asked her what she thought about taking a swing at a new and drastic form of radiation, still in the testing phase and a real long shot according to the oncologist, but Mrs. Plansky could see in his eyes how much he wanted her to say yes. Also in his eyes she saw that he was mostly dead already. She hadn't voiced that, had just simply given her head one little shake.

First, she sat down at her laptop and completed the application to drive for a rideshare company, the same rideshare company one of the waitresses at the club drove for and spoke highly of, and if not highly then at least without loathing. Second, she took out the jewelry box again, dumping out the contents on her bed. Mrs. Plansky didn't have a lot of jewelry but what she had was nice, and some of it very nice. Like this emerald-cut diamond ring in platinum, with a total carat weight she couldn't remember but it was up there. The ring had belonged to her mother and Mrs. Plansky had intended to give it to Emma on her twenty-first birthday or her wedding day or just some ordinary day. Maybe something else instead? But weren't there futures mapped out for everything in the jewelry box? This was where the steeliness came in. She had some cash in her purse and maybe five or six hundred dollars in the safe and that was it.

Down the road she could sell the condo and rent somewhere cheap, eking things out for the rest of . . . She left that thought unfinished. That was later and now was now.

Mrs. Plansky showered, brushed her hair, did her face, dressed in khaki slacks with a royal blue belt, light blue silk shirt, royal blue pumps, put her mom's ring in her purse, and drove to Frischetti Fine Jewelers, in the town center not far from her old house at 3 Pelican Way, and where she was known, at least a little.

Mr. Frischetti was alone in the shop, a loupe over one eye and a bracelet in his hand.

"Ah, Mrs. Plansky. So nice to see you. I heard you moved some time back."

"Hello, Mr. Frischetti. Yes, but not far. I'm down at Little Pine Lake."

"Hidden gem," said Mr. Frischetti. "Hey! Kind of funny for a man in my profession."

Mrs. Plansky didn't get it.

"Anything I can help you with?" he said.

Mrs. Plansky showed him the ring. He loved it, examined it with care, loved it even more and wrote a check for $29,000. Back in her car, she realized she'd forgotten to ask him the carat weight. But now she did get the hidden gem joke. "Everything evens out in the end," she said aloud, quoting what she thought was a bit of common folk wisdom. Just not in a way that we can understand, she added silently. She drove straight to Palm Coast Bank and Trust and deposited the check in the drive-through machine.

On the way home, Mrs. Plansky swung by Arcadia Gardens, checked in, and got up to the fourth floor without running into Jeanine, a lucky break. She knocked on her dad's door.

"That better be dinner," he called from inside.

Mrs. Plansky checked her watch. Two fifteen, perhaps a little early for dinner. "It's me, Dad."

"You?"

She opened the door and went in. Her dad, shirtless, had wheeled himself in front of a full-length mirror and seemed to be flexing his biceps.

"What are you doing here?" he said, not taking his eyes off the mirror.

"Just thought I'd drop in," Mrs. Plansky said. "Do I need an invitation?"

"I guess not. This isn't really my place, is it now? Not my own God-given place."

"Interesting you should mention that. The fact is—"

"It's not interesting to me. What I'm interested in is HGH. Can you get me some? Like today, if it's all the same to you."

"What's HGH?"

"Seriously? Don't you know anything?"

His gaze was still fixed on his own image so he missed the quick reddening of Mrs. Plansky's face, a reddening at first furious and then the precursor to a flood of tears. But she'd entered the time of steeliness and kept them inside. She crossed her arms.

"One thing going forward, Dad. There'll be no more *shekels* references or anything similar."

He glanced at her. "What are you talking about?"

"Anti-Semitism. I don't want to hear it."

"Me? Anti-Semitic? I deny it. Also I don't get it. Unless you're saying I think the Jews control HGH, which I absolutely do not."

Mrs. Plansky leaned against the back of her dad's TV chair, her legs suddenly weary. "I give up. What's HGH?"

"My hope and savior," said her dad. "Human growth hormone."

"You want to take human growth hormone?"

"Starting this very minute."

"Why?"

He gestured at her with his bare arms. "Look what's happened to my guns."

"Guns? Your arms are your guns?"

"More like just biceps. Never heard that expression? And you, a jock?"

"I'm not a jock."

"Sure you are. The only—one of the things I always loved about you."

Those tears also, Mrs. Plansky kept within. She came forward. "How would you like to come live at my place?"

A huge smile spread across his wrinkled, mottled face. It had the strange effect of making him appear more orc-like, but a lovable orc. "Really?"

"Really."

He wheeled around and zoomed over to his clothes closet.

"Not today, Dad. At the end of the month."

"Why the wait?"

"It's a matter of days. And I need the time to get things ready for you. Plus you're paid up here until then."

"So what's a few shek—"

He clamped his mouth shut.

"I'll come help you pack in a few days. Until then stay out of trouble."

"You're the boss."

Her heart sank. She was at the opposite end of that continuum. Safemo was the boss of her.

"What?" he said. "Something wrong?"

"Nope."

"The HGH, right? Don't worry about it for now. I'll hold off until the big moveroo." He gave himself a sort of celebratory hip shake, not so easy in a wheelchair.

"You know what makes me feel better about this?" said Mrs. Plansky's mother, on her deathbed, although Mrs. Plansky, much less familiar with dying back then, refused to believe what the doctors were saying, less and less euphemistically as the hospital days went on and on.

"You're going to be all right, Mama. Everyone says this round of chemo takes time to kick in."

"I hope it doesn't kick in when I'm six feet under."

Mrs. Plansky had smiled more than once in later years at the memory of that remark but she'd been stunned at the time.

Her mom patted her hand. "Just listen. What makes me feel better is knowing that when I'm gone you'll be living the life I could have."

"Oh, Mama, I don't—"

"Just look at you. I got the job done."

Those were just about the last words of her mother's that Mrs. Plansky heard. Now, driving away from Arcadia Gardens—which she had no desire to see ever again—she wanted the ring back from Mr. Frischetti. In one careless night she'd thrown away the life her mother could have had, or, to put it another way, Safemo had taken a piece of not just her but of her family, past, present, future. She wanted it back. Mrs. Plansky pulled over the first chance she got, coming to a stop in a parking lot. She scrolled through her phone until she came to Connie Malhouf, her lawyer—hers and Norm's—going all the way back to the first incorporation papers.

"Ah, Loretta. I thought I might be hearing from you."

"Oh?" said Mrs. Plansky, confused from the start.

"About—if I'm not telling tales out of school—Jack."

Jack? What in God's name was she—? Then the pieces started coming, in little shards that needed some help to form a whole. Cold chain? Ray and Rudy? $750K? Her will? Yes, Jack's call to Connie about her will, not a real big deal to begin with, and now irrelevant. Events had moved on.

"Loretta?"

"Right, Jack. I spoke to him. No problem. At least that isn't the problem. It's peripheral at most."

"What's the problem?"

Mrs. Plansky took a deep breath. She could feel Connie concentrating on the other end. Connie was one of those fierce concentrators, missing nothing and impossible to fool, impregnable, for example, to the Safemos of this world.

"I got this call in the middle of the night," she began, and out came the whole hodgepodge, so disorganized, disjointed, and dumb in the telling that no one could doubt that the teller was the just the type to have fallen for it. She came to the end, the part about no hope.

"Jesus," said Connie. "The FBI guy said that?"

"Not in so many words—which he actually did say."

"Jesus," said Connie again. Then came an expression of sympathy, totally sincere, and maybe more meaningful in her case, Connie not at all the warm and fuzzy type. But that wasn't what she wanted from Connie, or from anybody.

"What do you think?" Mrs. Plansky said.

"Beyond what I just said, you mean?"

"Yes."

"Is there something you want me to do?" Connie said.

"Fix it."

Had that sounded gross? Connie was silent for a few seconds. Yes, it had sounded gross.

"Are you raising the possibility of going after Newport Asset Management and or Palm Coast Bank and Trust for the losses?" Connie said.

Mrs. Plansky was doing precisely that but shrank from doing it aloud. It was weasely, cowardly, disgraceful. She said nothing.

"If so," Connie went on, "let me say three things. First, I do some work for Newport, meaning I couldn't represent you. Second, you might be able to find some lawyer to take this on. Third, I'd have to refresh myself on the case law, but any lawyer who'd say you had a chance in hell would be lying."

"Thank you," Mrs. Plansky said. In a strange way that turned out to be the answer she wanted.

That upright green turtle with a raised glass in its flipper was hard to miss. This time Mrs. Plansky turned in, parked, and went inside. She took a seat by herself at the end of the bar.

"Welcome to happy hour," said the bartender.

"Happy hour?" said Mrs. Plansky.

"Two for the price of one, now till six. What'll it be?"

For a moment she couldn't think of a single drink name. "Maybe a beer," she said.

"What do you like?" He recited a list that went on and on. Mrs. Plansky realized that she'd be getting two of whatever she ordered. Two beers were a lot of volume.

"Instead I'll do bourbon," she said, conscious of sounding like it was her first time in a bar.

"Any special kind?"

He was losing interest, and fast. She remembered the name of Norm's favorite. They didn't carry it, but had something just as good. He poured her two bourbons on the rocks from a bottle with a prancing thoroughbred on the label.

Mrs. Plansky sipped drink one. The Green Turtle Club was bright and airy, darkest at her end of the bar, with a Bahamian theme and free conch fritters. She had a weakness for conch fritters but she wasn't at all hungry. A guitarist began to play on the other side of the room and things got busy. Mrs. Plansky was aware of that. She moved on to drink two. All the seats at the bar got taken except for the one next to hers.

Mrs. Plansky was putting an end to drink five when someone behind her spoke.

"Loretta?"

Mrs. Plansky turned. Standing before her, wearing tennis shorts and a warm-up jacket was . . . was Kev? Yes, Kev Dinardo, lefty, wicked slice serve, pleasant manner, pleasant—even handsome—face.

"Hi, Kev. I don't usually—" Whatever that was going to be never got said, because in twisting around to see him better, she overbalanced, tipping the stool and heading for a crash on the tile floor.

Kev Dinardo, his white tennis shoes splashed with bourbon, caught her on the fly and set her upright on her feet. A bit of a hubbub rose and fell around her and she was aware of blurry faces. Mrs. Plansky made some sort of reassuring gesture, but lacked the stability to pull it off and started to go down again. And again he caught her.

He got her safely home, driving her car, with a taxi following to take him back. Mrs. Plansky sat in the passenger seat, seeing two of some things but picturing only one image of herself, a drunk old woman unable to take care of herself.

Kev glanced over. "No worries," he said. "That's why they call it *tipsy*."

She was silent.

At the Little Pine Lake condos he walked her to her door, made sure she got it open and that lights were on inside.

"Thank you, Mr. Dinardo," she said, making a big effort not to be slurry.

"Let's keep it on a first-name basis," he said.

Mrs. Plansky passed out fully dressed on her bed. She awoke in darkness and drank water right from the faucet, lots and lots of water. A wave of anger—real, hot fury—swept over her, anger directed only partly at herself. She found her laptop and opened a map of Romania.

SIXTEEN

"Did you hurt yourself?" Professor Bogdan said.

"No," said Dinu, back in the professor's office at the Liceu Teoretic for another English lesson.

"I only ask because you're limping."

Dinu did not know "limping" but he figured it out from the context. "It's these new boots. I have to break them in."

Professor Bogdan half-rose from his chair, gazed over the desk, took in the sight of Dinu's boots—cowboy boots, real ones, ordered online from a store in Santa Fe. Not only did the Americans have their own Georgia, but also their own Mexico, newer, better. Besides his cowboy boots, Dinu was wearing his new leather jacket, real leather with a red satin lining, and new ripped Levi's 501s. Only his socks, the Megan Thee Stallion ones, were old. Socks didn't show and at home the washer still wasn't fixed.

"Break them in?" said Bogdan. "That's very good American English. But I didn't teach it to you. Where did you learn it?"

Dinu shrugged. He'd actually ended up talking to a woman at the shop—she had a lovely, slightly slow way of speaking, had called him "honey"—and he'd learned it from her.

"No matter," Bogdan said. "The fact that your vocabulary is growing unconsciously is a good sign. Do you understand 'unconsciously'?"

"Yes."

"Define, please."

"Happening on their own, without knowing."

Bogdan sat back and nodded. "Even your accent is improving, as though you've been talking to native speakers."

"What are native speakers?"

"In this case, born Americans."

Dinu caught an expression on Bogdan's face that he didn't like. The professor knew damn well that he talked to native speakers. That was the whole point. Was he making fun of him?

Bogdan took out a notepad. "Let's forget about grammar today and simply converse. What do you want to talk about?"

"I don't know."

"Sports?"

"Okay," Dinu said. Then came an idea. "Explain baseball."

Bogdan laughed. "That I cannot do. A complete mystery, and do you know I attended a real game? Yankee Stadium—my brother took me on my last visit. He tried to teach me but it was impossible. There are thirteen ways to balk. Can you imagine?"

"What is 'balk'?"

"I have no idea but it ends in a big argument and the referee throws the coach out of the game."

"He throws him?"

"Not physically. He forces him to depart. But let's talk about something else. How about movies? Americans usually say movies, not films."

"Okay, movies."

"Have you seen many American movies?"

"No."

"What kind of movies do you like?"

Dinu shrugged. He hadn't seen many movies from any country. His mother watched a lot of TV, but not movies, preferring cartoons and game shows. As for going to the cinema, that cost money.

"I'm predicting that you'll like crime movies," Bogdan said.

Dinu sat back in his chair.

"There are many fine American crime movies—*The Maltese Falcon*"—the professor began writing on the pad—"*Double Indemnity, The Sting,* but you would probably like the more violent kind, like *Pulp Fiction, Reservoir Dogs,* or—"

"Can you put that out?" Dinu said, gesturing with his chin to the Chesterfield smoking in the professor's ashtray.

Bogdan looked up. Dinu made the chin gesture again. He didn't repeat the request, didn't bother mentioning the asthma, which had in fact been much better lately, didn't say please. Bogdan put out the cigarette.

The lesson came to an end soon after. Bogdan handed Dinu the list of crime movies. "Let's make this the last lesson," the professor said in their own language. "I've taken you as far as I can."

When Dinu reported for work that night, he told Uncle Dragomir that the lessons were finished.

"Who says?" said Uncle Dragomir.

"The professor."

Marius the bouncer was standing nearby, cleaning his fingernails with the knife he always wore in an ankle sheath, out of sight.

"Are you catching this, Marius?" said Uncle Dragomir.

"Pretty funny," Marius said.

"Funny?"

"Not ha-ha—the other kind. Want me to get him on the phone?"

Uncle Dragomir shook his head. "In person is always best in doing business. Go see him and have a talk."

"Just a verbal talk?"

"For now. I'm sure he'll be reasonable."

"What if he wants more for the lessons?"

"Now that's the ha-ha kind of funny. Tell him verbally there's a sale on the lessons—twenty-five percent off until further notice."

"Hey, there, Grampy, it's me, Robby."

Grampy in this case, not Grandpa or any of the other choices. Romeo's research was getting better all the time.

"My grandson Robby?" came the reply, the voice the thinnest, wobbliest, and scratchiest they'd come upon yet.

"The one and only," Dinu said. He, too, was getting better all the time. "How are things in Big Sky Country?"

"Colder than a well-digger's ass."

Wow. What a fabulous expression! Dinu glanced around the Cambio room at Club Presto to see if anyone else appreciated it, but not one of them—Uncle Dragomir, Romeo, Timbo, or Tassa—had enough English for that. Tassa, by herself in the back corner, had asked if she could sit in, a bit of a surprise, but a nice one, and Uncle Dragomir had said yes, also a surprise. Dinu felt totally relaxed, like a pilot landing his plane for the thousandth time.

"Pretty warm down here, Grampy."

"Still at Arizona State? Haven't heard from you in a while."

"Go Sun Devils. And I've been studying hard, but sorry for not calling. And sorry for the reason I call—I'm calling now."

"Huh?"

Dinu got going on the whole discurs, as they would say in his language. The DUI, the aggressive police, the $9,726.18—by now a lucky number to him—self-destroying password, Securo, the new Safemo, set up by Romeo in that clever and cautious way he had, always a step ahead. When Dinu came to saving the whales—his favorite part, his brain wave, as the Americans said—he glanced over at Tassa. And then came another surprise. She was staring at him, frowning so deeply she almost looked ugly. Maybe her mind was on other things completely, like her home life, just as messed up as his. But no time to figure that out now. The climax—this was like a Shakespeare play, always with a climax, according to Professor Bogdan—came: bank account, password, money—in this case the $9,726.18 plus the remainder in the account, slightly less than twenty thousand, but Dinu, busy with the thankful and affectionate denouement, might not have caught the figure right as it flashed on Romeo's screen. Bottom line, as the Americans said: nothing else, no real riches to mine, Romeo finding no other accounts, in other words just an adequate job.

Still, Uncle Dragomir seemed pleased. There were some high fives and then Uncle Dragomir told Timbo to hand out gift cards to Salle Privé, the deluxe restaurant next door, also owned by him. Dinu, Romeo, and Tassa stayed behind while Romeo got busy at several keyboards, erasing digital tracks and turning the event into a nonevent for anyone who came looking, even themselves.

"I'm starving," Dinu said.

The three of them went outside. It was cold and snowy. Dinu tried to take Tassa's hand, but it slipped away.

"Something wrong?"

She didn't look at him. "I lost my appetite."

"Come anyway. Maybe you'll find it again."

Tassa shook her head. When they reached the door of Salle Privé she kept walking.

"Tassa! Where are you going?"

"Home."

"But why?"

"I told you."

"Then just come sit."

She shook her head and walked on.

"Wait. I'll take you on the bike."

"To hell with the bike."

"What do you mean?" he called after her.

Tassa didn't answer, just hurried to the end of the block, rounded the corner, and vanished from sight.

"What's with her?" Dinu said.

"Maybe it's her period," said Romeo. Then he laughed. "You hope and pray, right?"

Dinu punched him on the shoulder, not gently.

"Ow! What's wrong with you?"

Dinu took a deep breath, got a grip. "Sorry."

They went inside, were taken to a nice corner table, ordered steak frites with Cokes to drink.

"We're getting good at this," Romeo said, his mouth full of frites.

"Yeah."

Romeo leaned forward. "Ever ask yourself why we even need Dragomir?"

"No," said Dinu.

"Think about it."

For dessert they had chocolate cake with chocolate ice cream. Romeo checked his watch and left soon after, but Dinu found he was still hungry and ordered another dessert, this time chocolate cake with maple walnut ice cream, which he'd never had. Maple, he knew, was a syrup that came from the Green Mountain State. He fell in love with maple walnut ice cream, tasting America in every bite.

Dinu was still eating when an older woman who'd been sitting at the bar came over. Older but not old, maybe in her twenties. Estimating the ages of older people wasn't easy. He'd seen this woman before. She'd been a dealer at one of the fancy casinos in Bucharest and was working with Uncle Dragomir on some sort of casino plan for here in Alba Gemina.

"Dinu, isn't it?"

"Yes." The smell of her perfume reached him. He felt like maybe his mouth needed wiping but his napkin had fallen to the floor. The woman wore a tight red dress, high translucent heels, had thick, wavy platinum hair, and a rose and bloody thorn tattoo on her shoulder; in short, she looked like a movie star.

"I'm Annika."

"Right, Annika. I've seen you at, um, next door."

"Correct. I hear, Dinu, you've got a head on your shoulders."

"Well, ah, I don't know about . . ."

"What else have you got?"

At first Dinu had no clue. Then a thought came to him. "Boots," he said. "Cowboy boots from Santa Fe." He stuck them out where she could see. She saw. The problem with Tassa—whatever it was— got very small very fast.

SEVENTEEN

 Mr. Santiago handled maintenance at the Little Pine Lake condos. Mrs. Plansky walked him through her place, explaining what her father could and could not do.

"Don't worry, Mrs. Plansky, I got this. Thirty years of maintenance in Florida—I've done every kind of these upgrades you can imagine."

"Good to hear. Any suggestions?"

"The time to install what you need for what's down the road is now. You'll save money in the long run."

"What's down the road, meaning further deterioration?"

"It never goes the other way in my experience. Who do you have coming in, don't mind my asking?"

"My father. I thought I'd—"

"Sorry. I meant coming in to help you out—a home health care aide, a professional."

"I'm pretty sure I can handle it, at least for now."

"I hear you," said Mr. Santiago. "If things change you might want to contact my sister-in-law Lucrecia. Experienced, reliable, hardworking, honest, and half the price of anyone you'd get from an agency."

"I'll keep her in mind," said Mrs. Plansky.

Mrs. Plansky's condo was a two-bedroom, master on the first floor and guest room upstairs. To avoid the stair problem, Mr. Santiago turned the little first-floor study into a bedroom. Her dad was delighted with it.

"This calls for champagne. I prefer Krug but I'm flexible."

"I don't have Krug. There may not be any champagne at all."

"That's gonna change. I'll buy some right now, on me. Where's your account?"

"What account?"

"Your liquor store account. I'll have them deliver."

"I don't have a liquor store account."

"Now I've heard everything."

A little later she found him in the pantry.

"No Fritos? Can't live without Fritos. Where's your account?"

Soon after that he got sleepy and Mrs. Plansky put him to bed. Over the next few days she observed that he did a lot of sleeping—morning nap, afternoon nap, and nighttime, which was really two long naps with a period of activity in between.

"I'll be quiet as a mouse," he promised about that active period. "You just get your beauty sleep. I won't wake you."

And he didn't wake her because Mrs. Plansky wasn't getting her beauty sleep or any other kind of sleep. Night after night she lay awake although her mind was dreaming, the same dream—in fact, a nightmare—over and over. This nightmare was like one of those noir-ish movies where everyone but the central character could see what was coming, a short little movie in this case that took place completely on the phone. Mrs. Plansky lay in bed, wide awake, sometimes soaked in sweat, sometimes shivering, never able to stop the movie. Over breakfast on day four or five—her dad had bacon and soft-boiled eggs every morning, stipulating three bacon strips and two eggs, although he never got past the first of either—he said, "No offense, but we're family, and all. You're not looking your best, Loretta."

When he went down for his morning nap, Mrs. Plansky called Mr. Santiago and got the number of Lucrecia, his sister-in-law.

*   *   *

"Dad, I want you to meet Lucrecia. She's Mr. Santiago's sister-in-law I was telling you about."

"In what context?" her dad said.

"Lucrecia will be staying here while I'm gone. Just a short business trip, as I explained."

"But you're retired."

"This is something new, remember?"

"No, but I'm listening."

"I'll have more details when I get back. For now please say hi to Lucrecia. Lucrecia Santiago, my dad Chandler Banning."

They shook hands. Lucrecia was in her fifties, looked something like Carmen Miranda, but a Carmen Miranda that never was, who eschewed makeup, fussing over her appearance, or glamor, bringing the inner strength of character into plain sight.

"Nice to meet you, Mr. Banning," she said.

He gazed up at her from his wheelchair. A sly look crossed his face. "Call me Chandler," he said.

"If that's your preference," Lucrecia said. "And please call me Lucrecia."

"That's my plan."

She smiled down at him. Her teeth were big and beautiful, gave her smile a lot of oomph, a complex sort of oomph that was only part-friendly. "Then we're off to a great start," she said. "It's like Ping-Pong."

"Ping-Pong?"

"Ping-Pong's my philosophy of life," Lucrecia said. "If you ping me that's what you get back, a ping. But if you pong me I pong you."

Mrs. Plansky's dad eyed her. Just as the silence was about to grow uncomfortable, he said, "I never used to like Ping-Pong."

That struck them all as very funny. They laughed and laughed. Mrs. Plansky put a lid on it when she felt tears on the way.

Mrs. Plansky no longer had much in the way of winter clothes. She went through what there was, folded neatly in a cedar chest at the back of the closet. She found shearling gloves, a knit hat featuring a logo with snowflakes forming the word ALTA, which had to date from their one ski trip to Utah, three decades ago, and a three-quarter length wool coat in navy blue that was warmer than it looked, as she recalled, and would have to do. Then, just as she was about to close the chest, she spotted a scarf tucked away in one corner.

Mrs. Plansky pulled it out. She herself had never gone for scarves but Norm had had many, only this one somehow surviving. It was a Scottish tartan, with autumnal hues laid out in a grid of little squares, one of his worst and frayed here and there. But when she tried it on and checked herself in the mirror, it looked right—or more accurately felt right—so it made the cut. Unlike Norm, when Mrs. Plansky traveled she traveled light, for this trip packing just the one suitcase, a hard-case roller type that could be jammed into the overhead bin. Shoes were always the problem. In the end she cut to the bone, taking only the pull-on low-heeled booties with the least tapered toes on the market, the warm, quilted indoor-outdoor mules in black, and her Italian ballet flats, which she just had to have.

Mrs. Plansky had her hair cut at Delia's on the Waterway, tipping more than usual on account of her booking the appointment so late. There had to be standards. Also she paid all the bills now due or that would become due for the next month, erring on the safe side, and withdrew $2,600 in cash—$1,600 covering two weeks' pay for Lucrecia and another $1,000 to give her for food and any other expenses—Mrs. Plansky shying away from checking the balance to see what remained. The other expenses seemed to already include a new Cuban place her dad had somehow heard of, although he always spoke disparagingly of ethnic food. There was no point wondering why on the suddenly Cuban part. The answer was the obvious one.

Mrs. Plansky booked a round-trip flight from Miami to Bucharest with a short stop in Zurich, leaving the return date open. On

Lucrecia's second day on the job—the first one having gone well, her dad taking over more of his self-care than he had in a long time, and also making the point that Mrs. Plansky needn't have stuck around—she rose before anyone was up, hoisted her suitcase into the trunk of the car, and drove down to Miami. She parked in an off-site lot, writing the space number in the notebook she'd bought special for the trip, took the shuttle to the terminal, and got to the gate with plenty of time to spare.

The man sitting next to her at the gate was on the phone, speaking an unfamiliar language. But Mrs. Plansky had taken both French and Latin in high school, and thought she was beginning to pick out some of the words. Frigorific, for example. That would be cold.

Eighteen

 Mrs. Plansky had a window seat in coach. Her phone pinged just as the plane was pulling away from the gate, and in came a text from Emma.

Grandma! Mom just told me the news! Is there anything I can do to help? I feel so bad for you. And also I'm furious! I want to hop on a plane to Bulgaria is it? Mom didn't seem sure. And shake those people down.

Mrs. Plansky texted back. Something to think about. Ha-ha. But I don't want you to worry about this for one second. How are things in your life?

She waited for a reply but none came before the airplane mode announcement. Mrs. Plansky put her phone away. Winter break had to be over now, meaning Emma was back in class at UCSB. What was her major? If Mrs. Plansky had ever known, she no longer did. But whatever Emma had chosen would have been the result of careful thought. Mrs. Plansky would never call her own daughter scatterbrained, but Emma was the opposite of what she wouldn't call her daughter, so Emma's mental discipline hadn't come from Nina. Nor had it come from Zach, Emma's dad, scatterbrained for sure, one example being that he'd forgotten on more than one occasion that husbands shouldn't sleep around, in his case leading to the Teds and now Matty and/or Matthew, who perhaps was better considered as two people, and with that thought came the certain premonition that the Matts, too, were temporary. Unless she somehow came through with the 250K! Maybe better to get off the plane this very minute and save Nina from the Matts!

Uh-oh. Had she spoken that last part aloud? It was just a joke. She had promises to keep. Mrs. Plansky glanced over at her seatmate, a gum-chewing boy of eight or nine, and quite literally a snot-nosed kid. He was watching her with what appeared to be mean little eyes. Mrs. Plansky gave him a vague smile. He turned away and got busy jabbing at the onboard screen, stopping when he came to the flight tracker. She was surprised to see they were already airborne, an inch or an inch and a half offshore. She looked out the window hoping for a sight of the Atlantic down below but they were above the clouds. "Why don't artists ever paint the clouds from above?" Norm had asked. She'd given him a nice print of Georgia O'Keeffe's above-the-clouds painting for his next birthday. Norm pretended to like it, but he could see she wasn't fooled. "It's a mathematical take," he explained. "That's what I do for a living." Mrs. Plansky gazed down at the cloud layer, like meadows of gold, and saw no math. If Norm had been seated next to her instead of the snot-nosed kid a very nice conversation might have been struck up now. Instead Mrs. Plansky took out her digital reader and opened a book on the history of Romania, downloaded yesterday.

There's losing yourself in a story and then there's getting lost in a story. Her experience with this history of Romania began with type one but after seventy or eighty pages descended into type two. Was it the writer's fault or did some countries just make better stories than others? The Romanian story, which she was in no position to judge a bloody mess, did seem to be both messy and bloody. The real Dracula, for example, often resorted to impaling. Mrs. Plansky looked up what impaling was, exactly, and put the reader aside for the moment.

She closed her eyes, resting them, in fact. Giving her eyes a little rest from time to time? That was new in her life. Her eyes had gone along for more than seven decades content to take their rest when the rest of her was resting—team players, the pair of them—but now they were making demands.

Rest when the rest of me rests, darn it! That was kind of funny. She thought of texting it to . . . to whom, exactly? Emma popped up first in her mind. Was it true that some traits skipped a generation? Mrs. Plansky had seen Emma far more in the early part of her life, then less, and now, in the past two years, hardly at all. You could say that's just the way things work nowadays. Or you could do something about it. She realized that she hadn't tried hard enough and decided there and then, skimming along over meadows of gold, to do something about it.

Emma's middle name was Loretta, one of the honors of Mrs. Plansky's life. Zach's mother's name was Emma. That part didn't bother Mrs. Plansky at all. The fact that Loretta was the middle name made it better—like a ring with a secret compartment.

At that moment, she thought of the emerald-cut diamond ring, intended for Emma, now in the hands of Mr. Frischetti. Her eyes decided they'd had enough rest. They snapped open and scanned the plane, saw everything in a new way, not how the eyes of a normal traveler for business or tourism would see, but more like the eyes of someone on a secret mission. And it was a secret mission in the sense that she'd told no one her destination. Mrs. Plansky never drank alcohol on planes, but when the drinks cart came around, she took one. She didn't order a martini, shaken not stirred, but she thought of it. She was going rogue.

When Mrs. Plansky awoke, needing to use the bathroom, the snot-nosed kid was gone, replaced by a sleeping and beefy middle-aged man in a tracksuit. He seemed to be the wide-stance type.

"Excuse me?" Mrs. Plansky said.

No reaction.

She raised her voice slightly and tried a few more times, also without success, then gave his shoulder a little nudge. His near eye opened slightly.

"Sorry to bother you." She made a little gesture toward the aisle. Sleeping next to the man was a beefy middle-aged woman, also in a tracksuit but with a narrower stance. He elbowed her. Ah, a couple. Soon they were both in the aisle. Mrs. Plansky got to her feet, with not close to her usual ease, and made her way to the back of the plane. On the way she glanced out the window for another sight of those golden meadows, but it was night.

"How much longer to the stop in Zurich?" she asked the flight attendant.

"Zurich?" said flight attendant with a marked German accent. "Zurich was an hour ago."

Mrs. Plansky resolved to be sharper, starting that very minute.

In Bucharest, she'd booked a room in a small hotel near the airport. It had Vila as part of a long name, which she presumed was like villa and therefore promising in her scheme of things, and also she'd liked the photo of the small breakfast room, with a few simple candlelit wooden tables and a buffet visible in the background. She was asleep five minutes after check-in, and didn't stir until daylight pinkened the insides of her eyelids.

When she awoke she saw she'd neglected to close the curtains. Outside was a very small patio with an alley beyond, partly obscured by a trellis with nothing growing on it. A rusty, tireless motorcycle leaned against the patio side wall. Snow was falling. The image— snow, motorcycle, trellis—somehow made her feel the foreignness of the place, deeply foreign, as though this visit was happening in the age before mass tourism. She closed the curtain, figured out the shower, got herself ready. Before Norm, back in college, she'd worked on a ranch in Montana one summer, the whole thing set up by her dad, the details now gone. There'd been a little fling with one of the wranglers—pretty much her sole venture into the flinging life—a wonderful rider although his passion was motorcycles. He'd taught her to ride his Harley Super Glide, an enormous howling beast that should have scared the bejeezus out of her, but did not. She'd been quite good at it.

The man at the desk called a taxi. It pulled up and Mrs. Plansky stepped outside, wrapping the Scottish scarf tighter around her neck. "Brr," she said as she got in the back seat. "Frigorific."

The driver glanced back in surprise. "You speak Romanian?"

"Only the one word."

He laughed, and then was quiet almost the whole way. Finally, slowing down, he said, "Here is another one. Noroc."

"What's that?"

"Good luck."

He pulled up in front of a large, low, gray building, actually more of a blocky compound, fenced and gated.

"U.S. Embassy," the driver said.

She paid him, tipping more than usual, encouraging noroc in a magical thinking way.

Mrs. Plansky presented herself at the reception desk.

"Hello," she said. "I'm Loretta Plansky from Punta D'Oro, Florida. I'd like to see whoever's in charge of cybercrime, please." She laid her passport on the desk.

The receptionist didn't touch it. "Do you have an appointment?" she said.

"No," said Mrs. Plansky. "But I'm happy to wait."

The receptionist nodded. "The problem is that in order to meet with anyone on staff, an appointment is required."

"Very well. I'd like to make an appointment with whoever's in charge of cybercrime as soon as possible. Preferably today."

The receptionist consulted her screen, the back of which was turned to Mrs. Plansky. The monitor hid the receptionist's face from below the eyes. The eyes, expressionless, were not moving. Time passed, perhaps the point of the whole exercise. Mrs. Plansky felt a twinge in her new hip.

"I'm an American citizen," she said.

"Yes," said the receptionist, glancing at the passport, still unopened. "I see that."

"Who has been," Mrs. Plansky went on, and then stopped herself. She didn't want to voice the word *victimized*, certainly not in front of this, well, child, a nasty designation she regretted. But still. "Who has been on the receiving end of a cybercrime. The FBI believes the crime originated in this country." Mrs. Plansky smiled in a way she hoped was encouraging. "Which is why I'm here."

"The FBI?" the receptionist said.

"Federal Bureau of Investigation," said Mrs. Plansky.

"That's not what I meant." The receptionist's tone, which had been right down the center began to veer toward the hostile lane. "Did the FBI send you?"

"Very much so," said Mrs. Plansky. "If indirectly."

The receptionist blinked. The reception desk was the circular kind. She rolled her chair to the other side and got on a landline phone, back turned and voice low. After a minute or two she hung up, wheeled to the front, handed Mrs. Plansky her passport, and said, "Please wait in the waiting area."

"Thank you."

Mrs. Plansky sat in the waiting area, her purse in her lap. A framed photo of the president hung on the wall. How confident he looked! Which was probably the point of presidential photos. On the other hand, picturing in her mind a photo of Lincoln, ol' Honest Abe hadn't been projecting much in the way of confidence and yet hadn't he inspired plenty of the real thing? Her mind was wandering along those lines when she realized she'd made a mistake. Her purse—brown leather, brass clasp—did not match the booties with the low heels and roomy toe boxes, which were black.

"Ms. Plansky?"

"Mrs.," she said, looking up.

A young man—although not as young as the receptionist—stood before her. He wore a subdued tie, gray flannels, and a blue blazer with a stars-and-stripes lapel pin. Some sort of gold badge was superimposed on the stripes, the writing on it too small for her to see.

"Mrs. Plansky, my apologies," he said. "My name's Jamal Perryman."

They shook hands. Mrs. Plansky rose. Still holding her hand, Jamal Perryman gave her a bit of a boost. She thought of resisting but her legs, which still seemed jet-lagged, took over the decision-making.

"Loretta Plansky," she added. "U.S. citizen."

"And currently residing here in Romania?"

"Oh, no. I live in Florida. Punta D'Oro. Are you in charge of cybercrime, Mr. Perryman?"

"Not in charge, but it's one of my duties."

"Are you with the FBI?"

"Secret Service." He tapped his lapel pin. Mrs. Plansky leaned forward. The words were right there.

"I thought you guarded the president."

"That, too. I gather you've been affected by cybercrime."

"Correct. I'd expected the file on my case would have already crossed your desk."

His eyebrows rose. "Are you telling me you flew over here especially for this?"

"That's right." She was a little confused. "Is it surprising?"

"Let's just say unprecedented, in my experience," said Mr. Perryman. "How about we go on upstairs and look into this?"

Mr. Perryman's small, tidy office was on the floor above. Through the window she could see a basketball half-court just inside the embassy perimeter. Two marines in full uniform were shooting hoops, a third one still clearing away the snow. On the shelves were what Mrs. Plansky took to be family photos—a smiling wife and two serious-looking little kids.

"Your children?" she said.

"Yes."

"Adorable. What are their names?"

"We don't divulge details like that."

"Ah. Sorry. I should have known."

"No reason why you should."

"Well, there is the secret part, after all. Right in the name."

He shot her a quick, less formal look. She'd gotten his attention. He pulled up a chair for her and sat at the desk.

"May I see your passport?"

She handed it over. He opened it, then turned to his laptop and got busy, typing and reading while Mrs. Plansky sat with her purse in her lap and clouds moved across the sky, darkening things a bit. Mr. Perryman had a handsome face, not closed off, not unfriendly, not uneasy, intelligent and maybe even predisposed to warmth. But that was the problem with human faces, and maybe also the reason they were so fascinating: you just never knew, beauty and truth maybe not being so congruent after all. Some famous movie stars turned out to be rather foul when the lights were off, if you could believe what you read. After Norm's death, in those many sleepless nights that had followed, she'd taken to reading Hollywood biographies, which she'd never done before or since. She was informed on the subject: that was the point.

Mr. Perryman looked up to find she was staring, perhaps staring hard, at his face.

"Whoa," he said. "Is something wrong?"

"No. Sorry. Well, yes. What happened to me was wrong."

He gestured toward the screen. "Yes, I see that. Can you walk me through the details of the contact?"

"You mean the phone call?"

"If you please."

"Certainly," said Mrs. Plansky. "But first—am I right in thinking you weren't aware of my case until I walked in?"

Mr. Perryman's face closed up the littlest bit. "I'm aware of it now," he said.

He looked her in the eyes. She did the same to him. After probably too much of that, Mrs. Plansky told herself to grow up, and started in on her story.

Some people are real good listeners, have an active way of doing it, as though a kind of ear magnetism is pulling the words right out of your mouth. Others are only listening for some sort of cue so they can jump in and take over the talking themselves. Mr. Perryman was the first kind, although his face remained totally formal the whole time. There was a slight shift of the eyes when she came to the part about saving the whales.

"Well?" she said.

"First," Mr. Perryman said, "I want to make sure I understand. There were actually two calls?"

"Yes, but the second one was very short."

"Can you go over that one again?"

"Sure, but I don't see how it's important. In terms of finding clues, I mean. Clues for solving the case, Mr. Perryman."

"Humor me," he said.

She couldn't help smiling. Mrs. Plansky decided they were beginning to hit it off. That had to be good.

"Start with how much time elapsed between the two calls," Mr. Perryman said.

"Five or ten minutes. The first thing he said was that he was free as a bird and out on the street."

"Did you hear any street sounds? Anything in the background?"

"Not that I remember. But the sound was better. I was happy, of course, thinking he was out of jail or the police station or whatever it was. I suggested he get a lawyer."

"What did he say to that?"

Mrs. Plansky thought back. "I can't remember. Maybe nothing.

Wait, no. At first he didn't seem to understand. I explained that he'd need a lawyer to represent him in court. When his case came up, you see. I thought he wasn't thinking things through. Like a typical teenager."

"Did he sound like a teenager?"

"Yes. And next he said it was a good idea and he said good night."

"In what way?"

"In what way did he say good night?"

"Straight up?" said Mr. Perryman. "Or—and bear with me—like he was amused inside?"

Mrs. Plansky felt stirring in the silo where the heavy artillery was stored. She knew at that moment she was done with crying. "Straight up, Mr. Perryman. You seem to think this second call was important. Mind filling me in on why?"

He tapped on his keyboard and a printer on a shelf behind him started up. "It's unusual," he said. "Maybe unique, and I see a lot of these cases. An awful lot. The point is we're always on the lookout for fingerprints. Not that the second call is a fingerprint for sure. But it's a candidate. Why make that second call? The game was over." He reached behind him for the printout, laid it on his desk, tapped it. "Off the top, I'm happy to say that your case has already been looked at here by one of my associates. She mentions the second call but doesn't seem to have flagged it as anything special."

"Shouldn't she be in this meeting?" Mrs. Plansky said.

"Ideally, yes, but she was posted back stateside two days ago. That probably explains the second call situation—she ran out of time." Mr. Perryman took out a red pen, and circled something on the page.

"So who's in charge of my case now?" Mrs. Plansky said.

"Good question. Let's see what I can do about that. Please wait here. I'll be right back." He rose and walked out of the room, leaving the door open.

Mrs. Plansky sat with her purse in her lap and waited. She remembered a recent appointment where she'd sat just like this, only at the DMV. She rose and went to the window. The marines were still shooting hoops. They were laughing and trash talking—she could tell that part from the body language—and having fun far from home but not far from boyhood. Mrs. Plansky took a closer look at Mr. Perryman's anonymous family and then wandered over toward the desk and sat back down. She gazed at the printout, the writing upside down from her vantage point, the font too small to be read from this distance anyway. But that was academic, the point being that you didn't read the paperwork on the desks of others. That would be snooping.

And snooping was wrong, end of story. Here, in this office of the Secret Service, Mrs. Plansky suddenly saw the irony. Snooping was wrong, yes, but this office was on a different planet, where snooping was the whole point! Therefore did refusing to join in make you impolite, a boor, brought up in a barn? Well, a stretch, maybe, but why take the slightest risk of being a boor if by merely rising and taking three or four little steps around the desk you kept your membership in polite society, at least polite society as it functioned on Planet Snoopy? Mrs. Plansky gazed down at the printout and was just starting to read when she heard footsteps approaching in the hall.

Something amazing happened at that moment, reminiscent of the tennis match not so long ago when she'd spun around and run down that lob without a thought to her new hip, which by the way seemed to be making its presence known since that late-night call. Mrs. Plansky didn't make the connection between that tennis match and what took place now until later, but the connection was absence of thought, the triumph of pure instinct—in the case of the tennis spinning around and running, in the case of the here and now whipping her phone out of her purse and snapping a quick photo of the top printout page.

She was back at the window, phone in purse, purse in hand, when Mr. Perryman walked into the room.

"The jarheads still shooting hoops?" he said.

Mrs. Plansky turned. "They're having so much fun."

Undercover ops? Was that the expression? She'd been born for this.

Nineteen

"My wife swears by your toaster knife," Mr. Perryman said when they were back in their places at his desk.

"How nice," said Mrs. Plansky. "Although we sold the company some years ago," she added, updating the research he'd just been doing.

"You and your husband?"

"My late husband."

"Sorry."

"Thank you."

Mr. Perryman glanced down at the printout. Mrs. Plansky suddenly wondered whether his office was equipped with security cameras. It almost seemed like a no-brainer, given his profession. She forced herself not to scan the room.

"I'm going to be taking over this case myself," Mr. Perryman said.

Because of his wife and the toaster knife? Whatever the reason, this was good news. Nothing beat face-to-face relationships in business. Why wouldn't undercover ops be the same?

He checked his watch. "I'll be reporting to you either by voice, text, or email as soon as I have any news, and I'll also be checking in once a week whether there's news or not."

"Great," said Mrs. Plansky. "Any chance you're free this afternoon?"

Mr. Perryman's handsome face wasn't formed for expressing

confusion. It came close to making him appear ugly. "Not following you."

"I was thinking we'd drive up to Alba Gemina. It looks to be about three hours away on the map."

Mr. Perryman folded his hands on the desk. "Why Alba Gemina?"

"Why, because of the Safemo connection." She gestured toward the printout with her chin. "Isn't that in there?"

Mr. Perryman didn't answer that question. Instead he said, "What do you know about Safemo?"

"Just what the FBI told me. Safemo's like Paymo or Venpal—a way to transfer money, except it was set up by the scammers, probably just for onetime use, they said." She saw in his eyes that she'd gone wrong somewhere. "They being the FBI, not the scammers," she explained. "But they—the scammers—made a mistake. It turned out that Safemo had in fact been used before. The FBI didn't tell me the details of that case, but in working on it they'd zeroed in on Alba Gemina. As the place where the scam originated from, is the point."

Mr. Perryman said nothing, just gazed at her.

"Oh, dear," she said. "Did I say Paymo? And Venpal?"

He nodded a slight nod.

"I meant the reverse, of course. Not reverse, but . . ." She let that trail off.

His gaze was on her but his eyes had an inward look. He gave his head a little shake. "I don't want to speak ill of a brother agency."

"Oh, go ahead," said Mrs. Plansky. "I won't tell."

Mr. Perryman's eyebrows rose slightly. Was a laugh on the way? It didn't come. Instead he said, "I'll have to ask you to forget about that initial Safemo hit, Mrs. Plansky, which should not have been mentioned. It resulted from another investigation, a classified investigation having nothing to do with cyberfraud."

"That's not what I was told."

Mr. Perryman had no comment.

"And I don't want to forget about it," she went on.

"Excuse me?"

"It's an important clue. How do you forget something like that?"

He sat back. He rubbed his hands together. His desk phone buzzed. He ignored it. "You're clearly an intelligent woman," he began.

"That won't work," Mrs. Plansky said.

Oh, dear. Had she spoken that aloud? She wasn't quite sure until she saw the hardening in his face, or more like a revelation of his inner self. Mr. Perryman was a tough guy—and why not in a job like his?—but also very smooth. He might have been around the same age as Jack, but he wasn't Jack, not close. She didn't even try to imagine Jack in a job like Mr. Perryman's.

"Okay," he said. "Let's skip on down to the bottom line. What happened to you has happened and will happen to huge numbers of people. I've seen the data. The perpetrators are all over the place, but especially in Eastern Europe, including this country, where Alba Gemina is a particular locus point. All you have to do is drive through it and see all the luxury car dealerships—like Brentwood, on a per capita basis, but there are no Brentwood-type jobs. The skill level is an important variable ranging from the crudest—just throwing out any sort of bait hoping to hook something—to sophisticated. Your case is on the sophisticated end. There are many indicators—the fact that they knew your grandson's name, to take one."

"How did they know that?"

"It just takes a little work—almost none if they've bought or designed an algorithm to crawl through social media twenty-four seven, three sixty-five."

Technology was good enough in, say 1959, thought Mrs. Plansky, a thought she held firmly to herself.

His phone buzzed again, and again he ignored it. "Any questions?"

Any questions? Didn't question time come at the end? Mrs. Plansky wasn't ready for the end of this meeting. She didn't want to be rude but there were still plenty of questions. She boiled them down. "What happens next?"

"On our end, we—meaning USSS and the FBI—will loop in our Romanian colleagues, specifically the Cybercrime Directorate, and open a joint file on the case. The actual boots on the ground are theirs. Our role is to provide technical and intel support. Plus encouragement, if necessary."

"Why would encouragement be necessary?"

"We're not at home, Mrs. Plansky. It's a different culture. We make mistakes if we make assumptions, even basic ones of right and wrong."

Mrs. Plansky was happy that such an intelligent and supple-minded man was carrying the standard of her nation overseas. On the other hand, she was unhappy with where he seemed to be headed.

"Is there any culture where stealing is okay?" she said.

Could a smile be somehow impatient? That was the expression she thought she saw crossing Mr. Perryman's face. "Not that I know of. I'm just trying to give you a heads-up on what might lie ahead."

"Go on."

"My goal is the same as yours—find the perpetrators, bring them to justice, recover what can be recovered. The goal of our Romanian colleagues is also the same but the context is different."

"How so?"

"The reasons for that are beyond my pay grade. That's what other people in this building, on the diplomatic side, work on for a living. Namely understanding another culture well enough to make their future actions predictable. What I'm trying to get across is the need for patience."

"You want me to be patient."

"A big ask, I know. But maybe now that you understand the situation it'll be a little easier."

Mrs. Plansky felt no easier, but had no idea what to say next. So she said what Norm would have said. "Finding the perpetrators, bringing them to justice, recovering what's recoverable."

"You've got it."

"Please estimate their probability, if you don't mind," she said. "In percentages, for example."

Mr. Perryman laughed, laughed—or at least she thought so—like the real Mr. Perryman inside, husband to the beautiful wife and serious kids on the shelf at his back. "I'm not going to do that," he said.

"I won't hold you to it," said Mrs. Plansky.

He just shook his head. "Now, as for you, I first want to say how much I admire you coming all this way, for being so proactive. It's really been a big help, and as I said I'll be in touch every week, at the minimum. I've booked you on a flight home at five this afternoon, first-class to Miami with that stop in Zurich, no nonstops, I'm sorry to say. Marine Corporal Avery will drive you to your hotel, wait while you pack and get ready, and take you to the airport." Mr. Perryman rose. "Here's your boarding pass."

"Is this the bum's rush?" she said.

"You're no bum, Mrs. Plansky. This has been a real pleasure. You've done your job, above and beyond. Now let us do ours. If it was any other season I'd say maybe stick around for a day or two, take in the sights. But winter's not the right time for Bucharest."

Mrs. Plansky rose. "Thank you." She took the boarding pass. They shook hands. "Noroc," she said.

"Sorry?"

"Uh, Romanian for good luck."

"Don't tell me you speak Romanian."

"Just a couple words."

"Same," he said.

Something in her chest seemed to make a sudden descent, like a too-fast elevator. Or her confidence in Mr. Perryman. He led her to the door. Marine Corporal Avery—no longer in uniform but she recognized him from the basketball half-court outside—was waiting in the hall. She hadn't realized how tall he was. Mr. Perryman introduced them.

"At your service, ma'am."

Corporal Avery walked her down the hall. His physical strength radiated a force field Mrs. Plansky could sense. She felt small. Counteracting that in some way was the knowledge that she had purloined and undoubtedly secret—if at a low level, far from the top, your eyes only—goods in her purse.

Back in her room—Corporal Avery waiting in the lobby—Mrs. Plansky took out her phone, went to photos, examined the picture she'd taken of the top page of Mr. Perryman's printout. She read it from beginning to end, a bureaucratic summary of her case prepared by a colleague of Mr. Perryman's with the initials FR in the appropriate box, now posted back stateside. Mrs. Plansky went over it a few more times, coming to the conclusion she was learning nothing new. Only the angle of incidence, as Norm would say, was different. Except for one little thing, a handwritten notation in the margin, with a handwritten FR at the bottom. This notation was what Mr. Perryman had circled in red.

Suggestion: Loop in Max Leonte in Alba Gemina? Then in parenthesis came a string of digits she took to be a phone number.

Mrs. Plansky took a deep breath and started entering in that number. But. But. There were so many buts circling around this little move. If she was going to take a shot—almost surely a one-shot sort of shot—shouldn't she maximize her chances? But how, exactly? There, one more but, just what she didn't need. Mrs. Plansky put away her phone and started packing. She'd emptied out her suitcase the night before, of course, hanging the hangables in the closet, with her mules and her ballet flats on the shoes shelf on the bottom and her foldables on the shelves above.

Mrs. Plansky went to the desk, found that Uncle Sam had taken care of her bill.

"This all?" said Corporal Avery, lifting her suitcase even though it had wheels.

"Yes, but you don't have to—"

"My pleasure, ma'am. My mom travels just like this, too, real light."

"She sounds like a very smart woman, Corporal."

"That's for sure, ma'am. No one messes with my mom."

Corporal Avery dropped her at the international doors at the terminal. Not quite dropping: in fact he carried the suitcase, walked her to the door, extended the suitcase handle, held the door.

"Safe travels, ma'am."

"Thank you, Corporal. Thanks for everything." Did her voice catch a bit, there at the end? She began to think this particular day was a strange one indeed.

Mrs. Plansky checked the board, saw that she had plenty of time, which was how she handled air travel. She got out her passport, stuck the boarding pass inside, entered the security line.

It turned out to be one of those slow-moving lines, through a not very big yet endless maze. But it was for this very type of situation that Mrs. Plansky allowed herself extra time! The line shuffled forward, halted, shuffled forward, halted. At the halts, she took to reading the purloined document, not technically purloined since she'd merely photographed it, but still. Then came a halt where she pocketed the phone, said, "Excuse me," and stepped out of line.

Mrs. Plansky reversed course and made her way out of security. A few minutes later she was at the counter of a rental car company she couldn't pronounce the name of. No one messes with Corporal Avery's mom. That was her guiding—if somewhat crazy—thought.

TWENTY

Almost all the available cars were stick shift. Automatic cost much more. Mrs. Plansky could drive stick, no problem, a bit of a surprise to the clerk. Way back in high school, the old guy who ran driver's ed insisted on all the kids learning to drive stick. "With automatic you're just sittin' thumb up your butt doin' nothin' and that's when the trouble starts." Even then the kids sensed he was a holdover from a previous age.

The clerk helped her program the route to Alba Gemina on her phone. "On your way to the mountains?" he said. "There's not much to see in Alba Gemina itself."

"The mountains sound beautiful," Mrs. Plansky said.

"The most beautiful drives in Europe, according to several polls. But there are many road closures in winter. Use caution."

"That's me," she said.

He laughed. "Bonne route, madame! The hard part is getting out of town."

That proved to be true. At least it was one of the hard parts. Also hard was just getting out of the airport. Then there were the road signs, the distance in kilometers, which meant multiplying by point six something or other, a task always done by Norm on their five or six European trips. She drove. He sat in the passenger seat and mused aloud, a driving trip always bringing that out of him. It was bliss. Sometimes they sang. He had a terrible voice, except for that Tony Bennett moment at the very end, but Mrs. Plansky could sing.

She'd been in various glee clubs and vocal groups straight through high school and college, could read music, carry different harmony parts, play a bit of piano and guitar and also harmonica, the only instrument she was actually any good at. All that in the distant past, except for the duets with Norm, in the more recent past.

Another problem with the road signs was the writing on them. Whenever a road sign appeared, she chanced a quick peek at her phone in its little holder on the dash to see if things were matching up, but the things, the words themselves, refused to make sense. The alphabet was the one she knew but while that was also true in Italy or France, the Romanian take was much more difficult. Mrs. Plansky decided to ignore the many diacritics and silently pronounce all words exactly how they'd be in English.

That worked. She kept to the speed limit on a fairly well-paved two-laner, at first dead straight through flat farm country lightly covered in snow, then getting curvier in some low hills. Traffic was heavy but then thinned out all at once, for no reason she could see. Mrs. Plansky even tried a bit of passing, overtaking an ancient truck with black smoke pouring from the tailpipe, and a horse-drawn cart with an old woman in black holding the reins, a not warmly-enough dressed little boy beside her, the breath of all three—woman, boy, horse—making tiny clouds in the bright sunshine.

The road began to climb in broad sweeping curves into what were probably the foothills of snowcapped mountains in the distance. Every so often a village went by, none looking prosperous, the houses and shops lining the road with very few buildings farther back, and always a church in the Orthodox style, the domes unpainted except for a single gold dome in one village. Mrs. Plansky drove carefully around a dog lying in the road and began to sing "I'm in the Mood for Love," one of her favorites. There were many versions but in a dopey kind of way the one she preferred wasn't Nat King Cole's or Jo Stafford's or even Billie Eilish's, but the doo-wop version by the Chimes, which she'd tried and utterly failed to teach Norm. Now she sang and sang, unaware at first that she'd driven up into fog, or that it had drifted down to her. She slowed way down. The fog grew thicker, and to her surprise she realized she was on a dirt road, quite narrow. That had to be wrong. Up ahead she could just make out what seemed to be a lookout off the side of the road. She pulled in and stopped the car.

Mrs. Plansky checked her phone, trying to figure out where she'd gone wrong. Was this a split she'd passed maybe ten kilometers back? Had she gone left instead of right? And what was this? Another split, this one a three-way, even farther back? And there she'd been, crooning away without a care in the world.

"Darn," she said. She didn't have the margin to do anything but devote full attention to what needed doing, full stop.

Mrs. Plansky got out of the car and headed toward what she assumed was the edge of the lookout, hoping to get her bearings. She thought she could make out a trash barrel, and headed for that. The fog thickened and thickened even though the wind was rising, a chilly wind. She tightened the Scottish scarf, feeling far from home. The silence was complete, like she'd been balled in cotton batting. Then from somewhere ahead came voices. She moved toward the sound.

Yes, she saw, a trash barrel for sure. Beside it she could make out the form of a man, leaning on something. And nearby another man, also leaning on something. She took a few more steps and the shapes of those two somethings resolved into bicycles. No, not bicycles. Motorcycles. What was hello, again? She'd memorized it on the flight, or meant to. But it wasn't there.

"Hello?" she said in English, wondering a little late if the Hell's Angels had overseas chapters.

The forms of the two men changed position, came forward through the fog. Small forms for Angels, and not men, but teenagers, one with a can of soda in his hand, the other munching on an end piece of dark bread spread with something garlicky she could smell. They were dressed similarly in jeans and leather jackets, the difference being in footwear, one wearing gold high-top sneakers, the other in cowboy boots. They gazed at her, mouths open.

"Hello," she said again. "Sorry I don't speak Romanian. Do either of you speak English?"

The one in the high-tops—plump, pimply, sixteen or seventeen—pointed to the other one—slight, fine-featured, with a James Dean–type forelock half over his eyes.

"Yes," said the slight one, hardly more than a boy from his appearance, "I speak English. Are you American?"

"I am," said Mrs. Plansky.

"From where in America?" said the slight one.

"Florida."

"Ah. The Sunshine State."

"That's right. Have you been there?"

"Only in my dreams."

The pimply one said something that sounded like "chay." The slight one spoke to him in Romanian. Mrs. Plansky was starting to get a feel for the sound, a mix of Italian, French, and some other more elusive element, but the only word she could identify was "Florida."

The slight one turned to her. "Is it sunny every day?"

"Not every day, but lots."

The wind rose a little more, not dissipating the fog at all but blowing scraps of newspaper and Styrofoam toward the edge of the lookout. The slight one seemed to be thinking. The pimply one downed the rest of his soda and tossed the empty can over his shoulder into the void.

"Have you been to the spring break?" the slight one said.

"Once," said Mrs. Plansky, "but a long time ago."

"You didn't like it?"

"No, I did, but spring break is for young people."

"Chay?" said the pimply one again, which she guessed was spelled C-E and probably meant *what?*

Again the slight one spoke to him in Romanian. A back-and-forth ensued, the pimply one growing more animated at what Mrs. Plansky assumed was a description of the goings-on at spring break. He turned to her and smiled, tapping his chest.

"Romeo," he said.

Uh-oh. No, it couldn't be. Some sort of wildly mistaken come-on based on a cartoonish image of female America, specifically the Florida spring break variety, combined with an adolescent inability to see what was in front of his face, namely a seventy-one-year-old woman, going on seventy-two? Just then, when she was about to try "You're not lookin' at Juliet, buddy boy," or something like that, he pointed to the slight one and said, "Dinu."

Ah. "Those are your names, Romeo and Dinu?"

They nodded.

"I'm Loretta," she said. "Nice to meet you."

They shook hands, Romeo and Dinu first removing their gloves—a polite gesture not lost on Mrs. Plansky—well-worn gloves with tears on some of the fingertips. Even though she hadn't been wearing her gloves, their hands felt cold in hers, meaning hers was warmer.

"Loretta?" Dinu said. There was something nice about how he spoke her name. Maybe it was just that he had one of those likable voices. "Like Loretta Lynn?"

"You know about Loretta Lynn?"

"Daughter of a coal miner. Excuse me—coal miner's daughter."

"Right, but how do you know about her?"

"Country music," said Dinu.

"You like country music?"

"Some. But the reason is for learning the right way of speaking English wrong, you know? For sounding like an American."

Mrs. Plansky laughed. "You're going to be very successful."

"I am?"

"Because that's a brilliant idea. I'll bet someone will monetize it, if they haven't already."

"What is monetize?"

"Turn into money."

"Ce?" said Romeo.

Dinu started in on an explanation of what Mrs. Plansky took to be country music, American language, and monetization. None of that appeared to interest Romeo much, certainly not to the level of spring break.

When that came to an end, Mrs. Plansky said, "Are you guys from around here? The truth is I'm a bit lost. I'm trying to get to Alba Gemina but I think I took a wrong turn."

"You were driving from Bucharest?" Dinu said.

"Yes."

"Then you took a wrong turn for sure but . . ." He paused, thought for a moment, and went on. "No biggie. In fact, you found the shortcut."

"Ce?" said Romeo.

This time Dinu didn't bother explaining. "We are from Alba Gemina. We will guide you there. Follow, please."

"That's so nice," Mrs. Plansky said. "But I don't want to interrupt your day."

"We have to go to work anyway," said Dinu.

"What is it you do, if you don't mind my asking?"

Dinu glanced at Romeo. Their eyes met. "Students," he said. "We're students. Where in Alba Gemina do you want to go?"

"I actually haven't made a reservation yet. Any recommendations?"

"For a hotel?"

"Or a B and B."

"What is B and B?"

"Well, it's . . . yes, a hotel. A hotel will be fine."

"There's the Duce," Dinu said. "It's very nice. All renovated. My uncle owns it." Mrs. Plansky hesitated. Dinu noticed that. "But the Royale is nicer. Also more expensive."

"Royale?" Romeo said.

He and Dinu got into a long discussion. Mrs. Plansky caught four or five hotel-type names but nothing else. The wind blew much harder and colder, opening a gap in the fog, and revealing a rather dramatic drop-off quite nearby, a matter of a few steps.

"How about this idea, Loretta?" Dinu said. "We can take you to the Duce. If you don't like it, the Royale is right across the square."

"Sounds like a plan," said Mrs. Plansky.

"Sounds like a plan. I love that one."

"Ce?" said Romeo.

Dinu launched into what must have been a translation of *sounds like a plan.*

Understanding spread across Romeo's face, followed by delight.

"Sound like plan!" he said in English. The two of them high-fived, then did it again, this time including Mrs. Plansky.

Mrs. Plansky followed them up through some switchbacks, the road still hard-packed dirt with gravel stretches, almost out of the fog, and into a golden haze. The boys—well, not boys, call them young men—led on their bikes, Romeo on the black one, Dinu on the red. From time to time the haze swallowed them up and she was alone, her wheels touching down on Georgia O'Keeffe's golden meadows. For a few moments Mrs. Plansky gave herself up to silly, grandiose thoughts, like "this is what travel is all about!" Then she rolled down her window—her car, the make of which was new to her and at the moment forgotten, equipped with the old-fashioned-type handles for the windows—so she could hear the motorcycles and not lose contact with these very nice young men. Mrs. Plansky felt good about her chances. The tide had turned, she'd turned the corner, was turning things around—all those turning clichés. The point was she was doing, not being done to.

The rest of the drive into Alba Gemina took place back in deep fog, unpenetrated by golden rays. Mrs. Plansky, trying to keep Dinu and Romeo in sight, could form only vague impressions of winding descent, flattening landscape, human structures, first rural, then urban. Toward the end they crossed a bridge, joined bumper-to-bumper traffic, turned into a quiet, cobblestone square with an equestrian statue in the center, and came to a three-story, slate-roofed, yellow building with blue drainpipes. Over the door—old, dark wood, brass studs—hung a gold-painted sign: DUCE. Romeo, waving goodbye, kept going with a slight wobble, across the square and down a side street, but Dinu stopped, put a foot down, and motioned for Mrs. Plansky to come alongside.

She drove up. Dinu's face was red from the cold. He pointed to the sign. "Hotel Duce," he said.

"Thank you, Dinu."

"And there," he went on, pointing to a bigger slate-roofed building on the other side of the square, this one blue with yellow drainpipes and also three heavy yellow columns, "Hotel Royale, ten stars."

"Ten?" said Mrs. Plansky.

"Whatever is the most," said Dinu. He laughed, maybe at himself in an ironic way. An unusual kid, thought Mrs. Plansky, laughing with him.

He revved the bike. "Happy traveling, Loretta!"

"Same you to. But—but wait a minute." She fumbled through her purse. She had no Romanian money yet, didn't even know if they had their own or used euros, but she found a twenty-dollar bill and held it out. "For you and Romeo."

"Oh, no, please," Dinu said, making a little gesture of dismissal, a gesture that struck her as aristocratic. He drove away, popping a wheelie. Maybe much more of a street urchin than an aristocrat, but an odd combo for sure. Mrs. Plansky eased forward between the lines of a marked space, getting herself properly parked, hauled her suitcase out of the trunk, locked the car, checked to make sure it was locked, and entered Hotel Duce.

TWENTY-ONE

The Hotel Duce lobby was small, with whitewashed stone walls, dark ceiling beams, a dark wooden floor, old and worn but highly polished. A few paintings hung on the walls, gleaming paintings all with the same subject, namely racing cars. Also there was a poster of Bela Lugosi, not in costume. Mrs. Plansky didn't recognize him at first. She liked this hotel already.

She went up to the desk. A very pretty young woman sat there, typing away on a laptop. She wore a tank top and jeans, an outfit that seemed a little scanty for the time of year. Pinned to the tank top was a name tag: ANNIKA. She looked up and said something in Romanian.

"Sorry," said Mrs. Plansky. "Do you speak English?"

"A little."

"I'm looking for a room for two or three nights, possibly more."

"No problem at all. Is winter." She handed Mrs. Plansky a brochure. "Available is the president suite."

"Oh, I don't need anything that fancy." Mrs. Plansky found pictures of the different classes of rooms. The presidential suite looked suitable for a very undemanding president. But simple and nice. All the rooms were that way, although the prices seemed rather high.

"Price is in lei," Annika said. "You are American?"

"Yes."

"Divide by five."

"Ah."

"And you can have president for regular deluxe rate. Off-season discount."

Mrs. Plansky did a quick calculation. They were talking around forty-five dollars a night. "That'll be fine," she said.

"Includes breakfast, Wi-Fi, and twenty-dollar gift card to Club Presto."

"What's that?" said Mrs. Plansky.

Annika gave her a close look. "Instead we do gift card to Salle Privé. Is nice restaurant."

Mrs. Plansky got out her passport and credit card. Annika was just finishing checking her in when a huge man entered through an inner door. Once she and Norm had signed on with an ad agency that had a relationship with a very popular former NFL lineman who starred in a TV barbecue show, and they'd ended up spending a lot of money hiring him to do a commercial. He'd turned out to match his image in terms of being relaxed and funny, and Mrs. Plansky had stood right next to him backstage, showing him how to use the knife. She'd felt like a member of some different species. This man—wearing a tight T-shirt that revealed enormous shoulder muscles rising up and sort of taking possession of his neck—had the same body type and size.

"Oh, Marius," Annika began, making what sounded like some sort of request.

"Ce?" said Marius.

Annika handed her the room key and the gift card. "Marius will take you to your room."

He came over, not in an enthusiastic way. "Hey, there," he said.

"Hi," said Mrs. Plansky. "You speak English?"

"Then and now," said Marius. He reached for her suitcase, plucked it up with just his thumb and index finger on the handle and led Mrs. Plansky across the lobby and up a flight of stairs covered in a threadbare oriental runner, stairs that creaked under Marius's massiveness. The pant legs of his jeans rode up slightly with his movements, revealing an ankle sheath with a knife in it, practically in her face. How interesting, she thought, two giants—the NFL lineman and Marius—had made a brief appearance in her life, with knives as—what would you call them?—props? Knives as props in both cases.

At the top of the stairs he turned down a hall, passing another poster of Bela Lugosi, this time in his famous role. They came to a door with a framed photo of a smiling Richard Nixon on the wall above. A planned juxtaposition by whoever had done the decor? Or just random? The fun she and Norm would have had with that!

"President suite," Marius said. He made a little motion with his fingers. She handed him the key. He opened up.

"Did he stay here?" she said. "Nixon?"

"Here no," said Marius. "Romania, yes. Was big moment in our history."

"He had lots of big moments in ours," Mrs. Plansky said.

Just a little joke, but wasted, Marius's face without expression. He rolled the suitcase inside but didn't enter, just gave her the key.

"Enjoy visit, lady."

"Thank you." She reached in her purse.

Marius made a windshield wiper gesture with his index finger.

"My goodness," Mrs. Plansky said. "Is there no tipping in Romania?"

"No tipping in Romania?" Marius laughed, a surprisingly high-pitched sound coming from him. "Very excellent joke. I tell the guys."

The presidential suite at the Hotel Duce turned out not to be a suite, but it did have a little seating nook.

The bed, a double, was a mahogany hulk from a past age with fluted posts and a canopy. Also, the presidential suite was very cold, one of the windows, a casement-style leaded window, being fully open. Mrs. Plansky cranked it shut, at the same time taking in a nice view of the square and the bronze equestrian statue, the horse and man both larger than life, the bronze old and oxidized, making for a deep glowing patina. The rider, in armor except for his *Doctor Zhivago*–style fur hat, was brandishing a wide-bladed sword. She locked the window.

After that she unpacked, hanging the hangables, folding the foldables, shelving her toiletries in the bathroom, which she'd expected to be tiny but was in fact as big as the bedroom, although it lacked a tub and was mostly empty space. Perhaps it had been its own room at a previous time. There was a door in the wall right next to the shower stall, an old, heavy wooden door with no knob or keyhole. Mrs. Plansky gave it a push. It didn't budge.

There was nothing more to unpack. She'd done all this careful unpacking because that was how she did things, but also as a way to postpone a tricky moment. Mrs. Plansky was well aware that she'd had plenty of time on the drive up from Bucharest to think about what was coming, but—and how lazy of her!—she'd waited for inspiration instead.

"And how did that work out, girl?" Out loud? No. She was almost sure.

Mrs. Plansky went into the sitting nook, sat at the desk—"back straight, feet together on the floor," as Miss Terrance had taught—and arranged the hotel notepad and pen in front of her. Then she took out her phone and looked over the purloined document once more. What had seemed like a great idea at the time no longer did. But it was her gut idea, and hadn't she always ended up going with her gut at the big moments? The truth was she really couldn't say. How was it possible to be this ancient and still not know thyself?

Suggestion: Loop in Max Leonte in Alba Gemina? And then in parenthesis what she took to be a phone number. But what if it wasn't?

"Why don't you just turn tail and go on home?" she said, out loud for sure, and angry, angry at herself. In her anger, Mrs. Plansky entered the number on her phone, stabbing out each and every digit. Except for the last one. Right then she had what seemed like a clever idea, just in case—well, just in case. Leave it at that. The clever idea was to change things up on her phone so her name would not appear to the receiver of the call. She was pretty sure it could be done, but how, exactly? Settings! Wasn't there some obscure region of the phone that dealt with settings?

Sometime later, not too long, her phone was set to go, now in a craftier mode. Mrs. Plansky dialed the number. It rang on the other end, wherever that might have been. Was there any reason to think this man, Max Leonte, was even in Alba Gemina right now? He could be anywhere, Washington, D.C., for example, which suddenly seemed more likely. Also phones no longer rang. Instead they made some sort of digital sound engineered and product-tested, no doubt, to induce a state of mind that—

"Da?"

Mrs. Plansky rose to her feet. Her hand, gripping the phone, had suddenly gone all sweaty.

"Da?"

A male voice, baritone, not exactly unpleasant, but certainly impatient.

"Da?"

Mrs. Plansky took a deep breath. "Hello? Do you speak English? I'm looking for Max Leonte."

"Who is this?" said the man, his English accented slightly but very good.

"Are you Mr. Leonte?"

"Who is this?" he repeated.

It was just a feeling but Mrs. Plansky didn't want to offer her name, at least not right now, and over the phone. This was a problem she hadn't foreseen, and foreseeing in general wasn't her strength these days. Maybe the foreseeing part of her brain had been wiped out in one of those silent strokes you heard about. She was only half-joking with herself about that, and during this little pause a sideways move occurred to her.

"My name wouldn't mean anything to you," she said.

"I am now ending the call," said the man.

"Wait! Don't do that. My name's Loretta."

"Just the one name? Like Beyoncé?"

"Not like Beyoncé," Mrs. Plansky said.

He didn't respond right away. Then he said, "What is it you want?"

"Well, first to know if you're Max Leonte."

"And then?"

"Maybe we could meet and talk."

"About what?"

"Cybercrime."

Mrs. Plansky expected some question about her interest in cybercrime or her relationship to it, but that was not what came. "Where are you?" he said.

"In Alba Gemina," she said. "Are you here, too? I'm talking about Alba Gemina in Romania."

"I know of no other," he said. "Where in Alba Gemina? A hotel?"

"I'd prefer to meet in some neutral place."

"Name it."

"I actually don't know of any yet. Maybe a coffeehouse?"

"There are many," he said. "In what part of town?"

She gazed through the window. "The old part. Is there a coffeehouse near the square?"

"What square?"

"With the equestrian bronze."

"*Michael the Brave?*"

Mrs. Plansky recalled the name from her reading on the flight, but the details, beyond many confusing and bloody battles, perhaps against the Ottomans, were gone.

"Possibly," she said. "Is there more than one equestrian statue in Alba Gemina?"

"Oh, yes," he said. "Is the rider brandishing his sword like a homicidal maniac?"

"Brandishing, yes."

"*Michael the Brave,*" he said. "Meet me at Café des Artistes, eighteen hundred."

"Is that the address?"

He blew out an irritated-sounding breath. "Six," he said. "Six o'clock this evening. Your hotel—the Royale, I assume—can give you directions."

"How will I know you?"

"I'll wear a billboard with a question mark."

Click.

Mrs. Plansky checked the time. She had two hours. In one of the desk drawers she found a map of the old town and quickly located Café des Artistes—down a street that led off the square, left at the second corner, halfway along the block on the right. She took the map over to the couch—more of a love seat, actually—and sat. Her legs were grateful for the move. Her whole body was grateful. She studied the map of the old town. There was nothing grid-like about it. Sun Tzu had written that understanding terrain was vital, as Mrs. Plansky had learned years ago while helping Jack with an essay for his college apps, in the end researching and writing it herself, more or less. More. But that wasn't the point, which was not to get lost.

Mrs. Plansky opened her eyes. It was dark, very dark for the bay window alcove across from the bar where she liked to sit on her chintz and maple love seat and gaze at the pond, even at night when, yes, she sometimes nodded off, although this deep darkness was unusual, the lights from the windows of the other condos reflected in the water and—

Mrs. Plansky sat up straight, a shock passing through her body, like she'd been paddled by one of those EMT crews. Surely not as bad as that, but . . . but what time was it? She rose, took a hurried step in the direction of the desk in this little hotel sitting nook. Where she was, of course, not back home at all! What was wrong with her? She took another hurried step, bumped into something, twisted around in a way that her new hip did not like in the least, and fell on the floor pretty hard. But—she took stock of herself—but somehow she'd gotten a hand, maybe both, out in front of her, breaking her fall without breaking her wrists, which, even with her mind in turmoil, she realized was the best way to fall, if she had indeed now reached the random falling-down stage.

Mrs. Plansky got to her feet—not so easily—her eyes now tuning in the weak light coming through the window overlooking the square. She switched on a lamp, saw that she'd tripped over a footstool, a footstool where she must have laid her phone and now there it was, on the floor. She snatched it up and checked the time. Twenty twenty-two? What sort of time was that? Then she realized her phone, much savvier than she, had already adopted European ways. Twenty twenty-two was 8:22 p.m. She was two hours and twenty-two minutes late. Had he called or texted? No. All she found were some unread texts that had come in from Emma.

Mrs. Plansky grabbed the map of the old town, threw on her coat, headed for the door, then stopped when she realized she was wearing the quilted mules. She kicked them off, put on the low-heeled booties, hurried out of the presidential suite, through the lobby, and into the square.

A cold wind was blowing. From the west? Didn't the European continental wind blow from the west in winter? Mrs. Plansky checked the map under her phone light as she walked, not as quickly as she wanted, the cobbles feeling tricky under her feet—and found no helpful indicators. Not important, but she always liked to know her compass direction. She reached the street leading off the square, checked its name on a plaque, but for some reason saw only the diacritics and none of the letters. The cobblestones came to an end and pavement began. Mrs. Plansky picked up speed.

Second left, and there it was on the right, Café des Artistes, the scripted letters of the sign followed by the image of a pen and two ink blotches, as though the sign painter had just finished work. A yellow glow leaked from the window and onto the street, otherwise dark. Mrs. Plansky had a strange feeling, like she was a time traveler on her way back. Was she losing her silly mind? She wrenched the door open with more force than necessary.

She had not gone back in time. For one thing, no one was smoking. The room, not big, was about half full. Mrs. Plansky sat at a side table, picked up a menu—a deceptive move of the type that would surely be in an undercover op's bag of tricks—and glanced around, then backtracked and glanced around again, less furtively this time.

The first thing she discovered was that she was the oldest person in the Café des Artistes, not even a close call. How old would the man on phone—maybe Max Leonte, maybe not—have been? Not a youngster, for sure, which eliminated most of the customers, who looked to be college age or the age of professors just starting out. Then there was a couple in their fifties, both wearing berets, two women maybe slightly older than that with shopping bags at their feet, and two bald men who seemed to be having a quiet argument. In short, not her guy, who surely would have been alone.

A waitress with a number of piercings on her face came over and said something in Romanian. Before Mrs. Plansky—who still wasn't able to take facial piercings in stride—could reply, the waitress switched to English for the undercover operator, who ordered coffee, the house blend with cream, although not extra cream, her usual coffee order. Those who missed meetings because they'd nodded off had to discipline themselves somehow or other.

The coffee was good. Two or three sips and she felt a change inside, like some rusted parts were getting oil. She checked those messages from Emma. The first one must have been sent during the flight:

Everything's good! I got accepted for a semester at Oxford! But sure you're ok?

The second: You ok?

The third: Mom says Pops says you're on a business trip? Everything all right?

Mrs. Plansky typed her reply: Short biz trip. Congrats on Oxford. Everything fine!!!

That was the first time she'd ever tripled up on exclamation points, or even doubled up. But she had to find the right breezy tone, somehow stop any worrying—actually any interference—on the home front before it got going. This was hard enough without all those people. Yes, the people she loved with all her heart, but each one lacking a certain capability or two, a fact she was now voicing to herself for the first time. The reasons for the capability gap, which might prove unsettling—especially if they had something to do with this new and troubling concept of the power of the giver—she would deal with some other time.

Mrs. Plansky caught the waitress's eye. The Oxford reference had triggered a little something in her mind. The waitress came over.

"Is there something I can get you?"

"Not just now. Wonderful coffee. I can't help noticing how good your English is."

"Thank you. I lived for two years in London."

"Ah." Mrs. Plansky glanced around. "I was supposed to meet someone here but I'm a little late."

The waitress didn't seem to find anything interesting in that. She gazed over Mrs. Plansky's shoulder at the next table.

"Maybe he was here and couldn't wait," Mrs. Plansky said. "He would have been sitting alone."

"We had several men sitting alone," said the waitress. "What does he look like?"

"Well," said Mrs. Plansky, her only idea being something about a blind date, a ridiculous response given her age.

The waitress caught a signal from another table. "Excuse me."

Not long after that, Mrs. Plansky was back out on the street. The night was colder and the wind stronger, a few hard, stinging little snowflakes in the air. She wrapped her scarf more tightly and headed back to the hotel.

TWENTY-TWO

Mrs. Plansky walked quickly, partly on account of the cold, but also because speed seemed to be making her new hip feel better, perhaps warming up all that titanium. How lucky she was! She knew other tennis players, men and women, who had replaced hips, knees, shoulders, even an ankle or two in the hope of getting back on the court. But often it didn't work out that way and yet there she was, playing the way she'd played ten or fifteen years ago! Naturally she'd need to check video to confirm that judgment, video that luckily did not exist. Mrs. Plansky was occupying herself along those lines when she got the feeling that maybe she should have reached the square by now. She checked her surroundings and recognized nothing.

It was a dim street, with old-fashioned lampposts here and there, most not working. A car went by, lighting up a few shops, all closed, and some two-and three-story structures that she took to be apartment buildings, but old ones from a middle-European past. She walked toward the nearest corner, hoping for a street sign, and wasn't quite there when she thought she heard footsteps behind her. Mrs. Plansky turned and saw no one, just a lot of shadows, some in humanlike form. But that was the way the imagination worked, often overcooking things. She reached the corner, looked for street signs, and found none. But around the corner a blue neon sign hung over a doorway: POLITIA.

Mrs. Plansky walked up to the door. Through a small window, she saw a uniformed woman behind a counter listening to a man standing on the other side, making emphatic gestures while he talked. A police station, for sure. She could go in and get directions, or . . . or do something more than that. A crime had been committed against her, a crime originating in this town. What did you do in a situation like that? You reported it to the police. Mrs. Plansky, feeling like whoever it was who'd sliced through the Gordian knot, opened the door and strode inside.

She was in a small lobby with a few plastic chairs, framed wall photos of half a dozen unsmiling men in uniforms with lots of braiding, and no one else except the gesticulating man and the female cop. The man was very annoyed about something but Mrs. Plansky couldn't pick out a single word. The cop was very patient or perhaps bored. She had her hair drawn back very tightly in a complicated bun, distorting her face a little and making her facial expressions hard to read.

Mrs. Plansky sat on a plastic chair, feet together, purse on her knees. It was nice and warm in the police station. She loosened her scarf and began organizing her little speech. Her mind didn't want to do that, instead wanted to think about distortion. For example, being in a foreign land was distorting. Wasn't that really the main attraction of travel? Yet people often came back saying, "When you get to know them they're just like us." So when they were distorted the foreigners were actually like us but we didn't know yet? Did we end up discovering our own distortion? Mrs. Plansky found she was confusing herself, perhaps proving the point.

A door opened on Mrs. Plansky's side of the counter but across the room. Inside was an office where a man who looked like he could have been in one of the framed photos—even down to the braiding on his uniform jacket—was sitting at his desk, glass in hand. An empty glass sat on the desk beside a whiskey bottle. A second man was at the door, on his way out, when the uniformed man said something that made him laugh. The second man replied. Whatever he said the uniformed man found very funny. He laughed and laughed and downed the rest of his drink. The second man closed the door and turned, taking in the scene at the counter. He caught her attention, maybe because of how imposing he was, how capable he seemed, with his large, square chin, nose that matched, large square hands, and a large square body, everything about him large and square, other than his eyes. His eyes were small, round, glinting, and not pleased with the goings on at the counter.

"Hei!" he said, his voice forceful but a little higher than she would have thought. For a moment she'd been wondering without any rational basis if this man might be Max Leonte, or more precisely the man on the phone, but their voices were very different—and not just in pitch but in sensibility, Mrs. Plansky allowing herself another unjustifiable mental leap.

The gesticulating man whirled around at the sound of that "Hei!" with something very aggressive on the way. At the sight of Mr. Squareman that aggression faded fast. He turned to the female cop, made a what-the-hell motion with his hand, said, "Ach," and walked quickly out of the building.

Mr. Squareman tied the belt on his black leather coat and pulled on black leather gloves lined in sheepskin. He headed for the door, then seemed to sense Mrs. Plansky's presence. He glanced her way. Those glinting eyes seemed to make a quick study of her with no attempt to pretend they were not, like some sort of scanning machine. He turned and walked out the door, not one of those big guys who was surprisingly light on his feet. She felt his strides through the soles of her booties.

The female cop looked over at her and said something in Romanian. Mrs. Plansky rose.

"Hello, Officer," she said. "Do you speak English?"

"No English," said the cop.

"I want to report a cybercrime," Mrs. Plansky said, speaking very slowly and distinctly, a caricature of an unsavvy tourist abroad for the first time.

The cop made an Italianate sort of elaborate shrug, most of her body involved.

Mrs. Plansky, a friendly smile on her face, approached the counter. "Does anyone here speak English?"

That got her a blank look from the cop.

"English?" said Mrs. Plansky, attempting a gesture meant to take in the whole building.

"Da," said the cop. "Capitan Romulu." She pointed to the office that Mr. Squareman had just left.

"Can I talk to him, please?"

No reaction.

Mrs. Plansky tried French. "Discuter?"

"Ah, discutu." The cop raised her fist, went *knock knock* in the air.

"Thank you."

Mrs. Plansky moved toward Captain Romulu's office. The sound of ice cubes dropping into a glass came through the closed door. She raised her fist to knock, now hearing the gurgle of pouring liquid. Her fist froze, all set to knock but not knocking. She thought of Agent Gatling, on his last day on the job and possibly speaking more openly than normal. *"But to the elite running the show over there the scammers are bad guys who also have a nice little industry going, bringing in the Yankee dollar and lots of 'em."*

Mrs. Plansky backed away from the captain's door. The tinkling of the ice cubes as the captain drank sounded impossibly loud. So was her heartbeat. She felt way too hot and a bit dizzy. Mrs. Plansky realized she'd entered a zone of extreme distortion. She walked quickly and somewhat unsteadily to the front door and out to the street. From inside came the voice of the female cop: "Hei!"

Mrs. Plansky hurried away, forcing herself not to run. As though she were guilty of something! That was how distorted this was. It seemed to be affecting all her senses. For example, she got a strange feeling between her shoulder blades, like she was being watched, but when she looked around she found herself all alone.

Mrs. Plansky retraced her steps, which didn't make sense since she'd already been lost when she'd taken them, but she kept going just because walking felt good. She was no longer hot or dizzy, and the distortion field, still present, was much weaker. What she needed now was a carefully thought-out plan. What she did not need were sudden impulsive moves made while lost on the dark streets of a town she didn't know. But where to begin?

"Think," she said, and at that moment turned a corner and strolled directly into the cobblestone square, her hotel on one side, the Royale on the other, like she knew what she was doing. Right away she felt more like herself, as though a dissonant soundtrack accompanying her had finally gone silent. The night was still cold but the wind had died down, and gaps were opening among the clouds. The moon came out, a half moon and very clear: she thought she could make out the missing half. Mrs. Plansky walked up to the equestrian statue and had a good look.

Michael the Brave gazed down at her. So did the horse. Their bronze eyes were sightless of course but the moonlight was playing tricks with that. *Michael the Brave* looked fierce and medieval, although not a particularly good listener. That didn't stop her from speaking to him. "I could use someone like you, Mikey."

No answer from Mikey. Mrs. Plansky began to think she preferred the horse, also fierce and medieval, but somehow more approachable. She moved closer and reached up. The horse seemed to have been caught in a cantering pose, hooves up high, but she could just touch a rear one, icy cold.

From behind came the voice of a man. "Going for a ride?"

And now Mrs. Plansky came through for herself. Although all the usual clichés applied to her state of mind—she jumped a foot off the ground, almost had a heart attack, was scared to death—

none of them showed. In fact, she turned quite slowly, in a measured way.

Standing before her was a somewhat younger man. He had dark hair, quite long but at least somewhat kempt, in a style she associated with European intellectuals, although she'd never met one. While there might have been only a hint or two of gray in his hair, his closely trimmed beard was pure white. He was sturdy of build and his eyes appeared to be the color of the moon.

"You're American?" he said.

Maybe because of the fright she'd kept inside, Mrs. Plansky forgot her manners and made a rude gesture, backhanding his question away. "I recognize your voice," she told him.

He didn't seem offended, but neither did he answer, but just watched her closely.

"Are you Max Leonte?"

He kept silent.

She raised her voice, simply couldn't help herself. "Yes or no?"

He smiled, his teeth also moon-colored. "Yes or no—it doesn't get more American than that. No need to see your passport."

"You haven't answered the question."

"First please explain where you got that name."

That was a tough one. The true answer, very complicated but climaxing with the purloining of a document, wouldn't do. "It . . . it came up in the course of an investigation."

"Who is conducting this investigation?"

"Well, me." The truth of that hit her as she spoke, the tongue somehow barging in front of the mind. But it was good to hear. Somewhat intimidating, certainly, but she had taken charge. And whose life was it, after all?

Meanwhile her remark seemed to have had an effect on this man as well. "Don't tell me," he said, putting his hand to his chest. "A member of the tribe?"

What tribe was that? Did he think she was of Romanian heritage? That was her only thought. "Tribe?" she said.

"Metaphorically," he said. Other than slight differences in how he spoke the vowel sounds, shortening some and lengthening others, his English seemed as good as hers, or better. "But I should have said fraternity. That's more accurate and expresses the spirit of the thing."

"What thing are you talking about?" Mrs. Plansky said.

"The journalism thing," he said. "But I can see you're not a journalist. It wouldn't be your style." He held up his hand before she could react to that. The moonlight turned it silver, like another sculpture in the square, this one airborne. "Not that I'm criticizing your style, not in the least." He lowered his hand, held it out. "Max Leonte, at your service."

In the shadow of *Michael the Brave* his hand was no longer metallic, so clearly flesh and blood. Mrs. Plansky took it in her own. They shook. Their breath clouds rose and merged in the air.

TWENTY-THREE

"Loretta Plansky," said Mrs. Plansky, letting go of his hand. Did he show any reaction to the name? None that she could see. "You've been following me."

"Oh, yes," Max Leonte said. "A circuitous course that tired me out. From the Café des Artistes to the old town precinct house, and now to here. I was a little concerned you'd skipped our meeting and gone instead to perhaps see Captain Romulu, who works late but not hard. In fact, I'm still concerned."

"Why?"

"That depends on what you're investigating."

"You're a journalist?"

"Correct."

"Who do you work for?"

"At one time several print and television outlets, here and in other parts of Europe. Now—freelance."

"Meaning you're self-employed?"

"Correct again. I'm working on a book."

"What's it about?"

"Corruption. Specifically in Romania and other countries with close connections to Russia, historically, culturally, geographically—only one of which is necessary in my formulation, but they share the fact that the closeness was in all cases involuntary. My hypothesis, not set in stone, is that the closer those ties the greater the corruption."

Mrs. Plansky was out of her depth. She wasn't the type to ever think herself the smartest person in the room—or even think in those terms at all—but she'd always felt she could hold her own with most people. But not this one. He was one of those European intellectuals, for sure. Still, she plunged ahead.

"Does corruption include cybercrime?" she said.

"Very much it does," said Max Leonte. "Why do you ask?"

Mrs. Plansky had a little internal debate with herself before answering. On one hand, the appearance of Max Leonte's name on Mr. Perryman's document now had some context. On the other, it was a dark, cold night in a strange town far from home. But hadn't she just been asking *Michael the Brave* for help? If not this guy—probably not as violent as Mikey but almost certainly smarter—then who? There was just one thing to be nailed down.

"I'm assuming you're against cybercrime," she said.

He laughed. "Is there any reason we couldn't continue this conversation somewhere warmer?"

"I'm staying at the Duce. I think there's a bar."

Some thought seemed to pass just beneath the surface of his eyes. "Let's try the Royale. Their bar is nicer."

The bar at the Royale had a nineteenth-century hunting lodge decor, with lots of dark wood paneling, thick, smoke-blackened wooden beams, period photos of unsmiling hunters posed over their kills, and weapons—from spears and bows and arrows to shotguns with gleaming barrels—hung on the walls, interspersed with the mounted heads of brown bears, boars, wolves, and something sheep-like with enormous curving horns and contemptuous eyes. Although that part about the eyes might have been just an unusual reflection from the light of the fire in the stone fireplace—an enormous fireplace although the fire itself was rather small.

They sat close to it, Mrs. Plansky in a soft leather chair, the arms studded with the brass caps of shotgun shells, and Max Leonte on the stone hearth itself, with no one else in the room except the waiter, scrolling on his phone.

"Have you tasted tuica yet?" Max Leonte said.

"What is it?"

"Plum brandy. Our national drink. You could try it now and maybe never again, but at least check the box."

He ordered two plum brandies. They came in crystal mugs with a twist of lemon and a drop or two of honey. Mrs. Plansky took a sip and started to warm up, from the inside out. Their eyes met. His turned out not to be the color of the moon, but more like the pale blue of the sky in winter.

"What should I call you?" she said.

"Max. And may I call you Loretta?"

Mrs. Plansky nodded. "What I'm investigating, Max," she said, "is a cybercrime. It involves myself, the victim." How she wished there was another term. And just when needed, it arrived: potential victim, since she wasn't done yet. But would it sound ridiculous? She kept it unsaid.

Max nodded. "Go on."

Mrs. Plansky took another sip of her tuica, actually much more than a sip. Once they'd gone to a talk by a famous writer, she and Norm. After it was over, she'd seen the famous writer in the cloak-room, picking up one of the bookstore clerks with hardly a word, a woman of college age, or even high school, decades younger than the writer. That was disappointing, but now she remembered something he'd said in the talk: "When telling a story leave out most of it."

She started in on her story. She left out Norm. She left out her entire family, except for Will. She left out the toaster knife, her financial obligations, the promises—implicit and explicit—she had to keep, and her deep feeling of humiliation. All the rest she included, meaning the details of the crime as seen from her end, the amount that was stolen—because how could you discuss a theft and omit the amount?—Safemo, her conversations with the FBI agents, Rains and

Gatling, her visit to the embassy in Bucharest, her talk with Mr. Perryman. Well, she left out some of that, namely the important parts, like the purloined document and the fact that Mr. Perryman probably thought she was safely back home by now, and also the very name Mr. Perryman.

"That's pretty much it," she said, taking another big drink. The drink or something else began to ease her burden a little, and even if that was just momentary she gave herself to the feeling.

Max hadn't made a sound the whole time, or even moved at all, although she knew there was movement going on in his mind. His eyes told her that. Wintry blue, large yet not obtrusively so, symmetrical, but none of that was especially meaningful. If the eyes really were the window to the soul, then he was soulful. That was the important part. Journalists could be soulful? That had never occurred to her. Did learning go on right to the last breath? Mrs. Plansky didn't know but she wanted to depart that way herself. She had plenty of time for these irrelevant thoughts because Max was in no hurry to speak.

Finally he set his crystal mug down on the hearth and said, "Tell me about yourself."

Mrs. Plansky hadn't been expecting that. "There isn't much to tell," she said. His question seemed at odds with the famous writer's storytelling advice.

Max smiled. His teeth looked white and cared for, but one of the incisors was very crooked. That fit nicely with the European intellectual part.

"I'll tell you why that can't be true," he said. "I've looked into dozens of cyber scamming cases, am familiar with the details of hundreds more, and know enough about the tens of thousands, the hundreds of thousands originating in central and Eastern Europe to be almost certain that you're the first victim to come looking. That makes you special, so there must be something about yourself to tell after all."

She was the only one? How strange! That couldn't be. "I can't think of anything," Mrs. Plansky said. "I'm just an ordinary American woman." That didn't feel quite right. She made a slight edit. "Ordinary older American woman."

Max picked up his mug and took a drink, watching her over the rim. The fire, reflected at many angles through the crystal facets, lit his face in a devilish way. "I guess I never met one before," he said, lowering the mug. "Since I'm starting from zero, please tell me what you hope to accomplish."

She'd come for her dignity, of course. Did that sound melodramatic? Ridiculous? Unhinged?

"I'd like the money back," Mrs. Plansky said.

Was he about to smile, like she'd amused him in some way? That was her first thought, but it was wrong. Instead he simply said, "It's a lot of money."

"Yes," said Mrs. Plansky.

"Is it a lot of money to you?"

"I don't understand."

"The three point whatever is the exact digit million. What percentage of your wealth is it?"

Mrs. Plansky made allowances for her jewelry and this and that. "Do you want me to include the value of my home?"

"No," he said.

"Then it's about ninety-seven," said Mrs. Plansky.

Max seemed to think that over, and while he thought it over she began to get angry, a very rare event in her life. "But even if it was only one darn percent what does it matter? We earned that money, my husband and I."

He raised both hands, palms up. "Oh, certainly, certainly. I was only thinking from the angle of risk and reward."

"Okay, then." Her anger melted away.

"If I may ask, why didn't your husband come with you?"

"He's dead."

"Ah. I'm sorry."

"Thank you."

"Similarly, I lost my wife. Not to death, but to another man."

Mrs. Plansky had no idea what to say to that.

"But very different, of course. I apologize for being . . . what is the word?"

"Self-dramatizing?"

He looked shocked, then hurt, then amused, the changes coming so fast she almost couldn't keep up. "I was searching for flippant, but yours is better."

"I didn't mean—"

"No, no, I'm glad."

And he looked like he was having fun. One thing about being in Max's company, so far: she was wide awake.

A loud popping sound came from the fire and an ember flew out and landed on the floor. Max squished it out under his shoe. "What's your plan for getting the money back?" he said.

Mrs. Plansky faced facts. "There is no plan."

"Because you don't have enough information yet?"

She grabbed at that. "Yes, that's it."

"So you've come to find out what goes on in the enemy camp."

"Exactly," she said. He was making her sound very shrewd. Inside she felt the opposite, like a fake.

"Is that why you went to the police tonight?" Max said. "To find out what's happening on the ground?"

"Well, yes. But only after failing to meet you at the café."

"There was no other reason?"

"Like what?"

"I was at the café. I sat for forty-five minutes. Then I went outside and waited nearby."

"And you followed me to the police station?"

He nodded.

"How did you know it was me?" she said.

"Let's just say you look the way you sound. I mean that as a compliment. But that won't stop me from making sure your visit to the police station had no ulterior motive."

"I don't understand."

He gave her a careful look, making no effort to hide the fact that he was examining her. An odd feeling came over her. She let herself be examined.

"I have—I don't want to say enemies, but certainly not friends, among the police in this town. Captain Romulu, who I happen to know was the duty officer tonight and would have been the only English speaker there at this time of year, is the least friendly. Naturally I'm interested in what you told him."

"Nothing," said Mrs. Plansky.

"You didn't speak to him?"

"No."

"You spoke to someone else?"

"Just the lady at the desk, to find an English speaker. She pointed toward his office. But I left instead."

"Why?"

"This may sound harebrained," she began.

He interrupted. "That's one expression I've never understood."

"H-A-R-E," said Mrs. Plansky. "Like bunny rabbit."

Max smacked his forehead, so loudly that the scrolling waiter turned to look from across the room. "What an idiot!" he said, and started to laugh, a low sort of rumble deeper than his speaking voice, and surprisingly pleasant, as though the bassoon was taking the lead for an unexpected bar or two. Tears came to his eyes. He wiped them away. "Go on, Loretta. It can't be too harebrained—H-A-R-E!—for me."

"It's just that I'd already seen Captain Romulu through the doorway," Mrs. Plansky explained. "I didn't like the look of him."

"Very wise," Max said. "Captain Romulu would not be the contact you want to make."

"Who would be?"

"Good question," Max said. "I'll have to do some digging. We need to know as many of the answers as possible before we start with the questions. That probably makes no sense at all to someone like you."

"I've met a few people who operate that way," Mrs. Plansky said, omitting the fact that she'd never liked them.

"I don't like them, either," said Max.

Oh, no. Had she said the second part out loud after all? If not, he'd surprised her in a big way, so big she was almost missing something that had to be important: he was speaking of "we."

Was this a moment to be coy, shy, a wallflower? Absolutely not. "So," she said, "are you going to help me?"

"Obviously," said Max Leonte.

"Sorry to be so slow," Mrs. Plansky said. She felt a tremendous relief inside.

"Well, Loretta, I would have expected you'd know the first rule of journalism, the kind of journalism that gets read—put a face to the story."

"I'm the face of your story?"

"With your permission."

Mrs. Plansky nodded. She leaned forward. "In that case you should know a couple of things. First, I assume you're acquainted with Mr. Perryman at the embassy."

"We've spoken a few times but never met."

"He thinks I've gone home."

"Ah," said Max. "And I assume you got my name from him?"

"Not directly," said Mrs. Plansky. "Which brings us to the second thing." She told him her purloining story.

A smile spread across his face as he listened. That crooked tooth of his seemed to draw her gaze like something magnetic. "Therefore I won't be contacting Mr. Perryman," he said when she was done.

"Not about me," Mrs. Plansky said. "What do we do next?"

"Next you go back to your hotel, have a good sleep, and tomorrow perhaps take in the Museum of Carpathian History. There are a number of potential suspects but I'll try to narrow it down, based on what you've told me, and call you by four at the latest. Here is my card. I will add the home address." He patted his pockets, found nothing to write with. Mrs. Plansky opened her purse and handed him a pen. Max wrote on the card and gave it to her.

"Keep the pen," she said.

He read the writing on it aloud, as though intoning a mystical spell. "New Sunshine Golf and Tennis Club." He tucked the pen in his pocket. "Is there anything else you can remember about that second call?"

That second call again. Mr. Perryman had flagged it, too. "There's not much to remember. It was very short. Is it important?"

"Important? I don't see how. But interesting, yes, for the reason that it was unnecessary to the business at hand. So the question is—why?"

"You tell me."

"I have no idea." He laid his hand on his chest, right over the heart. "But I think Roma, romance, romantic, Romanian."

"You lost me."

"It's about our ancient legacy. Some ancestral relic in our minds, a deep feeling that always seems to rise up at the wrong time." He picked up his mug. "But enough of rambling. What shall we say? To justice?"

"Maybe something less highfalutin," said Mrs. Plansky. "How about noroc?"

His eyebrows rose, dark eyebrows, like his hair. "You're full of surprises."

"That's the lone one."

They clinked their mugs and downed the rest of their tuicas.

"Oh, and one more thing." He got out his phone and took her picture. "The face of the story."

"I wasn't smiling," said Mrs. Plansky.

Twenty-four

Dinu was high as a kite. They had the same expression in his language and Dinu liked it better, preferring the sound of zmeu to kite. He'd been high as a zmeu for two days, although he hadn't messed with any drugs or alcohol. It was all on account of Annika, the croupier from Bucharest who'd come to help Uncle Dragomir with his casino idea, and was also taking a shift or two at the Duce. Dinu had run into her on the street on a rainy morning, he coming out of the pharmacy—sent by his mother and Aunt Ilinca for aspirin, both of them suffering from splitting headaches, no mystery why—and Annika struggling with her umbrella, blown inside out by the wind. Without a word he'd taken the umbrella, gotten it straightened out, and handed it to her.

"Well, well, Dinu," she said. "What an efficient young man. Which of course I already knew. Here, you're getting wet. I'll save you." And she'd pulled him in close, under the umbrella, one hand on the umbrella grip, the other around Dinu's waist.

"That's all right, I'm—"

The hand around his waist gave a little squeeze. Looking back, that was the instant when the kite began to rise. It was like Annika's hand was a master communicator, sending a message from an earthly heaven he hadn't even known existed.

"Where are your cowboy boots?" she said.

"I don't wear them in the rain," said Dinu.

"So smart! What a good husband you'll make!" She drew him

out of the rain, under an awning, but kept the umbrella up as well, making for a strange feeling of privacy even though they were in the middle of town—as though they were tenting at a remote campsite. "How is that pretty girlfriend of yours?"

"I haven't seen her in a while."

"No? But she's such a peach. Don't you like peaches, Dinu?"

Annika looked up at him. He was a little bit taller. She was so beautiful, her skin so alive, her eyes impossible to look away from.

"Well, peaches, I haven't really—"

"Maybe you're not handling the situation well," she said. "Peaches like to be squeezed and kissed. Are you a good kisser? It's very important. Yet they don't teach it in school. What does that tell you?"

Dinu had no idea. He didn't know what to say or do, but also was in no hurry for this little camping trip to end.

"Here is Annika's lesson number one in the art of kissing," Annika said. "Your little peach can thank me later."

Her free hand slid upward, rounded itself over the back of his head, not gently, and kissed him, a deep kiss involving tongues and force and some sort of exchange of intimate knowledge he didn't understand, and that wasn't all he didn't understand. Then with a bright little laugh she was gone, leaving him under the awning, fully clothed, of course, although not ready for a public appearance. A minute or two passed before he descended into that state, although inside, the zmeu was almost in orbit.

"You don't think Annika's involved with my uncle, do you?"

"Involved?" said Romeo.

"You know."

"Well, there's his wife, Simone, plus the Polish girlfriend and the Moldovan girlfriend, so just from the time management angle I'd say no."

They were in their new and private office under the apartment block where Romeo lived with his older brother and his wife and kids, an apartment block even shabbier than Dinu's, but down in the subbasement was a storage room, long walled off, where Romeo had cut out a hidden back entrance. Now, sitting opposite each other at a card table cluttered with Romeo's equipment, they were all set for their very first operation, just the two of them.

"What about Annika?" Dinu said. "Do you think she has a boyfriend? Or—or maybe even a husband?"

"I don't know," Romeo said, switching on an array of monitors. "What difference does it make?" He glanced over at Dinu. "Hey, are you crazy? She's thirty years old."

"She is? How do you know that?"

"I took a look at the payroll. She's there because of helping out at the Duce."

"You took a look?"

"Hacked," Romeo said. "I hacked into the payroll." He slipped on his headphones. "Now can we get started?"

Dinu reached across the table. They bumped fists.

"Like those two guys who started Apple in their garage," Dinu said.

"Hewlett Packard," said Romeo. "But yes, like that."

Dinu checked his script. He wasn't nervous in the least. His English was getting better all the time, but it wasn't just that. He was good at this, had a knack. Had he shown a knack for anything else in his whole life? Well, maybe riding motorcycles. The two knacks went together in a way. He felt very strong at that moment, standing tall on his own two legs.

A phone rang, far away in the Cornhusker State.

"Hello?" said some little old lady.

"Hi, Granny. It's me, Eric."

"Eric?"

"Your grandson Eric. My goodness! Have you forgotten me, Granny?"

"Oh, no. I think of you so often, Eric. But it's been some time since I heard from you, that's all I meant. I hardly recognized your voice."

"I'm so sorry about that, Granny. I promise to do better. And the connection from here is pretty bad."

"Where are you?"

"That's the problem, Granny. And after so long I hate to be calling you about this, but there is nowhere else—but I have nowhere else to turn."

Dinu explained. Twenty-two minutes and seven seconds later—Romeo had decided to time all the calls and keep a record as part of their business plan—$38,492.17 had been deposited in an account he'd set up in Qatar, which Dinu now knew how to pronounce and find on a map.

"Hewlett," said Romeo, raising a hand.

"Packard," Dinu replied. They high-fived.

Dinu rode his bike to Bijoux Parisien in the old town, next door to the Porsche dealership. He'd been to the dealership a number of times, just to stare through the display window, but now he didn't even take a glance. Inside Bijoux Parisien he asked to see something nice. The woman gave him a friendly smile, then checked out his cowboy boots, the smile fading a bit.

"For your mother or girlfriend?"

"Oh, girlfriend."

"Were you thinking of rings? Bracelets? Necklaces? Brooches?"

Dinu hadn't gotten that far.

"How much did you want to spend?"

"I don't know. Three thousand, maybe?"

"Lei?"

"Dollars."

The friendly smile returned at full strength. Not much later he walked out with a sapphire necklace on an eighteen-carat gold chain—the first sapphire he'd ever seen!—beautifully gift-wrapped in a velvet lined box. Just the one single sapphire hanging on the chain, but a very nice one as the woman had explained and Dinu could see with his own eyes. For a few hundred dollars more, $3,600 in all, he could have had the same sapphire with a platinum chain, but Dinu rejected the idea, not because of the added cost but because platinum looked just like silver and everyone knew gold was better than silver. Platinum was a scam. The idea of him falling for platinum was pretty funny.

Uncle Dragomir's casino was going to be in the old Hotel Metropole, which had gone out of business and which he now owned and was renovating. It stood on a rise overlooking the river, not far from the bridge, and Dinu rode by at the end of that day, when work would be wrapping up. And well, well, well. There was Annika, walking away from the site, a roll of blueprints under her arm. He pulled up from behind.

"Hey, Annika."

She whirled around, annoyed, like he was some sort of pickup creep.

"Oh, Dinu, it's you."

"Yes. Hi. Can I take you somewhere?"

"On that?"

"You don't like the bike?"

"Riding around on the back of some guy's motorcycle? Do I look like the type?"

Didn't all girls like riding on the backs of motorcycles? Then he remembered she was thirty. So by thirty they were past that? Dinu filed the fact away.

"I guess not," he said. "Can I buy you a coffee?"

Annika checked her watch. "Sure, if we make it quick. Very nice of you. And please take off that ridiculous helmet."

He whipped it off.

A coffee place was just a few steps away on the other side of the street, with a patio, glassed in for the winter, by the river. They took the table with the best view, ordered coffee, Dinu also asking if they still had prajitura piersici, the little peach-shaped Christmas cookies, and being told no.

"Too bad about the cookies," he said, as they sipped their coffee.

"You have a sweet tooth?" said Annika.

"Well, no." He shrugged. "But peaches, that's different."

She showed no reaction, just added a little cream to her coffee, a faraway look in her amazing eyes. Faraway looks like that could happen when someone's mind was on something else, but Dinu would have bet anything that she was thinking of peaches, specifically the . . . the peachy moment they'd shared! That made this the perfect moment. He reached in his pocket.

"I have something for you."

"Oh?"

Dinu handed her the little gift-wrapped box, the paper thick and creamy, the bow deep purple. Annika took it. He noticed that one of her fingernails was dirty.

"What is this?"

"Only one way to find out," he said, and in English. Yes, he had a knack for sure.

"What does that mean?"

"Open it."

Annika untied the bow, removed the creamy paper, gazed at the gold lettering on the box: Bijoux Parisien.

"Dinu?"

He said nothing, just smiled the mysterious smile of an in-charge type who knew what was coming.

Annika took the top off the box. She stared at what was inside.

"To a peach," he said, a remark designed to be offhand and cool but his voice broke in the middle.

Annika looked up. "This is for me?"

"Uh-huh," he said. She was bowled over. That was plain to see.

"From you?"

Dinu tried to think of another cool, offhand remark but none came to mind so he just nodded.

"You shouldn't have," she said.

He shrugged, a cool, offhand shrug. That was more like it.

Their eyes met. Her eyes: so amazing, and now so full of emotion, including, he saw to his surprise, something like fear. Dinu made an astonishing mental leap: thirty-year-old women, especially of the beautiful and yes, sexy kind, like Annika, could have feelings so strong it scared them.

"Put it on," he said, taking control, like he was the thirty-year-old and she was the kid.

Annika glanced around, maybe not wanting their privacy disturbed at such a moment, but they had the glassed-in patio to themselves. She took out the necklace, gave it a close look, her eyes now revealing nothing, and put it on, fastening the clasp behind her neck with one simple twist of her fingers. Annika had taken off her coat, now hanging on the back of her chair. She wore a tight-fitting sweater of some soft material, maybe cashmere—a somewhat low-cut sweater. The sapphire nestled between her breasts. Dinu knew this was a sight he would never forget.

"Do you like it, Annika?"

"Oh, it's beautiful all right. You've chosen very well. But too generous."

"My pleasure," said Dinu.

"I mean it, Dinu. Too generous."

He spread his hands in an openhanded gesture that meant, Hey, what can I do? Hitting peak offhand cool without speaking a word. He felt, for the first time in his life, like a man.

Now she was looking at him again, again with a complicated expression in her eyes.

"What?" he said.

She leaned across the table and kissed him. Not a kiss of the peachy kind, actually more like one of his mother's pecks on the cheek. But he knew there was peachiness to come, lots and lots of peachiness.

"It looks great on you."

"It would look great on anybody."

"Well, thanks."

"No. Thank you."

"My pleasure," he said again, unable to top it with something else. "So what do you want to do?" he said.

"Excuse me?"

"Now," he said. "Well, not now, but after here, when we're done. We could go for a walk." He realized as he said it that the rain was coming down hard, beating against the glass walls. "Or maybe you're hungry? What restaurants do you like? Or—" He stopped himself, on the verge of inviting her back to the flat. What a terrible idea! A gem like her in a place like that.

Meanwhile she was reaching for her coat. "Now, in fact, I have a meeting with the builder."

"And, um, after?"

"A very long and involved meeting, followed by a good sleep, please, God. I have another meeting at seven in the morning. But of course you'll be at school in any case."

"Well, not so much these days."

"Naughty boy."

She rose, removed the necklace, placed it carefully in the box, tucked the box in her coat pocket. He tried to help her with her coat, but too late.

They went outside. Annika opened the umbrella but did not pull him under. He stood in the rain, getting soaked but not feeling it.

"I'll call you?" he said.

"All right."

"I don't have your number."

"Call the desk at the Duce. Leave a message if I'm not there."

"Okay, good. Um, don't get wet."

"Goodbye, Dinu."

Annika crossed the street, headed back to the Metropole. She hadn't taken the creamy wrapping paper and the ribbon, left behind on the table. Didn't girls like to hang on to stuff like that? Maybe not by the time they were thirty. Dinu put on his helmet and rode home on his bike.

Dinu knew he was dreaming but it was delicious nonetheless. In this dream he and Annika were on the bike on a mountain road high above the valley where Tassa's sister and brother-in-law had their farm. He could see the roof of the farmhouse from where they were—a kite was flying above it—but otherwise it didn't figure in the dream, just one of those strange things that happened in dreaming. The important part was how much fun he and Annika were having, she clinging to him, and him sometimes driving no hands. They weren't wearing their helmets, in fact weren't wearing anything at all. Except for the sapphire necklace, which kept getting bounced against her breasts and his bare back, a rather exciting back-and-forth that could only lead to something very good.

But before it did, a commotion started up.

"What are you doing?" his mother said. "You have no right."

His mother was in the dream? That wasn't possible. Not enough room on the bike, for one thing, and this was no time for mother to be in the picture. A door banged open. There were no doors in the dream. He smelled cologne.

Dinu sat up in bed. The door to his room was open, with two back-lit silhouettes in the doorway. One was Mama. The other was the silhouette of a man, bigger than Mama but not terribly big, although he had a way of standing like something powerful was coiled inside. His mama was tugging on the man's shoulder.

"You must leave here this minute," his mother said. "Or I'll call Dragomir."

The man laughed. Dinu already knew who he was, of course,

just from the cologne and the stance, but he knew the laugh as well, kind of soft, gentle. By now Mama lay on the floor in the hall, nightie askew, nose bleeding.

Dinu jumped out of bed. The bedroom light went on. There was Timbo in the doorway, an unlit cigarette dangling from his lips, his handlebar mustache, maybe freshly waxed, seeming to glow in the light. In the background Dinu could see the front door, hanging on its hinges.

Dinu yelled something—he didn't know what—and charged at Timbo, fists raised. Timbo made no move to defend himself. Dinu punched him in the mouth, or at least aimed a punch that way. It never landed. Instead Dinu felt a sudden and very sharp pain in his other hand, not the punching one, and the next thing he knew he lay on the floor, the baby finger on his non-punching hand sticking out sideways.

Timbo lit his cigarette, took a deep drag, shook out the match flame, and dropped the match on the floor. "You are not a type-A employee after all. Get dressed."

TWENTY-FIVE

Uncle Dragomir owned eight or nine cars. Dinu didn't know exactly how many. One was a black F-350 pickup, far too unwieldy for the many narrow twisted streets they had in Alba Gemina. Timbo drove. Dinu sat in the passenger seat.

"What's going on?" he said. "I don't understand."

"Seat belt," Timbo said.

Dinu fastened his seat belt, taking extra care that nothing touched that horribly bent pinkie finger on his left hand. The whole hand was throbbing, and in the midst of that came shooting pains all the way up his arm.

Timbo said nothing more. He turned out to be a poor and anxious driver, squeezing the wheel tightly, braking and speeding up at all the wrong times. He didn't look Dinu's way even once. Dinu considered unbuckling, flinging open the door, leaping out, running home to his bike, parked in the basement garage of the apartment block, racing off to where? Hungary? Serbia? He went on considering, but did nothing except try to control the pain. He was no longer high as a kite, had trouble believing he'd ever felt that way.

Timbo pulled into an unlit alley and drove a few hundred meters until he came to the back of Club Presto. No lights shone inside, meaning it was very late. The loading bay door rolled up and Timbo drove inside. The door rolled back down. Timbo cut the lights. That brought total darkness to the loading bay.

"Get out," Timbo said.

"I can't see."

"Don't be a baby," Timbo said. He opened his own door and the cabin lights went on. Timbo lit a cigarette and looked at him. His eyes could have been those of a stranger. "Or be a baby. It doesn't matter now."

Dinu got out of the car. It went totally dark again, except for the glow of Timbo's cigarette. Dinu followed that glow to a door that led inside the club at the basement level and the Cambio office. The name was a funny joke. Dinu had missed that all this time. Meanwhile Timbo was unlocking the door, his back turned. Dinu considered cracking him over the head with something, a hammer, say, or a brick, neither of which he had, of course. Timbo opened the door. They went in. A low light burned partway down the hall that led to the Cambio room, but Timbo didn't go that way. Instead he went down a rough, unfinished staircase that Dinu had never taken, lit by a naked hanging bulb. Dinu followed him down to a sublevel with an earthen floor to another door. Timbo held it open. Dinu went in. Timbo closed the door behind him, leaving Dinu by himself.

Dinu was in a small room lit by a floor lamp with a yellowed shade, the room itself like something out of a peasant's hut from long ago—earthen floor, two crude wooden chairs, a crude wooden table. He walked around. No windows to climb out of, not down underground like this, but there was another door. Dinu tried the handle. Locked. He sat in one of the chairs, holding his left wrist in his right hand. He considered trying to wrench the finger back into place. That would hurt, but he was already hurting. What if afterward, instead of better it was worse? And was there some trick, some right way of doing it? For the first time in a long while, he thought of the father he really hadn't known, except for a memory or two, and missed him.

The door to the hallway opened and Uncle Dragomir walked in. He was wearing the sapphire necklace.

"How do I look?" he said.

Dinu rose. "I . . . I don't understand."

"No? How do I look? It's a simple question. You're supposed to be smart. So let's hear a smart answer. How do I—your uncle and the brother of your father—look?"

Dinu got the idea the right answer could save him, like in some fairy tale. "You . . . you look angry, Uncle Dragomir."

"Really?" said Uncle Dragomir. "That surprises me. I don't feel angry, not the least bit. Do you know what I feel?"

"No."

"Think. How would you feel in my place?"

Dinu realized he had no idea how Uncle Dragomir felt at this or any other time, not a clue. "I'm sorry. I just don't know."

Uncle Dragomir pulled up a chair and sat down facing Dinu, an arm's length away. "What am I?" he said.

Dinu knew the answer to that one. "The boss," he said.

"Sure, the boss. But to you, pusti?" *Pusti* being like *kiddo* in their language.

"To me?" Dinu said. "You're my uncle."

"Now we are talking." Uncle Dragomir reached out and touched Dinu's knee very lightly. The sapphire swung freely out from its little nesting place in his chest hair—Uncle Dragomir wearing his shirt with the top buttons unfastened—and hung between them. "We are flesh and blood. Look at me."

Dinu looked at him.

"Am I the kind who could ever harm his own flesh and blood?"

Dinu knew the correct answer was no, you are not that kind. But it wasn't the right answer. How could it be, considering the time, quite recently, when Uncle Dragomir had punched him in the ribs? Dinu couldn't remember why. Something about showing up late for work? All he knew for sure was that the ribs still ached a bit. Then there was the tooth that got knocked out, and now this matter of the finger, both Timbo's work, but acting under orders, for sure. All that added up to the correct answer and not the right answer being the one to go with, beyond any doubt.

"No, you are not that kind."

Uncle Dragomir withdrew his hand. "Very good. Now we are on the same track, you and me, and I can freely tell you how I feel." He tucked the sapphire back inside his shirt. "I am disappointed, pusti."

From somewhere through the walls came what sounded like a groan.

Uncle Dragomir smiled. "Do you know why?"

Dinu shook his head.

"I'll tell you a story. Some people understand better from stories." Uncle Dragomir took a cigar from his pocket, cut it with a gold cigar cutter, lit it with a gold lighter. He blew a stream of smoke in Dinu's direction, but maybe not deliberately. Dinu started having trouble with his breathing right away. "But stop me if you've heard this. What do you know about how your old man died?"

"It was in Hungary," Dinu said. "He died trying to save some people in a fire."

Uncle Dragomir smiled. "And who told you that?"

"My mother."

"Did you know she wasn't always a drunk?"

Dinu didn't like that question. As for a response, he could think of none, except for violence. It wasn't exactly that he was afraid of violence. But he was afraid of Uncle Dragomir. Plus there was practical matter of his finger, the pain worsening.

"It's true," Uncle Dragomir said. "Before she was a drunk she was a slut."

Dinu rose from his chair, balling his right fist. The punch he had in mind never got thrown, because without getting up, Uncle Dragomir leaned forward a bit and gave Dinu's finger a wristy backhand flick. Dinu thought he might faint. He subsided on the chair, accepting the fact that he wasn't much of a puncher. He refused to cry out.

Uncle Dragomir tapped a little cigar ash cylinder onto the floor. "The Hungary part is false. It was Moldova. But there was a fire, although not part of the plan. Your old man—what a character he could be!—knew some gamblers over there. This was when we were just starting out, didn't really have a plan. It was like our high school years in this business." He took a drag off his cigar, sent more smoke Dinu's way. "Now I have my doctorate." Uncle Dragomir nodded to himself, pleased with this thought. "But back to your old man and his idea. These gamblers held a big poker game on Saturday nights, fixed, of course, but it attracted rich guys from all over—Odessa, Varna even. Rich guys who thought they were smart because they were rich. Those are the chickens the gamblers feed on, but we didn't care about any of that. We went in late at night, wearing masks—my idea—and throwing smoke bombs— his idea. This kind of operation you want to go fast fast fast. Not like you were thinking with Annika, huh? I've had some of that one. Not that good, believe me. Anyway, fast fast fast. Which was how it happened. At first. We scooped up all the cash in sight, thousands of euros, real money for us back then. But just as we were headed out the window—this was on an upper floor, with a fire escape—your old man spotted a safe on the wall and turned back. To find someone among all these panicking card players who could open the safe, you see. Meanwhile something had caught fire. I yelled forget it let's go. But—and this is the point of the story—he was greedy. My last sight of him he had a knife to the throat of some girl, maybe the girlfriend of one of the guys who ran the place. He could be persuasive, your old man. Then comes this tremendous boom. I was lucky to get away with my life. So, the moral of the story—don't be greedy." Uncle Dragomir tapped off another cylinder of ash, this time on Dinu's knee. "You are greedy, just like him."

Dinu did not believe the story. In his mind he changed it up a bit, making Uncle Dragomir the one with the knife, but he couldn't make it come out right like that.

"You shouldn't have gotten greedy," Uncle Dragomir said. "Your future was bright."

Dinu shook his head. "I just don't know what this is about."

Uncle Dragomir held out the sapphire. "Where did you get the money for this?"

"I—I've been saving."

"That's your answer?"

Dinu looked Uncle Dragomir in the eye. "Yes."

"You see, I was hoping you had sold your motorcycle and raised the money that way. But I am told the motorcycle has not changed hands. So one more time. Where did the money come from?"

"Savings. I've been saving all my life."

"You have talent, no question." Uncle Dragomir rose. "Come, please."

Dinu followed him to the door, not the door to the hall, but the other one, locked. Uncle Dragomir knocked. The door opened right away. Marius stood on the other side. This room was just like the other one—earthen floor, lamp, crude wooden table and chairs. Romeo sat in one of them. It was bad, what they'd done to him.

"Hello, Marius," Uncle Dragomir said. "Could you ask Romeo to kindly look up?"

"Hey, look up," said Marius.

Uncle Dragomir corrected him. "Kindly look up."

"Hey, kindly look up."

Romeo raised his head. One of his eyes was swollen shut, but the other found Dinu.

"Here's your friend Dinu," Uncle Dragomir said. "We have a little mystery happening now. Let's call it the mystery of the necklace bought from Bijoux Parisien right here in beautiful Alba Gemina for three thousand one hundred ninety-five American dollars. Maybe you can kindly help us solve our little mystery. Will you do that for us, Romeo?"

Romeo nodded, a very slight nod, but enough to start his nose bleeding.

"Thank you, Romeo." Uncle Dragomir came forward, removed the necklace. "Take it."

Romeo reached out, his hand shaking, and took the necklace. A drop of blood from his nose landed square on the sapphire.

"It's nice, isn't it?" Uncle Dragomir said. "Do you know the name of that stone?"

Romeo shook his head.

"Tell him, Marius."

"Jade," said Marius.

Now, for the first time since this horrible episode began, Uncle Dragomir did look angry. "What is wrong with you, Marius? It's a sapphire."

"Sorry, boss."

Uncle Dragomir turned to Dinu. "See how hard it is to find good help? That's what makes this all so upsetting." He turned back to Romeo. "Here's the question, Romeo. Your friend—or should I say business partner?—claims he bought this necklace for—do you remember the amount I told you?"

"Three thousand one hundred ninety-five U.S.," said Romeo, so quiet Dinu could hardly hear.

"Notice, Marius, how Romeo recalls the exact amount, just from hearing it once."

"He's a smart son of a bitch," said Marius.

"They both are," said Uncle Dragomir. "That's what's killing me." He sighed. "So, Romeo, Dinu claims that amount you just mentioned came from his savings over the years. Do you think that's possible?"

Romeo gazed with his one good eye at the necklace in his hand and said nothing.

"Or is it possible that it came from the profits of a little side business? Wasn't Romeo telling us about that business earlier tonight, Marius?"

"For sure," Marius said, stepping forward. "Do you want me to get him to tell it again?"

"Stop," Dinu said.

"You have something to say?" said Uncle Dragomir.

"That's where I got the money. And the side business was my idea."

Uncle Dragomir patted Dinu on the back. "That's the boy. So now let us all go up to the Cambio office where Romeo will transfer the total of the funds from your little side business into an account of mine, and we will be all square."

"As long as you keep the . . . the jewel, too," said Marius.

"Now you're thinking." Uncle Dragomir took the necklace from Romeo's hand. "Oh, and one more small matter. It's about your business partner's poor finger. Have you seen what happened to it, Romeo? Show him, Dinu."

Dinu raised his hand slightly.

"Your partner and your friend, Romeo. Before we go upstairs, let's take a moment to fix it."

No one moved.

"Meaning you, Romeo. I want you to fix it."

"I don't know how," Romeo said.

"It's easy," said Marius, holding up his own hand and sticking out his baby finger. "You just give it a pull at the same time you slide it back. Use some force, sure, but that's the trick, the pull. A real sharp pull."

Romeo lowered his head and shook it, blood dripping to the floor.

"That's disappointing," Uncle Dragomir said. "I'm afraid Romeo needs some persuading, Marius."

Dinu walked up to Romeo and held out his hand. "Just do it."

TWENTY-SIX

Breakfast at the Duce was served buffet style in a room with several tall potted plants on the floor—none of them doing well—and Django Reinhardt doing very well on the sound system. As Mrs. Plansky, the only customer, helped herself to coffee and a slice of black bread with plum jam, forgoing the only other offering, a dish that looked vaguely eggy, she remembered a movie she'd seen where a character playing Django had made an appearance. But that was all she remembered, the rest of the movie gone. If she saw it again would it all come back to her after the first minute or two? Or would the whole thing be brand-new? In that case, she'd reached a stage where just one movie would do. In death there were no movies, so the progression made sense: many movies, one movie, none. Death simplified things, no question. Mrs. Plansky understood something as she sat at a window table that was partly screened off from the rest of the room by one of the potted plants: she didn't particularly care about simplifying life. Complication was fine with her, and if more complications meant longer life, then bring them on! Meanwhile her foot was tapping to the music. She realized she was having one of those little happiness bursts that popped up inside her from time to time. But now? In her present situation? She must be mad. Mrs. Plansky bit into her toast. She'd been a sliced-white-only gal before Norm, like living in a bread desert. He would have loved this Romanian black bread. She spread on some more plum jam—anything plum appearing to be the way to go in this town—and laid her phone on the table, waiting for Max's call.

Annika, the pretty woman from the front desk, entered, poured herself a cup of coffee, and sat at a corner table away from the window side, partly screened from Mrs. Plansky's view by the potted plant. Even so, Mrs. Plansky could tell Annika wasn't happy today. Did all humans speak the same body language? She didn't know, but Annika had one of those faces where unhappiness made everything turn down, giving a preview of how she'd look after two or three more decades of gravity had done their work. Mrs. Plansky checked the reflection of her own face in the bread knife and saw what gravity could do when it got its hands on a real serious chunk of time. Then she focused on just the eyes, and everything was all right.

A man in a long black leather coat entered, helped himself to coffee, and sat down opposite Annika at her table. Mrs. Plansky, allowing her imagination to run free, said to herself that if they were romantically involved all those downturns on her face would now flip the other way. They did not, although there was a change, perhaps from unhappiness to caution. Did the man seem familiar? Mrs. Plansky peered between the dried-up, dusty, dying leaves of the potted plant, peered unobtrusively, undercover ops' style. Although not even turned toward her, his face with its big features, none remotely recessive, seemed to radiate power, and not simply brute power. But plenty of that, too. It was Mr. Squareman, from the police station last night, a drinking buddy of Captain Romulu, who was not to be trusted, according to Max. Mrs. Plansky sipped her coffee, watching over the rim of the cup. She knew, of course, that despite the leaves and the cup, if she could see them then they could see her. But they weren't looking.

Mr. Squareman and Annika talked in low voices, Mrs. Plansky catching just enough to know they were speaking Romanian, so they might as well have been shouting at the tops of their lungs. He seemed to be telling her a story of some kind, an involved kind

of a story with a this-happened-and-then-this rhythm, a story that
Annika seemed to like less and less as it went on. At one point Mr.
Squareman attempted a sort of pantomime, taking the pinkie finger
of one hand and bending it way down, as though trying to snap it
off or something. The only interpretation Mrs. Plansky could come
up with involved breaking a wishbone, meaning Mr. Squareman's
story probably had to do with some dinner, perhaps at Christmas,
and assuming that Romanians had the same ritual. But how to explain Annika's reaction, putting her hands to her face in horror and
disbelief?

That took Mr. Squareman by surprise. He'd clearly been expecting something different, maybe laughter, the little pantomime being the punch line to a shaggy dog joke.

"Annika!" he said, raising his voice, followed by something with
the tone of *oh for God's sake, lighten up.*

Annika did not lighten up. Instead, she pushed back from the
table.

"Okay, okay," he said in English, then raised both palms in a
pacifying gesture.

"Okay?" she said. "Is not okay."

Mr. Squareman frowned, a muscle bunching on his forehead,
above the bridge of his nose, bridge of the nose being very apt in
this case since his nose was like the prow of a ship. Then he said
something with a *will-this-change-your-tune* tone, reached into his
pocket, and took out a piece of jewelry, a necklace, maybe or . . .
yes, a necklace, the chain gold, the jewel some blue stone. He held it
out for Annika to take it. She shook her head, pushed farther back
from the table.

Mr. Squareman got angry. He said something that sounded
mean, possibly even disgusting, and smacked his huge hand on the
table. Annika's cup bounced in its saucer, like from an earth tremor,
and she shrank back. Just a little—she was a strong woman, but
afraid of Mr. Squareman. He jumped up and marched toward the
doorway, Mrs. Plansky losing sight of him behind the potted plant.

Then, through the leaves, she spotted something flying through the air, something blue and gold, the necklace, of course, but there was a little beat before Mrs. Plansky realized that.

In the little beat, Mr. Squareman stalked out of the breakfast room and the necklace landed on Annika's table with a soft thunk. The stone separated from the chain and came bouncing crazily across the floor, between two potted plants and coming to rest right at Mrs. Plansky's feet. She was wearing her ballet flats at the time.

Mrs. Plansky bent down, her skeleton picking this moment to make a creaking sound or two, and picked up the blue stone. Ah, a sapphire, and a nice one although not very big. One of the ladies at the club had a huge sapphire ring that she wore while playing. Sometimes it refracted the sunlight—an unfair advantage, Mrs. Plansky had said one day, a joke that made the other players laugh, although not the ring wearer, who perhaps transferred to the Old Sunshine Country Club soon after.

Meanwhile Annika was coming her way. She dangled the gold chain between finger and thumb, away from her body, like it had a bad smell.

"Here," said Mrs. Plansky, extending the sapphire. "This, um, fell on the floor."

"Ha," Annika said. "Sure. A fall for sure."

She made no move to take the sapphire, in fact looked a little pale. Mrs. Plansky didn't say anything, just pulled out a chair. Annika sat down. Mrs. Plansky went to the buffet table, poured a cup of tea, set it before Annika.

Annika reached for it, but the chain had gotten entangled in her hand and for some reason she couldn't get rid of it. Mrs. Plansky did it for her. Her fine motor had always been pretty good. She was deft at sewing on buttons, for example, or getting twisted-up shoelaces untied—how often she'd done that for Jack when he was a kid!

Annika took a sip of her tea, a tiny wave slopping out of the cup. She looked up, her eyes clearing, maybe really taking Mrs. Plansky in for the first time.

"You're the American lady?"

"An American lady, yes. My name's Loretta."

"In the presidential suite?"

"Right. It's very nice."

"Of course, of course. I apologize for being so . . . so malorganized."

"No apology necessary." Mrs. Plansky laid the sapphire on the table. "Drink some more tea."

Annika sipped her tea, this time spilling none. "I have met only a few American men. They are nicer."

"Nicer than . . . ?"

"Our men." Annika gestured toward the table on the other side of the room. "I don't know what you saw."

"Oh, not much. Nothing really. Not worth thinking about."

"I wish for that. That it would be not worth thinking about." She pointed to her name tag. "Annika."

They shook hands. Mrs. Plansky broke off some black bread, spread it with plum jam, gave it to Annika. Annika bit into it.

"Oh my God, so hungry," she said. "Sometimes you find that out when . . ." She finished the sentence by holding up the bread.

"You haven't been eating?" Mrs. Plansky suddenly realized she was sounding like a Jewish mother, in fact like Norm's mother. Fifty years late, give or take: if she'd pulled this one out of the bag back then maybe she and Norm's mom would have gotten off on the right foot.

"So much work to do, is the problem," Annika said.

"Is it busy here?"

"Oh, not the hotel, not in winter. But that is just my gig side."

Gig side. Mrs. Plansky liked that, and was also liking Annika. "And your main gig?"

"Main gig is the big job?"

"Yes. Your English is very good. I'm sorry I don't speak Romanian. I only know two words—noroc and frigorific."

Annika smiled. "With those you will do well here."

Mrs. Plansky pushed the sapphire a little closer to Annika. "This is very nice. I've always liked sapphires. They make me think of summer."

"Then you should keep it."

Mrs. Plansky laughed, a laugh she cut off as soon as she noticed the expression on Annika's face, the expression of someone thinking she'd stumbled on a good idea. Or was it possible this was one of those cultures where if you admired some object the owner was obligated by tradition to fork it over?

"Even if you meant that, I could never accept," she said.

"Why not? Is from Bijoux Parisien, a very nice store and not just for this town. The cost was three thousand one hundred ninety-five—and not lei but dollars."

"All the more reason, then, it being so valuable," Mrs. Plansky said. "And there are others. Supposing the gentleman in question and you patch things up? Or maybe he's your husband—so you're patched whether you like it or not! And then he discovers that some tourist is now wearing the thing. What an interesting situation that would be!"

Annika sat back. "I don't know to laugh or to cry," she said. "Patched whether you like or not! I will never forget that. But the gentleman, as you are putting it, is not my husband. Or even boyfriend." Some sort of cloud passed beneath the surface of her eyes. "Except on one—I don't know the word."

Mrs. Plansky could think of several that might apply. She went with the blandest. "Occasion."

Annika nodded. "Occasion, yes. And there will be no repetition. But we are patched in business so I have to build walls. Not real walls. Walls inside my head. You understand this meaning?"

"I do," said Mrs. Plansky. "What sort of business, if you don't mind my asking?"

"Casino business," Annika said. "We are building a casino here in Alba Gemina, in the old Metropole. I am partner—minor partner and employee for now." She made a gesture encompassing the hotel. "And why I am here. But my knowledge is casinos, from the Palace in Bucharest and WinBoss in Odessa."

"Ah," Mrs. Plansky said, understanding the business part but no further ahead when it came to the sapphire necklace. Was Mr. Squareman hoping for another occasion with Annika? And on an unrelated subject, had his meeting with Captain Romulu been about the casino? She'd been to a casino once but hadn't enjoyed the experience, and not because of the way Norm's foolproof black-jack method—which he'd worked on for days before their Las Vegas trip—played out. He'd lost his entire stake—$270—in eleven minutes. That part she'd actually enjoyed. Not that he'd lost, of course, but the look on his face after, so sweetly crestfallen. He was superb. But the feeling inside the place, like being trapped in a hellish spaceship stalled in the void—that she hadn't liked. None of that was relevant now and she hoped all this thinking was happening in a flash. The point was that all she knew of the actual business part of the casino world behind the scenes she'd learned from *The Godfather*. Hadn't there been a shady police captain somewhere in part one, or maybe part two? She was considering some question about Captain Romulu when Annika picked up the sapphire and the chain and stuck them in her pocket.

"Ah," said Mrs. Plansky again.

Annika shook her head. "Not for keeping. But returning to the owner."

"Even though—" Mrs. Plansky stopped herself. It was none of her beeswax. Of all things, late in life, was she turning into a nosy parker? On the other hand, wasn't that in the undercover ops hand-book, perhaps the most important chapter: Be a Nosy Parker!

"Even though," she went on, "that didn't go so well the first time?"

Annika looked confused.

"Returning the necklace to the owner," Mrs. Plansky explained. And then she got it. "Oh, I see, you mean the jeweler, Boutique, um . . ."

"Bijoux Parisien," Annika said. "And no, not there. But also not to Dragomir."

"Dragomir is the man in the leather coat?"

Annika nodded. "Dragomir Tiriac, my partner, businessman in town, owner for example of this hotel."

So Dragomir Tiriac was the actual name of Mr. Squareman, but somehow not the owner of the necklace? One puzzle solved, another rising up in its place. Mrs. Plansky was wondering what the undercover ops handbook might have to say to that, when a recent fact popped up in her mind, unfortunately not related to the necklace but kind of interesting on its own. One of the motorcycle boys—the good-looking one—had told her that his uncle owned this place, owned the Hotel Duce, possibly the reason he'd recommended it. What was the boy's name again? Mrs. Plansky remembered the name of the other boy, the pimply one, no problem. Romeo—who could forget? Now if she could just for God's sake come up with the name of the good-looking boy she could say to Annika, Hey, do you know X? But the name seemed to be gone, at least for now.

Meanwhile Annika was dabbing at the corner of her cheeks with a napkin and pushing back her chair.

"I must go, Loretta. I have much enjoyed our talk. Thank you. It is a help to me."

"Very nice getting to know you a bit."

"And if there is anything you need while here," Annika went on, "anything at all, here is card with personal number."

Mrs. Plansky took the card. "Thank you, Annika. And good luck."

Annika walked away. She'd reached the arched entry way leading to the lobby, when the name came to Mrs. Plansky: Dinu!

Hey, Annika, do you know Dinu? He's Dragomir's nephew. But Mrs. Plansky didn't say it. Why not? Was it in some way the sight of the back of Annika's bared neck, quite lovely but also vulnerable? Or the fact that Dragomir and Captain Romulu appeared to be pals, even drinking buddies, and Max had warned her about the captain? Or was it the memory of that bloody horse's head in *The Godfather*? For whatever reason, Mrs. Plansky kept silent. She thought of lending Annika her Scottish scarf.

TWENTY-SEVEN

Einstein said—well, Norm said Einstein said, not a caveat in Mrs. Plansky's mind but absolute proof—that if you went real fast—real real fast—then time would slow down. Now, back in her room after breakfast, time had pretty much come to a standstill. That should have meant Mrs. Plansky was currently speeding along, but she was not. She sat perfectly motionless, gazing out the window at the statue of *Michael the Brave,* also motionless. But at least he had plans, all about cutting off someone's head with that wide-bladed saber or whatever it was. She herself had no plans, other than waiting for Max's call. What would Einstein do in her place? He was probably in a league of his own when it came to mathematical problems, and hers was at least partly a mathematical problem, take the Safemo angle, for instance, algorithms and all that. On the other hand wasn't it also a people problem? She half-recalled something about Einstein: math wiz, yes; people wiz, especially female-type people, no. At that moment something clicked into place. That second call! Mrs. Plansky sat a little straighter. The second call, flagged by both Perryman and Max as being unnecessary, was a people thing. That was what made it so interesting, or anomalous, or important. Or all three. Drilling down, as they said in the consultancy world—she and Norm had once hired a consultant, very briefly—it was a thing about one particular person, namely the Will masquerader. Therefore even if Einstein had been around and hanging out in this very room, he couldn't have helped.

Mrs. Plansky decided to go for a walk. It looked cold and windy outside, but dry. She made a second decision, choosing the warm, quilted indoor-outdoor mules over the booties.

Yes, cold and windy. Mrs. Plansky turned right out of the Duce's entrance so she could have the wind at her back, discovering when she checked her map a few blocks later that the Museum of Carpathian History, ostensible object of the excursion, lay in the opposite direction. She kept going, the wind giving extra zip to her pace, like she was decades younger, or at least a year or two. Then, all at once, she found she was passing Bijoux Parisien. She stopped to look in the window.

The first thing Mrs. Plansky saw was her reflection. Oh, dear. She patted her hair into shape, or at least a shape of sorts. Then, changing the angle of view slightly, she got rid of the sight of herself, now replaced by the window display. She saw a string of pearls she liked— big, fat, excessive pearls—and a gold ring set with little rubies that looked like a throwback to the time when the Ottomans were in charge around these parts, although in fact she knew nothing about the Ottomans or—

Mrs. Plansky became aware that someone in the store was trying to get her attention. She peered beyond the display case. A woman—neatly dressed and very presentable, as Miss Terrance used to say—with a big, friendly smile was waving her in. Mrs. Plansky had no intention of—or means for!—buying anything, but did an undercover op remain aloof from the people or . . . or come in from the cold! Mrs. Plansky entered Bijoux Parisien.

"Welcome, madame," the woman said in French, a language Mrs. Plansky understood pretty well. "Better to look and be warm at the same time, no?"

"It certainly is," said Mrs. Plansky in English. She could have said the equivalent in French, but speaking it was laborious and the sound of her accent always made her feel like a female Pepé Le Pew.

"You're American?" the woman said, switching to English.

"Yes."

"Probably the only American in Alba Gemina today. Were you looking for anything in particular?" The woman's expert eye scanned her for jewelry. There was nothing to see but a plain little emerald ring and Norm's wedding ring, which she wore on a chain around her neck. Her own wedding ring she'd buried with Norm.

"What nice earrings, by the way," the woman said.

Oops. Mrs. Plansky had forgotten the earrings, also plain little emeralds—hardly even visible—and matching the ring, although she'd bought them much later.

"Thank you," Mrs. Plansky said. "You have a very nice store."

"Merci, madame. Please look around."

Mrs. Plansky pretended to look around, all the while working hard on a move that was taking shape in her mind, but not quickly.

"Recently, but I can't remember where," she began, and oh how pitiful, right from the start, "I saw a necklace I liked. A gold chain with a sapphire, I think it was oblong cut."

The woman's eyebrows, works of art deco type art all by themselves, rose. "Was it here in Alba Gemina where you saw it?"

"I—I really can't say," said Mrs. Plansky.

"Because just the other day I sold a piece very like what you are describing."

"Really."

"Yes. Unfortunately it was one of a kind. I do have a very pretty brooch with three sapphires, square cut in Italian style."

"That sounds nice, but I've just never worn brooches." Mrs. Plansky laughed gaily. The falsity of that sound: at that moment she was neck and neck with Judas. "Maybe you could put me onto whoever bought the necklace!"

"Pardon?" said the woman, back in French. *Pardon* in French cut to a depth *excuse me* never could.

"Just a thought," Mrs. Plansky said.

"A thought to contact my customer?"

"More as an after-market type of thing."

"After market? I do not understand."

"Well," said Mrs. Plansky, plunging ahead, "it's about the sapphire necklace. If I knew the buyer I . . . I could make him an offer he couldn't refuse!" The reaction she was hoping for did not appear on the woman's face. "Or her," Mrs. Plansky added, on the slim chance that was where she'd gone wrong. But it wasn't that, either. She was considering an explanation involving *The Godfather* when she caught a lucky break. A new customer entered the store and the woman went off—hurried off—to attend to her. Moments later Mrs. Plansky was out on the street.

The wind was blowing harder now. She took her phone out of her pocket to check the time but fumbled a bit, came close to dropping it. That could have led to all sorts of things, none good. Mrs. Plansky hurried across the street to a recessed doorway and tried again. Time: 14:11. Text and voice mail messages: zero. And there she was, reflected in another window, a lady with messy, windblown hair, not looking her best, in fact appearing a little lost, confused, apprehensive, even afraid. What did she have to be afraid of? Nothing. At least nothing concrete.

"Pull yourself together." Had she said that aloud? Just in case she hadn't she did it again, making sure this time. "Pull yourself together!" Then, in the midst of this—what should she call it? collapse?—she caught another lucky break. The etched sign on the window glass read: SALON DE COAFURA. *Coafura:* so close to the French *coiffure.* Not a sign on a window but a sign from above! Still she hesitated. Hadn't she had her hair done just the other day at Delia's on the Waterway? Could she afford this indulgence? Absolutely not. But Delia's on the Waterway was another world, and taking a closer look she spotted a price list card on the window shelf. If those numbers were in lei then this place was a bargain, if in dollars it was like Beverly Hills. Alba Gemina was not Beverly Hills. So far, Mrs. Plansky thought as she went inside, she was preferring Alba Gemina.

Twenty minutes later, hair washed, blown, and dried for a cost of twelve U.S. dollars including tip, unless she was messing up the math, she was back out on the street, feeling much better and looking, in her estimation, slightly European. And not only that, but the mysterious type of European woman, like, for example, Catherine Deneuve. Mrs. Plansky was well aware that she and Catherine Deneuve were on different planets when it came to beauty, and she had never felt in the least mysterious inside, but now, by God, she did! And what if Catherine Deneuve actually didn't feel that she was mysterious inside, and often thought, Oh, Catherine, what a bore you are! Unlikely, yes, but things had a way of evening out, as everyone said. Mrs. Plansky checked her phone again. Time closing in on 16:00, still nothing from Max. She was setting off at a nice pace, a spring in her step, when she noticed a woman walking quickly in the same direction, only on the other side of the street. It was Annika, wearing jeans, sneakers, and white jacket with red sleeves and a fur-trimmed hood.

Could you tell something about a person from how they were walking? That question had never arisen before in Mrs. Plansky's mind. Annika's head was down. Her arms weren't swinging, but held close to her sides. Yet she was moving fast. Mrs. Plansky deduced that she was on her way to do something she didn't want to do. Was there any reason to follow her? No, not a one. And at any other moment in her life, Mrs. Plansky would not have followed. But this moment was special, Mrs. Plansky feeling for the first time mysterious. Staying on her side and keeping her distance, she followed Annika down the street, the wind cold, but at her back.

TWENTY-EIGHT

An undercover op would surely have many tricks for following without being seen but Mrs. Plansky knew only one: don't get too close. That seemed to be good enough and in any case Annika never looked back, just kept clipping along in that stiff posture, perhaps moving even faster than before. Yes, faster for sure, and increasing the distance between them. Mrs. Plansky, losing sight of Annika as she came to the end of a long block and turned down a side street, realized the don't-get-too-close trick came with a drawback. She picked up the pace, but suddenly found herself huffing and puffing. How could that be? She played tennis three or four times a week, almost always doubles, true, but was never out of breath, also had never before felt this strange tightness in her chest, nothing she would call pain. But still. A short, round woman dressed all in black and carrying two shopping bags in each hand passed her with no sign of any effort at all.

Mrs. Plansky reached the end of the block, turned, and failed to spot Annika among the pedestrians, of which there seemed to be dozens, maybe more. Then, at least a hundred yards ahead, she caught a red-and-white flash: Annika crossing the street. Mrs. Plansky—who had once broken twenty-four minutes in a 5K—tried to walk faster but could not, not without provoking the tightness in her chest. Tighter and tighter. She lost sight of Annika, although she couldn't be sure because her vision had gone a bit blurry. Mrs.

Plansky stopped, her back to a lamppost, and tried to catch her breath. That took some time.

Meanwhile, the wind was dying down and the light was fading. She checked her phone: 16:00 on the nose, no calls, no texts. Feeling better, although strangely detached, she walked on, in the faint hope of picking up Annika's trail, but at the leisurely speed her body seemed to prefer right now. She became aware that she was leaving the old town, the architecture changing from faded grandeur mixed with a sort of medieval hipness to something more dismal that she thought of as Stalinist, four-and five-story apartment blocks separated from each other by bleak empty plots, with lots of litter scattered here and there. She knew almost nothing of Romanian history but felt she was somehow absorbing it by osmosis on this walk. Mrs. Plansky was lost in thoughts like that when she saw Annika, standing at the entrance to an apartment block across the street, not twenty yards away. Mrs. Plansky stepped behind a skinny leafless tree, planted in a tiny dirt plot cut into the sidewalk and reeking of pee.

Annika had her phone to her ear and was gazing up at the bleak façade of the building. No balconies? That was rather grim, in Mrs. Plansky's opinion. A face appeared in a window on the third floor, the face of a man, possibly young. He withdrew. Annika pocketed her phone. She appeared to take a long, deep breath.

The entry door to the apartment block—a plain, steel door with no pizzazz whatsoever—opened and a man came out. A youngish man in sweats and a T-shirt with what might have been the image of a skier on the front. One of his hands, the left, was wrapped in some sort of bandage or splint. The wind blew a forelock of his hair over one eye. Oh, and also he was wearing cowboy boots. Mrs. Plansky took a closer look at his face. Hard to be sure at this distance but he looked a lot like one of the motorcycle kids, not Romeo, but . . . but the other one, his name once again elusive. So frustrating! But in her moment of frustration Mrs. Plansky had an inspiration. She took out her phone and snapped a photo of the scene! How brilliant was that! Seconds later, using her thumb and index finger on the screen in a motion the designers probably considered instinctive—getting it wrong in her case—she expanded the image. Yes, the other boy, for sure. And then came his name: Dinu! She was on a roll.

In tennis you don't change a winning game. Applying that rule to the here and now, Mrs. Plansky kept watching the scene across the street through the screen of her phone, taking photos from time to time. A discussion was going on, Annika pointing to Dinu's bandaged hand and Dinu holding it behind his hip, like he was trying to hide it from sight. She reached out and touched his shoulder, kind of tentatively. He turned away, now had his back to the street and Mrs. Plansky. There were tears on Annika's face, silver in the fading light. She reached into her pocket, withdrew something Mrs. Plansky couldn't quite make out, just a tiny flash of blue and gold, and tried to give it to Dinu. He backed away, didn't want it. Annika took his good hand, which he'd folded into a fist, gently opened it, pressed the blue and gold object on his palm, folded his hand back up. Then she turned and ran off down the street. Dinu watched until she was out of sight. He went back inside the building, the steel door closing behind him.

Mrs. Plansky stood behind the skinny, leafless tree in its mephitic little patch of dirt. She was stunned, amazed, bewildered. Where to begin? Dinu knew Annika? Well, perhaps not actually a surprise. His uncle, Dragomir Tiriac, owned the hotel, and Annika filled in there from time to time, on breaks from the casino development job. Mrs. Plansky slowed down her mind, laying down all the little details as she would have before a presentation to a prospective client. Slow thinking, she'd learned, was best for planning, fast thinking for emergencies. But stop! Her undisciplined old mind was wandering. This was not the time. She turned to her phone and went through the pictures she'd just taken.

First, the flash of blue and gold. Yes, the sapphire necklace. She had clear images of it in Annika's hand and on Dinu's palm. Also, before going back inside the building, he'd opened his hand to give it a look. Somehow she'd missed that in real time, but here it was. And the expression on his face at that moment? So complicated, such an odd combination of very grown up and not grown up at all. Mrs. Plansky, who hardly knew the boy and had no clue about what was going on, felt bad for him. She zoomed in on his injured hand, bandaged and with the last three fingers splinted together.

She went over the facts she knew. Someone bought the sapphire necklace at Bijoux Parisien, paying $3195 U.S., not peanuts anywhere, and certainly not here. Dragomir Tiriac tried to give the necklace to Annika, an idea that seemed to have appalled her. Now Annika had given it to Dinu, who hadn't wanted it, either. The necklace was like some talisman in a fairy tale, a new one for Mrs. Plansky, in a language she didn't know.

She expanded another photo, this one of Annika with tears on her face. They both—Dinu and Annika—had expressive faces, almost like actors. Somewhere she'd read that actors, or maybe just movie actors, had faces that were big in proportion to their heads, which didn't seem to be the case with Dinu or Annika. But there went her mind again, off the leash. What did she see on Annika's face? That was the point. What she saw was grief, as though someone had died.

In this same photo of tear-faced Annika, Dinu had his back to the camera. There was something written on his T-shirt. Mrs. Plansky enlarged the image some more and read the words: BOGDAN PLUMBING AND HEATING, NUMBER 1 IN THE GRANITE STATE. Mrs. Plansky studied that little inscription, as though it held a hidden meaning. It was often strange and even funny to see how foreigners glommed on to bits of American culture, but what was their angle? Satiric? Ironic? Mocking? Mystified? Or maybe sometimes a T-shirt was just a T-shirt. Still, Mrs. Plansky couldn't quite completely let go of Bogdan Plumbing and Heating. Something about it bothered her, but she couldn't think what. Was it the Granite State part? Once, when she was a kid, she'd been stuck alone on a chair lift on a class ski trip in the White Mountains, hovering high over a gnarly slope for over an hour with the wind blowing and the temperature in single digits. But she hadn't thought of that episode in years, decades. Could whatever was bothering her be that far back? Mrs. Plansky doubted it, and in any case had no desire to roam around her life in search of unresolved traumas.

She checked the time: 16:22. No call from Max, no texts. She considered entering the apartment building and looking for Dinu. But why? Yes, she seemed to have stumbled on a little mystery, but it had nothing to do with her mystery. Even so, she scanned the building until she found the number of its street address: 971. She took a picture of it. Then she walked to the nearest corner and took a picture of the street sign: Strada Izvor. There! A tangible fact, almost certainly irrelevant yet it made her feel good anyway, like she'd accomplished something. Dinu lived at 971 Strada Izvor. And then she realized she knew the address of someone else in Alba Gemina, namely Max Leonte. Wasn't it written on his card? She dug through her purse and found it.

Max's card was written in Romanian and English and had a little line drawing of his face at the top left, not a bad rendering at all, catching his intelligence, which she'd seen in person, and perhaps something judgmental, which she had not. MAX LEONTE, JOURNALIST, AUTHOR, SEEKER OF TRUTH, it read. Then came his phone number, already captured by her own phone, and the address he'd added with the New Sunshine pen—56 Strada Vulcan, Alba Gemina. She checked the map, found Strada Vulcan, a minor street that backed onto the river, not far from the bridge she'd crossed when she'd first entered the town. Aha! The geography of the town began to make sense to her: the Soviet-style part where she was now, on the eastern side, and then moving west the old town, the main shopping district, the river. She texted Max—**haven't heard from you**—and started walking, steadily but not fast at all.

Fifty-six Strada Vulcan turned out to be near the top of a steep hill, which wasn't apparent from the map. Mrs. Plansky found she—or rather her lungs or heart or some other internal traitor—

wanted to stop for a rest on the way up. Nothing like this had ever happened before. What was going on? Then it hit her: delayed jet lag. She'd read about that in *AARP* magazine, which she didn't subscribe to but came anyway, like the AARP folks wanted to make sure she was under no illusions. So, now that she'd figured it out, no reason to extend this little break for one more second. Mrs. Plansky treaded up the hill, keeping the huffing and puffing under wraps, or at least their sound.

Strada Vulcan was lined with new-looking one-and two-story townhouses, all of them simple and quite similar although their colors were different, even numbers on the river side, odd on the east side where Mrs. Plansky was walking. Through the gaps between the townhouses she caught glimpses of the river, deep red in the dying light. The sky was almost fully dark, a few stars already visible. Fifty-six came into view, one story and painted pink. The windows were dark but a car was parked outside. Mrs. Plansky paused to send another text: **Max? I'm about to knock on your door.**

The very next moment that door opened. Mrs. Plansky had just enough time to think *now we're getting somewhere* when a man came outside, not Max but a much bigger fellow. He went quickly to the car—a bunch of papers and what might have been a notebook in his hand—squeezed in, being so big, and drove away, not looking once in her direction. She knew this enormous man, those shoulder muscles unmissable even at a distance and in poor light. It was Marius, who'd carried her suitcase up to the presidential suite, discussing Nixon and refusing a tip. Reluctantly carried her suitcase, as though it wasn't in his job description. So what was?

Mrs. Plansky stood watching number 56 from across the street, waiting for something to happen. Nothing did. After a while, she slung her purse over one shoulder, dusted off her hands, and got down to business, crossing Strada Vulcan and knocking on Max's door.

No answer. She knocked again. "Max? You there? It's me, Loretta." Perhaps she'd whispered that. She tried again, in a normal tone. Why not? Was anything abnormal going on? Not that she could define. She knocked again, harder. He'd promised a call by four. Was this the kind of country where you expected unpunctuality? Not to her knowledge. "Max? Max!"

No answer. Mrs. Plansky tried turning the knob, a move she'd seen in lots of noirish movies. Norm had a thing for noirish movies. If there was a shot of a rainy street on a dark night, he was in. But Max's door, unlike the doors in all those movies, was locked.

Mrs. Plansky glanced around, like someone up to no good. Which she was not. No need to be furtive! Especially since no one was around. She circled to the back of the townhouse like she had every right.

Max had a nice little patio behind his place, not unlike hers on Little Pine Lake with a similar wrought-iron glass-topped table. An empty beer bottle stood on the table, beside a paperback book. She checked the label on the bottle. The maker's name was long and full of diacritics but from the small print, all in Romanian, she gathered that the beer itself was a pilsner from Transylvania. The book, in English, was a guide to Florida. Mrs. Plansky picked it up and leafed through, stopping at a page with the corner turned down, a page devoted to her town, Punta D'Oro. There was a photo of the library, the oldest building in the county. Standing on the front step was Eleanor Fuentes, the librarian, who Mrs. Plansky knew to say hi to. She got a strange feeling out there on Max's patio, kind of lonely.

Mrs. Plansky turned to the back of the house. Max had glass sliders, also not unlike hers, with closed curtains behind them. Maybe for that reason she'd missed what she should have seen right away, a perfectly shaped round hole in the glass, the size of a dessert plate, near the frame and about halfway up. She went closer. Yes, perfectly shaped, like it had been cut by some tool designed for the task. She remembered a home-security commercial where she'd seen it done by an actor portraying a bad guy. He'd used a round stick-on hockey puck–like tool and something like an X-Acto knife.

Loud alarms sounded right away. Out here on the patio it was quiet. Mrs. Plansky could hear the river rippling and gurgling. She didn't know what to do.

What would she do at home in a situation like this? Well, at home she wouldn't be in a situation like this. At least not before these recent events—the Will masquerader, Safemo, !NorManConQuest!, all the rest. But wasn't that the point, the new square one of her life? All those recent events had happened! Did that change everything? At home and in the last square of her previous life, she would call the police. Was that a good idea here in Alba Gemina, where Captain Romulu might end up on the call? That was point one. Point two was that even back home she wouldn't have been able to resist a peek behind that curtain. You had to know yourself at least a little bit after all this time. So, being true to herself even in strange circumstances, Mrs. Plansky carefully stuck her hand in the dessert plate–size hole.

She got hold of a small handful of curtain and tugged. Nothing doing. She tugged harder. The curtain was stuck. Maybe little annoyances like flawed curtain track design were the same the world over, an unexploited human unifier. Mrs. Plansky reached around to the inside of the frame, where the locking mechanism would be, and finally realized that the slider would be unlocked. Which was the whole raison d'être for the hole in the glass! She blushed from embarrassment, then withdrew her hand and slid the damn thing open.

Mrs. Plansky stepped in and flung the curtain open as well. She was in a small living room, lit by a single table lamp. That lamp was not on a table, but lay sideways on the floor. The whole room was that way in some form or other, trashed: couch and chairs overturned, bookcase knocked sideways with books—many, many books—scattered all over the floor. The only undisturbed object was a framed photo of Max with a younger woman who looked a lot like him, especially the eyes, both of them laughing.

Mrs. Plansky went down the hall, switching on a light or two. She looked into a bedroom where the mattress was slashed, the kitchen, where all the cabinets were open and all the pots and pans had been knocked off their wall hooks, the bathroom, where the medicine cabinet door hung on its hinges, and a tiny office, where all the desk drawers had been torn loose and their contents dumped out. What she did not see was any sign of a fight, such as blood, for example. But she was no expert. She thought of Marius hurrying away with his armful of papers.

Mrs. Plansky left the way she'd come, closing the curtain and the slider. On the way she righted the table lamp in the living room, mindful of the risk of fire. Don't give fire a place to start was one of Miss Terrance's most important rules, and Mrs. Plansky never forgot.

TWENTY-NINE

Mrs. Plansky walked and walked, trying to find some benign explanation for what had happened at Max's place, and failing completely. She held up her hand and saw how unsteady it looked in the moonlight. Mrs. Plansky tried to subdue the unsteadiness—not just in her hand but all through her, mind and body—with rational thought, and maybe that, or all the walking, or something else, deep in her nature—maybe even something screwed up, such as optimism with blinders on, calmed her, at least to the point of realizing she was hungry.

Mrs. Plansky had never been one for skipping meals. On the way back to the hotel she made a slight detour to the Café des Artistes, mostly because she knew how to find it, but also in the hope that Max would be there, a forgetful and tardy foreigner after all. He was not. She ordered lamb chops and a glass of something red and Romanian. The first bite, the first sip: what power they had sometimes, especially, she now realized, when you'd left the beaten track of your life. She gazed into the wineglass, not seeing anything but thinking of all the times Norm—not a big eater, even fussy—said, "I love watching you eat." Her reply, often with her mouth full, was always the same: "Gotta keep my strength up."

A text came in from Lucrecia, back home: Hope you're having a good trip. Quick question—three cases of Krug champagne got delivered today from Al's A1 Liquors. Your dad says you have an account.

I checked and you do—you opened it yesterday? Just checking this
is OK?

Mrs. Plansky's finger hovered uncertainly over the screen, waiting
for a signal from her brain. Her brain was confused. No matter what,
this latest shenanigan—if the word could be singular—of her dad's
was not okay. But in her former life she would have just said what the
hell, made some private arrangement with Al's A1 Liquors governing
future orders, and moved on. Now, just weeks or even days away from
a rapid and permanent descent down the financial ladder unless she
came up with something close to a miracle, those three cases of Krug
were not okay. Mrs. Plansky downed the rest of her Romanian red,
the taste earthy, rough, foreign. She plunked down her glass with a
firm thunk and decided to bet on herself. OK, she texted. Cheers. Al,
if there was an Al, was depending on her, too. She had a grandiose
thought: she was performing a duty to society. She quashed it at once.

Back at the hotel she was crossing the lobby when Annika came
hurrying over from the desk.

"Ah, Mrs. Plansky. I've been looking for you."

"Oh?" She hoped that Annika wasn't about to offer thanks for
giving her a shoulder to cry on that morning. That would feel uncomfortable given that later in the day Mrs. Plansky had been spy-
ing on her. This was probably a routine situation in the life of an
undercover op, even a good sign. She needed to toughen up and get
smarter. Starting this very moment.

But that wasn't where Annika was going. "My boss would like to
buy you a welcome drink."

"Your boss—meaning the gentleman from the breakfast room?"

Annika's eyes showed nothing. "Exactly. Mr. Tiriac. He happens
to be in the bar right now."

The brand-new toughened-up and smarter Mrs. Plansky lined
up the facts. Mr. Tiriac was Annika's boss, but also Marius's boss,
and drinking buddy of Captain Romulu, the iffy cop, according to

Max, who was now hours late making contact, and whose house had been ransacked, almost certainly by Marius. What would any self-respecting undercover op say at a moment like this?

"Why, certainly. Very nice of him."

Mrs. Plansky climbed the stairs to her room, freshened up, changed from the mules to the ballet flats, and came back down. Annika escorted her to the bar, a small dark room with more potted plants, framed prints of French music hall posters, and no one there except for the bartender and two men at a round corner table, one of whom was Dragomir Tiriac. She made a mental note to look up the derivation of Dragomir.

"I present Mrs. Plansky," Annika said. "Mrs. Plansky, Dragomir Tiriac, the patron, and Professor Bogdan."

Professor Bogdan rose. He had a small upside-down crescent bruise under one eye, purple and yellow, the color of healing after a black eye.

"Nice to meet you both," Mrs. Plansky said, shaking hands. Professor Bogdan's hand was thin and damp, Dragomir's immense and dry.

"The professor will translate," Annika said. "He is a teacher of English."

The professor bowed his head and sat down. Annika turned and left the room. Mrs. Plansky pulled up a chair.

"Drink?" said Dragomir in English.

"Yes, thank you," said Mrs. Plansky.

"Champagne is good?" Dragomir said.

"Very," Mrs. Plansky said.

Dragomir snapped his fingers. The bartender hurried over. Dragomir spoke to him in Romanian. The bartender clicked his heels—the first time in her life Mrs. Plansky had actually seen that—and headed back to the bar.

"You American?" Dragomir said in English. Everything about him seemed oversize and formidable, excepting his eyes, small, round, glinting—but also formidable.

"I am," said Mrs. Plansky.

He spoke to Professor Bogdan in Romanian, something that was more of a command than a request.

"Where in America?" said the professor.

"Florida."

The professor's tone changed, became more natural, like he wasn't translating but speaking for himself. "Have you ever been to New Hampshire?"

"Oh, yes." The question didn't surprise her. She'd been thinking of New Hampshire—and Dinu's T-shirt—from the moment she'd heard the professor's surname. "Why do you ask?"

Professor Bogdan looked like he was about to reply, but Dragomir interrupted with something in Romanian.

"Welcome to Romania," the professor said.

"Thank you."

Dragomir spoke to the professor.

"Mr. Tiriac asks if this is your first visit to our country," Bogdan said. His look was not formidable—a thin old guy—well, quite possibly younger than Mrs. Plansky, but an indoorsy type with nicotine-stained fingers and a neck too small for the buttoned-up collar of his shirt. He also wore a wool tie and an ancient-looking tweed jacket with a pack of cigarettes in the chest pocket.

"It is."

"And he would like to know your impressions."

Mrs. Plansky decided—based on nothing—that Dragomir understood English fairly well and so spoke directly to him. "It's too soon to have any opinion at all, but so far the country looks beautiful and the people are friendly."

Dragomir nodded. Professor Bogdan translated. Dragomir nodded again and spoke to the professor for a minute or two.

"Mr. Tiriac is glad you like the country so far," the professor said. "He notes that it's somewhat unusual to see tourists here in Alba Gemina at this time of year. Is there any special reason for your visit? Or maybe more American to say, what brought you here?"

Whatever this nice little welcoming get-together was about, Mrs.

Plansky—old version and new—knew one thing for sure: the truth was not the answer. But which untruth was best? "No special reason," she said. "I was in the mood for a quick getaway and saw some cheap flights to Bucharest."

The professor relayed that to Dragomir. He gazed at her for a moment, a sizing-up gaze, in Mrs. Plansky's interpretation, that found her on the shallow side. That had to be a good thing. She had every confidence that she could pull off the shallow persona without breaking a sweat.

"Is cold," Dragomir said. He crossed his arms and shivered. The sight, to her surprise, was kind of charming. "Cold winter."

Mrs. Plansky flashed him a smile she hoped was a little too bright. "When you live in Florida you don't travel for the weather."

Dragomir turned to the professor. "Ce?"

Bogdan started in on an explanation. Dragomir made a dismissive gesture, his hand so big Mrs. Plansky felt a tiny breeze from across the table.

"For what reason Alba Gemina?" he said in English.

"Oh, that," Mrs. Plansky said, hoping that whatever was coming next came soon. And then it did, just perfect, as though the goddess of ditziness was watching over her. "I'm interested in equestrian statues and happened across yours in a guidebook. I wanted to see it in person."

"Ce?" said Dragomir. But the professor looked baffled.

"Ours?" he said.

"Right outside—*Michael the Brave*."

"But no one here pays the slightest attention. It's nothing but a copy—and a bad one, if I may say so. The original was blown up by the Nazis or possibly the Russians. The facts are forever in dispute."

This seemed like a handy cue for the too-bright smile. "That makes it all the more interesting!"

"Ce?" said Dragomir.

The professor began an explanation, soon interrupted by Dragomir who asked what sounded like an impatient question. Mrs. Plansky understood nothing except for one word. It sounded like *E.D. Ought*, and didn't come together at first. As for the context: possibly good if he was asking Bogdan if he thought she was an E.D. Ought; or bad, if he was saying only an E.D. Ought would believe her.

At that moment the waiter arrived. Professor Bogdan, Dragomir, and Mrs. Plansky watched the popping of the cork and the pouring of the champagne—except for Dragomir, who mostly watched her watching, as Mrs. Plansky was aware of without looking.

They clinked glasses. "Sănătate," the professor said, which Mrs. Plansky took to mean health.

"Si bogatie," said Dragomir.

"What's that?" Mrs. Plansky said.

"Wealth," said the professor.

"They rhyme in English," she said. "Health and wealth."

"Health and wealth?" Dragomir said, not getting the *th* sound right. "Hey! I like you!" If so, his eyes hadn't gotten the message. He drained his glass of champagne in one go and set it down. "Si acum Leonte," he said.

"Excuse me?" Mrs. Plansky's heart started racing, reacting before her brain.

"Mr. Tiriac would like to know your relationship with Max Leonte," Bogdan said.

"Well, my goodness," said Mrs. Plansky. "Are you talking about the writer?"

Bogdan nodded.

"How strange." The word in her frightened little heart was not *strange,* but *terrifying.* Here Mrs. Plansky took a chance. "I have nothing you would call a relationship with him. I came across his work and emailed a couple of questions through his publisher. Why are you asking?"

That led to a long back-and-forth between Bogdan and Dragomir. Mrs. Plansky had plenty of time to think of the holes and minefields in her little bit of improv. For example, did Dragomir somehow know she and Max had been in the bar of the Royale the night before? If he did, what would be the sign? If he didn't, how had he put them together? Right now all she heard in his voice was annoyance.

They both turned to her, catching her in the middle of a nonchalant sip of champagne, a lucky break, Mrs. Plansky's timing perhaps not usually one of her strengths, if she had to rate them.

"Why we ask," Bogdan said, "is that this man, Leonte, is not a good type. It is better—"

Dragomir interrupted, saying something that sounded like "moolt."

"Much better," Bogdan went on, "much better not to know him, certainly for you, such a respectable lady tourist."

"I'm a bit surprised," Mrs. Plansky said. "Not a good type in what way?"

"The man is not a patriot," Bogdan said. Dragomir nodded. "In fact, he is in league with a foreign power to harm the Romanian people."

"Really? How so? I'm curious."

That led to another exchange between Dragomir and Bogdan.

"By meddling in our internal affairs," Bogdan said. "Spreading false information. Raising doubts. Romania has a long history of which we are proud, but much of it is troubled. This explains our strong desire for stability. Do you understand?"

"I do."

Dragomir tapped the table twice with his middle finger. Bogdan leaned forward.

"So that is why," he said, "as good citizens we must ask you—are you yourself an agent of a foreign country?"

Mrs. Plansky was still for a moment. Then she burst out laughing, hand to her chest. "Me? Do I look like . . . like a spy? Good grief! You're joking, right?" For the first time, the expression in Dragomir's eyes, a changing combination of impatience and intelligence, with something violent a constant under the surface, grew a little murky, possibly confused.

"Therefore your answer is no?" Bogdan said.

"Do you want me to sign an affidavit? Watch out I don't use invisible ink!"

"What is an affidavit?" Bogdan said.

"Pardon me, just a joke," Mrs. Plansky said. "I am not an agent of a foreign power. In fact I have no job at all. I'm retired."

While Bogdan relayed that to Dragomir, Mrs. Plansky wondered whether to ask where they got the notion she knew Max, or to say nothing and let them conclude she was too dumb to think of the question. The answer seemed obvious. Meanwhile Dragomir was making another of his dismissive hand gestures.

The professor turned to her. "It's been a pleasure to meet you," he said. "Mr. Tiriac wishes you a pleasant stay." Dragomir took an envelope from his pocket and handed it to Mrs. Plansky. "And here is a gift card to Club Presto, which he owns also."

"Well that's very nice." Mrs. Plansky rose. "And thank you for the lovely champagne, gentlemen. Good night."

Mrs. Plansky walked out of the bar. In the lobby, she encountered Marius, just coming in from the street, a sheaf of papers in his hand.

THIRTY

Mrs. Plansky heard noises in the night. At first, still mostly in dreamland, she thought the noises were coming from the square, even had the crazy idea that the Nazis or the Russians had come again, this time to destroy the replica. But then she realized she was wrong. Yes, the sounds were real, but they weren't coming from the square. They were much closer than that. She sat up in bed and reached for the lamp on the bedside table, her hand encountering nothing. That was because she'd reached for where the lamp would have been at home. Here in the presidential suite, it was on the other side. She was shifting over in that direction, somewhat tangled in the sheets, when it struck her that the sounds were coming from inside the room. She went still.

Scratch, scratch, scratch scratch. Was there something metallic about that scratching, like a key was having trouble getting into a lock?

Scratch, scratch. No, not from inside the room, but close, behind the wall, maybe from an adjoining room. Or . . . or her own bathroom. Very quietly she got out of bed, the tile floor cold under her feet. How could she have forgotten to pack her slippers? She moved toward the bathroom, that enormous bathroom, and heard the scratching sounds more clearly, although they weren't coming from inside the bathroom. They seemed to be on the move, getting softer, fading away, perhaps on a staircase, descending. What sort of adjoining room had a staircase? A royal suite? That was her only thought, totally unhelpful.

Meanwhile her eyes—not so fast these days when it came to adjustments—were getting used to the darkness, not a total darkness, moonlight entering through a tiny gap in the curtains. She saw she was standing next to the shower stall, right in front of the old, heavy wooden door with no knob, no keyhole. Once again, Mrs. Plansky gave that door a push. Once again it didn't budge. She put her ear to it and heard nothing. She had the weird feeling that she'd traveled back to the time of Michael the Brave, whenever that was, exactly.

Mrs. Plansky went back to bed. But it was hopeless. Never mind sleep. Her eyes wouldn't even close. To pass the time—or even soothe herself to sleep—she decided to think about Norm and things they'd done together, something she did now and then, and in fact quite often, floating along on reveries. But now, for the very first time, her mind wouldn't go there. It refused to dwell on some memory of Norm, would not even begin, wouldn't try. No matter what she did, her mind could not be steered in the direction of Norm, like a sailboat that would not come up into the wind. Mrs. Plansky sat up and put her hands to her face. She was alone.

Self-pity? Oh, dear. "What is wrong with you?" She said that aloud, loud and clear, no question. Lowering her voice she went on a bit. "Think of what some people go through. You've had it way too easy. Spoiled! Spoiled frickin' rotten."

She got out of bed and marched to the bathroom, no moonlight now, the suite darker than before, but without thinking she knew the way. She turned on the tap, splashed cold water on her face. Had she really, for the first time in her life, said "frickin'"? She was falling apart. "Don't be a punching bag. Punch!"

Mrs. Plansky threw a punch in the darkness.

"Ow!"

Her punch, meant to hit nothing but air, instead struck something hard and unyielding. Well, perhaps not totally unyielding. She heard a splintering sound, not loud, very minor. Mrs. Plansky felt along the wall, found the switch, turned on the light, and looked around, blinking into the brightness. What she'd punched was the heavy old knobless door. Now it was open about an inch, like she was Mike Tyson. Mrs. Plansky rubbed her hand, sore already. Did boxers have to just live with sore hands? She'd always felt bad for them. She gave the heavy old door a little push. It creaked open another inch or two.

Mrs. Plansky stepped forward and peered into the little gap. In the narrow beam of light escaping from the bathroom, she could make out a cobweb forest, and through the cobwebs what seemed to be a stone wall a few feet away, old and rough-hewn. She felt a slight, cool breeze. It carried the faint scent of cigars. She stuck out her finger and tried another push. Now, without a sound, the door swung open some more, just enough for a person of her size to step through. Brushing cobwebs aside, Mrs. Plansky stepped through.

She stood in the little pool of light from the bathroom and looked both ways, the light on either side quickly swallowed up in darkness, but she could see this was some sort of stone-floored passageway, a stone wall on one side and a wooden one on the other. Mrs. Plansky crouched down, looking for footprints. She saw none. But hadn't someone been out here? Perhaps going somewhere? It was a passage-way, after all. Room service, maybe? Or could there be rooms along the passageway, servants' rooms dating back to the Middle Ages, perhaps now used for the staff? But then why all the cobwebs? Mrs. Plansky had no other ideas. She took a few steps to her right and entered total darkness.

Some travelers, much savvier than her, took lots of gadgets on their trips, Swiss Army knives, for example, or mini-flashlights. A mini-flashlight right now would have been very useful. Instead, Mrs. Plansky just stood there in her nightie, bare feet getting cold on the stone floor, the faint, cool breeze in her face, and again feeling she'd gone back to the time of Michael the Brave. Wasn't that part of the lure of travel to some places, that you also traveled in time? Mrs. Plansky was wandering around in thoughts like that when it suddenly hit her that her phone was also a flashlight.

She went back into her room, found her phone, slipped into her flats, returned to the passageway. She got the phone light working and shone it to the left. The passageway petered out only a few yards away, ending in a narrow bricked-over wall. But in the other direction, to the right, it continued beyond the range of her light. Mrs. Plansky was about to set off that way when she remembered she was in her nightie, a rather short nightie but very comfortable, and of course no one ever saw her in it.

And no one ever would. Mrs. Plansky went back into her room and changed into her black woolen slacks—the wool thin but nice and warm—and gray cashmere mock turtle. Then she returned to the passageway, pushed the door closed, and began following her light beam through the darkness.

After not very long there was a change in the passageway, the flat flagstones of the floor replaced by bumpy cobbles, as in the square. The passageway narrowed and soon after that her beam seemed to be probing emptiness. Mrs. Plansky moved on, slow and cautious, until she came to a descending staircase. She followed it down, actually counting the steps, which struck her as a rather clever idea. There were fifteen. At the bottom she panned the light around, found she was in a sort of cellar, dirt-floored and dank. Huge wooden casks, very old and worn, lined one wall. She went closer, fixed her beam on something branded on the side of one of the casks: MDCLXXXIV. Ah, Roman numerals. M was a thousand, D had to be five hundred, C one hundred, L fifty, making what so far? Mrs. Plansky got lost in the Roman numerals—as the Romans, if they were being honest with themselves, probably did, too. Bottom line, the meaningful one: the feeling of long ago came close to being real in this place, like some historical character—Dracula being an obvious candidate— might step out from behind the casks at any moment. Here was just one reason why wandering around in too-short nighties was a bad idea. She sniffed the air, searching for some ancient boozy smell, but picked up only that faint cigar scent. When she tapped the cask the sound was hollow and empty.

Beyond the last cask a rectangular space was cut in the stone wall, leading to what looked like another staircase, this one wooden. Mrs. Plansky had to duck down to get through the space but once through she could stand upright. She shone the light up the stairs, very steep and roughly-made, but not old. The walls were made of plywood. She started up, once again counting the stairs. There turned out to be thirty-one and Mrs. Plansky, huffing and puffing, had to pause for breath at the top. She shone the light back down the stairs. Standing on the cellar floor, front paws on the first step, and staring up at her, was an enormous, very long-whiskered rat, its claws also enormous and glinting in the light. Mrs. Plansky's heart jumped in her chest. "Shoo!" she said, in a sort of furious whisper that had no effect on the rat. She brandished her phone at it, the beam of light streaking back and forth in a way that must have struck the rat as violent. It darted away, out of sight. *Scratch, scratch,* went those enormous claws, *scratch, scratch.*

Mrs. Plansky turned around, but with the phone still at her side and pointed down, so its strong beam didn't drown out the faint light that lay ahead. She switched off the phone light. Her eyes again took their time to catch up, but eventually she saw she was at the end of a long corridor, the floor linoleum and the walls plaster. The faint glow began about twenty feet farther ahead, flowing in from the right. She walked toward it.

Mrs. Plansky came to a window on the right hand side, a fairly narrow window, maybe only two-and-a-half-feet high, but very long horizontally, going on as far as she could see. She leaned forward and took a quick peek through the strangely dark glass.

Mrs. Plansky didn't understand what she was seeing at first. Down below was a huge room, the ceiling hung with unlit chandeliers and also some mirror balls, not rotating, a highly polished red-and-black-squared marble floor, glass-topped gilt tables, a stage with music stands, and a long translucent bar, all of this lit only by a couple of wall sconces. The last thing she noticed was what she should have noticed first, a neon sign behind the bar reading CLUB PRESTO. She was gazing at that sign and feeling some re-arrangements going on in her mind when she became aware of move-ment down below. A woman in a head scarf had entered from the other end of the room, carrying a mop and pail. She set them down and began lifting all the gilt chairs onto the glass-topped tables. A woman perhaps of Mrs. Plansky's age? She moved stiffly and—

And all at once, without the slightest warning, the woman in the head scarf turned her head and looked right at her. Mrs. Plansky froze, learning in that instant an important lesson: in total panic, that's what humans did. In partial panic they ran about wildly. She began preparing a little story involving her gift card. The woman—too thin and much younger than Mrs. Plansky had thought—turned away and went back to work.

Meaning? Meaning she hadn't seen Mrs. Plansky, although of course Mrs. Plansky had seen her. And therefore? The woman was blind—a complete nonstarter given her job, the way she moved, the look in her eyes—or this window was in fact the one-way kind, a window on Mrs. Plansky's side, a mirror on the Club Presto side.

Aha! She moved on and after twenty feet or so reached the end of the window, as well as the corridor itself. Ahead stood an unfinished wooden door with a spray-painted sign: CAMBIO. Cambio was a word you saw on signs all over Europe, meaning a place to exchange currency. In Mrs. Plansky's experience, this was not the usual type of location. She stood before the door and listened, hearing nothing. Cambios would be closed in the middle of the night, and of course locked as well. She tried the door knob. It turned. She gave a little push. The door opened easily and soundlessly. On the other side was a small room with a bit of light coming in from another dark window, not big, about the size of the window by her kitchen sink at home, with its nice view of her sunny little plot of black-eyed Susans, doing so well.

There was nothing cambio-like about this small room. It had no furniture at all except a single card table chair by the window. Along the back wall was a lot of musical equipment—mic stands, amplifiers, a few keyboards, a stand-up bass leaning against a bass drum. A broad shelf stood at the bottom of the window, and on that shelf were an ashtray containing cigar butts and a half-full bottle of Johnnie Walker Blue. She went closer, noticing a mesh grill, postcard size, built into the shelf, with a red button beside it. Mrs. Plansky looked through the glass.

Down below lay a room that looked like some combination of a radio studio and a mission control setup for sending astronauts into space. Mrs. Plansky tried to make sense of it all—the many screens, the stacks of blinking modular boxes connected by coiling cables, the mics, headphones, and so much other digital-type equipment she had no names for. Was there such a thing as bitcoin mining? So maybe this was some sort of cambio after all? She was trying to remember something about bitcoin mining, or bitcoins in general—anything at all, really, just one measly solid fact—when a door along the far wall of mission control opened and people started filing in. Mrs. Plansky knew them all except for the man who entered first, a wiry little dark-eyed guy with a waxed handlebar mustache. The others were Marius, Romeo, Dinu, and Dragomir, in that order. The way they came in, the way each one took his place, like the home side trotting onto the diamond at the top of the first inning—they were a team.

And taking a closer look, Mrs. Plansky saw there was something of the locker room about the setup—a few crushed soda cans on the floor, someone's hoodie rolled up in a corner—and even of a teenage boy's basement in a home lacking supervision. She thought she could make out a grimy sheen on the keyboards. It was actually kind of dirty down in that room.

Dragomir sat on a lumpy chair in one corner. Beside it stood a side table with a bottle and a glass. He took a cigar from his pocket. Marius sat on a stool in the corner diagonally across from him. He drew the knife from his ankle sheath and began cleaning his finger-nails with the tip of the blade. The wiry guy with the mustache stood with his back to the far wall. He looked all around, his gaze passing without a pause right over Mrs. Plansky. Her heart, already beating too fast, speeded up a little more, even though she knew he couldn't see her. Something or other—possibly the human geometry—gave her the idea that the three of them, these tough, and yes, dangerous men—didn't even like each other. She knew—from stories Norm had told her—that could be a team thing. Hadn't two famous Yan-kees hated each other? She thought so, but the names wouldn't come.

As for the boys—and the presence of the three men brought out the boy in them and blotted out the man—she could see they were friends just from how they walked together. Neither looked good at the moment. Dinu's face was pale. His hand was still splinted. Perhaps it was hurting. As for Romeo, poor Romeo, he wore a thick bandage over his nose, taped to his cheeks, and his upper lip was horribly swollen and purple. Had they been in a motorcycle wreck? That was the only explanation that came to mind.

They sat beside each other at the radio studio–type table. Romeo produced a printout. The boys went over it together, their heads al-most touching, Romeo pointing things out, the two of them talking from time to time, although Mrs. Plansky couldn't hear through the glass. After a couple of minutes or so, Dinu nodded and Romeo set the printout aside and got busy with the stack of modular compo-nents, disconnecting and reconnecting cables, switching switches, dialing dials, gazing at screens, all of them full of what might have been numbers, some flashing. Dinu pulled the table mic a little closer. Meanwhile, leaning against the wall at their backs, the wiry man with the handlebar mustache never took his eyes off them.

Mrs. Plansky found she was sitting in the card table chair by the window, her head inches from the glass. Dragomir's lips moved. Romeo hunched forward, seemed to be trying to do whatever he was doing faster. At last he sat up and nodded to Dinu. The boys put on headphones. Dragomir lit his cigar. Marius stopped cleaning his fingernails and sheathed his knife. The wiry guy leaned against the wall and watched the backs of the boys' heads. Romeo pressed a big button on one of the modules. Mrs. Plansky really wished she could hear what was going on. Then, perhaps a little later than most people would have done, she realized she had a button of her own, this red one by the mesh grill on the shelf by the window.

She pressed it. Nothing happened. Her hand, maybe getting impatient with her brain, took over and gave that button a twist. Ah, a dial. The sound of static came through the mesh grill. But that only lasted a few seconds. Then came a sort of unmarred and somehow vast silence, followed by something like a dial tone.

Yes, a dial tone for sure, followed by the sound of a phone ringing on the other end. It rang four times and Dinu and Romeo were just exchanging a possibly nervous glance when there was a little click, followed by the voice of a woman.

"Hello?" she said in English.

THIRTY-ONE

"Hello?" said the woman again, an American woman, not young. And from somewhere down South—Mrs. Plansky knew that from just those two syllables. "Hello?"

Dinu leaned closer to his mic. "Hey, Gram." He glanced at the printout. "It's me, Andy."

"Andy?"

"Yeah, Gram, your grandson, Andy. Have you forgotten me?"

Romeo's eyebrows rose. He gave Dinu a thumbs-up.

"Oh, no, honey, what a thing to say! But I haven't heard from you—gosh, in ages—and you sound so far away."

Romeo turned a dial.

"Well, jeez, Gram, the Beaver State is far away."

"Beaver State?"

"The Beaver State—Oregon. I'm at college in Oregon, Gram."

"Of course, of course. I knew that. It's just been so long. But that's not important. It's so good to hear from you, Andy. It can get a bit lonesome here, time to time. How's college life treating you?"

"Pretty good, Gram. I'm learning so much! Real things! Although there's a problem right now."

"Oh, dear. What kind of problem? Is there anything I can do to help?"

No, no, no, don't say that! Mrs. Plansky could hardly breathe. Anything but that! Or nothing, nothing at all. Gram! Hang up!

"Well, that's why I'm calling, Gram. You're the only one I can count on."

Yes, mission control, or something like that. They were landing a plane and now it was just touching down. How horrible! That poor grandchild-loving grandmother! This was so wrong. Mrs. Plansky wanted to bang on the glass and shout: Stop this instant! She's a human being just like you! Think what you're doing! Of course she was too cowardly to protest out loud, or lift a finger to—

But suddenly Dragomir was looking up, right in her direction, as though seeing her even though she was invisible. Mrs. Plansky couldn't turn away, like his eyes had taken her gaze prisoner. Was it possible she'd actually spoken those thoughts, her protest? No, no, she couldn't be that far gone. But maybe she had let out some sound? She didn't remember making a sound, but how to explain the fact that Dragomir now said something to the wiry man, quiet, in Romanian, and drowned out by the goings-on between Dinu and Gram, Mrs. Plansky picking up only the first word, which was "Timbo?" Possibly a name? And now Timbo, if that was his name, was headed toward a door on his side of the room. He opened it and went through—all his movements compact and swift—kicking the door closed with his heel in a quick movement Mrs. Plansky might have called elegant in another situation.

But not this one. She rose, so slowly, like one of those animals easily hypnotized by a predator, and glanced around. There was only one door to the Cambio, leading back to the corridor overlooking Club Presto. She moved—like through molasses—in that direction, but had taken no more than a couple of steps before she heard a door closing somewhere nearby, followed by the sound of soft and rapid footsteps in the corridor. Mrs. Plansky froze, again undone by total panic. She came close to hating herself at that moment, and in her anger came alive. There was only one thing to do. She hurried over to the stacks of musical equipment lining the back wall, got down on her hands and knees—not so easy—and crawled between the stand-up bass and the big bass drum. Then she made herself very small.

Mrs. Plansky heard the Cambio door open. Then came footsteps. The man himself appeared, at least partially. Mrs. Plansky, on her hands and knees, had a slight view from around the lower curve of the bass drum, a dim shadowy space where she was exposed, but only from the eyes up, all the rest of her completely concealed. Should she try to wriggle her way a little farther behind the drum? Drums could be loud, if you knocked them over, for example. She stayed where she was.

Meanwhile her eyes were fixed on what she could see of Timbo—at first just his lower half. He wore sneakers, form-fitting jeans, and a belt with a heavy gold buckle. His legs and his stance were those of a champion in some sort of sport.

Meanwhile, down in mission control, Dinu was working his way toward the climax, his dialogue with Gram coming through the speaker on the shelf by the glass.

"The password?" Gram was saying.

"For the account, Gram. It will encrypt and vanish faster than . . . than you can say Jack Robinson!"

Timbo turned toward the speaker. "Hei!" he said, and continued on with what sounded almost like baby talk. He headed toward the window, and that was when Mrs. Plansky noticed something new in the room. Standing next to the red button on the shelf—actually a dial—was a rat. A huge, long-whiskered rat, with enormous, curving claws—yes, her rat. Had it followed her the whole way, right at her heels? Or had it found another route? Now here it was, and it had Timbo's full attention.

"Hei," he said again, moving toward the rat, Timbo's top half coming into Mrs. Plansky's line of sight. His waxed handlebar mustache, such an extreme grooming statement, diverted her gaze from the rest of his face, but now she took it in. There was nothing unusual about any of his features and in his eyes she even thought she saw a gentle expression. Somehow it made his presence even more disturbing.

Timbo approached the rat and he was speaking to it for sure, in Romanian baby talk. The rat, which had been standing on all fours, now rose into a sitting position, its tail, very long and rather reptilian-looking for a mammal, curled around the red knob. Timbo laughed softly and kept moving. Mrs. Plansky had no idea what was going on and didn't want to find out, but she couldn't look away. In midstride, Timbo reached out, not especially speedily, took hold of the end of the rat's tail and—

But oh, the nastiness. Mrs. Plansky, too late, turned away. He'd—he'd dashed the animal headfirst against the edge of the shelf. Now he held it dangling, the animal lifeless, blood—not much—dripping from its head.

Through the speaker came Dinu's voice. "All done, Gram. Thank you so much!"

"You just take care of yourself. Bye now, Andy."

"I will. Bye bye!"

Timbo walked out of the Cambio room, the rat still dangling from his hand, and closed the door behind him with that same slick flick of the heel.

Mrs. Plansky didn't move. Well, that wasn't quite true. She didn't change her position, but if shaking was movement then she was moving. But not puking. Mrs. Plansky had always had a strong stomach.

A click came over the speaker and then there was silence. She rose and walked toward the window, stepping carefully over the trail of blood drops. Down below in mission control Timbo was holding up the rat, as for a show-and-tell, explaining how he'd found the culprit in the observation room. Marius laughed, Dragomir showed no reaction, the boys looked a little sick, and in Romeo's case also afraid. Then Dragomir stubbed out his cigar in an ashtray, rose, and dropped a few brightly colored bills in front of the boys. The men left the room, the boys staying behind. Dinu gathered up their paperwork. Romeo started switching off the machines. There were tears on his cheeks. Mrs. Plansky had a brain wave. She took out her phone and snapped a picture, capturing the next moment, when Dinu laid a hand—his splinted hand—on Romeo's shoulder, comforting him. Romeo wiped his cheeks on his sleeve. At that moment she abandoned the motorcycle wreck explanation. Romeo gathered the money, divided it up. The boys headed out of mission control, shutting off the lights.

That left Mrs. Plansky in total darkness. She didn't dare turn on her phone light, trusting herself to find her way to the Cambio door without it, which she did, expecting that on the other side she'd again have the light from the wall sconces in Club Presto, but they, too, had been switched off. Well, no matter. She remembered how this went. First would come this long narrow gallery, followed by the thirty-one stairs down to the ancient cellar, where it would surely be safe to use the phone light. Voilà! So nice to have a plan. Although Mike Tyson—again, and so soon?—said everyone has a plan until they get punched in the mouth. She realized something important. I already got punched in the mouth, Mike. But I'm still here, planning away. She made a mental note to keep the braggadocio strictly to herself.

Mrs. Plansky moved slowly along the narrow corridor, sometimes running her hand along the plaster wall to her right. This went on longer than she'd expected and she was starting to wonder if she'd made some sort of mistake, when her hand touched what felt like a doorknob. Mrs. Plansky came to a halt. A door off to the side in the corridor? She had no memory of that, but could easily have missed it. Not that it made any difference. Her job now was just to get to the thirty-one stairs. And she was taking the first step when she heard a sound from behind the door, a human sound, the sound of a muffled groan.

Mrs. Plansky stood still, although her body was already weighted toward movement. There was such a thing as pushing your luck, according to gamblers, and she'd been very lucky so far on this little excursion. Therefore, Loretta, get on the stick! Maybe you imagined the groan, and if it was real what were the chances that the groaner was a bad guy, or whatever was going on behind that door was something beyond your understanding and best left alone? There! Her analysis was impregnable. Her toes rose to take that first step. And then came the groan again.

Damn, thought Mrs. Plansky. She turned the knob and gave the door a little push. On the other side was a small room with an earthen floor, a crude wooden table and chairs, the only light coming from a low-wattage lamp in one corner. A man—she was assuming that from the sound of the groan—his face hooded, was duct-taped to one of the chairs. So much duct tape, winding from his ankles all the way up his neck. Mrs. Plansky could sense that he was aware of her presence, or at least that the door had opened. She steeled herself, marched forward, and pulled off the hood.

It was Max.

Their eyes met. They'd duct-taped his mouth so he couldn't speak but in his eyes she saw amazement, and also pain.

Mrs. Plansky took hold of a corner of the duct tape strip over his mouth to gently peel it off. It wouldn't be gently pulled off.

"This will have to be like a Band-Aid," she said, and ripped off the tape.

Max didn't cry out, or make any sound at all. He closed his eyes for a second or two, then opened them. "Thank you." He kept his voice very low.

"Certainly." Mrs. Plansky glanced around, looking for something sharp. There was nothing like that in the room. She got to work on the duct tape with her bare hands.

"What are you doing here?" Max said. "And, please, a little more quietly."

"You first," said Mrs. Plansky, lowering her voice.

"I behaved like an American. I should have been devious, like a European."

"We're not devious?"

"You're clumsy when you try, at least from our perspective. I approached Dragomir directly—Clint Eastwood–style." Max's shoulders were now free. He shrugged, wincing at the motion.

"Are you hurt?"

"Nothing to speak of. My own fault. I told him I'm writing a book on cybercrime and wanted to get some quotes, anonymous, of course."

Max seemed rather talkative given the goings-on. But he was a writer, so it was probably to be expected. Mrs. Plansky, trying to move things along a little faster with the duct tape, had trouble taking it all in.

"For example," he was saying, "I asked if he kept records of the identities of the victims. He blew up. There are no victims, he shouted, only happy customers. I hardly had time to argue with that before Marius, the big one, was on me. They blindfolded me and brought me here." Max glanced around. "Wherever here is. And questioned me—mostly about who my book contract was with, who else I'd spoken to, nothing I couldn't dodge fairly easily. They also asked about you."

"Oh?"

"No worries. I gave the impression you were one of those readers."

"What readers are you talking about?" By now Mrs. Plansky was on her knees, having trouble with the duct tape that bound his arms to his sides.

"The kind who develop obsessions."

"What sort of obsessions?"

"Like . . . like a groupie."

"You told him I was a groupie?" A long strip of duct tape finally split down the middle, tearing the top off one of her fingernails in the process.

Max nodded, kind of sheepishly. "We have borrowed your word in Romanian."

She stared up at him. His gaze slid away. "That's one of the stupidest things I've ever heard," she said.

"But he believed it without question. So we know for sure they don't retain the names of the victims. They probably destroy all the records. It would make sense."

Suddenly much stronger—groupies being young, among all the rest of it—Mrs. Plansky ripped off the remaining duct tape in seconds, then rose, her knees cracking loudly but without pain.

"Can you get up?" she said.

"Yes."

But it turned out he couldn't, not without help from her.

"Maybe we should let you rest here for a bit," she said, getting his arm across her shoulders and taking a lot of his weight.

"Oh, no, no," said Max. "I will be okay. They'll be back, next time with an associate named Timbo."

That couldn't happen. Mrs. Plansky stepped forward, pretty much dragging Max along. She felt him gathering his strength. He leaned on her, but not as much. Together they walked out of the earthen-floored room.

"Where are we going?" he said.

"You'll see."

"I can't see a thing."

"Trust me."

What an odd thing to say! It had just popped out, like from the mouth of someone who knew what she was doing. The real Mrs. Plansky wasn't even sure she was back in the corridor, or had wandered off somewhere else, into a dungeon, for example. She felt her way along the wall with her right hand, her left arm around Max's waist. Trusting her or not, he kept his mouth shut. After a while, Mrs. Plansky felt a faint and slightly damp breeze in her face. She stopped, fished the phone from her pocket, turned on the light. And there, a half step away, was the void. Trust me—ha! A scary second or two, but it was the right void. She aimed the beam a little lower, illuminating the thirty-one steps.

"What's this?" he said.

"Concentrate," she said. "No rails."

"They took my phone."

"Of course. They're crafty."

Mrs. Plansky went first, but also took his hand, guiding him down step by step. In the beginning his hand felt awkward in hers, but by the time they got to the bottom it was perfectly normal.

Mrs. Plansky shone the light around the cellar, pausing over the enormous casks.

"My God," he said, still holding her hand. "I had no idea."

"And the end of all our exploring," Mrs. Plansky said, *"will be to arrive where we started and know the place for the first time."* She'd always loved that one. And now, to have a chance to actually say it? Things were looking up. Meanwhile Max's gaze was on her. She didn't have to see, just felt it.

"And here we are," said Mrs. Plansky, her voice low, just above a whisper, as she got a fingertip between the edge of the knobless door and the jamb, and pulled the door open. They entered her bathroom. "Welcome to the presidential suite," she said, switching on the light. Max's face was very pale, the blue of his light blue eyes faded almost to nothing. But he smiled.

"The one with Nixon's photo on the door?" he said.

"Correct."

He limped to the sink, turned on the tap, lowered his head to the flowing water, drank, and drank. When he finally raised his head he looked a little better.

"What are we going to do?" he said. "The truth is—and I'm not complaining—I'm still in something of a trap. Any ideas?"

"Sleep," said Mrs. Plansky. "We'll have ideas in the morning."

As things played out, ideas began arriving sooner than that. There was nowhere for Max to sleep but the love seat, much too small, but Mrs. Plansky removed the cushions and arranged them in a bed-like form on the floor. Then she added one of the pillows from her bed, covered him with an extra blanket, got him settled. While all that was going on she tried to give him a concise recap of what she'd witnessed in Club Presto and what it meant, but she wasn't sure he was taking it in. After that, she hung the Nu Deranja sign on the front door and went to bed herself.

It was very quiet, the hotel, the town, what remained of the night. The only sounds were those Max made, trying to be comfortable, trying, she could tell, in ways that wouldn't disturb her. After quite enough of that, she made a pragmatic decision.

"You'll sleep better up here."

"Oh, I don't really think I—"

"Are you arguing?"

She could hear him rising, crossing the floor with some difficulty, climbing into the bed. Of course there was no touching or anything like that. For goodness sake. Just think of all the reasons.

So, no touching or anything like that. Not at first. But hadn't something like this happened in *For Whom the Bell Tolls?* When Mrs. Plansky first encountered that scene way back in English 101 she hadn't bought it. Now was different.

The Scottish scarf hung discreetly in the closet. Norm had always been—and seemed to be still—a very tactful man.

THIRTY-TWO

"What are we going to do?" Romeo said.

"About what?" said Dinu.

"Everything." Romeo took out his share of last night's pay—400 lei—and laid it on the kitchen table. They were at Dinu's place, an overcast, gray dawn just breaking and Dinu's mom still asleep. The walls were thin. They could hear her snores. "I mean look at this. Now we're serfs."

Dinu had boiled up instant coffee. He filled their cups and sat down. "It's just for now. He'll get over it and we'll be back to normal."

Romeo sipped the coffee and put down his cup. Dinu could tell the heat hurt his puffy lip. His own hand, which hadn't been bothering him, or at least not much, now started throbbing.

"Maybe we'll go back to what we were getting paid before," Romeo said, "but we'll always be on a leash. How is that fair? We're the talent."

"You are," Dinu said.

Romeo shook his head. "Your English is so good now."

"How would you know?"

"Bogdan was telling him."

In truth, Dinu knew his English was getting good, like he'd crossed some sort of language bridge and there was no going back. He would thank the professor the next time he saw him. Even if he could no longer turn English into big money, he'd come to like it for itself. Putting lipstick on a pig, for example, or shooting the breeze.

"You knew Marius tuned Bogdan up?" Romeo said.

"Yeah. But why?"

"Because Bogdan forgot he was a serf, that's why. It was for reminding him."

"How much does he get paid?" Dinu said.

"Shit, like us."

"What was the take last night?"

"From the old lady? Fourteen thousand dollars and a bit. We emptied the account. Not too bad but it didn't lead to anything else. Like with that other old lady—when was it? They all get mixed together. What was her name?"

Dinu shrugged.

"The people, not the numbers. The numbers I don't mix up. It was three million eight hundred thousand. Highest in almost three months. But I've been having this idea."

"For what?"

"For using AI to narrow down the field to just those that will lead to something else. I've even roughed out some of the code. But I'm putting it aside."

"Why?"

"Because." Romeo tapped the 400 lei with his finger. Gazing at the money, he said, "There are lots of Romanians in Hungary."

"So?"

"Not just in the border towns. In Budapest, too. I have cousins in Budapest. Ever been?"

"No."

"It's nice. More western."

"What are you saying?"

Romeo looked up. His swollen eye seemed to be on the verge of tears but his other eye was dry.

"You know what I'm saying."

"You're thinking of going to Hungary?"

"Not exactly. I'm thinking of both. The two of us go to Hungary."

"And do what?"

"What we do but for ourselves. We already know it works. You've forgotten? Thirty-eight thousand dollars in one go, Dinu! Just multiply!"

"What about school?"

"Hungary has schools."

"We don't speak Hungarian."

"So? We'll learn. We'll hire tutors. Pretty ones."

At that moment, Dinu's mom appeared in the doorway to the hall, wearing a frayed old tiger-stripe robe, and still in her hairnet.

"Pretty tutors?" she said. "What are you boys talking about?"

"Nothing," Dinu said.

She took a closer look at Romeo. "Oh my Jesus. What happened to you?"

"He was on the motorcycle when I had the accident," Dinu said, raising his splinted hand.

"You didn't tell me that."

"I'm telling you now."

Romeo rose. "Thanks for the coffee," he said. He turned to Dinu's mom. "Nice to see you, doamna."

"Be more careful," Dinu's mom said.

She sat down at the table. Dinu rinsed out Romeo's cup, poured in fresh coffee for her. She spooned in lots of sugar.

"What's going on?"

"Nothing."

"Everything's all right with Dragomir?"

"Why wouldn't it be?"

"Don't be rude."

Dinu didn't have the patience for her this morning. There seemed to be new lines on her face every day. So he felt sorry for her as well as impatient. Did he have to go on feeling sorry for her forever? He reached into his pocket and gave her half of his miserable take from the old lady in whatever state it was.

"What's this?" said his mom.

"What does it look like?"

His mother stuffed the money in the pocket of her robe. "You're sure about Dragomir? I mean no problems, and all?"

Dinu raised his voice. "Stop asking!"

"Don't you dare talk to me like that!"

They glared at each other across the table. That had grown less common lately, but only because he hadn't been around much. He took a gulp of coffee.

"We're going to Hungary."

"What?"

"You heard me."

"To Hungary? When? For how long? Who is we?"

Dinu, about to go into the details, changed his mind. The less she knew the better. "Not for long, but soon. We'll make money. I'll send you some." He nodded toward the pocket of her robe. "More than that, much more."

With no warning she burst into tears, sobbing, snot, the whole performance. He hated thinking about it in those terms but how often did he have to see this? "If only your poor dad hadn't died in that horrible fire! They should never have gone to Hungary. Don't you go, either. It's bad luck."

So she really didn't know the truth about how her husband died? "But it was Moldova, not Hungary," he said.

"Who told you that? Dragomir? But of course he doesn't like the mention of Hungary. He can't go back there."

"Why not?"

"They will arrest him for what he did that night. Here he is safe." She made the little money-talks gesture, rubbing thumb and index finger.

"What did he do that night?"

"All the bad things that got blamed on your poor dad. But in Hungary, not Moldova. There's no money for stealing in Moldova. In Hungary, yes, money." She buried her face in her hands.

Dinu didn't know what to believe. He went into the bathroom and took a shower. There was no hot water. By the time he was dressed, teeth brushed, hair combed, she'd gone back to bed. He gave in to an urge he'd been having but not given in to and called Tassa. She didn't pick up.

When he went outside he found that the wind had risen and snow was falling, not much snow but at a sharp angle, the flakes stinging his face. No one was around. The whole street looked so shabby. He texted Tassa: Can I come over to your place? The answer came back right away. No.

Dinu crossed the street. A woman he hadn't noticed was standing by a twisted little sidewalk tree. An older woman, wearing a navy-blue coat too nice for the neighborhood, and a scarf around her neck, the kind of scarf with one of those Scottish patterns, like in *Braveheart*. She was watching him. Was there something familiar about her? Why, yes. The American woman from the lookout, whom he and Romeo had guided into town. A very nice lady—she'd tried to tip them. And the name, like the coal miner's daughter. A career idea came to him: spinning country music records for a European audience! Out of some little studio in Budapest! Radio Free Dinu! He hurried over to her.

"Hey, Loretta! It's me, Dinu!"

She slapped him across the face.

Had that really happened? Mrs. Plansky would never have believed it, but there was all the proof anyone needed—the left side of Dinu's face bright red, her right hand hot and tingly, and the look in his eyes. The silo had opened at last and the heavy artillery had come rolling out.

Dinu reeled back, blinking. "Loretta? Dinu, remember?"

"There's nothing wrong with my memory." Well, not precisely true, but the only route forward in this conversation.

He put his hand to his cheek. "Then why did you do that?"

"Because you deserved it! What you did to that poor woman—disgraceful!"

"Poor woman?" Dinu looked baffled. That made it even more callous.

"Really?" said Mrs. Plansky. "You've forgotten already? It was only last night."

Dinu's mouth opened and closed, no sound coming out. It was easy to see him as a ten-year-old kid at that moment. Mrs. Plansky overrode that part of her nature.

"Gram, Andy? Think back. Gram, down in Alabama maybe—the Cotton State as you're no doubt aware? Gram, who gets lonesome from time to time and was so cheered up to hear from her loving grandson, unaware he was ruining the rest of her life? Is this how you live with yourself? By erasing the . . . the deeds right out of your mind?"

The deeds? That sounded so melodramatic, like from a Victorian potboiler. She was shaking—not from fear but with rage, a first in her life, terrifying in a way but also a strange kind of high—and should have been calling him out in the most vulgar language possible. Mrs. Plansky knew all the right words, of course, but even now she couldn't quite make herself voice them.

Meanwhile Dinu had turned white, except for the mark of her slap. "How do you—where—I don't understand."

"Same here." Mrs. Plansky lowered her voice, but it now sounded—at least to her—all the more dreadful, like something on the boil in a tightly-lidded container. "I don't understand lots of things. Start with you not calling Gram back. How come no second call?"

"Second call?" Dinu said.

"Stop sounding so stupid. I know perfectly well you're not stupid. That's not your problem. I'm talking about when you call back after the first call, after you've stolen all you can get your hot little hands on."

"But why would I—what sense would that be? Even, uh, suppose—supposing all that other what you say is true? What's going on? Was it all recorded? Did you see a tape?"

Mrs. Plansky laughed. She just couldn't keep it in. "One thing for sure—don't you ever testify in court. It won't go well."

Dinu glanced around, as though the paddy wagon might come careening around the corner any second. "Are—are you from the police?"

"The honest police," Mrs. Plansky said. "In spirit. Are you saying you never make a second call?"

Dinu gazed at her. He, too, was shaking, but in a little boy sort of way, like he was about to be sent to the principal's office, which probably didn't even happen anymore. He gave a tiny little nod.

"But Dinu, you called me back. You made a second call to me. Why?"

"Loretta? Is it . . . ? Are you—are you one of the people?"

"Loretta Plansky, one of the people. That name—Plansky—doesn't ring a bell?"

He shook his head.

"You've forgotten the night you were my grandson Will, locked up in some little Colorado town, desperate for bail money? Your research is good, by the way. Who does it, you or Romeo?"

Dinu's eyes shifted one way, then the other. "Romeo," he said in a small voice.

"So you remember?"

He nodded.

"Say it! Say I remember!"

"I remember."

Mrs. Plansky took a breath, composed herself. "Very well, then, let's get to that second call. Why?"

"I don't know."

"Think."

He closed his eyes tight, a ten-year-old thinking his pathetic hardest. "Did you tell me to get a lawyer, for representing in court?" He opened his eyes. In them now was a new look, a look she interpreted as asking for help.

"Yes, but obviously you weren't calling about that. What was the point? You had the money, three million, eight hundred thousand and whatever the hell else it was. Why, Dinu? You owe me an answer."

"Is that why you've come? You came all this way just to find out the reason for calling back?"

"Don't be dense," said Mrs. Plansky. "I came for my money. Mine, not yours. I want it back. So give."

What Dinu gave her was an unusual look. The longer it went on the older he seemed, even aging beyond where he was now. "No matter what was the subject of conversation—in the first place and everything—I . . . I liked talking to you. Like, you know, I really was . . ."

"Was what?"

He shrugged. "The grandson. Yours. There. That must be it. You can believe or not."

Dinu waited for a response. She said nothing.

"And now can I ask a question?" he said. "How do you know about last night?"

"The answer to that will depend on how things go between you and me." How menacing was that! Mrs. Plansky had amazed herself. "Here we are in person," she went on. "All we need now is the money and then we can start talking again, this time on even ground. Where's the money?"

"Gone. I'm sorry, Loretta."

"Sorry is not what I want from you. Gone where?"

"But I am sorry. Seeing you here. You came all this way?"

She nodded.

"To get your money back?"

"I already made that clear."

"No one does this."

"It's upsetting, isn't it?"

"Upsetting is . . . ?"

"It disturbs you."

He looked down, his gaze on his cowboy boots, or maybe right through them.

"Why?" she said. "What's so disturbing?"

Dinu looked up. His face seemed slightly disarranged, like tears were on the way, but his eyes were dry. "I would give you back the money if I could. I promise you that."

"Would you give Gram back her money, down in Alabama? And what about all the others? Would you give them back their money, too?"

"No," Dinu said. "Just you."

Mrs. Plansky, on this cold and windy day on a dilapidated Soviet-era street, hard little snowflakes stinging any exposed skin, laughed. "What are we going to do with you, Dinu?"

He thought for a bit, treating it as a real question. "I would like to live in America."

And just maybe it had been a real question. In any case, wasn't there a real vision in his answer? A potential deal began to take shape in Mrs. Plansky's mind.

"Let's put that in a box for now," she said.

"What box?"

"A box in our minds, that we can open when the time is right. But the time won't be right until we find out where the money is. Matter can neither be created nor destroyed—did they teach you that in school yet?"

"I don't think so."

"Never mind. It means the money must be somewhere."

Dinu gave that some thought, too. He did some more glancing up and down the street. There were a few pedestrians around, hunched against the wind, paying them no attention. "We could go see Romeo," he said. "He likes you, too."

Good grief. What was with the men of this country, or at least some of them? They seemed to have—but it couldn't be!—something of a thing for her. She thought of the look in the eyes of Max—her captive lover or whatever he was, she almost blushed to think—when she'd left that morning, the NU DERANJA sign firmly in place on the door to the presidential suite. What if she'd grown up here? She tried to imagine an alternate life, growing up as a glamorous figure. And failed.

Romeo turned out to have a dank and rank sort of office somewhere beneath the apartment block where he lived. Getting there involved a trial by ordeal—cobwebs across the face not once but many times, stepping on squishy things, never escaping the smell of pee, well-aged and brand-new. At last the three of them were sitting around a card table, the only light coming from Romeo's many screens. A long back-and-forth got going in Romanian between Dinu and Romeo. Romeo had a face made for dramatic reaction. Mrs. Plansky thought she could follow things pretty well just from his changes in expression. In the beginning there was lots of shock, amazement, fear. At the end his eyes were bright.

He leaned toward Mrs. Plansky. "Money you no make or destroy, only move around. I am loving that."

"I told him what you said," Dinu explained.

"I gathered that," said Mrs. Plansky.

Romeo laughed and pointed to a screen showing columns and columns of numbers. "There!" he said.

"What's there?" Mrs. Plansky said.

"Your money," said Dinu.

Mrs. Plansky peered at the screen and was no wiser, but what a nice moment anyway! She followed it by bringing up finder's fees, a notion the boys were unfamiliar with but grasped immediately. The three of them joined hands across the table, one of those hand stacks you see in the locker rooms of big-time teams. That was another nice moment. Then the subject of Hungary came up. After that, Romeo rummaged around and found a coil of nylon rope, thin but strong— and also black, which couldn't have been better. That led to a round of high-fiving. The boys were getting excited. Mrs. Plansky knew that too much excitement on the eve of big plans was not good.

"How am I going to rein you two in?" she said.

"Rain?" said Romeo, holding out his hands under an imaginary sky. "Is no rain!"

Dinu thought that was hilarious and started laughing. The laughter spread to Romeo and even to Mrs. Plansky herself. What was happening to her?

"Oh, and account," Romeo said.

"Account?"

"Bank," said Dinu, "plus password."

"We're doing it now?" she said.

"Not now," Dinu said. "The very last thing. But we must be all set."

For the second time but under different circumstances, Mrs. Plansky gave Dinu her banking information. She enjoyed a full-circle moment of accomplishment.

"Norman Conquest with exclamations?" Dinu said. "I remember that one."

"She keeps same password?" Romeo said.

The boys started laughing again, popping her accomplishment bubble. This time Mrs. Plansky did not join in. She half-remembered Allison Suarez calling to tell her to change the password immediately.

THIRTY-THREE

 "Lazybones," said Mrs. Plansky, entering the presidential suite and finding Max still in bed, leafing through a glossy hotel magazine.

He looked up and smiled. A very handsome man for sure, and that one crooked tooth was just the kind of thing that caught her attention and wouldn't let go.

"Lazybones?" he said. "I love it. Yours?"

"You mean did I make it up? Good grief, no. It's a common expression."

"But there's nothing common about you." He patted the empty side of the bed.

Mrs. Plansky ignored that completely. "I've brought sandwiches from Café des Artistes," she said, taking a paper bag from her purse. "Smoked brisket or zacusca, I think it's called—roasted eggplant, onions, red peppers. Smells delicious. You pick." She set the bag on the empty side of the bed and took off her navy-blue woolen coat. Wound over one shoulder was the coil of black nylon rope.

Max's smile faded at once. "What's that?"

"The reason for the sandwiches," said Mrs. Plansky. "You need to keep your strength up."

"Oh?" he said, the smile returning. "I wasn't aware you had a problem with the upness—if that's a word—of my—"

"Stop right there," said Mrs. Plansky.

She went to the window. Outside lay the square with *Michael the*

Brave still on the warpath, snowflakes swirling around his head. It was a very public place, but there was no avoiding it. The problem was on the anchor end. There were no potential anchors. Mrs. Plansky went into the bathroom.

"What are you doing?" Max said.

"Just eat."

Mrs. Plansky checked the view from the bathroom window. Pretty much the same as from the bedroom, but an old-fashioned radiator stood right below the sill. She unwound the rope, tied one end to the thick pipe entering the radiator from the floor. Mrs. Plansky knew knots from Miss Terrance's class. *"A half hitch for a temporary hold, girls, but a rolling hitch for something that lasts."* She tied a rolling hitch, coiled the rope, and tucked it neatly under the radiator.

When she returned to the bedroom, she found that Max had polished off the smoked brisket sandwich and was patting the corners of his mouth with a paper napkin.

"Now I feel absurdly strong," he said.

"Store it up for tonight."

"What happens tonight?"

Mrs. Plansky sat on the edge of the bed. "There have been some developments."

Max sat up. "Should I put on clothes?"

Not just yet. That was Mrs. Plansky's first—and unruly— thought, a thought she kept strictly to herself. She said, "That's always best."

He raised an eyebrow—for some reason Mrs. Plansky's interest in him grew a lot at that moment—and lay back down. "What developments?"

"Do you remember last night?" she said.

"I'll never forget."

"Stop. I'm talking about what I saw in Club Presto."

"The scam in action?"

"Exactly. Do you recall the part about the boys?"

"Dinu and Romeo."

"Correct. I met with them a couple of hours ago."

"How did that happen?"

"Blind luck. Well, with a nudge or two."

"A nudge from you?"

"Yes."

"You're a good nudger. World-class if I might—"

"Zip it. The point is we have a plan. Have you ever been to Hungary?"

"Certainly. And you?"

"Tonight will be my first time. The hinge point of this whole thing is a kind of karma, if it all works out. Recently the boys decided it would be a good thing to set up on their own."

"Jesus."

"Dragomir found out, of course, and now, after actual physical punishment, they're back working for him, with the pay reduced—much reduced, I gather. Dragomir also made them give him all they'd gotten on their own, upward of thirty thousand dollars. But he had Romeo do the actual moving of the money to an account on something called the dark web. Is there really a dark web?"

"I'm working on a chapter about it right now."

"Oh, good, then this is all real," Mrs. Plansky said.

"Not real like you," Max said.

Their eyes met. "Why are you looking at me like that?" she said.

"You know."

"Well put a lid on it."

"Ha!"

"And stop acting like an adolescent. You have to concentrate."

"I am concentrating. The point is Romeo now knows how to get into the dark web account and Dragomir's too impressed by how frightening he is to have any concerns about Romeo. You're going to get your money back. Maybe you're paying a finder's fee. Maybe they plan to set up again across the border and make so much money they don't need a finder's fee. Maybe it's simply that they're still kids. Maybe it was just the way you are. But the transfer will happen at the very last minute, right before the four of us take off for Hungary. Is that it?"

"Pretty much."

"What I don't understand is why Hungary."

"Because Dragomir can't go there. He's wanted for some crime years ago."

"I'm getting so much material from you."

Mrs. Plansky gave him a severe look. "Not everything is printable."

"What about your photo?"

"Forget it."

"You didn't say that before."

"I'm saying it now."

Max nodded. "A deal. But in return for your help."

"What sort of help?"

"With the book. How to organize the story. The world of cyber-crime, but personal."

"You don't need me for that."

"Oh, I do. Let's think."

"Just like that? Think and the book happens?"

"You can help it along."

"How?"

"For example, it's well known that humans think better lying down."

Mrs. Plansky laughed. Then she lay down. "But my clothes stay on."

A knock on the door. Mrs. Plansky opened her eyes. Perhaps she'd dreamed it. She felt odd, possibly because she never slept during the day. Odd, but actually quite good in a way. She glanced over and there was Max, fast asleep, the last dim fading daylight coming through a gap in the curtains and lending a reddish glow to his close-cropped white beard. What would he look like with it shaved off? Hmm. That raised a potential—

Knock knock knock.

Mrs. Plansky sat up.

A voice called through the door. "Mrs. Plansky? Mrs. Plansky?" It was Annika.

Max began to stir. Mrs. Plansky placed her hand over his mouth. His eyes popped open. She let her other hand do the talking, first making the quiet sign over her lips, then pointing toward the door. He gave her a slight nod.

"Coming," Mrs. Plansky called. By now she had a plan. "Just a minute."

She got out of bed, discovering that not all her clothes had come off, although what remained was in disarray. She quickly made herself presentable, at the same time signaling Max to get up. He was naked, articles of his clothing here and there on the floor. She made get-those-picked-up-for-God's-sake gestures. He started gathering the clothes. She gave him the hurry-up sign, followed almost immediately by the quiet sign again, then grabbed his hand and led him into the bathroom. His eyes were full of questions. She dismissed them all with a wave of her hand—perhaps a little on the impatient side—and moved to the knobless old wooden door. She gave it the quietest push she could. It opened.

"Mrs. Plansky? Mrs. Plansky?"

"Coming! Coming!"

Now she gave another quiet push, this one propelling Max through the doorway and into the passageway. She closed the door and pulled the towel rack in front of it. Patting her hair into place, she went into the bedroom, and, on the point of opening the front door, wheeled around in a swift detour and straightened the bed covers. Then, kicking the love seat cushions in the direction of the love seat on the way, she returned to the front door and opened it.

Annika stood in the hallway, but not alone. Timbo was behind her, his eyes not on Mrs. Plansky, but trained, in a questing way, on the room.

"Sorry to bother you, Mrs. Plansky," Annika said.

"Oh, no bother, no bother at all."

"Thank you. It seems that a previous guest may have left a thing of value behind. He has sent Mr. Timbo here to perhaps do a quick search."

"Why, of course," said Mrs. Plansky, stepping aside.

"You may leave the room if you like," Annika said. "I can send champagne for you into the bar, compliments of the hotel."

"More champagne? Goodness, no. But thank you. I'm happy to stay. What was the object of value, if I may ask?"

Annika turned to Timbo and spoke to him in Romanian. His eyes shifted. Really? Mrs. Plansky thought. Not prepared for such an obvious question? Finally he said something to Annika. She relayed it to Mrs. Plansky. "Mr. Timbo says it was a box of cigars."

"They must be Cuban," said Mrs. Plansky.

That led to another brief exchange in Romanian.

"Mr. Timbo says the box is platinum."

"Ah," said Mrs. Plansky. "Naturally, if I'd seen something like that I'd have brought it down to the front desk."

"For sure, for sure," Annika said. She made a little motion and Timbo entered the room. Mrs. Plansky gave him a smile, like she was the hostess. He didn't look at her, but went immediately to the closet, which he opened and saw all there was to see, namely the neat shelving of Mrs. Plansky's clothes. While he gazed into the closet, Mrs. Plansky's own gaze wandered around the room and came upon Max's underwear, lying in plain sight halfway between the door and the bed. She strolled over there and stood on it, looking as nonchalant as possible.

"Is it still snowing?" she said to Annika.

"A little, but more to come."

"Well, well, there's always the weather."

Annika looked at her like she was an idiot, and rightly so. Meanwhile Mrs. Plansky made a few foot movements—please, God, let them be subtle—to render Max's undies completely invisible. Norm always wore boxers of the loose-fitting kind. Max, it turned out, wore briefs, a rather brief form of brief that ordinarily would have given her pause, but were ideal in this situation. On the other hand, he'd left them right out there when his orders—well, not orders, more like a suggestion—had been to collect all his clothes. Mrs. Plansky had never been the type to generalize about men, and for that reason only, let this subject go.

Meanwhile, Timbo was on his hands and knees, peering under the bed. Under the bed had actually been Mrs. Plansky's first idea, which gave the lie to the old rule about the first thought being the best. She glanced over at Annika, who was scrolling through her phone.

Timbo went into the bathroom. Mrs. Plansky's mood, which had been rather breezy, like she was a character in a farce, a stupid character who had forgotten what Timbo was capable of, changed completely, her heart beating way too fast and a trembling starting up in her fingertips. She listened for the sounds of Timbo moving around and heard nothing. But he was so quiet on his feet, could have been doing anything in there. Was it possible he knew about the secret door? Not a secret, actually, known and obvious to anyone who saw it, but just as obviously not a working door, lacking knob and keyhole, so clearly—please clearly—a vestige, a remnant, made obsolete in some long-ago remodel, even centuries ago. And don't forget, Loretta, those cobwebs, so dense, the first time you entered the passageway. So Timbo! Enough! There's nothing to see!

Timbo came out of the bathroom. He walked right by Mrs. Plansky, again without a glance, and out the front door, also without a glance at Annika. She looked up from her phone.

"Well, then," Annika said, "I guess no cigar."

Mrs. Plansky laughed. She caught a look in Annika's eyes, a sort of yearning. But Mrs. Plansky couldn't help her. "I'll be leaving tomorrow, Annika," she said, her voice soft, even gentle. "Please prepare my bill."

"Certainly. I'll text it to you. You can pay by phone. I hope we'll see you again."

"Thank you," said Mrs. Plansky.

Annika closed the door and went away. Mrs. Plansky took a deep breath. She could never skip out on a bill. That went without saying. But it was also a clever—well, not all that clever—misdirection, because the real checkout time was going to be much sooner. Yes, clever, damn it, all that clever! She scooped up the too-brief briefs and marched into the bathroom.

"I've never had any actual mountaineering experience," Max said. "Have you?"

"No," said Mrs. Plansky. "What's your point?"

They were in the bathroom of the presidential suite, lights off, Max fully clothed, standing by the window, Mrs. Plansky tugging on the free end of the black nylon rope to make sure the knot around the radiator pipe was good and tight, and Max gazing into the night.

"Isn't this called rappelling?" he said. "That's a mountaineering term."

"Let's not overthink," said Mrs. Plansky.

"What do you mean?"

"The alternative is waltzing out through the lobby. That's what I mean."

"You don't have to get angry."

"I'm not angry."

How quickly they'd advanced to the bickering stage! But bickering was part of life. Mrs. Plansky felt full of life at the moment. She tied the free end of the rope with a half hitch to the handle of her suitcase, now fully packed.

"Ready?" she said.

"Yes, Commandant."

She gave him a little punch on the shoulder and then opened the window—the casement type—nice and wide. The square was dark and deserted, the wind still blowing, no snow falling but a light coating on the cobbles and the few cars parked in front of the hotel, the most distant being her rental. Mrs. Plansky checked the time, now exactly thirty minutes since Dinu had sent his text: **Blast Off!!!** She took hold of the suitcase and raised it up to the sill.

"Allow me," Max said.

He really was polite. Mrs. Plansky stepped back. Max swung the suitcase outside, then began lowering it, the rope sliding slowly through his hands—hands that were quite beautiful, strong, and finely shaped. She moved closer, watched her suitcase touch silently onto the cobbles.

"Now you," she said.

"But don't you think—"

"I do not."

"At times you can be a slight bit controlling."

"Think what you like."

Not a bad joke, in her opinion, a joke Max got at once. He laughed and swung one leg up over the sill, twisted around so he was straddling it. After that he took the rope in both hands, raised his other leg up and over, all his movements very smooth, like he was used to exits of this sort. And just like that he was facing her, hanging outside by the rope.

"À bientôt," he said, and began lowering himself, not bothering to walk his way down, feet against the façade of the hotel, but simply using his hands, hand under hand. Mrs. Plansky knew one thing for sure: she couldn't do that, not that way. Maybe Max realized that, too, because when he reached the bottom he changed the plan, quickly freeing the suitcase and making a gesture for her to haul up the rope.

What was à bientôt? French, and familiar, but the meaning wouldn't come. Meanwhile, down in the square, Max was pantomiming the new plan, much more involved than doing it his way, a plan that began with tying the rope around her waist. Mrs. Plansky found she was already doing that. She tied it nice and tight, secured with a half hitch, then got one leg over the sill, as Max had done. Well, not with the ease or speed, or grace, no fooling herself about that. Not too much later she was sitting astride the sill, her body with absolutely no idea of how to get fully outside and turned around. Meanwhile her new hip was not liking this position at all, fast on the way to finding it intolerable. With the rope around her waist what was the worst that could happen? It would be different, of course, if she'd tied the rope around her neck, but she'd been too savvy for that. Mrs. Plansky realized for the first time in her life that there was a strand of goofiness in her makeup, had been there from the start. Her mind was still occupied with this revelation as she got her inside leg over to the outside somehow or other and started down, a somewhat controlled fall partly broken by her hands trying to squeeze the rope as it slipped rapidly through them, by her low-heeled booties scrabbling for traction against the façade, and finally by Max, catching her in his arms. He was too much of a gentleman even to grunt.

"Nice work," he whispered. He pointed. "But you should have dropped that down first."

Mrs. Plansky found she'd done the whole thing with her purse slung over one shoulder. She needed her purse, of course. Dropping it out of windows could never be good.

She untied the rope. It swung back and hung straight down from the bathroom window, almost invisible. With any luck no one would notice until daybreak, and by that time she'd be having a nice breakfast, goulash waffles, or whatever was served in Hungary. They walked over to her car. Mrs. Plansky opened the trunk. Max loaded the suitcase inside. They glanced around. The boys should have been here by now. She checked her phone. Nothing from Dinu.

Max spoke softly in her ear. "They'll be coming up Strada Piata." He took her hand, leading her to a street off the square. After only a few steps Mrs. Plansky heard strange noises, squeaky and rumbling, in the distance. Then out of the night came the boys, pushing and pulling some sort of cart. They passed under a streetlamp. Not a cart but a small flatbed trailer, and on the trailer the two motorcycles. The motorcycles? Had anything been said about the motorcycles? Not a word.

Max ran forward.

"Hei!" Romeo called, oh, so loud.

"Shh!" said Max, also loudly.

By the time Mrs. Plansky arrived they were in the middle of a sort of hissing conversation. Max turned to her. "They want to bring the motorcycles."

"I see that."

"Romeo made a connector. He says it will work with any car."

"Okay. Let's go."

They headed back toward the square, Max and Mrs. Plansky in front, the boys following with the trailer. But when they reached the end of Strada Piata and started to turn the corner, Mrs. Plansky saw there had been one big change. Another car, engine running, was parked right behind her rental. This car had a light on the roof, not shining at the moment. The front door opened and a uniformed man got out. It was Captain Romulu. He switched on a flashlight and began circling the rental.

Mrs. Plansky shrank back. So did Max, giving the boys the stop sign as he did. They gathered together by the trailer.

"What are we going to do?" Dinu said.

"Are the bikes gassed up?" Mrs. Plansky said.

Romeo nodded.

"I don't know how to drive a motorcycle," Max said.

"That's all right," said Mrs. Plansky. "You get on the back with Romeo, I'll ride with Dinu."

Dinu raised his splinted hand. "I can't drive."

Then came a long moment, in which they heard Captain Romulu speaking, perhaps on a phone or that police car device, the name not coming to Mrs. Plansky.

"I can," she said, and there was plenty of truth, or at least some, in that. You could argue that she'd learned on a Harley Super Glide on that ranch in Montana when she was nineteen years old and now she was what she was and the bike was a Yamaha, but that was the half-empty-glass response. She looked in the eyes of the three and saw no doubt at all. Was that because of some image they had of American womanhood? Or—oh, for God's sake: it must be that strange effect she had on these guys! One thing for sure. She'd fallen in love with this country.

In the event, there turned out to be big differences between the bikes and between nineteen and seventy-one. But not insurmountable! After one or two false and noisy starts, they were off—Romeo with Max on the back in the lead, and Mrs. Plansky following with Dinu—and rolling away from the square, leaving all the big pieces of luggage behind, including her suitcase containing, among other things, the Italian ballet flats. By the time the river bridge appeared, she knew that this bike was easier to handle than the Super Glide. The thumb throttle for one thing—a nice innovation. Crossing the bridge she moved into the lead. Dinu, his hands lightly at her waist, leaned forward and spoke in her ear.

"You're a good biker chick."

"Where's your helmet?" said Mrs. Plansky.

"Must have forgot. But there were only two. And with you I have no worries."

"God in heaven." She checked for her purse, found it was snugly over her shoulder.

"Second right after the bridge," Dinu said.

"How far to the border?"

"One hundred and fifty kilometers. An hour and a half if you stay one hundred all the way. Oh, and by the by. Or is it by the way?"

"Depends."

"Such a smart lady. In any case, you have your money back. Romeo made all the arrangements. It's in your account at the Palm Coast Bank and Trust, three million eight hundred thousand and a little more, I forget the exact number."

She inhaled a deep, deep breath. His **Blast Off** text had meant the same thing but hearing him say it was so much more real. A thrill passed through her from head to toe, so profound she felt embarrassed. Strangely enough, and hard to explain, it had nothing to do with the money.

Mrs. Plansky took the second right after the bridge and they were soon out of Alba Gemina, riding up and up into the mountains and with no traffic except for Romeo, lagging behind. But she wasn't hitting one hundred kilometers or anything close, first because the road—a two-laner—was so winding, and also because the snow was falling again, although not hard, tiny flakes as before. These were big and fat and thick. Things were getting slippery under her tires and it was harder and harder to see. Sometime later, rounding a curve and topping a crest, she caught the flash of a faraway light in the side mirror. At first she thought it was Romeo's headlight, but how could he be so far back? Then his light popped into view as he came around the curve. The distant light was much farther away than Romeo, although perhaps not quite as distant as she'd thought.

They wound down the side of one mountain, started up another. The snowfall thickened and the pavement got slipperier. Mrs. Plansky leaned forward, geared down, throttled back, peered ahead, the snowflakes black in her headlight beam. Once or twice she caught light reflected in her mirror: Romeo falling farther and farther back now, and the other light, a double, not a single, getting closer and closer.

"That's the F-350," Dinu said.

"What F-350?"

"My uncle's. It's good in the snow." He patted her side. "But we are close. One last mountain and then a flat part and then the border."

Please, thought Mrs. Plansky, a please directed to no one in particular. She started down a series of switchbacks, leaning into every one, going as fast as she dared, Dinu leaning with her, moving together. Romeo fell farther behind. The F-350—Dinu had to be right about that—was getting closer and closer. The road leveled out and entered a small village, stone walls on either side, not a light showing. Mrs. Plansky hit 140 on the dial and kept it there all the way through the village and on the lower, easier part of the mountain on the other side. Then came a series of long curves, up and up, forcing her to throttle down. Down down down, all the way to forty. My God! Forty? She checked the mirror. Several curves below the double headlights had caught up to the single, and yes, a pickup, she could see that clearly now. Eyes back on the road, Loretta! She found she'd drifted left, almost off the road and into the rocky embankment. She turned the wheel, in fact over-turned it, and they went skidding sideways. Mrs. Plansky knew anything she did now would only make it worse. She just let it happen. The bike skidded back across the road—Dinu sucking in his breath—and then the tires found their grip and straightened things out on their own. A few hundred yards farther on was a short straightaway. Mrs. Plansky took a chance and checked the mirror. Now the F-350 was only one curve back. Much farther behind she spotted the single headlight. They'd gone right past Romeo and Max, hadn't even bothered. There'd be plenty of time later for mopping up.

That angered Mrs. Plansky, perhaps unreasonably, but the feeling was very real. She throttled back up, the bike roaring as it climbed and climbed, the road now covered in snow. All at once they were caught in a much mightier roar, and the powerful beams of the F-350 lit them up. Mrs. Plansky throttled up some more, far more than she dared, through one last switchback, the wind howling, her bike howling, the F-350 howling. And right at the crest, before the start of the first descending turn, nothing but the void in view, the F-350 came up beside her. She could see their faces, Dragomir at the wheel, Marius beside him, Timbo in back. Dragomir looked right at her, the fury inside him distorting his face.

Someone else, not her, took over at the controls. Someone comfortable enough at a time like this to thumb that throttle way way up and then at the last second or later, take the thumb right off the handle and gently, oh so gently, touch the brake pedal. The F-350 stayed right beside her—until that touch of the brake pedal. Then it shot ahead, Dragomir now, too late, hitting his own brakes. The F-350 went airborne, off the crest of the mountain and into the void. Oh, what a terrible sight, although it barely registered with Mrs. Plansky in real time. She and Dinu went into another skid, so far over that her throttle hand touched the snow, and kept skidding and skidding right to the edge, where they bumped, not hard, into an old stone mile marker, Mrs. Plansky the merest of passengers at that point.

The motor conked out. There was nothing to hear but the wind. Mrs. Plansky lay half buried under the bike and snow, depleted, utterly spent, undone. She would have burst into tears but she didn't have the strength.

Dinu crawled out from underneath and pulled the bike off her.

"Loretta? Loretta? Are you all right?"

"We should know pretty soon," said Mrs. Plansky.

THIRTY-FOUR

The weather changed very quickly.

"That's how it is in these mountains," Dinu said. "Transylvanian mountains, in case you didn't know."

"I feel like I know them very well."

They stood side by side near the old stone milepost, whatever had been written on it now eroded away. The wind died down, the snow stopped falling, the clouds thinned out, and the moon appeared, spreading silvery light into the void that had been so dark. A heavily forested canyon opened up before them, the sides steep, the trees snow-covered. The F-350 had cut a road through those trees, shearing off branches and splitting whole trunks, and now lay upside down wedged between a massive tree trunk cut off at human head height, and two huge boulders. A very big and muscular body, Marius-size, lay facedown and motionless at the base of one of the boulders, the snow all around him dark red. Timbo was close by. He'd been—oh, no—impaled by a spear-shaped branch. Just recently Mrs. Plansky had been horrified by reading the mere definition of the word. Now the real thing would be the stuff of nightmares.

"I don't see him," Dinu said.

She knew who he meant. "Me, either."

He turned to her. "You're shivering."

"Not really."

"Where is your coat?"

She glanced down at herself, surprised to see she wasn't wearing her coat. Yet somehow her purse was still hanging off her shoulder? How was that possible? And she was still wearing the Scottish scarf? Wasn't it dangerous to wear scarves on motorcycles? She really could be clueless at times.

"Here is my jacket."

"Very kind of you, but no."

She set off in search of her coat, Dinu trailing after her.

"Loretta? Your purse—it's open."

She glanced at the purse, indeed open and twisted around almost behind her in an awkward position. Her fingers, too, were awkward, somehow unable to get the thing closed. Dinu came closer and fumbled around for a bit with the purse. "There we go."

"Thank you, Dinu."

"Do not mention it."

They were still looking for the coat when Romeo drove up with Max on the back of the bike, the faces of both of them stone-colored like the moon. A lot of excited talk started up, mostly in Romanian and mostly between Dinu and Romeo. Mrs. Plansky was aware of Max's gaze on her from time to time, but mostly she just felt detached. She couldn't even summon much interest when Max went down in the canyon, searching for Dragomir. There was no sign of him, not a surprise to Mrs. Plansky. Her mind was on a pair of fox-lined mittens that had belonged to her mother. Those mittens would be handy. What had become of them? They all climbed back on the bikes.

Mrs. Plansky didn't start feeling more like herself until a few hours later in a small town in Hungary, the dawn breaking and the four of them in a little café, Max, who turned out to be fluent in Hungarian, ordering her toast and jam and a bowl of hot chocolate. She stretched out her legs.

A little later Max rented a car and arranged for the bikes to be trucked to Romeo's cousins in Budapest. Then they drove there themselves, Max behind the wheel, Mrs. Plansky beside him, and the boys in back.

"Before you guys fall asleep," Mrs. Plansky said, "we better finalize this matter of the finder's fee."

"Oh, no, not necessary," Dinu said.

"Maybe only a little bit?" said Romeo.

Dinu elbowed him, quite hard.

"Huh?" said Romeo.

"I understand about Tassa," Dinu hissed at him, an inexplicable reaction from Mrs. Plansky's point of view.

And perhaps from Romeo's as well. "Huh?" he said again.

"Who is Tassa?" Max said.

No answer from the backseat.

"First, Dinu," Mrs. Plansky went on, "this doesn't take the place of my promise. I will get you into the U.S. one way or another, at the very least on a visitor's visa. Second, a normal finder's fee is ten percent. In this case, ten percent for each of you. Any thoughts?"

The boys seemed to have no thoughts, but Max did.

"I beg your pardon? You propose to give them in excess of three hundred thousand dollars? Each?"

"I do."

"But think what will happen! They are children."

Mrs. Plansky considered that for a while. "Good point," she said at last. "I will give each ten percent of the ten percent now, and the rest when they turn twenty-one. I'll have my lawyer make the arrangements first thing when I get back. Deal?"

"Deal," said the boys.

She handed her phone to Romeo. "Do it now, the ten percent of the ten percent." She felt Max's gaze—perhaps an incredulous gaze—on her face. "Eyes on the road," she told him.

Romeo worked out the numbers and transferred the finder's fees into an account for him and an account for Dinu, all in what seemed like seconds. He handed back the phone, at the same time having a quick conversation in Romanian with Dinu.

"Romeo wants you to change your password."

"Now, please," Romeo said.

"The cursor is at the correct place," Dinu said. "Just type it in and save."

"Really? I don't see—"

"Now, please," Romeo repeated.

Mrs. Plansky caught a break. A password came to her, out of the blue. She made a slight revision, then typed it in and saved. Presi-DentialSweeT! Notice the pun? And the capitals mixed in? Plus that exclamation mark, giving the whole thing actual meaning? Pretty damn clever. Mrs. Plansky felt quite pleased with herself.

The boys fell asleep. There was a nice feeling in the car, like this was a family trip, one of those families that got along.

"What now?" Max said.

"Well, drop off the boys at Romeo's cousins, and then me at the airport, if you don't mind. After that I assume you'll head back to Alba Gemina."

"Not until I know it's safe," Max said. "And what if I do mind dropping you at the airport?"

She turned to him. His eyes were on the road. He really was a handsome man, and that soulful look in his eyes was no illusion. She knew that for a fact.

"How old are you, Max?"

"I don't see what difference it makes."

"Max?" She was prepared for something young, even as low as sixty-one, or God help her, fifty-nine.

"I will be forty-seven in November."

"Oh, Max," she said. She leaned across the console, wrapped her arm around his neck, and kissed his face. And kissed it again. "I'm seventy-one."

"But I knew that."

She disengaged, returned to her own side. "You didn't and you still don't."

There was silence after that, all the way to the first appearance of a distant spire in the west.

"What if I happened to come on vacation to Florida?" he said.

Mrs. Plansky thought about that. Vacationing in Florida? Millions of people did that every year. What heart could be so shrunken as to forbid it in his case? "That would be very nice," she said. At that moment she remembered the meaning of à bientôt—soon, as in see you soon. She came close to saying it out loud.

On the drive home from the off-site airport parking lot, Mrs. Plansky stopped at the first branch of Palm Coast Bank and Trust she saw. She went in, produced her driver's license, and asked to see her balance.

"Could you write it out by hand, please?" she said.

"By hand?"

Mrs. Plansky made a little writing motion. The teller wrote out her balance and gave her the slip. It was all there, less the two 10 percents of the percents. She stuck the slip in her purse. That was when she discovered—hidden in a fold way down at the bottom—the sapphire necklace. How had it gotten there? When? Ah.

"Have a nice day," the teller said.

"I'm home!" she called, entering her condo on Little Pine Lake. She found her dad at the kitchen table, enjoying a rather large Cuban sandwich.

"Oh, hi," he said.

His feet were bare. So were the feet of the woman sitting opposite him, a woman of her dad's age or even older. She, too, was eating a Cuban sandwich. One of his bare feet was resting on one of her bare feet.

Lucrecia came in, carrying two open beer bottles.

"Loretta! Welcome back! Did you have a nice trip?"

"Yes, thank you."

"I want you to meet my mom, Clara." Lucrecia set the beer bottles on the table. "Mama, this is Loretta I was telling you about."

"Hola!" said Clara, raising a bottle.

"She and your dad seem to be hitting it off," Lucrecia said. "Can I bring in your suitcase?"

"That won't be necessary," Mrs. Plansky said. Or even possible. She kept that to herself.

But amazingly, her suitcase turned up a couple of weeks later. Agent Rains brought it.

"I've had some extremely interesting conversations with Jamal Perryman," she said. "He heads our Secret Service post in Bucharest. You're familiar with him?"

"Slightly."

"First, he wishes me to pass on the message that Dragomir Tiriac has not reappeared. He may be in Russia and we're trying to substantiate that. But more important, what we'd very much like to do is debrief you, Mrs. Plansky, just have you run through the whole story in your own words. Mr. Perryman believes, and I strongly agree, that your experience will be most helpful in our battle against cybercrime."

"Meaning the others will get their money back?"

"Wouldn't that be nice?" said Agent Rains. "But no. Mr. Perryman actually sat down with the boys in our Budapest embassy and they went searching for the money but there wasn't a trace. We'd still appreciate your thoughts."

"Certainly," Mrs. Plansky said. "As soon as we nail down visa arrangements for Dinu. Something permanent would be best."

Mrs. Plansky's family was dynamic, meaning changes never stopped. First, it appeared that Nina and Matt, Matty, or Matthew had broken up. There were several stories, one with him meeting someone else, another with her meeting someone else, and a third with both of them meeting someone elses. But the upshot was that the $250K for the Love and the Caribbean start-up was no longer needed.

As for Jack, his cold chain partners out in Tempe, Ray and Rudy, had been indicted by the federal government on a number of charges—wire fraud, tax evasion, money laundering, and another category or two she couldn't remember. So the $750K was also not needed. Jack did send her a brand-new tennis racket model to try. Waving it around in the kitchen, she began feeling hopeful about him.

Nina and Jack were happy that her trip had gone well, which was their takeaway, but were both too preoccupied to press her for details. The grandkids, Emma and Will, showed much more interest. Will had whooped loudly on the phone, actually deafening Mrs. Plansky in one ear for a day or two, and Emma had called her the bravest grandma in the whole U.S. of A. Mrs. Plansky made a mental note to send her the sapphire necklace on her birthday. Then she had a selfish thought: but I want it. "Get a grip," she told herself. The necklace was Emma's, full stop.

Meanwhile, she took to wandering around her place a lot, like she was missing something. One morning she stopped in front of a photo of Norm she had, a lovely photo of him, head thrown back and laughing.

"Any advice?" she said.

And yes, he had plenty, all good. She read the message in the pixels of his eyes.

Later that same morning, even within the hour, Kev Dinardo called.

"I hear you've been away."

"I'm back."

"Great. I know this is a little late but friends of mine, a married couple, good tennis players, are going to be in town tomorrow and I thought you and I could show them how the game is played. Say, four o'clock at the club? And after if you like I could take you to dinner. That new sushi place by the marina is supposed to be good."

Well, why not? Good grief. She loved tennis, had a new racket to try, and Kev was a fine player with excellent manners on the court. "Thank you, it sounds like fun," Mrs. Plansky said. Despite all that rationalization, she felt like the whore of Babylon. Oddly enough, it wasn't all bad.

ACKNOWLEDGMENTS

Many thanks to my agents, Molly Friedrich and Lucy Carson, for their enthusiasm for Mrs. P when she was just an idea; to first readers nonpareil Diana, Meggy, and Alan; and to Kristin Sevick and the whole Tor Publishing Group team. No writing man is an island.

READING GROUP GUIDE

1. If you were Mrs. Plansky, would you agree to fund your children's risky start-ups (such as Nina and Matt/Matty/Matthew's Love and the Caribbean? or the cold-chain partnership touted by Jack and his buddies)? How do requests for money usually play out in your family?

2. What were your first impressions of Dinu? How did your opinion of him shift throughout the novel, including the revelation about why he made the second call?

3. What made Mrs. Plansky vulnerable to cybercrime? On the flip side, what gives her the strength to take on her thieves—with far more success than the authorities achieved? What traits make her the ideal sleuth?

4. As Mrs. Plansky cares for her cantankerous dad (Chandler Banning) and recalls her mom's final moments, what do we discover about her relationship with her parents? How did they shape her expectations for herself as a mother and wife?

5. Dinu was born into the tragic legacies of his parents and the cruelty of Uncle Dragomir. Nina and Jack were born into a stable, loving family. What does this tale of two families say about nature versus nurture in determining a person's outcomes in life? Are Mrs. Plansky's grandchildren more like their parents or their grandparents?

6. What do Annika and Tassa mean to Dinu at various points in his life? How do both women attempt to ensure their own survival?

7. We meet Norm through Mrs. Plansky's memories of him. What does she miss about him the most? What aspects of her life before marriage is she able to reclaim when she goes to battle against the scammers?

8. Dinu is successful because he pays attention to details in his research of American culture. What does he understand about his targets that no amount of coaching from Professor Bogdan can fulfill? What are the most significant distinctions he discovers between American and Romanian culture?

9. Max's card identifies him as a "journalist, author, seeker of the truth." Why is he the perfect ally for Mrs. Plansky? And why are journalists vital in a quest for the truth?

10. Discuss the moment when Mrs. Plansky realizes her financial security has been shattered. As she makes a personal inventory, what does she realize about the truly valuable parts of her life? If you were to experience a similar situation at that stage of life, what would be the most difficult possession to part with, and what would be the most challenging lifestyle change to make?

11. Which is worse: trying to scam an elderly stranger or trying to sweet-talk an elderly relative into supporting a doomed financial venture?

12. What do you predict for Mrs. Plansky's tennis date with Kev? What makes them a good match (on and off the court)?

13. Spencer Quinn is a prolific author, including the beloved Chet and Bernie series featuring a special bond between a detective and his dog. What is distinctive about Quinn's approach to crime stoppers and storytelling? In what ways does Mrs. Plansky's journey beautifully balance a serious topic with laugh-out-loud humor?

Guide written by Amy Root Clements

Turn the page for a sneak peek
at the next Chet & Bernie mystery

A FAREWELL TO ARFS

Available summer 2024 from Forge Books

One

Who wouldn't love my job? You see new things every day! Here, for example, we had a perp clinging to a branch high up in a cottonwood tree. That wasn't the new part. Please don't get ahead of me—although that's unlikely to happen, your foot speed and mine being . . . very different, let's leave it at that with no hurt feelings.

Where were we? Perp in a cottonwood tree, nothing new? Right. Nothing new, not even the little detail of how this particular perp, namely Donnie the Docent Donnegan, was styling his shirt and tie with pajama bottoms. Seen that look once, seen it a . . . well, many times, just how many I couldn't tell you since I don't go past two. Not quite true. I have gotten past two the odd time, all the way to whatever comes next, but not today. No biggie. Two's enough. We're the proof, me and Bernie. Together we're the Little Detective Agency, the most successful detective agency in the whole Valley, except for the finances part. Bernie's last name is Little. I'm Chet, pure and simple.

We stood side by side, as we often do, and gazed up at Donnie. "Donnie?" Bernie said. "No wild ideas."

Donnie said something that sounded annoyed, the exact words hard to understand, most likely on account of the thick gold coin, called a doubloon unless I was missing something, that he was holding between his teeth. Donnie the Docent, an old pal, was an art lover with an MO that was all about museums. On this particular occasion our client was Katherine Cornwall who runs the Sonoran Museum of Art, also an old pal but not a perp, who we met way back on a complicated case of which I remembered nothing except that it ended well, perhaps only slightly marred by an incident in the gift shop involving something that hadn't turned out to be an actual chewy, strictly speaking. Katherine Cornwall was a woman of the gray-haired, no-nonsense type. They don't miss much. You have to keep that in mind, which can turn out to be on the iffy side.

I should mention first that the gold coin between the teeth was also not the new part of this little scene, and second, that this was the time of year when the cottonwoods are all fluffy white and give off a wonderful smell, a sort of combo of thick damp paper, sweet syrup, and fresh laundry. There's really nothing like rolling around in a pile a fresh laundry, possibly a subject for later. Also our cottonwood, standing on the bank of an arroyo, wasn't the only cottonwood in the picture. On the other side of the arroyo rose a second cottonwood, just as big and fresh laundryish or maybe even more so. In between, down in the arroyo, we had flowing water, blue and rising almost to the tops of the banks. That was the new part! Water! I'd seen water in some of our arroyos before but only in tiny puddles, drying up fast under the sun. I'm a good swimmer, in case you were wondering. There are many ways of swimming, but I'm partial to the dog paddle, probably goes without mentioning.

Meanwhile, high above, Donnie seemed to be inching his way toward the end of the branch, which hung over the arroyo. As did, by the way, a big branch on the far-side cottonwood, the two branches almost touching. Below the far-side cottonwood sat Donnie's ATV, engine running. How exactly we'd gotten to this point wasn't clear to me, even while it was happening, and was less clear now.

"Donnie?" Bernie said. "It's a fantasy."

Donnie said nothing, just kept inching along the branch, the gold coin glinting in the sunshine. His eyes were glinting, too, glinting with a look I'd often seen before, the look in the eyes of a perp in the grip of a sudden and fabulous idea. There's no stopping them after that.

"Donnie! Middle-aged, knock-kneed, potbellied? Is that the acrobat look?"

Donnie glanced down, shot Bernie a nasty glance. Then—and this is hard to describe—he coiled his body in a writhing way and launched himself into the air, his hands grasping at the branch of the other cottonwood. Wow! He came oh so close. I couldn't help but admire Donnie as he went pinwheeling down and down, landing in the arroyo with a big splash and vanishing beneath the surface. Also showing no sign of coming back up.

Bernie ran toward the water, but of course I was way ahead of him. I dove down, spotted Donnie at the bottom, flailing in slow motion, grabbed him by the pant leg and hauled him up out of there. Cottonwoody white fluffy things came whirligigging down and drifted away on the current. Case closed.

It turned out Donnie didn't know how to swim, so you could say we'd saved his life, but he forgot to say thanks. Maybe that had something to do with the fact that he'd gotten the gold coin stuck in his throat, although he'd soon swallowed it, but after X-rays at the hospital had established to Katherine Cornwall's satisfaction that it was still inside him but would appear in a day or two, she cut us our check—a woman of the no-nonsense type, as perhaps I didn't stress enough already.

"Very generous, Katherine," Bernie said. "It's way too much."

"I'll be the judge of that," Katherine said. I found myself in a very strange place, namely not on Bernie's side. "There's evidence that this particular doubloon was once in Coronado's personal possession."

Bernie's eyebrows—the best you'll ever see and there's no missing them—have a language of their own. Now they rose in a way that said so much even if I couldn't tell you what, and he tucked the check in his pocket, unfortunately the chest pocket of his Hawaiian shirt. The Hawaiian shirt, with the tiny drink umbrella pattern, was not the problem, in fact was one of my favorites. The chest pocket was my problem. The check belonged in the front pocket of his pants, the front pocket with the zipper. I pressed my head against that pocket, sending a message. Bernie had great balance and didn't even stumble, hardly at all.

"He's so affectionate for such a formidable-looking fellow," Katherine said.

"True," said Bernie, dusting himself off, "but this is more about chow time."

Chow time? It had nothing to do with chow time. But then, what do you know? It was about chow time! Chow time and nothing but! When had I last eaten? I was too hungry to even think about it. I eased Bernie toward the Beast. That's our ride, a Porsche in a long line of Porsches, all old and gone now, one or two actually up in smoke. The Beast—painted in black-and-white stripes in a rippling pattern, like a squad car showing off its muscles—was the oldest of all. We roared out of the museum parking lot, Bernie behind the wheel, me sitting tall in the shotgun seat, our usual setup, although once down in Mexico we'd ended up having to pull a switcheroo. This is a fun business, in case that's not clear by now.

ABOUT THE AUTHOR

Diana Gray

SPENCER QUINN is the pen name of Peter Abrahams, the Edgar Award–winning author of forty-seven novels, including the *New York Times* and *USA Today* bestselling Chet and Bernie mystery series, *Mrs. Plansky's Revenge*, *The Right Side,* and *Oblivion,* as well as the *New York Times* bestselling Bowser and Birdie series for younger readers. He lives on Cape Cod with his wife, Diana—and Dottie, a loyal and energetic member of the four-pawed nation within.